Fully Booked
A Novel by **Run + Jump Books**

Copyright 2013 / All Rights Reserved

Fully Booked / Genn Pardoe

The author and her family will be donating ten per cent of sales from this book to Boston's therapy dogs. When you bought this book, you donated too. Thank you for celebrating these furry champions. We are not strong, we are Boston Strong.

Fully Booked / Genn Pardoe

"We ask ourselves, *Who am I to be brilliant, gorgeous, talented, and fabulous?* Actually, who are you *not* to be?"
$$\text{Marianne Williamson}$$

Fully Booked / Genn Pardoe

1. Charly Briar Takes the Scenic Route to Adulthood

Cut to me on the floor writhing in pain from a hernia thanks to a badly executed rebound with a total stranger. Was it time to re-evaluate my priorities?

Perhaps.

I'd finally worked up the nerve to extricate myself from my first "big" relationship. Now, admittedly, I didn't *really* want to dump Ethan Charge, but I felt it was the right thing to do on account of his Olympic-level cheating. I felt I had no choice in the matter and I was left devastated, betrayed, and very thirsty.

So, I did what any level-headed college girl would do. I mustered up all my remaining dignity and went to the campus bar to throw myself at the first guy who bought me a drink on two dollar martini night. Fast forward a couple hours: I've got a massive hangover and a best-in-show hernia.

We're talking dark times, people, dark times.

What started as a much-needed night out ended in traction and the extent of my paralysis was matched only by my excruciating pain. I *seriously* considered ending it all in some unnecessarily dramatic fashion—like doing a tuck-and-roll out of a very fast moving car—but I didn't, because:

a) I couldn't move,
b) I did not have a car, and
c) I'd already RSVP'd to a massively fabulous party at the Fairmont next week.

Be that as it may, it was clearly time for me to take my destiny into my own hands. If I'd learned one thing from wasting all that time on a guy like Ethan Charge, it was that I couldn't leave things up to fate. Clearly, the universe and I were not on the same page in terms of what constitutes a good boyfriend. If I was going to find my soul mate, I'd have to do the leg work myself. I decided at that very moment that only *I* could determine my future. The first step, I thought, was to make a list:

To Do List:

1. Embark on a life-changing journey of self-discovery, and,
2. stop getting hernias from strangers.

"I don't think what you have there constitutes a hernia," said Nikki Temple, my best friend at college.

Her cigarette smoke wafted in my general direction and nearly caused me to vomit (again) due to the profundity of my hangover. Nikki was very happy that Ethan and I were over and wasted no time celebrating this fact.

Everyone has that *one* friend who confesses that your boyfriend was about as fun as a canker sore mere minutes after you break up.

Information that would have been useful to me over two years ago please and thank you…

"I knew he was a cheater the second I met him," affirmed Nikki with vindicated confidence.

"Information that would have been useful to me over two years ago," I moaned. "Can we get back to my hernia?"

Nikki responded in her best *I'm a hernia expert* tone, "That's not a hernia! A hernia is an affliction for, like, old and fragile folks, you know, when they get startled or lift cookbooks. And I'm no *sexpert*, wait, no, actually I am... anyway, let's just say that *you* are doing something *very* curious in the bedroom if *you* are the one doing the heavy lifting."

"Ha, ha," I groaned as I tried to change the channel on my TV with my hot fuchsia painted big toe. "Argh, what was I thinking?"

"Well you probably just needed a little rebound to get that jerk off your mind. Personally, I'm happy you're finally done with Ethan, he was *such* a loser. Anyway, a little fling is never a bad thing, you're young, you're in college—"

Yeah," I interrupted. "I get *that*, I meant my toe nail color. Fuchsia? What was I thinking?"

"Um, yes," Nikki scrunched her nose, "I wasn't going to say anything, but it's almost more tragic than your choice in men."

I stuck my tongue out at Nikki, promised myself a pedicure, and proclaimed, "I can't help but feel that Ethan should cover the cost of my Percocet. Isn't he culpable for the state I'm in? Yes, I dumped *him*, and yes, I hooked up with a stranger to take the edge off, but, *he's* the one who cheated. I mean, c'mon, shouldn't there be some kind of retribution in the form of free healthcare?"

My other best friend (and roommate) Alégra DeVrees entered the room smiling softly and with great sympathy—the complete opposite of Nikki. Alégra nodded and agreed that Ethan should, at the very least, pick up the tab for any and all prescription pharmaceuticals for the next six months, at minimum.

"It would be the courteous thing to do," Alégra said supportively as she fluffed up the pillow under my knees and tried to make me comfortable.

Nikki, on the other hand, was not one for sensitivity, "Sure, Charly, and in return, *you* should pay for the crab shampoo to alleviate whatever Ethan is no doubt picking up from the nearest girl with daddy issues as we speak."

I couldn't help but smile.

"Get over it!" Nikki exclaimed. "You just went on a diet and lost 180 pounds of douche, you should be happy."

She *did* have a point...

Okay, must change pattern. But how?

I spent the next six hours staring at the ceiling in a Percocet haze. My mind wandered and I started to think about all of the life choices I had made that culminated in the moment in which I found myself: I was temporarily handicapped and lying on a floor having just had a meaningless rebound to mask the pain of my cheating boyfriend. Oh, and I was totally high on a pain killers. Where had I gone wrong? How had I derailed myself before I'd even begun? This didn't happen to people like me! This isn't how people like me are made... People like me are made in the following way:

1. Take Two Over-Educated WASP's aged to Baby Boomer, pragmatic and quirky with self-deprecating humor, both Professors of Cultural Anthropology, annoyingly still madly in love.

2. Add a dollop of Socially Acceptable Alcoholism (also known as "Irish Charm").

3. Be sure to drain Daddy Issues, Eating Disorders, or "Bad Experiences with Boys" prior to mixing.

4. Simmer in a quiet suburban setting with *just a hint* of teenage awkwardness (so as to avoid tartness).

5. Throw in a dash of over-active imagination that comes from being an only child.

6. Send off to Boston University for a *much encouraged* Major in Cultural Anthropology.

By early twenties, results should yield a painfully normal Bostonian chestnut-haired girl named Charly.

Bon Appétit!

Aside from my profound burrito addiction—which I prefer to keep private (burritos are proof that god and every other deity wants us to be happy and anyone who disagrees is either in denial or uninitiated), and just the *tiniest* little tendency to exaggerate my dedication to Pilates, I'm not *that* much off track. I mean, I was finishing up college and I'd soon land a great job, probably at a painfully cool public relations agency specializing in luxury travel or eco-chic hiking gear made from free range Alpaca (*details TBD*). Then one day, in would walk Mr. Fabulous—probably a client, maybe a financier—and he'd be absolutely floored by my perfectly put-together outfits, my Pilates-shaped figure and my holistic vegetarian glow. He'd exclaim, "Charly! My God! Is there anyone more perfect than you? Come explore the world with me. Adventure! Romance! Burritos! Let's go!"

This, of course, would happen after I actually took up Pilates...

...and switched to veggie burritos...

...oh, and figured out how to put an outfit together.

Anyway, the point is that I'm simply too big for Boston! Too fabulous! Too worldly! I crave exotic adventure and wild romance (and fashion sense). I knew it was out there, *the real me*, I just didn't know how to find it. My parents, of course, had the perfect solution for my desire for adventure: be a complete dork and study indigenous tribes and the clay pots they make in the world's most malaria-ridden countries and other gross stuff like that.

(Notice how no one has ever said, "You had me at cholera."??)

"You know, Charly," my mother once said, "it's only when we immerse ourselves in the unknown that we truly discover who we are."

"Are you suggesting that I *go native*, mom?"

"Oh, stop it," she laughed. "You know, before I met your father I had a little exotic romance in—"

"Yes, great, that's fabulous I'm going to stop you right there," I cringed.

"All I'm saying, Charly, is that your father and I fully support you taking off and exploring the world for a couple years. Travel is a much more constructive use of your time."

"Than what, mom?"

"Than organizing launch parties or writing tag lines for some culturally vapid travel company or whatever it is you're thinking of doing after college," she said as she topped up her pre-dinner cocktail.

(Throwing launch parties and writing tag lines actually sounds awesome, but whatever...)

"Fine," I conceded as she topped up my pre-dinner cocktail as well. "I get what you're saying."

I did not get what she was saying.

Little did I know, I'd be thinking a lot about that conversation during my hernia-recovery week. With little else to do as I lay there on my dirty college room floor—the kind that was so dirty it hadn't been vacuumed since the Maxi dress was in style, the *first* time around—I finally decided to give my mom's words some consideration. I looked at my To Do List again:

To Do List:

1. Embark on a life-changing journey of self-discovery, and
2. stop getting hernias from strangers.

Why couldn't I have started with something simple, like, *switch to decaf*? Argh, must lower expectations of self in order to increase sense of accomplishment!

Okay.

Enough excuses.

Maybe it was the culmination of breaking up with Ethan, my mom's words echoing in my mind, and the fact that graduation was fast approaching, but I suddenly felt a sense of great urgency. I glanced at my To Do List for a third time and realized that this was a pivotal moment, a moment of decision, a moment of action.

First realization: I can't embark on a life-changing journey of self-discovery in rainy old Boston! Let's be honest, if I stay here I'll just end up with another douche-kabob like Ethan in a boring job and recurring back pain.

Must stop cycle.
Must take ownership of destiny.
Must get the heck out of here.

Second realization: After graduating from college I must embark on a mission. A mission to have a life-changing experience. The kind of experience people have when they jump head-first no snorkel into the unknown. The kind of experience people have where they come out bursting with worldly wisdom and glowing skin. Like at an ashram or one of those mean spas in Arizona.

Yeahhhhh, I said to myself as I stared at the ceiling completely stoned on pain killers, slightly hallucinating, and most likely drooling, *that's perfect.*

But how should I get started? Where to begin?

And most importantly, where to find the catalyst to push me into a life-changing journey of enlightenment and self-awareness and general betterness-than-the-average-girl? (You didn't think I'd go alone, *did you?* Forget that! What's the point of embarking on a journey of self-discovery if there's no one to tell me when I've, like, discovered myself?)

This is when the *great* thinking really got started...

Third realization: My most important packing item would be a guide. Yes... I like it. A partner of some sort to jump into the unknown with me. My own personal Yoda, Buddha, and Fortune Cookie all rolled into one.

But who could this person be?

A therapist? Too preachy! A Sherpa? Too short. A psychic? Too phony. I needed a lifeguard in the truest sense of the word.

I needed someone who would act as an objective observer and cheerleader as we travelled together on my amazing journey....

Enter lightning bolt.

A boyfriend!
Of course!
Perfect!

A boyfriend is only one person—much easier to manage than a group of friends—and a boyfriend will be dedicated to me and only want what's best for me. And here's the best part: if I don't like him anymore, I'll just get another one!

Amazing!

Genius!

I shall fetch myself a boyfriend to bring along with me on my awesome journey of self-discovery.

Brilliant!

There's no possible way this can end badly and no, this "total moment of clarity" is <u>not</u> connected whatsoever to the fact that I just broke up with my boyfriend of two years who made a national sport out of cheating on me and I'm not entirely sane at the moment!

And noooo, this has nothing to do with the fact that instead of getting the much-needed super hot rebound I so totally deserved, I am at present moment, totally incapacitated thanks to some doofus who didn't know his left from his right!

And nooooooooo, I'm not desperately looking for anything — anything at all — to validate my hopeless existence and make me feel good about myself!

And PS: no no nooooo, I will not be sharing my Genius Penis Plan with my besties because, well, they just wouldn't get it...

I smiled to myself with inebriated pride: despite the hernia and the dirty carpet lying, this was turning out to be a *hella* productive week....

2. Wicked Classy

One week later my self-reflecting and dirty carpet lying had come to an end (although my subsequent limp and enthusiastic Percocet use had *not*) so my best friends Alégra DeVrees and Nikki Temple helped me hobble my handicapped ass to the party of the year. It was at the Fairmont Hotel and it was for—actually, I have no idea but since I believe hotels to be the *only* acceptable venues capable of hosting worthwhile parties, I was in. It's not that I'm too *chi chi* for pubs or bars (I like those too!) I just appreciate the views, the well-lit bathrooms with, *ahem*, free towels, and the waiters' near-pious level of patience with drunk patrons. (And yes, sometimes I like to get tipsy and run down the swanky hallways pretending I'm in a French perfume commercial.)

Highly recommended!

As we made our way, Alégra offered some words of advice with regards to my current situation, "Growing up is a tricky dance between resistance and acceptance. Unfortunately, Charly, you've got two left feet."

"Well, *that* answers the question as to whether we're done talking about my *situation*," I joked.

Nikki fiddled with the straps of her silk romper, visibly annoyed at having to dress up for the evening. An *actual* dress was out of the question for Nikki, and Alégra considered it quite the accomplishment that Nikki—the natural beauty if there was one to be named among us—had dressed up at all.

Nikki contributed to the conversation absent-mindedly, "I think I read it on a mug, or maybe it was in a PMS pamphlet, but apparently, one day you'll laugh at the things that used to make you cry."

"Well aren't you two Head of the Association of What's Blatantly Obvious," I winced as the seconds passed between the last pain killer wearing off and the next one kicking in. These are my best gal pals and I adore them:

Nikki Temple: the private-to-the-point-of-reclusive girl who looks like an early nineties Calvin Klein model with her raven hair (mostly worn in an unintentional chignon), frighteningly wild green eyes, and slender anemic frame maintained by red meat, vodka, and cigarettes.

Alégra DeVrees: a perfectly put together Pollyanna with soft golden features, like a rich French pastry or a sweet fawn puppy. Either way, you just want to squeeze her in the hopes that some of her sunshine will transfer.

(But she's not without her quirks: Alégra answers the question *what would the love-child between a Ritalin-addicted Barbie and Martha Stewart look like?*)

And then there's **me**: a perpetual grass-is-always-greener ragamuffin with an ever-so-slightly-over-active imagination, a penchant for burritos, an unused class pass for Pilates, and an obsession with finding my one big true love.

So I'm told...

"It all sounds so charitable, so *giving*," Alégra cooed as she leaned against a high top table in a much-practiced stance that allowed her royal blue silk dress to highlight her curvaceous hips and early twenties breasts in equal parts.

Not two minutes into the party of the century and Alégra had already been abducted. Some philanthropic type was laying it on thick for her and he was right to: every man in the room was tripping over himself to get to Alégra.

In addition to being a total knockout, Ali had a timeless look that made her age impossible to guess. And as such, she could play arm candy to the established forty-something broker just as easily as gal pal to the cute but nerdy biology PhD. The male world was Alégra's oyster; this made Nikki roll her eyes and order another round. It was already a given that Nikki would not be interested in talking to any men at the benefit that evening. Nikki Temple's dating style was slightly more below the radar. Actually it was more like totally über-stealth...

Where Alégra and I gushed endlessly about the men in our lives, Nikki Temple's romantic affairs occurred in total clandestine fashion. In fact, the only evidence that these rendezvous, meet-ups, and flings actually *did* happen were Nikki's juicy tales—and sometimes scars—from the battlefield.

Her love life, just like all the other parts of Nikki's life that made her *her*, was kept under lock and key. Sometimes Alégra and I wondered when, if ever, the real Nikki would appear...

"Alright," Nikki said in a conclusive tone after about seventeen minutes, "I'm off. I've got to get some stuff done."

It was code for *I have a date and no, I'm not going to talk about it*. I said goodbye to Nikki and spent the next ten minutes staring blankly into my Seven & Seven (yes, I drank Seven & Sevens at a super swanky party, an amateur's mistake, I know that now. On the other hand, I can't really regret it because of what happened next).

"Drink-this-not-that," a painfully beautiful British supermodel (think early Naomi Campbell) blinked at me with a disapproving half-smile. She handed me a big glass filled with wine, "That tacky cocktail says *Hi, I'm here for the Roofy-ing*."

The girl was about a million feet tall with pitch black espresso bean skin, blue shimmery eye shadow and soft pink nails. She was wearing a pale thigh-high satin dress with a deep V on both the front *and* the back.

It fell flawlessly on her and outlined her elegant but precise chin-length coif. She was perfect.

"You're so cool," I blurted out like a total idiot.

(Give me a break. I'd been on a week-long binge of Percocet and *harsh* self-reflection; two things I prefer to stay away from.)

"Um, okay, thanks *dahling*," she laughed in a polished British accent. "Anyway, we just don't want photographers shooting young ladies such as yourself looking, um, *inelegant*. Alright, well, have fun! Cute dress by the way."

"No! Wait!" I near-shouted after the girl in what must have looked like the beginning of a lesbionic lovers' quarrel.

I couldn't help my platonic girl-crush. This girl was swathed in glitter, like one of those golden age Hollywood starlets, or people from Monaco. They're just inherently awesome. I *had* to know who she was and why she was at the party.

"Are you one of the princesses rumored to be here?" I whispered conspiratorially.

She threw her head back and allowed a genuine laugh to escape, "not quite, I'm the hotel PR girl."

Hotel.
PR.
Girl.
Oooooooooh...
I like that!
"Me too," I said with confidence.
What?!

No you're not, dumbass!
Why would you say that?
Stop trying to sound cool.
You better fix this!
Back-peddle!

"I'm sorry," I collected myself. "What I mean is, I am currently in college and I would *like* to pursue a career in public relations in the hospitality industry."

I would? Since when?

"That's great!" the British girl cheered, "Well let me give you my business card, let's keep in touch, we're always hiring."

We shook hands and I almost passed out.

"Edifice Luxe Hotels & Resorts?" I stammered as I read the card, painfully aware that I was in the presence of cool.

"Oh, yeah," the girl shrugged easily, "I don't work for the Fairmont. I'm *in* hotel PR, just not *this* hotel. The organizer of the party is a dear friend of mine and I'm just helping out. Edifice Luxe owns many smaller, you know, more upscale boutique hotels. Anyway, I'm not surprised you haven't heard of us, and that's where I come in! I'm on a year-long global media tour."

OMG this girl is the coolest person I've ever met!

She continued nonchalantly, "I go from hotel to hotel with travel writers, editors, and journalists — if you can call them that! — to show them everything fabulous that we offer. You know, the usual, elephant safaris, snorkeling with dolphins, trekking with Sherpas, ultra-luxury spa getaways, it sounds amazing but it's exhausting. My job is to make sure the media *adore* Edifice Luxe hotels, no matter what. I swear sometimes I feel as though I'm babysitting drunken perverted children. I live in a never-ending 5-star hell, I tell you! Actually, *shoot*, I am totally rambling, sorry, darling, I should be heading out, early flight tomorrow. It never ends! Seriously, call me. I'll set something up. *Ciao ciao!*"

I was left spinning.

Spa Getaways?

Ultra-Luxury?
Sherpas?
Dolphins?
5-star hell?
Sign.
Me.
Up.

Two things became immediately clear. One, I would never again drink a Seven & Seven. Two, I was going to be the next jet-setting public relations girl for Edifice Luxe.

Talk about figuring it all out in a matter of moments!!
How perfect is this?

I could embark on my amazing journey of self-discovery without ever getting dirty *or* study the mating habits of goat farmers along the southern Ganges (sorry, mom and dad).

Life plan solidified? Check!

The British mystery girl had given me another piece of my existential puzzle! I already had the *what* (amazing journey of self-discovery), the *who* (a boyfriend, which shouldn't be too hard to find) and, thanks to this amazingly stylish stranger, I now had the *how* (jet-setting hotel pr girl). Now I just needed the *where*! I drank two (or three?) more glasses of wine in celebration as I blissfully absorbed the serendipitous curveball the universe had thrown me. I couldn't help but fantasize about the exotic destinations I was going to visit as a hotel PR girl. I'd be taking esteemed members of the media to Edifice Luxe hotels in Southeast Asia, Russia, and Africa.

Maybe all three!

Yes, that makes sense, they'd probably have me flying all over the world, liaising with fabulously interesting people like travel writers and photographers. I'd show them monkey sanctuaries and ultra-luxury spa retreats hidden high up in the mountains.

The media would all want to come on my press junkets because I'd throw the *greatest* island parties and gala events and grand openings and chic soirees — *oh my!*

We'd all become great friends and say things like, "Look me up next time you're in Honduras, I'll be surfing there this winter." Or maybe, "If you make it to Laos, I know a great little whiskey bar in Vientiane, ask for PukPuk, tell him Charly sent you."

Holy F Cakes I was about to have the coolest life ever!

Finally, Alégra was ready to leave and we both floated home: me on a cloud of infinite possibilities in my new life as a world traveler and Ali in the reassured bliss that twenty or so men desperately wanted to get it on with her. I told Ali all about the mysterious British girl I'd met but she was too busy deciding which guy to blue-ball for the next month or so. But then I realized it wasn't Alégra who I wanted to share my news with. It was my recently dumped boyfriend, Ethan Charge.

(My freshest ex is usually my person of choice for making ridiculously drunk and deluded statements of grandeur to.)

Three (or four) nightcaps later I'd mustered up the courage to call Ethan... I woke him up, and, through marvelously inebriated and somewhat medicated tears of triumph, I announced that I was entering the jet-setting world of hotel public relations and just a heads-up, but I'll probably never be heard from again.

Go me!

(True, I was taking a *pretty* fancy gamble telling Ethan all that stuff considering I had no tangible means by which to *actually* embark upon this life-changing journey of self-discovery, *yet*. But I had a plan. And I think that's the point. Anyway it doesn't matter because it all worked out.)

Well kinda...

Fully Booked / Genn Pardoe

One Year Later...

> From: Scott Lansdowne (s.lansdowne@edificeluxe.com)
> To: Charly Briar (c.briar@edificeluxe.com)
> Subject: Hotel Job
>
> Attachment 📎 Hotel PR – Job Description
>
> Hi sweets!
>
> I thought you might be interested in this... I know how much you "love" working as a copywriter. Your little PR ship has come in!
>
> You'd be based out of Bangkok traveling to all the Edifice Luxe properties in Southeast Asia as the PR Liaison. Remember what Eden was doing when you gals met at the Fairmont? Same idea, smaller market.
>
> Basically you'd be hosting travel writers on various tours and your only job, basically, is to make sure they have the best time and give Edifice Luxe a good name in their magazines, newspapers, etc.
>
> See attached for more details and compensation. It's not a full "expat package". You have to get your own place to live, but the pay is decent, you should consider it. It's only a six month contract, you can test out life as an expat!!
>
> It starts at the end of your current contract: in August. I'm <u>tight</u> with the HR girl in Bangkok, it's yours if you want it girl!
>
> *Scott Lansdowne,*
> *Marketing Manager, Sales & Marketing,*
> *Bumi~Spa~Aquas, A Subsidiary of Edifice Luxe Global*
> *Boston Headquarters*

I chuckled at the thought of Scott being *tight* with the HR girl in Bangkok. Scott was *tight* with every girl and according to office gossip he was the biggest ladies' man in the entire Edifice Luxe Hotels & Resorts family. This was a pretty impressive accolade for the biggest hotel chain in the world. What made it *even more* impressive was that it was totally untrue. Scott Lansdowne: gorgeous, sweet, chestnut-haired blue-eyed farm boy from the mid-west, was/is/always will be, gay.

Unofficially, that is. As coworkers and now good friends, Scott and I had become close over the past year. Eden Quinn—his original *gal pal*, the third member of our at-work gang, and the British supermodel-esque world traveling fashionista who got me into this business—and I kept his secret from judgmental colleagues and his super conservative family. In return, Scott kept us full of Pinot and gossip at lunchtime.

**There's only one acceptable grape persuasion when it comes to Pinot, by the way, don't make me say which. One is vile, the other is fabulous, and if it were socially acceptable to put it in my breakfast cereal, well then I'd start eating breakfast.

I filled the space between throwing my back out in college and the moment I received that email from Scott by backpacking around Europe with Alégra, seriously contemplating becoming a yoga teacher and/or wine master, and two relationships. To top it all off, I was halfway through my contract in the first year of my first *real* job and not to toot my own horn, but I was rocking it!

Go me!

I was the East Coast Communications & Strategic Initiative Brand Ambassador Edifice Luxe Hotels & Resorts Worldwide, (pretty big mouthful for a lowly copywriter but no one needed to know that). Okay, I wasn't technically *in* PR, but I was PR *adjacent* and besides, Scott's email might just be the opportunity I had been waiting for. Until then, I was happily situated in the Edifice Luxe Boston office. Specifically, I worked for their line of upscale eco-spas and wellness sanctuaries: Bumi~Spa~Aquas.

With only fifteen or so properties worldwide, Bumi~Spa~Aquas was by no means the biggest or most impressive brand owned by Edifice Luxe, but I eagerly accepted a one-year contract as copywriter and dove right in. From day to day, I instructed would-be vacationers to:

"Dive into extravagant minimalism, embrace modernity in an ancient landscape, and abandon yourself in a journey of self-discovery at Bumi~Spa~Aquas"

Okay, okay...
I'll admit it was *slightly* on the fluffy side of things (and my parents never let me forget it) but it was a start. What's more, it was a start at Edifice Luxe: the biggest, most chic hotel brand on the planet. Plus, the job had a commuting time of about seven minutes from my bed to my cubicle (I *will not* commute) so I happily overlooked the not so intellectual aspect of my job. (Had I known that the job would lead me to the love of my life, I probably would have been a lot more appreciative, and *maybe* visited the Pilates Nazi at my local gym too...)

So a year and a bit later I had some life experience in my soul, a little traveling under my feet, and some relationship experience in my heart. All good things... but not *great* things.

I *still* hadn't had *that* life-changing journey of self-discovery; I needed to experience something that would set me apart but also make me fit in. Something that would make me see the world, and myself, in a different way... I was excited about Scott's email and wondered if it just might be the catalyst for change I was seeking.

I quickly IM'd him back and said I'd give it some serious thought to which he responded that he and Eden were meeting for after-work drinks in five minutes.

It was 3pm. It was Thursday.

I love my work friends.

The three of us laughed our way through two and a half bottles of Moet at the Fairmont's Oak Room (rule number one of working for a hotel: make at least a miniscule effort to *not* get sauced on company property. Trust me, it's *way* harder than it looks...)

Scott, Eden, and I were celebrating absolutely nothing and having fabulous fun irritating everyone in the immediate vicinity with our big laughter and offensive humor.

"You are such a little tramp, Eden!" Scott squealed as he listened to Eden recount her latest conquest with excruciating clarity. Personally, I was feeling a little dirty just *hearing* the details of my friend's recent tryst. Despite Eden's gorgeous looks and effortless grace, she was quite the, um, complete man-eater.

"Oh, Scott, how else do I make new *friends*," Eden quipped. "E-network on LinkedIn? I.don't.fucking.think.so, *dah-ling*."

Eden Quinn
The Public Relations & Media Outreach Ambassador at Edifice Luxe and the *most* beautiful and *most* British girl I've ever met in my life. With the regal deportment of a lioness, Eden was fiercely gorgeous and fiercely fierce. She had a wide reaching reputation for eating men (and members of the media) alive. To me she was the big sister I'd never had. She was cool, traveled, protective, and totally acid-tongued. (She was also the girl I'd met just over a year ago at the party that Ali had dragged me to; so it was thanks to her that I was part of the EL family.)

"So, are you still with this guy?" I dug for gossip, wanting to know if Eden's newest boy toy actually lived up to his nickname: *The Angry Inch*.

"Of course I'm not still *dealing* with that insufferable wankshaft!" balked Eden, "I knew it was over when we were out having drinks and he had the *raving* audacity to tell me it was 'okay to leave some wine *in* the glass.' Well, naturally I thought he was joking. He wasn't. So I called him a total fascist and suggested he join a Prohibition rally at the corner of Main St. and 1922. Can you imagine anything so insane?! I mean, honestly, I knew I'd have to lower my standards when I came to America, but *my* lord…"

We all laughed. Hotel bars are the best spots for after-work (or before-work) drinks. I can't understand why anyone would go anywhere else. They are the chicest watering holes with the most interesting clientele and the waiters have an unnaturally high tolerance for abuse.

(Hotels are also a great place to pretend you're wicked classy on a boxcar hobo's budget: I could *never* afford to hang out in such an elegant setting if it weren't for Scott's company card.) We talked about everything and nothing during our Thursday afternoon rituals. But the topic of conversation in recent weeks had unfortunately become quite predictable: my dry spell. I resisted vehemently but apparently war, famine, and *even* fashion took a back seat to my relationship status which was at that point, non-existent.

The Dry Spell

A "dry spell" for someone who takes time off in between relationships to grieve and get perspective (um, like a *normal* person), can be anywhere from three months to three years.

I, however, was on a deadline. I was committed to finding the perfect boyfriend to join me on my journey of self-discovery and I saw no need to waste time "letting it all sink in" between relationships. I had to get back on that proverbial horse as fast as possible and besides, I could always deal with the baggage later, when I had more time. It's not that I *can't* be single it's that I don't *want* to be.

Why in the name of liquid lunches would anybody want to be single?
Seriously.

If it's so awesome being single, why are there 54 million people dating online? Is it because they're so hyped about being completely alone that they are dying to broadcast it on the Internet? I don't think so, people...

I call BS.

You see, for people like me (let's call us *serial daters*) a dry spell is a seriously slippery slope. It can easily evolve into a dry season, and god forbid, a draught. It was obvious to me that I couldn't risk taking actual time off in between relationships. The entire essence of my being as a serial dater hinged on dating one guy after another after another after....

If I dated one guy, and then nobody, well, I wasn't a very good serial dater then, *was I*? Ever since I had decided back in college that this was a critical step in my amazing journey of self-discovery it had always been pretty clear to me that a dry spell could have a monumental impact on my schedule.

(I was hoping to have completely found myself by twenty-seven, or so, twenty-eight, at the latest).

"Cheers, girls," I said to Eden and Scott. "It's the beginning of the end for me and my life as we know it. This morning I found myself sneering jealously at two pigeons mating. I'm totes devastated guys! I think I'm having a quarter-life crisis."

"Quarter-life crisis, huh?" Scott laughed as he ran perfectly manicured fingers through his Moroccan-oil scented hair. "So you're going to live to be ninety-nine years old?"

We both laughed. Scott crossed one Gucci loafer over the other and readjusted his tan cashmere sweater. I looked down at my nails—which were rocking the *chipped chic* look—and I was pretty sure I was catching wafts of last night's chicken vindaloo in my hastily washed tresses. Eden and I could never figure out how Scott's hair and wardrobe were impervious to weather: it was a classic March in Boston and yet somehow, Scott was able to pull off suede, cashmere, and dark Ken Doll hair.

"*What-ever*," Eden said in her highly affected *Aristobrat* accent. "Charly doesn't *need* a new man every five minutes. She's an independent woman."

"Like Beyoncé?" Scott chirped hopefully on my behalf.

"No," Eden shook her perfect chin-length coif. "Like an agoraphobic, or a lesbian."

"You two see that I'm sitting *right* here don't you?"

I exhaled faux-hopelessly as strands of brown fringe flew up and then settled back down in front of my eyes. *Ugh*, I thought as I looked down at my long hair, deep mauve shift dress, navy tights, and brown slouchy boots. I looked like one of those *Emo* girls who will only do things ironically.

Must get new look!

"You know what I mean, my little darling," Eden topped up my champagne flute and gave me a big-sister wink. "We just adore you and we want to see you with a *proper* man."

(Some women were serial monogamists, some were sporadic monogamists, Eden was a never-monogamist... so her idea of a "proper man" kinda scared me.)

"Why don't you try wearing a push-up bra?" offered Scott cheerfully as checked out a cute guy that walked by.

Like a mother about to tell her much-adored gay son that the Saks Fifth Avenue Fall Collection just went up in smoke, I sighed, "I *am* wearing one, honey."

Scott frowned and suggested carefully, "Maybe, um, uh, how to say this... lay off the burritos?" I shot a horrified look to Scott who quickly added, "I mean, don't get me wrong, you have a tiny frame. Quite frankly I don't know where you put it, but Mexican food on the regular is, like, *mucho* unattractive."

"Are you *high*?" I snapped at such a ridiculously insane suggestion but then collected myself quickly. "Sigh! It's useless. I'm condemned to a life of solo holidays and sitting at the kids' table well past the age of what is considered appropriate."

"Stop being so *dramatic*, you've only been single for a couple of weeks!" Eden's reality check fell on deaf ears.

"It's over for me. I should probably go buy a cat," I huffed as I contemplated the last time I had a pedicure or facial (*ack, or a waxing*).

"Sweetie," Scott tried to cheer me up, "you're totally dateable. Just give it time... maybe we need to shake things up, you know, find a new hot spot, join a new gym..."

"Eventually my hoo-ha will grow over and I'll become a virgin again," I sank further into my comfy wingback chair and for the first time, looked at the other patrons in the room.

It was busy, even for a Thursday, and equally divided between tourists and businessmen.

"That actually happened to a friend of mine," Eden forewarned. "Totally re-virginized."

"Well," Scott said earnestly, "at least that's one sexual issue Eden will never have to worry about!"

"*Amen!*" Eden cheered.

I was about to beg that we change the subject—I wasn't sure if I was more tired of having a dry spell, or more tired of talking about it—when Scott's BlackBerry chimed in.

Scott squealed and, for a second, I thought my ears might bleed, "O M F G! My old college roommate is coming through Boston on business and he wants to meet for drinks. Wanna come, Charly?"

"*OMFG!* Honestly," Eden guffawed loudly, "how can your parents *not* know you're gay? Doesn't their house catch on fire every time you visit?"

After a second Scott smiled, "Ohhhh, because I'm flaming. Good one, Eden. At least I don't have junk that swallows men whole. That thing is like a *Whoretex*: men go in, but they never come out!"

Eden and Scott both burst out into laughter as they mock-echoed into her crotch, "**Hello!**Hello!Hello!"

(Sometimes I thought that Scott and Eden would make the best couple because they never had all the issues that come with sex.)

"Now, Charly," Scott turned his attention to me after they had settled down, "are you coming?"

The thought of playing third wheel to Scott's romantic man-reunion was about to make my freshly drowned dry-spell frustrations resurface when Scott set me straight, "he's a breeder, like you! Totally straight. Totally New York born-and-bred. He's an investment banker, he's super hot...."

"Oh, thanks a lot, you *tosser*," interrupted Eden with a huge pout. "Why am I not invited?"

"Because, Eden," Scott said like a caring father doling out love and discipline in equal parts. "You do okay for yourself. Charly is teetering dangerously on a dry spell—according to her—and says she needs my help."

"Details, details," Eden waved a hand as though the truth were nothing more than a fruit fly.

Classic Eden.

"Well," I began, clearing my throat and tasting my mid-afternoon buzz, "I guess it would be *rude* to decline an invitation."

We made a date for eight but not before Scott suggested a steam bath to drain my complexion of Baby Duck.

"You look as though you've been off with Captain Baccardi on a rum binge. I know there's a beautiful swan in there somewhere, my little ugly duckling."

"Hardy har harrr," I said dryly as a tiny little drop or two of champagne found its way out of my glass and onto my lap.

Scott paid using his company card and I headed to the door propelled by thoughts of vegetating all afternoon in a glorious steam bath. The only reason I lived in a condo *chic* enough to have a steam bath, by the way, had everything to do with my roommate Alégra DeVrees and literally nothing to do with me.

Get ready for this: As the product of an extramarital affair between her mother and a rich industrialist with a guilty conscience, Alégra received a monthly allowance equivalent to the GDP of a small country *and* a stunning condo overlooking the city.

How lucky is that!?

Alégra was *also* a buyer for Liam & Olivia, my *most* favorite label of all time; so we had more slouchy boots and big bags than we knew what to do with.

"Thanksssss for the drinksssss Scott," I slurred as Eden buttoned up my navy pea coat, "I *will* pull it together for tonight!"

"What would you do without me?" Eden tisked, "You are about as useful to yourself as a vagina is to Scott." Then she leaned in and whispered extra-harshly, "Just be sure you're not getting into another Tyler Kee situation..."

Fully Booked / Genn Pardoe

4. The Tyler Kee Situation

Almost two months ago I went on my first real business trip. *It was amazing!* Every year, Edifice Luxe sends its marketing and media relations departments to a massive week-long conference and training seminar in Singapore. The event was *always* held in Singapore—because that's where the brand originated from—and although most of my older, more seasoned coworkers tried to get out of going, I was beyond excited to attend. Eden invited herself over to help me pack, and since I'd never been to Singapore, or to one of these conferences, I welcomed any and all advice. (I also had to be extra nice to Eden because she was babysitting my little Boston Terrier, Kermit the Dog.)

Round, furry, and full of kisses; I'd yet to find a man who compared to Kermit and he let me know it. Kermit was the first and final say with *all* my boyfriends. (If he didn't get Kermit's approval, he didn't get mine.)

I found Kermit, or rather, he found me on the last day of college. I was outside Nikki's house on her porch, waiting for her to get ready for brunch, when a fat little terrier trotted by. He was covered in mud and quite frankly, crap, and he looked scared but at the same time determined.

He came to a full stop when he saw me, turned on a dime, marched right over, and plopped himself down beside me on the porch steps. We just sat there silently for a while, exchanging half-glances out of the corners of our eyes. I didn't want to look at him full on, or pick him up, for fear of scaring him off. After a while, he sighed and leaned his muddy little body into my lap. He had no tags and I swear on a stack of studded headbands that I put posters up. But three weeks later, he had yet to be claimed. I officially adopted the little guy and named him after my first love: a little green frog who never gave up on his heart's desire for true love. We've been sharing burritos ever since.

"Now darling," Eden brought me back to packing as she shot a moderately disapproving look at Kermit—who snored intermittently on the bed...

"The retreat is seven days of conference room chairs, conference room cookies—the ones with the totally suspicious red jelly in the middle—and torturous seminars. Avoid. Avoid. Avoid. This is a massive event with countless employees, trust me, *no one* will notice that you're off sightseeing and shopping and, and—what *is* all this crap in here?"

Eden's brows furrowed as she riffled through the contents of my suitcase without apology. I wasn't aware that there would be a baggage search but I felt as though Eden was about to explain the ways of the hotel world to me so I tried to listen as intently as possible without being too distracted by her repacking efforts. She explained how to avoid getting caught by signing the attendance sheet and dropping a business card in the fishbowl, sitting in the back during the opening spiel, and then ducking out at the first break. I knew that what she was saying was helpful and yet I couldn't help but stare wide-eyed at the disaster Eden was make out of my meticulous packing job.

"Are you listening?" Eden snapped playfully, "Of course you're not. Americans have the attention span of dust bunnies. In my country you wouldn't be trusted with children's scissors."

Kermit and I sat on the edge of my bed watching my suitcase being unpacked and repacked as Eden tossed aside my favorite Miss Piggy pajamas and replaced them with a Victoria's Secret slip. She gave me *you'll thank me later* wink as I frowned slightly.

Sigh.

I love The Muppets.

"I am so jealous of you lot," Eden sighed. "All of the Edifice Luxe properties in Singapore are booked up, so you are staying at The Raffles Hotel. You'll *adore* the Raffles, the décor is breathtaking and they make *the most fantastic* Singapore Slings. It's where they were invented, after all."

"Well, I'll really miss you!" I said as I curled up with Kermit and pouted because Eden wouldn't be there.

"I know! It's *such* a shame I can't make it," Eden frowned. "Damn press tour. Who comes to Boston in January? Ugh, I can't believe you actually *want* to work in PR. You do realize PR attracts completely vacuous, anorexic, alcoholic, back-stabbing evil idiot-girls, yes? I mean, aside from me of course. I'm an angel."

We both laughed.

"Easy for you to say, Eden," I sighed. "Your job seems amazing compared to mine. Today I was tasked with an internal communications project: update the current *please don't flush your feminine products down our toilet* signs."

Eden rolled her eyes and made a barf-face.

My specific instructions had been to "make it sound classy" and at that point, I was pretty sure that babysitting supposedly perverted travel journalists in exotic locales beat trying to find something that rhymed with 'applicator'.

"Can we please get back to packing?" Eden pleaded.

"Of course," I said. "But you're throwing out all the good stuff!"

Much to my protest, Eden tossed aside a pair of comfy moccasin slippers and a flannel housecoat and scolded me, "Charly Briar! You are going to the *swish* Raffles Hotel in Singapore, not an incontinence convention in Boca Raton!"

I was thankful for Eden's help but didn't have the heart to tell her that she was packing from my Skinny Drawer.

The Skinny Drawer

The Skinny Drawer contains skirts, jeans, and tops that once fit me nicely but over time have become snug and awkward.

I'm not fat, *okay?!*

I'm just not seventeen years old anymore…

I guess that's something I'll have to come to terms with eventually. And, rather than toss out my fabulously form-fitting clothes, I relegated them to the Skinny Drawer. This was done in the hopes that I would one day contract a hellacious case of food poisoning and violently excrete those pesky seven pounds that stood between me and eternal bliss.

A girl could dream.

I checked back in to realize that Eden's epic speech was finally reaching its dénouement. Having drifted off, I was unsure if she had just outlined the Edifice Luxe Annual Retreat or a plan to assassinate upper management.

I glared in mock-horror as she took a mini curtsy and zipped up my suitcase, filled to the brim with clothes that didn't fit. The next day, I left for Singapore…

¤ * § * ¤

The flight was long but totally worth it. I arrived in Singapore with a group of more than a hundred Edifice Luxe employees hailing from all over the world. Everyone was pretty much the same age as me, or maybe a bit older. I guessed that senior EL employees were put up in actual Edifice Luxe properties around Singapore. Either way, I had no complaints about being sent to The Raffles: it was the chicest place I'd ever seen. I wasn't sure where to start. It was so overwhelming; I wondered if the rest of Asia was this impressive. I walked into the grand entrance and sighed happily.

An expansive oak wraparound veranda, a fragrant courtyard peppered with delicate rose blossoms, the smell of frangipane and oolong tea, fresh white linens and sharply dressed porters, the timeless colonial décor... This place was plucked out of another era and I loved it!

After my fellow conference attendees and I endured the long process of check-in, we were given the week's itinerary: seminars on marketing, training sessions on customer service, a networking dinner... None of it seemed appealing and I immediately began to search for escape routes.

"This schedule looks pretty painful, eh?" said a cherub-faced hottie who'd sidled up to me out of nowhere.

Whoa.
Hello to you!
And your name is?
Who cares actually... let's just makeout.

"Um, yes, it does. I'm trying to think of a getaway plan," I near-whispered, in part to sound conspiratorial, in part because I was breathless from his good looks.

Who is this guy!?

"Well aren't you a regular badass," he chuckled as he casually bent down to pick up my luggage.

Such a gentleman.

While he was down there being gentlemanly I took the opportunity to steal a glance at his ass. It was very Tom Cruise early years; like a Jockey underwear model and totally *not* a Metrosexual's *derrière*, which I have no time for.

It looked so supple yet firm with the perfect amount of curvature, I wondered if he'd let me use it as a pillow later...

Whoa.
Calm down.
Don't let your desperation get the better of you.
You don't even know his name.
He doesn't even know yours —

"C'mon, Charly Briar," said the cherub-faced hottie as he carried my valise for me.

"How'd you know my…"

Oh.

My name tag.

Idiot.

I glanced at his: Tyler Kee.

I repeated the name to myself dreamily for what felt like an eternity as I imagined us making out on a magical horse-drawn sleigh over a sea of clouds and shooting stars…

When I regained consciousness I realized that Tyler was halfway up the red carpeted staircase and I rushed to catch up.

"So, what do you do for Edifice Luxe?" I asked maybe a little too keenly.

Tyler Kee told me that he was Get-Up-And-Go Ambassador at Edifice Luxe's newly acquired brand: OM Luxe.

In English please?

He was the sports manager at a modern boutique resort that was owned by Edifice Luxe.

The only thing I really knew about OM Luxe resorts was that it cost a lot of money to stay there because they're super minimalist and don't offer much beyond a vegan menu and hot yoga instructors. I actually remembered helping out with a backgrounder for a media enquiry about OM Luxe a couple months back. I wrote that the properties "carried the timeless Edifice Luxe DNA with an updated suite of offerings for the post-modern eco-voyager."

Eco-voyager? I mean, *really!* The OM Luxe property that Tyler worked for was in the Maldives and he looked as though he'd been on vacation for the last six months. I had heard of that resort before, it was totally isolated and full of rich desperate housewives looking to grope the staff's um, *staffs*.

I sarcastically offered my sympathy at having to work under such horrible conditions. He gave the same response that I do when asked why I work for Edifice Luxe: perks.

"Working at OM Luxe isn't exactly *broadening* my horizons," Tyler smiled at me and I practically melted into a puddle of hot, happy, goo. He continued, "But the pay is decent and the expatriate life is awesome. And I'm a recent grad so it's good to get out and travel, you know?"

"I'm a recent grad too! Well, kind of," I tried to sound casual but came off sounding as cool as those people who wear socks with sandals and eat honeydew melon with cottage cheese in the center.

Ugh.

For reals?

"Hey," Tyler leaned in towards me and gave a smile so hot it would have Alaska sprouting palm trees in no time. "Wanna ditch this luggage and skip class with me?"

"Would love to," I said without a moment's hesitation as I finalized the details of our destination wedding in my mind.

We wandered around the hotel for about two minutes before deciding that "it was probably safer" to go into hiding. After all, we couldn't risk being caught by Edifice Luxe executives on their way to boring seminars. Eventually we made our way to a second floor balcony overlooking a lush courtyard that seemed unchanged since the 1800s. It was like a setting from a Theroux novel: foreign and unknown, exotically perfumed and inviting. In the far corner sat two oversized tan wingback chairs that we claimed as our own, sinking deep into them with big contented sighs.

"Perfect," Tyler said as he looked at our surroundings.

"Yes, it is," I said as I looked at him.

Ugh...

I know...

It's so pathetic...

I become such a perv when I'm teetering on a dry spell...

"Homemade Singapore Sling?" Tyler asked as he produced fruit punch, soda, and Duty Free gin from his backpack.

"Close enough," I smiled easily and from there, the conversation just flowed.

Two hours, and several Singapore Slings later, Tyler asked frankly, "So, what do you look for in a guy?"

"Oh, wow that came out of left field," I said.

His question sobered me up so naturally, I was a little put off.

"Oh, no," he chuckled, "that's not what I meant. I'm just making conversation. What I mean is… why don't you have a boyfriend?"

"Because in the real world, Tyler," I laughed, "ridiculously hot guys like *you* would most likely use girls like *me* as a one-time slam piece *at best*."

And then I humped his leg.

No I didn't.

I just blushed.

I also wondered how I could translate my inner monologue into real words without coming across as an escaped mental patient from the Hospital for the Serial Dating Obsessed.

"I don't know," I said casually. "I guess I just haven't found the *right* guy yet."

Perfect answer, Charly, much better than the first option.

As a general rule, I don't engage in this conversation with guys I've just met. Talk about Friend Zone…

Must change subject.

"Anyway—" I started.

"Would you date me? Um, for example?" Tyler smiled and I was practically whisked away on a tidal wave of my own arousal. It's not fair that some people are so good looking *and* so sweet.

Would I date you, Tyler??

Would I date you, Tyler!!

Would I date you, Tyler?!

"Does a zoo have a fence around it!?" I *wanted* to blurt out.

But miraculously, despite my homemade Singapore Sling buzz and temporary loss of motor skills due to his excessive hotness, I summoned up enough strength to shrug my shoulders and smile sweetly, "I don't know Tyler, we barely know each other."

Brilliant execution!

I rolled with my newfound confidence, "Maybe you're too cool for me, too much of a party animal, or maybe you're too serious."

Good playful jab, Charly.

It shows you're flirtatious but not easy.

Tyler chuckled warmly and emptied the remaining contents of booze into tumblers he had stolen from a room service cart, "Too hot, too cold, jeez, you are the Goldilocks of Men."

"I'm just discerning," I faux-scolded him as I readjusted my fawn-colored wraparound dress to reveal *just the right* amount of knee and lower portion of upper thigh.

Not as easy as it looks.

Alégra had it down, I was still an amateur...

"And by the way," Tyler near-whispered as he leaned in and barely brushed his finger tips over my freshly exposed knee, "I promise you, Goldilocks, I'm *just right*."

I felt a thousand volt shock run through my entire body originating from where he had touched me. I immediately changed the subject for fear that I might pass out from a sexually charged electrocution, "Where are you from in the States?"

"I'm not," he smiled. "I'm Canadian."

"Oh, really?" I said as I slurped the last of my Singapore Sling and tried to put it back on the table as steadily as possible without much success, "Weird."

Argh!

Weird?

Why did you say that?!

Moron!

He smiled softly, "Oh, c'mon *eh*, we're not so different."

"I somehow doubt that," I did my best coquettish smile but worried that it came across less *sexy mysterious chick* and more *psychopathic pirate glare*.

Gah!

I'm such a dolt!

Must practice sexy stares in front of the mirror!

"Well, Goldilocks," said Tyler with a sexy smile. "Why don't we grab a couple of real drinks at the bar downstairs and try to overcome our cultural differences?"

"It's worth a try," I grinned and accepted his outstretched hand.

While we didn't resolve any international disputes, Tyler and I *did* manage to engage in a little free trade between two friendly nations...

Self-high five!

On our third night after a particularly sweaty session in his hotel room, Tyler rolled off of me and announced that his birthday was the following day, "a bunch of us are going to Clarke Quay at night, it's gonna be fun, you should come."

As I lay beside him he rolled onto his back and put his naked Canadian body on display. It was a body that made me wonder if he was raised on a farm or by a lake with loving parents, lullabies, and a diet high in dairy and leafy greens.

Tyler had naturally rosy cheeks and thighs so strong that I would definitely cling on to them in the event of a flash flood. I mean, he was so well built I wondered if his penis might have its own six-pack.

Happy sigh.

It's moments like this that make me wish I could give myself a high-five... I kissed Tyler for the millionth time and then got up slowly from the bed.

I smiled at him over my shoulder as I crossed the room to shower his perspiration from my body. Once in the tub, I told him I'd love to come to his b-day bash.

"Great, it's a big one for me," he said as he joined me moments later. He kissed me on the forehead and I smiled, I hadn't realized that Tyler was older than me.

So gorgeous AND mature?!
I totally rock!
Go me!

I was in my mid-twenties and I had pegged him for about the same. Either way, I was happy to help Tyler ring in his thirtieth. The big *three-oh*, definitely reason to celebrate...

I turned to face the shower-head as he stood behind me and sighed as he reached around and cupped my breasts softly, "I can't wait to be eighteen. I know that's like, so retarded to say that, but it's like, off the *heezee*."

O.

M.

G.

The next day I found the Business Center and quickly signed onto to g-chat in the desperate hope that Nikki would be online.

kermitandcharly@gmail.com

Nikki says:
    Hahahahahahahah, that's precious. You're such a cradle robber.

Charly says:
    I didn't know! How was I supposed to know? THIS is why I stick to serial monogamy.

Nikki says:
    Ugh, more like *serial monotony*. Ugh. Seriously, how could you not know this guy was an Ashton? Couldn't you have at least asked the tadpole if he was aware that 90210 is a *remake*?

Charly says:
    Funny, that never came up. I *did* find it intriguing that his flawless complexion didn't seem to have any pores... And when he said "I'm a grad"... Oh god, he meant high school...

Nikki says:
    LOL you're SUCH a pervert. So, the real question is: are you going to call it quits now that you know how old he is?

Charly says:
    Well... I don't want to discriminate based on age... I mean, he's really sweet and aside from the age thing we actually do have a connection. Maybe if the situation was different we'd end up together...

Nikki says:
> You just keep telling yourself that, Chester the Molester. Well, either way, good for you, it's been awhile. Did he have to use a broom to clear the cobwebs from your hoo-ha?

Charly says:
> Hardy har. No... it was a Dustbuster.

Nikki says:
> Cool, I can actually say I'm friends with a pedophile. I don't know how they do it in Singapore, but in my neighborhood you have to register with some online creep site...

Charly says:
> Back to my dilemma please...

Nikki says:
> If the baby bootie fits...

Charly says:
> I already feel horrible about this....

Nikki says:
> Why!? If the genders were reversed in this situation they're be high-fives all around... Why do men get to have all the fun while my vagina is a second-class citizen?

Charly says:
> Lady, your vagina welcomes more delegates than the United Nations.

Nikki says:
> At least the delegates are of the age of consent!

Charly says:
> Touché.

Nikki says:
> So are you guys going to stay in touch?

Charly says:
> I gave him my info, I don't know. We'll see.

Nikki says:
> Coolio. Gotta go. Safe flight home. xo

Charly says:
> Bye, see you soon! xo

I could always count on Nikki for comic relief. Through every one of my romantic entanglements since elementary school, Nikki had been there to offer sage advice and less-than-sensitive commentary. Sometimes she was just there to laugh at my expense. But I honestly never took offense. That's because Nikki and I did not exactly share the same approach to men: she had no use for them beyond two or three weeks.

Nikki wasn't a "never monogamist" like Eden or a "sporadic monogamist" like Alégra, and she definitely wasn't a "serial monogamist" like me, Nikki was her own brand of woman who refused to adhere to social conventions. I often wondered how Nikki got through her day being so confident and so humbly above it all. But of course, I already knew…

Fully Booked / Genn Pardoe

5. One Night In Boston...

Let's just put that Tyler Kee situation aside, *for now*.

Back in Boston (almost two months after my trip to Singapore) and following a particularly saucy Thursday with Eden and Scott—and subsequent forced steam bath at the condo I shared with Alégra—I was getting ready for my date with Scott's mystery man. Tyler Kee and the Singapore trip had faded into a distant, moderately embarrassing, memory and I was looking forward meeting someone new. With my precious Kermit the Dog asleep on the couch and Alégra in the other room, I was preparing for my night out the same way I always do: to music. I put on my makeup to early nineties pop, get dressed to eighties party anthems, fix my hair to power ballads of the seventies, and apply finishing touches (as well as the mandatory humming and hawing about wardrobe) to classic Motown tunes. I like the process of going backward in musical time and have never truly caught on to anything past 1999.

Truth be told.

"Nobody knows you better than your own music collection," my grungy college boyfriend (the one before Ethan) had once said. Needless to say, his wise words enjoyed a longer lifespan than our relationship.

What a meat-stick he was.

Anyway, I'd decided to sport the classic go-to outfit for first encounters of the casual-but-hopeful kind: skinny jeans tucked into black equestrian-chic boots, and a tailored white dress shirt. Since my trip to Singapore, Eden had become my official wardrobe consultant and so naturally, she came over to comment.

"You look like a lost member of the Gestapo Marching Band," the words flew out her mouth as I answered the door and grasped at the bottle of Pinot she had brought over. "No more Project Runway for you, missy. Auf Wiedersehen."

I mock-congratulated Eden on her blunt wit as she slipped out of an incredibly gaudy fur coat (*ew!*) to reveal a ballerina-esque frame covered in nothing but faded skinny jeans and a burnout white tee, no bra.

Kermit wiggled excitedly at Eden's arrival but she breezed by him nonchalantly and headed straight for the kitchen. Along the way she waved hello to Alégra who was preparing for a third date with some banker type named Teddy.

Alégra's routine differed from mine: it consisted of watching TMZ, sausaging herself unnecessarily into spanx, slathering cover-up onto an already perfect complexion, and carefully affixing hair extensions, each strategically placed and fussed over.

"Damn, girl," Eden joked to Alégra as she sat on top of our kitchen island and easily crossed her bare feet into Lotus pose. "Fake hair, fake nails, fake boobs… Were you made in China?"

"Oh, aren't you clever," Alégra smiled warmly — with just a titch of sarcasm — at her polar opposite. "Some of us actually envision a relationship lasting longer than *by-the-hour*."

"Why?" Eden cocked her head sideways with genuine confusion.

Ali shook her head in mock-disappointment and joined us in the kitchen, "Drinks, ladies?"

I placed three wine glasses on the counter as Eden uncorked the bottle she had brought. Alégra declined in favor of warm lemongrass water.

To each her own, by which I mean... more for me.

I happily accepted my wine and hopped on top of the counter to join Eden. Kermit posed in front of me on the floor and did his best: *I haven't eaten in three weeks* pose. I pretended to buy it and fed him cubes of Gouda and Smoked Gruyere. He eked out tiny farts in appreciation... it was our thing.

"So, I hear you have a new man, Ali," Eden prodded. "I just hope he's not like the last one. I have told you a million times, dating men who say '_____ *is the new black*' is not acceptable."

"Oh, Declan? C'mon, Eden, he was sweet. Too skinny — which of course made me feel fat — but very sweet."

Alégra reminisced dreamily as she curled her eyelashes and blinked heavily while shifting her head from left to right, as though testing the different angles of her curls.

"Ugh," Eden scoffed, "I always wanted to ask him: *do you think you may have gone just a little overboard with your staff discount at Suburban Hipster?*"

"Eww!" Alégra squealed with a disgusted look. "Declan didn't work in retail! He was a curator at an art gallery."

Eden burst out laughing, "Oh, he was a *gayer*, even better! That explains why you two were always *talking things out*. I'm surprised your periods didn't sync up."

"Ha!" Alégra fake laughed. "And dare I ask, how's *your* love life going, Miss Quinn?"

"Absolute perfection!" Eden cheered excitedly. "Oh, darling, why don't you come out with me tomorrow? I'm going trolling for my next conquest."

"Hmm, *thanksbutnothanks*," Alégra smiled and looked in my direction. "Anyway, Eden, don't you have someone to dress?"

Eden untangled her Lotus pose, rose gracefully in agreement, and faux-cackled, "Come with me, my pretty!"

I let Alégra get back to her primping as Eden and I headed towards my room with Kermit in tow, dragging his slobbery Miss Piggy blanket and letting out cheese-flavored farts.

I wish more men were like Kermit; so straightforward and uncomplicated. Over the last month or so my favorite dates had been the ones with him: we'd take a walk through the Common and stop for a shrimp burrito with extra cheese.

(I was careful never to order jalapenos when we ate together.) Then, we'd sit on a bench side by side and people-watch as we shared the world's greatest food. Sometimes we'd happily waste away an entire afternoon together. What I liked about Kermit was that we shared the same taste in cuisine, *burritos*, and we enjoyed the same hobbies, *people watching*. Sometimes I doubted I'd ever find a guy as simple, sweet, down-to-earth, and full of unconditional love as Kermit...

Jeez lady, get a two-legged date!

It suddenly dawned on me that I was a bit out of practice. Okay. Minor freak out: what if I was totally out of sync with the dating world? Oh crap, who exactly *was* Scott's mystery guy and why I had never heard of him?

What if he turned out to be the love of my life?
What if we got married?
What would our kids be like?
Whoa. Calm down.

"Hey, smitten kitten," teased Eden. "I can *see* you fantasizing about all the little *wanker banker* babies you two are going to have. Just take a breath. It's only a drink. Let's get you sorted, shall we?"

I nodded sheepishly and she got to work. When Eden was finished she stood back and admired her project: tousled chignon, Audrey makeup, cashmere wraparound sweater over cream silk chemise, navy skinnies, and sky-high ankle boots. Almost *everything* by Liam & Olivia (from Ali's closet, *obvi*) and *almost* nothing owned by Charly. Eden made a *mwah!* gesture with her fingers—as if admiring a dish of Spaghetti Bolognese—reminded me that I owed Alégra my life for access to such a great wardrobe, and rushed me and my new-and-improved outfit into the living room to show me off.

We rounded the corner to see that Nikki had joined the party. As different as Alégra and Eden were, Nikki and Eden were *that* similar. The girls exchanged big embraces and immediately erupted into a frisson of girlie gossip which was normally so unlike both of them, except for when they were together. It naturally left Alégra somewhat out of the group, so I joined her in the kitchen as Nikki and Eden traded war stories that would make even my dog blush. Kermit, on his part, assumed his regular spot in front of me and went back to eating cheese bits off the floor and farting in thanks.

"Nikki! How *are* you, darling? Tell me everything! What's new? Who's been messing about in your naughty bits?" Eden still had her bare arms wrapped elegantly around Nikki.

Both girls were effortlessly slender, but Eden certainly took the cake when it came to exuding natural grace; an irony I think helped dilute her crass demeanor.

Nikki, who was sporting a harshly-tailored navy blazer and over-the-knee black boots, plopped down on our over-stuffed couch and lit a cigarette as Alégra frowned from the kitchen. Nikki rolled her eyes playfully at Alégra, cracked the nearest window a bit in response, and turned her attention to Eden.

"Bitch, I'm fucking amazing. I just had a high-colonic and hot fling with the concierge in my building. Not in that order, *obviously.*"

"High-colonic? What *is* that?" Alégra whispered to me as she stole a tiny sip of my wine.

(Alégra believed that food or drink belonging to someone else contained no calories.)

"Oh, Ali, you are *much* too cute for your own good," I said as I topped up my wine glass.

"If I'm so cute, then how come I haven't found *him* yet?! I mean, Teddy's great, but it's only our third date. Who knows what will happen!? I have to meet his parents, friends, I mean, there's a lot of effort on my part! It's exhausting searching for love!"

Alégra continued to pout as she fussed over a wisp of perfectly manufactured golden fringes.

"Oh, hunny," I kissed Alégra's forehead (and in doing so, left a tiny trace of glistening lip gloss that would make her sprout a second head if she saw it), "You'll find him. You're smart, funny, stylish, and you're like, annoyingly gorgeous. What man wouldn't be lucky to date you?"

"Beautiful? Ha! I'm a size *six*. SIX! I'm *humongous*! Nikki and Eden are so tiny and gorgeous and perfect and they don't even try!"

I smiled sadly at Ali. It was unfortunate but true. Our two besties were classic *stunners*; they literally had to beat men away with a stick. I've actually seen Nikki do it more than once... What's worse, they didn't care. This, of course, made men fall to their feet even more. *Vicious cycle indeed.* I wished that the universe would give Alégra some of the confidence that Eden and Nikki had. She deserved it. She was truly one of the 'good ones'.

"Alégra," I sighed, "first of all, size six is not humongous. You're a teeny tiny thing but you're like me, and the *rest* of the *human* women on the planet, we have to work at it *just* a little bit. So? That's okay. It's better to be healthy than have *vodka* as your blood type like Drunk & Drunker over there. Secondly, you *will* find him. Don't rush things and *don't* compare yourself to others. It's an exercise in wasting the person you are."

Of course I could say that with confidence...

I was about to meet my betrothed...

I was so happy that night. I felt as though I was *finally* taking the first steps on my journey of self-discovery, I was seriously considering Scott's email (the offer to go to Bangkok) and I had a mystery date with my future husband. (Oh, and I *totally* reeled in a super-hot Canadian tadpole earlier this year.)

Ali smiled as she finally poured herself her own glass of wine. "You're right. Thanks, Charly and—"

"Eden, I am *telling* you," Nikki's raspy voice boomed over ours. "The stench from his crotch would kill a vulture, a cockroach even!"

Eden burst out laughing and Alégra looked at me helplessly, "And *she's* the one who always has a date on Friday? Like, seriously! She has *no* class!"

"I heard that, Pollyanna," chuckled Nikki hoarsely in Alégra's direction. "And, I'm *classy as fuck*, baby."

"Oh, I can see that," Alégra laughed as we made our way into the living room to join the girls. "Okay, okay, I give up! What are you two ladies talking about?"

"Well," said Nikki, "*I* was updating Eden on how I just broke up with this douchebag and now I'm terrified that *I am* a douchebag because I slept with one."

Nikki looked to her friends with genuine concern.

"Like, am I sullied by his douchebaggery? Does that stuff spread? Is douchebag-ness communicable? Is there, like, some kind of Mexican under-the-counter antibiotic I can take to rid myself of douchebag cooties?"

Alégra cleared her throat and genuinely put forth her best effort, "Okay, first of all, stop saying *douchebag* and second of all, no, I don't think so. It's not like herpes, or bad fashion sense. It's not contagious so you don't need worry."

"Hmmm," Nikki considered Alégra's words thoughtfully, "you're probably right."

"Right," I tried to collect the attention of the group. "Can we please have one final verdict on the outfit before I go and meet Scott's friend, otherwise known as, my husband-to-be?"

"Super cute!" Alégra squealed. I mouthed a *thank-you* to Ali and turned towards Nikki.

Now for the final verdict...

Nikki cleared her throat and declared with authority, "That outfit says, *although I am relatively easy, no, I do not have daddy issues, so, unfortunately for you, we will not be sleeping together on our first date so like, too bad for you.*"

"That's *exactly* what I was going for," I teased Nikki as I stole a drag from her cigarette—*only when I'm nervous, I swear.*

Eden assured me, "You look lovely, just lovely. Now come on my little Charly girl, I'll drive you."

That was great news because I felt myself gently swaying back and forth, final glass of Pinot in hand.

"Bloody lush," huffed Eden. "Good thing you've got me to chauffeur you about. Besides, it's colder than my mother out there."

I had no problems being *chauffeured about* in Eden's luxury SUV: it cost more than my parents' combined annual salary. Actually, all of my friends were super-moneyed: Scott was a trust funder, Eden was practically royalty, Alégra was supported by a very rich absentee father, and Nikki, well, I'll get to *her* later…

"Oh, can I come?" Alégra asked as she wrapped her alpaca Liam & Olivia cape around her shoulders and slid on chic slouchy boots. "My date isn't for a couple hours, he's working late."

"And by *date* you mean *bootie call*," Nikki teased. "I might as well come too, I'm out of cigarettes."

Alégra stuck her tongue out at Nikki—who grinned widely and linked arms with her Liam & Olivia-draped friend—as we made our way out of our condo and into the cold.

Minutes later Eden's Escalade pulled up in front of a tiny wine bar and I couldn't help but wince as I opened the door. Freezing winds swirled about in Eden's toasty ride, causing everyone to shiver.

"Ah!" Eden exclaimed, "I simply *cannot* take it anymore. I am of African descent, *after all*. I'm in *dire* need of clement climes and sunny vistas."

"African?" chirped Nikki. "If you're African, I'm the last Mohican."

"*What-Ever.*" Eden said in Mockney slang, the accent *de rigeur* of British youths.

They all burst out laughing as I double-kissed their cheeks and hopped out.

"Have fun, Charly!" Alégra, who is love's greatest cheerleader, smiled and waved at me eagerly.

"Thanks for the drive!" I said into the wind.

I scuttled away as Nikki cracked open her door to shout something about the importance of prophylactics. I raised a finger in sarcastic acknowledgement and burst through the storm doors. Inside it was quiet and I immediately spotted Scott. He was in mid-conversation with a well-fed Gucci model who seemed to have lost his way *en route* to Fashion Week…

Fully Booked / Genn Pardoe

6. Okay so here's how Nikki Temple got through her day...

Oh, *right*, back to Nikki.

...to get through her day, Nikki Temple went to some pretty great lengths. For starters, she changed her entire identity.

Pause for scandal...

Born Nicola Templeton, daughter of Dusty Templeton of *the* Templeton Industries (only the world's largest shipping company and controller of most oceanic navigation routes from here to Auckland), Nikki's family was one of the last true dynasties in the modern world.

I know! Crazy, right?

Over the last five generations, the Templetons had migrated from England to every major port in the world. LA, Toronto, Singapore, Cape Town, London, Hong Kong harbor, I mean, they even had stake in the Shat al Arab. No big deal.

Huge deal.

Over the course of a hundred and fifty years or so, the Templetons had slowly but surely built an empire, establishing control over most everything that was transported by boat. In the majority of the countries where they had presence—New Zealand, Singapore, England, and South Africa—the Templetons enjoyed a privileged but relatively quiet existence.

No such luck for the American branch of the Templeton family tree. This was thanks to Nikki's dad...

In his day, Dusty Templeton was a wild playboy who drank excessively and bedded every Hollywood A-lister he could get his hands on—the result of which was more children than he and the family cared to acknowledge. Except Nikki. Nikki was his favorite. This was most likely because Nikki neither looked nor acted like a typical Templeton. Where all of the other Templeton women were blonde and voluptuous, Nicola was a natural waif with raven-hair and electric green eyes. But like every teenager, Nikki had gone through a period of wanting to fit in—at any cost. She was able to hide her true self thanks to implants, contacts, and ample amounts of bleach. (Luckily none of these false attributes became permanent fixtures—especially the implants.)

Then came the media...

While her older siblings and cousins were happy to be snapped by photographers as they fell out of bars and Maybachs, Nicola preferred to be at her father's side. Growing up, Nicola understood that part of being a member of the Templeton family meant being the object of admiration, awe, and scandal—depending on how the media skewed it that week.

But it never really suited her, in fact it terrified her. Even though she'd been in the public eye since before she could walk, Nicola loathed the mass amounts of attention and did everything she could to avoid it. But by the age of 13, fate had other plans for Nicola Templeton: she was named the future leader of the company as per her father's dying wishes. (Don't stress. It turned out to be a false alarm in the form of bad indigestion. Dusty Templeton remains very much alive and is a huge supporter of his daughter's choice to lead a private life. Having said that, Dusty still expects his favorite daughter to take charge of Templeton Industries one day...)

Pressure much?
Like, seriously!

By the age of 13 Nikki was already armed with the knowledge that she would eventually take the helm of the world's largest shipping conglomerate. So it's no wonder that an overwhelmed teenage version of Nikki dove into a tailspin for a couple years. Drugs, alcohol, and other things that are just too weird to mention — it all happened at once for Nikki.

Suddenly, it was Nicola falling out of bars and Maybachs and being snapped by hungry paparazzi...

For three years, there wasn't a tabloid magazine that didn't have an image of a drunken Nicola — eyes half closed, breasts mostly exposed — on the cover at least once a week. By the time she'd reached 17, she was burnt out. It was time to make a change.

Of her own volition, the young heiress approached her father with the following proposal: say goodbye to Nicola. And that's how the transition from a bubbly blonde with a serious drinking problem — Nicola Templeton — to a sardonic bitch business major with a, um, less serious drinking problem — Nikki Temple, began.

If she could make it on her own, away from the scrutiny of public life, she'd return to the family at the age of 30, and properly take control of her birth right. But until then, she'd rather be just another fish in the Boston harbor.

Reluctant to let his little girl go into the world all alone, Dusty Templeton made Nicola promise to check in every day and visit him at the country house no less than once a month. She dutifully obliged and in return, Dusty invested for the first time in a Templeton woman's education (plus more-than-generous living expenses) and enrolled his daughter in Boston University under the name Nikki Temple.

It wasn't that tough getting her into the school. After all, half of the buildings on campus were named after him. On her end, Nicola Lillian Blythe Templeton had no trouble becoming Nikki No Middle Name Temple. Her father and the family's publicist, on the other hand, had some work to do.

Eventually however, they pulled it off...

In the eyes of the average Boston gossip magazine reader, troubled heiress Nicola Templeton had moved to the family's home on 'the continent'. (To a refurbished seventeenth century villa in Genoa, to be exact.)

Nicola was presumed to be either avoiding the public eye or living out her days as a vapid trust fund party brat until she'd eventually marry an equally vapid trust fund party brat, probably from the famed Smythe-George name (the only family remotely in the same stratosphere of affluence as the Templetons). It would make a logical alliance, the tabloids had concluded. The story went on and on....

At one point Nikki read that she was pregnant with twins and living on a commune in the Azores. She didn't care. She'd long ago morphed back into the flat-chested raven-haired outliar she'd once been and didn't even consider herself to be Nicola Templeton anymore. In her own way, she was happy. (Even though 'happy' to the naturally melancholy Nikki looked more like bottomless depression to the average person.)

As months became years, Nikki grew increasingly confident in herself as independent from the Templeton family. And although she never forgot where her good fortune came from, she refused to share her true identity with anyone, even Alégra.

Especially Alégra...

7. In Which Charly Briar Meets the Love of Her Life (and so early on in the story, too!)

Kai Kostigan remained seated and casually shook my hand, making the shape of 'Hi' with his mouth but not really saying it. I did the same as I finalized the details of my *Breakfast at Tiffany's*-inspired wedding shower.

I sat down in between Scott and Kai and ordered a glass of Pinot amidst unicorns prancing on rainbow-colored clouds with dancing babies in hats.

Um, love at first sight?

Yes.

Okay first off, the immediate attraction was that we both remembered the eighties (which is more than I can say about that yummy Canadian puppy who, er, shall remain nameless). But it was so much more than that.

Over the next three hours I learned that Kai was a witty New York-based investment banker who made Matt Damon look like an illiterate boxcar hobo. Kai was traveled, educated, smart, funny, and painfully good-looking. Basically, I was dealing with a living tribute to the Greek, Roman, *and* Gucci gods…

OMG!

As I listened to Kai Kostigan talk about himself I realized that I was sitting with every girl, cougar, and sexually confused teenager's ultimate fantasy. In his worn jeans, grey V-neck, and chocolate brown loafers, Kai looked more like a well-fed supermodel than an awkward *wanker banker*, as Eden had predicted.

Kai was soft spoken but sharp, and *just the right* level of charming for me to cross *emotionally deranged freak* off my list of *must-not* haves.

Score!

I kept winking *thank-you's* at Scott and made a mental note to give him a kidney if it ever came up. When Kai talked, he did so unhurriedly and carefully. He asked intelligent questions and gave thoughtful answers. And, he looked in my eyes *only* when emphasizing a point, the rest of the time gazing profoundly into space, or at his beverage. (A sign of true intelligence.)

I was thankful for that because it gave me a chance to admire Kai's flawlessness without blatantly appearing to stare. As I blatantly stared at Kai, I couldn't help but drink in his crisp apple hair and sweet sugar cookie eyes...

Okay, I seriously need to stop drunk baking.

Kai was *so* flawless and *so* statuesque that I didn't want to tell a joke for fear that his perfectly chiseled face would crack and shatter on the sidewalk. So instead of pulling out my usual witty quips, I resorted to staring dreamily at him while fantasizing about having, like, a thousand of his babies.

And he was so interesting!

Kai captivated me with his ambition and subtle humor. It almost made me feel as dull as matte lipstick when I was called upon to speak about myself. But I *did* make headway as I recounted my pre-Edifice Luxe days as a wandering traveler with Alégra in Europe.

"Well aren't you rare and well aware," Kai cooed as he drained a scotch that was older than me.

Oh swoon.

"Am I?" I said as coolly as possible.

"Yes," he confirmed with confidence. "I've always wanted to travel, *especially* for work."

"Me too!" I exclaimed.

I think I might have even clapped my hands together like a plumpy child at a birthday party when the loot bags are brought in. I can't quite remember the details because I was completely inebriated on a deadly cocktail of libations and love...

Yes, love. (I know!)

All night the conversation literally fell out of our mouths. There were hardly enough seconds in each passing minute for Kai and me to tell each other everything we wanted the other person to know.

Kai was one of those people you *just have to* tell everything to. I couldn't believe he felt the same way about me. And then it happened...

"You are achingly beautiful," Kai whispered into my ear when Scott was busy ordering another round.

Um, excuse me?

Huh?

I absolutely could *not* believe that Kai was referring to *me*. I immediately glanced over my shoulder, expecting to see some smoking hot Scar Jo/Kate Hudson hybrid lingering annoyingly in the background.

No Hottie Hybrid.

No nobody.

Just me.

There must be some mistake.

In my long brown hair and Cleopatra bangs I was 'the cute girl', in my borrowed Liam & Olivia frocks I could pull off being 'the stylish girl', and, in my enthusiasm for alcohol and capacity for witty banter I was 'the girlfriend girl'.

But there was nothing I owned or behaved like that made me 'the achingly beautiful girl'. Kai must suffer from night blindness, I decided, or maybe he was on drugs, or perhaps he was having a stroke.

I was truly confused.

Just over a month ago it was Tyler Kee in Singapore, now Kai Kostigan in Boston, what's next? Will I open my door to find Tom Hardy and Jake Gyllenhaal naked wrestling each other to the ground for my affection?

Something was not right...

Why was the universe being so generous with its hotties? Had I been blacking out and signing away my entire salary to Greenpeace? Had I accidentally donated all of my organs to those less fortunate? Had I forgotten that I volunteered to drive the Meals On Wheels van for the next ten Christmases?

Was this simply the universe trying to tap me on the head and tell me I'm a complete and total idiot for even *thinking* that I was in a dry spell?

Why was Karma being so nice to me?

When the hour was late and Scott had abandoned us some time ago, it was clearly time to make a move. After a break in the conversation, Kai sighed and rubbed his hands along his designer denim covered thighs, giving the signal for the night to come to a close. I reciprocated by reaching for my slouchy clutch and smiling dumbly. As I was about to thank him for the drinks and bring up the awkward next step of catching one cab or two, Kai suggested we go back to his hotel for a late dinner.

Thank god Eden dressed me.

(Before she came over I was wearing Spanx and my old bra that Kermit often used as a chew toy.) As we rode in the taxi back to his hotel, he placed his hand on mine and I was sure that I was in love.

¤ * § * ¤

"Crikey," Eden exploded at me and my hangover the next day at work. "Blonde hair, blue eyes? Charly, you're making him out to be the poster boy for the National Socialist Party. Either that, or a Swedish robot assassin from the future."

"Shhh! I gushed to Eden, who made the international symbol for bulimia. "Now tell me how this story ends!"

I tried to tie the story together as I soothed my aching head with a diet soda and ramen noodles, the perfect cure for the morning after the night before.

"We stayed up all night eating room service. We talked about everything and nothing. Oh-my-GOD-I-am-so-in-love!"

"You are so mental," Eden laughed as I tried to stifle my squeals of joy and elation.

OMG. So in love!

"Anyway," I continued, "he left at six in the morning to catch a flight on some kind of investment banker mission and dropped me off on the way to the airport." The only physical contact came in the form of hand-on-hand in the cab and an *I'm leaving for war, wait for me my love* style kiss. It was perfect!"

"Filthy liar!" barked Eden, loud enough for a few heads to pop up over cubicles.

I pulled her deeper into my cubicle area, "I am not! Nothing else happened. Wait. Why did nothing else happen? OMG. No!"

"Well he's gay, darling, obviously he's totally gay. Why didn't Scott tell you he was gay?"

Ever the problem solver, Eden wheeled my chair (and me) out of her way and IM'd Scott on the intra-office message system. Within seconds my computer beeped with a flashing message from Scott informing us that indeed, Kai was *not* one of the *chosen ones* and, by the way, he told Scott that he had an "unforgettable time with the stunning Charly Briar".

OMG!

Boy gossip!

Is there anything more precious??

Scott then informed Eden to quit hijacking my computer and go back to work, lunch at 2pm? We both responded *yes* and I tossed my soppy noodles in the garbage. Over lunch, Eden interrogated Scott as to why Kai had rejected me.

Before I could protest—I felt as though 'rejected' was a pretty strong word—Scott launched into a suspiciously natural soliloquy about Kai's reputation for not really committing.

"*He's just not that into you,*" I said in my Scott-voice.

"Shush! That's not what I said! He *is* into you, Charly. Trust me. I saw it last night when you walked towards us." Scott tried to assure me, but I was unconvinced. He continued, "Kai was awestruck. Seriously I've never seen him so taken with a girl before. It's just that… Well… Didn't he tell you about his ex?"

"Yeah," I began slowly, "he said she was eaten by a hippo while on safari. I think he was being facetious."

"Ya think?" Eden quipped.

"Hardy har," it was my turn to be cheeky.

"Exes are an inescapable part of that ridiculous serial dating game you like to play, my dear," said Eden as she picked at her lunch, a very big and very raw piece of fish.

"Not for me," I shrugged. "I don't think about ex's once I'm done with them, never have. That's just not how I'm built. Sure, I wish them all the best, but I don't actually *care* about them."

"Oh, *please!*" Scott and Eden both said in unison.

"No, truly, I don't." I said honestly. "I like to exhaust all attempts at salvation from *within* the relationship, so when it ends, I know it's over… for *good*. I never understand why people are so bummed when a relationship is over. When have you *ever* seen a perfectly content relationship end? Two people love each other more than anything… so they break up? No. Of course not. That would never happen. That's not how it works. Only crappy relationships end… because… wait for it… they're *crappy!* I see it as a good thing. It paves the way for the next, and possibly marriage-worthy, relationship to begin."

Case in point: Ethan Charge, that barnyard animal I dated for two ridiculous years. He might as well be on a space station or embarking on his own version of *Eat, Pray, Love* for all I care. I'm over it. I'm over him. Why? Because it was *crappy!*

"I'm not buying this," said Scott quizzically. "There's not one guy—not one single guy—who has ever gotten under your skin?"

"Nope," I shook my head truthfully. "I guess I just see the bigger picture, I guess."

"C'mon! What about that minor you molested in Singapore last month?" asked Scott. "I saw his picture, *yummy!*"

I stuck my tongue out at Scott and pushed thoughts of Tyler out of my head, *again*.

"Oh please," Eden answered for me.

I was thankful that she was on my side...

Eden continued, "I'm sure Charly has had more memorable times going solo than with the kabobs she brings 'round."

Oh, well, not exactly what I was going for...

"Thanks, Eden," I accepted her backward compliment. "That so beautifully articulates exactly what I was getting at. The point I'm trying to make is that I don't get hung up on all that end-of-relationship drama. And I've never cried over an ex, *ever*."

"That's because you've *always* got a new guy waiting to take the place of the old one. You never give yourself time to grieve," Scott said softly, but firmly.

"Grieve! Grieve? It's a *penis*, not my grandmother," I chuckled.

"He's right," agreed Eden. "You never get closure."

I'm sorry, what?

"Scott, did you seriously just drop the *C-word* on me?! Closure? Closure? Are you kidding me right now?" I raised an eyebrow and shook my heard. "Okay, like, honestly, this is *me* rolling my eyes at *you*."

Okay. Here we go.

Yet again.

I'm going to try and walk *everyone* through this *very, slowly*, so that we can finally get on the same page on the closure issue. The ~~concept~~ fallacy of closure is best explained via a comparative look at people like me (serial daters) and people like my adoring bestie, Alégra DeVrees (sporadic daters). Okay, let's get started:

The Serial Dater

Aw, my people.

When we exit a relationship we want to be darn sure it's over. No more soft and cuddly feelings, no questioning of our judgment, no residual sexual attraction, and above all else, no tears.

Ever.

A Serial Dater leaves a relationship feeling sorry for the next girl who has to date her moron ex, not feeling jealous of her. After all, beyond the extremely brief readjustment period (like, two weeks, max.) there's no room for ill-will towards the ex-boyfriend or his new waitress / dancer girlfriend.

Am I right?

Or am I right?

You see, the Serial Dater doesn't have to sink to jealousy because: the facts speak for themselves. When the evidence is so clear, (a.k.a. "we broke up because he suffers from profound douchebaggery and his new girlfriend earns a living through her work on a website") well, like I said, there's nothing to be jealous of....

Serial Daters don't mess around with breakup sex, drunk dialing, or falling asleep with the aid of Ambien and half a pack of cigarettes while clutching a bottle of raspberry-flavored Smirnoff and sobbing hysterically about the end of the world and the collapse of the universe.

We don't even cry!

Ever.

It's no joke.

Tears are *seriously* frowned upon in the Serial Dater world, and I for one wholeheartedly support tear-shaming, by the way.

It's just not done!

I didn't cry when Ethan and I ended things, not even when I had a hernia, and the fact I *was* crying when I called him to announce that I was embarking on a jet-setting journey of self-discovery, well, those were just tears of triumph.

Serial Daters leave a relationship the way they leave a Sample Sale: "*Meh*, it was okay, I suppose. I can't really remember most of what I saw, it was all a happy blur, but it's over now and I certainly don't miss anything. In fact I don't even really recall what brought me there in the first place... seemed like the right thing to do at the time. Oh, well, whatever. I see there's another Sample Sale next week. Perfect. Bring it on!"

Much like the golden rule that no calendar is complete without the next Sample Sale jotted down in it, no Serial Dater's social life is complete without the next potential boyfriend on the horizon. It's just common sense, people. It's called being prepared. And besides, having the next guy waiting in the wings cuts down on "emotional baggage"—words I hate almost as much as "closure". Where Sporadic Daters, like Alégra, carry around emotional baggage for the next three evolutionary stages, Serial Daters don't have time to cry over spilled boyfriends. We need to get things moving! I make it a rule to never, *ever*, loiter about in my own past. Who knows what I'd find back there.

Yikes! I have shivers just thinking about it, and besides, doesn't living in the past inhibit your ability to move into the future? Doesn't being a Serial Dater seem like a way better approach to dating? It saves on time *and* effort. It's like the Prius of dating: totally sustainable, totally chic. Now, to become a Serial Dater all you need to do is think like one. That's all. It's that easy! Here's what you need to do and honestly, when I learned about it, my life changed. It's a simple mantra, and when said correctly, it can be the most empowering phrase ever uttered. Ready to make your transformation?

Okay...

At the end of your current relationship, walk to the mirror and repeat the following vow three times:

"Wow, I must have suffered from temporary but profound alcoholic-infused retardation to give [guy's name] the time of day let alone date him." That's all it takes!

You suck.
I rule.
Magnum Extra Large?
That's adorable.
I can't believe you think your penis is above-average size.
Or even average...
Haven't you heard of Google, boy!?
Next!

Unfortunately, not everyone can see the light... The sad mantra of Sporadic Daters is as follows: "I'll simply never find another heart and/or mind and/or penis as majestic as his."

Gag me.

The Sporadic Dater
See: Alégra....

Sporadic Daters are those people who take time off in between relationships to absorb and reflect, maybe even have a rebound (an exercise I clearly fail at executing, see: hernia.) and then they *ease* their way into their next relationship equipped with the lessons they have learned from their past....

Oh, sorry, I <u>literally</u> fell asleep while writing that.
Boring! Seriously!

In some circles, Sporadic Daters are referred to as "normal people", and honestly, I have no idea why. Let me drop a cold hard fact on you adorable wackos: just because there's more of you, doesn't make you normal. Sporadic Daters are the people who obsess *forever* after the break-up and drag their friends through *hell* during the mourning period. They're also involved in nothing short of *harassment* when it comes to their ex. (Good luck to the gal pals if the ex-boyfriend has a new lady right away.) Even *I'm* embarrassed at how many times Alégra has dragged me on a ~~night stalking mission~~ excursion to "randomly" bump into an ex and his new date.

Stalking is way more exhausting than it looks!
Seriously...
Carb up, people!

And here we arrive at my central thesis....

It is my position that this *all* has to do with Sporadic Daters' obsession with the asinine notion of *closure*. This mirage they keep chasing—that conversation or gesture that will make the end seem like an amazing idea and one that is mutually beneficial for both people; as if they *both* came up with it in the first place.

Sad shake of head...

Sporadic Daters say things like, "He was just holding me back and, actually, he is *such* an amazing guy to let me go so I can dedicate myself fully to my career as a dental hygienist," or "She's so focused on yoga teacher training right now and I'm really proud of her. She just doesn't have the time for a serious relationship. I'm sure we'll reconnect in the future, she *said* we would."

Um...

Okay...

No.

You people used to touch each other's privates and throw around hypothetical names for your mediocre-looking future children—you made promises to each other! And now he's broken up with you because he's a moron and thinks he can do better—he's smashed all those pretty dreams to bits—and you think you're going to stay in each other's hearts forever as you hold hands and ride magical friendship-unicorns over a beautiful rainbow into the land of....

Oh please!

Have you been sipping paint?

It's over.

And that's okay.

Don't worry. You'll be fine...

I swear. For reals....

You lived like a relatively normal functioning human *before* him and you'll most likely go back to that *after* him.

Hell, you might even discover a *better* version of yourself.

So stop peeing your pants over this meat-head!

Maybe you'll take up Pilates or get a new hairstyle. Perhaps you'll enroll in culinary school or finally take that cycling tour of a wine region you've always wanted to visit. The wrong relationships have to end to make room for the right one. I mean, you can't marry all the guys you date—that did occur to you, right? By far the majority of your relationships will end. That's kind of the point, *no?*

Yes.

And for those girls who require closure from a guy who treated them like utter crap—why are you empowering that douche-cake even more? If he wasn't good to you *during* the relationship, what in the name of side-swept fringes makes you think he'll be genuine and decent *after* the relationship?

Cold hard fact number two: he owes you nothing. It's not up to him to make you feel better, you *dingbat*. It's up to you, wine, your friends, and maybe the hot rebound you're about to have. I don't know—haven't had one. But the point is, it's up to *you* not *him*.

Anyway, of all the bizarre rituals propagated by Sporadic Daters, the "we're having one last lunch together, you know, for closure" is the one that gives me the biggest headache.

I don't even know where to begin on this one…

Like, honestly…

Okay, here we go…

The idea that an entire relationship can be summed up, rationalized, and tied neatly in a Tiffany-colored bow—leaving no question unanswered and no feeling remotely bruised—over a California Roll and Diet Coke is *the* most bat shit crazy thing I've ever heard. And why, in eight out of ten breakups, does the quintessential *closure lunch* consist of soda and sushi? I guess it's French cuisine to rendezvous, Italian to *besame mucho*, and Japanese to say *sayonara!* I guess for Sporadic Daters, Pacific-caught salmon and carbonated aspartame really takes the edge off of a breakup. (Word to the wise: if you're breaking up with me, nothing says, *we're over, buddy* like Surf & Turf and a big glass of Pinot. Just saying…)

Bottom line: there's *no* such thing as closure.

I used to argue this with Alégra all the time.

"Of course there is!" she'd say. "Everybody needs closure at the end of a relationship, it helps you move on. You know, you meet for coffee, or grab some sushi..."

Did I call that or what?

"...and both people have a chance to go over the reasons for breaking up when they're in a calm state of mind. It's very cathartic and the process ensures there are no hard feelings. It's healthy, Charly."

"It's doesn't exist, Ali, I'm telling you." I tried to explain.

"How are you so sure?" Alégra guffawed.

"Are you *sure* you want to know?" I cautioned.

"Yes, of course!"

"Ali, there's no such thing as closure," I began, painfully aware I was about to burst my dear friend's love-bubble. "Because the only person asking for it, is the one who's been dumped."

OMG!

Light bulb!

I continued, "Closure is simply a bullshit courtesy that the dumper extends to the sad sack they've just left."

"Whoa," said Alégra, her eyes widening.

"I know," I nodded.

"I mean," she asked with furrowed brows. "It's not *always* like that, is it?"

"It's *always* like that," I confirmed.

I hated to be the one destroying my friend's perfect vision of love and relationships and break-ups and "staying friends... but I felt that in the long run, I was doing her a favor.

"Even if it seems like *you're* the one doing the dumping, if you ask for closure, it was already over."

"Shit."

"I know."

¤ * § * ¤

"Can we please get back to talking about Kai's ex," I whined as I ordered another glass of lemon water.

My head was pounding from lack of sleep and too much Pinot.

It'd been completely worth it though...

I was so totally in love with Kai—I think, I'm pretty sure—and I couldn't wait to tell Scott and Eden all about it.

"So," I began, "here's what I know about Kai's most recent relationship: it ended almost six months ago and she left him for some job in a country that ends in *'eesia'* or *"ikistan*. Kai said the break-up was amicable but I think he suspected cheating... do you know if he caught her?"

"Nope," Scott shook his head in a way that suggested he had intimate knowledge of the story I was telling. "But I remember that Kai didn't wait around to find out. The only thing he said was, *When there is doubt, there is no doubt.*"

"Ohhhh, that's so profound," I pined.

"Yes it is," balked Eden. "Profoundly moronic." She rolled her eyes and reduced Kai to yet another *wanker banker*. "I *told* you!" she stated triumphantly. Scott tried to reassure me that Kai in fact *did* have a great time, he *was* going to call, and his ex-girlfriend might *as well* have been run over hippos—it was *that* over. Still, it took Scott most of lunch to convey this message because Eden kept interrupting with gestures of doubt. As we walked back to the office, I tried to make sense of my encounter with Kai amidst growing insecurity, thanks to Eden.

Why did nothing substantial happen?
Had I missed his cues?
Had I done something to change his mind?
Had he just wanted a drinking buddy for the evening?
So much for the love of my life...
Sigh.

I guess my evening with Kai was nothing more than one of those bizarre, *unqualifiable* (I know that's not a word but it should be) nights that would become diluted by the passage of time.

By the end of the walk back to the office I doubted if I'd ever see Kai again. *Dammit.* I was so confused. This morning I'd felt so sure about us. But now, as the day wore on, I feared I'd made the whole thing up.

Crap.

I had already filled out the online bridal registry at Tiffany & Co. Only in my mind, that is.

Obviously.

I'm not crazy.

I made a mental note to call the bridal consultant and cancel the registry. That's, like, the third time.

Whatever… next!

Who cares about stupid Kai Kostigan? I should be thankful. At least I avoided another Ethan Charge Debacle…

Fully Booked / Genn Pardoe

8. The Ethan Charge Debacle, Part I

When serial monogamists, like me, look over their 'List' there's always one name that screams, *What in the name of LBDs am I doing here!?* Even thinking about this name makes one think, *Gee, I must have been blackout drunk the entire time we were together and all the Clorox in the world won't get your cooties off – and out – of me!*

For me, that name was Ethan Charge. *His* was the name I called after the party at the Fairmont to announce that I was going to be a jet-setting PR maven and would never be heard from again. *His* was the name that made me realize I needed to embark upon a life-changing journey of challenge, discovery, and opportunity.

Yes indeed, if I could stick a pin in the precise starting point of my whirlwind journey, Ethan Charge would be the prick that started it all. Ethan and I met in university through mutual friends. He was two years older than me, in the business program, and at the top of his class.

After graduation he was recruited by a top-tier consulting firm and moved to an amazing condo overlooking Back Bay. I visited him when I could, but for the majority of our relationship, I was in school and he was away on business. This made it staggeringly easy for him to cheat on me.

Ethan was blonde and huge; the kind of guy who looked like domestic abuse might be part of his cardio routine. He was also responsible for my attraction to blonde-haired, blue-eyed, emotionally unavailable and socially withdrawn men with commitment issues and really big secrets.

Thank you very little, Ethan.

Our first date was at a local pub, the kind with peanuts on the floor that reeked of draught beer, early 20s promiscuity, and unbearably loud music by an excruciatingly awful Celtic band. Barely a word could be understood—this forced patrons to drink vast quantities of alcohol and confuse themselves into thinking they were having a good time.

I was having a *great* time.

Ethan was engaging, intelligent, and hilarious (although I couldn't understand the majority of what he was saying due to said noise level).

But I didn't care.

When the bar closed we went to a late night pizza dive and stood in line for what seemed like ages. It was a complete contrast from the dark bar we had just left and I became starkly aware of the profundity of my inebriation.

Yup, I was drunky drunkerson.

At one point I caught my reflection in the window and nearly fell over; my carefully applied makeup was running down my face—as though it was on a toboggan propelled by the alcohol seeping out of my pores.

My dishevelment was further confirmed when I looked down and realized that my strategically placed blouse had come half undone. Great, I thought, I'm standing in a pizza parlor at 4am with a guy I barely know and my breast is half-ways exposed. (For some reason, *boobus escapus* became a chronic issue I'd find myself confronted by more than once over the coming years.) Thankfully, we were distracted by familiar voices.

"Charly!"

It was Alégra and Nikki.

"Hey!" I exclaimed, thankful for the interruption so that I could put myself back together. "*This* is Ethan."

"Hi girls," he said politely. "How's it going?"

Alégra started up a conversation with Ethan. They were both in the same Young Business Starters Club or something equally stupid that people join in university thinking it will make a difference to their résumé in the real world.

I availed myself of the opportunity to whisper in Nikki's ear, "Help! I've got wandering boob. Ethan is going to think I'm so crass!"

Nikki responded with a laugh and shook her head. The girls got their pizza to go and we said goodnight while Ethan and I sat at a high-top table and shared a slice.

"So, what did you say to your friend about me?" Ethan asked casually as he peppered the entire slice with chilies (rendering it completely inedible for me).

"Sorry, what?" I asked nonchalantly.

Ethan smiled at me hard like an angry mama gorilla, "I heard you say *he's an ass* to your friend Nikki. Is that what you think of me?"

It suddenly got very silent in the pizza parlor.

"No, no! I would never say that!" I laughed awkwardly.

Ethan had obviously misheard "crass" for "ass" and I tried to explain my situation, hoping he'd find the humor in my *boobus escapus* conundrum.

He didn't.

Ethan slammed the pizza on the floor and screamed at me, "I'm not a fucking ass! Do you hear me? Do you fucking hear me?"

And then he stormed out.

All of a sudden I was left all alone with inedible pizza and a very confused look on my face.

Like, for realsies…

What just happened?

Now, a normal person would have chalked Ethan up to a completely deranged psychopath who most likely spent the better part of his childhood in a basement closet when not being felt up by a perverted uncle, and *bolt* from the scene faster than immediately.

But, as I've been told, I took the scenic route to adulthood... It hurt me that Ethan would think I could say such a thing, especially after we'd had such a fantastic night and seemed to click so well. I had to clear things up.

Right?

What proceeded was a chase scene down Commonwealth Ave. with Ethan—tears streaming down his face—in the lead and me calling frantically after him. This is the most perfect encapsulation of *the first half* of our relationship I can think of: me chasing him. A representation of the second half of our relationship would be the exact same scenario, in reverse. When I finally caught up to Ethan he was huddled on a stoop with his hands around his knees hiding his face in his lap and crying hysterically.

Again, even a person of minimal intelligence would have been able to see that this was not a good situation. I should have kept right on walking by and never looked back. But, I was a sucker for tears back then and I couldn't stand the thought of being misunderstood. Sounds like *somebody* could have benefited from one or two psychology classes along the way...

But all I could think was, *what if Ethan told people that I was a bitch?*

Then, all of those people from university that I never *ever* kept in touch with after graduation would have a misinformed opinion of me.

The social horror!

I couldn't risk having an unwarranted bad rep among people who today, I could literally trip over and not recognize.

Damn you, Insight!

Where were you in my early twenties?

And Perspective, I'm not happy with you, either....

"Ethan, you *have* to believe me," I pleaded. "This whole thing is just a miscommunication. I said *crass* not *ass*. I said I thought you'd find me crass 'cause of my—"

"Never mind, it doesn't matter. I *am* an ass. At least, that what my parents told me every single day of my dammed stupid life."

Oh boy.

And *that's* the point where even a deaf-blind laboratory baboon with no cognitive skills whatsoever would have called it quits. That baboon would be like, *fuck this, I'm out.*

And yet, like some kind of gigantic moron hell-bent on self-destruction, I persisted, "But I *don't* think that Ethan, I think you're great, fantastic actually."

"Really?" he palmed his eyes with his humungous gorilla hands and looked up at me hopefully.

"*Really*," I confirmed.

"Because, um, Charly, can I tell you something?"

"Anything, Ethan."

"I'm totally in love with you."

"Oh, uh, wow," I was totally caught off guard.

Don't say it don't say it don't say it!

"Ethan," I couldn't help myself. "I love you too."

It was love at first fight.

Fully Booked / Genn Pardoe

9. And it begins...

"Charly! Hello? Ms. Charly Briar! Care to get out of your head and join us over here?"

Eden's voice brought me back into the moment: we were back at the office after a Kai-dissecting lunch. I was tired, doubtful, and a mixture of hungover and the teeniest bit love-sick over a guy I'd just met. A small crowd had gathered at my desk.

"*Somebody* sent you flowers," Scott said in a sing-song voice. "*Told you* he's not like other guys, Eden!"

I swatted both Eden and Scott away and turned back to my desk to find a tightly wound bouquet of short blue roses (*interesting choice*) with a gold-trimmed ribbon, a little package wrapped in pink paper, and a card. I ripped open the package first. It was a hot pink Liam & Olivia wallet. I had casually mentioned last night that Liam & Olivia means more to me than anything—except for Kermit the Dog and burritos, obviously—but definitely more than most friendships, family members, and career aspirations. Obviously I would have to lose about a hundred pounds, shave my legs and marry this man immediately.

I read the card:

Charly B.

Feeling a little blue without you.

xo
Kai

Hence the blue flowers....
Because he's blue, without me.
So poetic!
Oh, you sweet, sweet man.

In an instant all my doubts washed away. I placed the flowers on the corner of my desk, sat down, and sighed blankly (for the next three hours). I wondered where Kai and I would live once we got married. Would he want to live in California or stay in Boston? Maybe we'd move to Paris. I guess it depended on how many children we were going to have and whether or not they'd be in public or private education.

What am I saying?
This is crazy talk!
We'd *obviously* have to be in Chicago, or perhaps New York or Hong Kong, wherever the big stock markets are. Oh, I was going to make the best wife *ever*.

That afternoon the phone at my desk rang...

"It's a wicked day at Bumi~Spa~Aquas. This is Charly Briar, how can I make your day *totes* better?"

It was the mandatory salutation and I *hated* it. The temptation to answer my phone with a fully erect middle finger was almost overwhelming.

"Charly, *please* tell me they make you say that," it was Kai.

I perked up, instinctively smoothed my dress, and crossed my legs, "Oh, hi! No, I mean yes, *yes*, they make us say that," I laughed uncomfortably at my own awkwardness.

"So, Charly, tell me, how is the most beautiful girl in Boston?"

"Oh, well," I blushed hard. "I um, I—"

"I can't stop thinking about you," Kai near-whispered.

Oh – my – god!

I could practically hear him smiling on the other end of the phone. I laughed softly. Was this really it? This was it, this *really was it*. I immediately became flushed and broke out in the kind of sweats usually reserved for when I eat too much ham or mayonnaise. Thankfully, Kai and I were talking on the phone and not in person.

He spoke again, "I have something to tell you."

"Yes!?" I stuttered excitedly.

I couldn't wait to hear what Kai Kostigan—the future father of my children, the love of my life, the greatest husband of all time—had to say to me.

Of course at that second—the second that Kai Kostigan was going to profess his undying love for me just a day after we'd met proving that there really is such a thing as true love at first sight—another call was coming in on line 2. Calls are monitored at Edifice Luxe, ignoring it was *not* an option.

Ugh!

Of all times!

"Kai, I'm sorry. I am so, *so* sorry to do this to you. I'm at work as you know because you, er, called me here, and I, have to take this call. Wait here, or, on the line I mean, I'll be right back, Okay?"

"Sure thing, Charly B," he said without emotion.

Gah!

"It's a wicked day at Bumi~Spa~Aquas," I began in my *most* IBS-inspired voice. "This is Charly Briar, how can I make your.."

"Hey, Charly," said a familiar voice.

"Scott! Get off the phone, I've got Kai on the other line!"

"Then why'd you pick up?"

"Hello! We're at work!" I was three kinds of frustrated. "What do you want?"

"Top top *top* management wants to know about the offer—"

No idea what Scott was talking about.

I was *totally* preoccupied with thoughts of Kai and our Super Model Astronaut babies...

"I can *hear* your blank stare," laughed Scott. "Bangkok. The job that starts in five months. In August. You. Expat life. Journey of self-discovery yada yada yada.... PR rep at the Edifice Luxe hotels in Southeast Asia. *Hello?* I knew you were in love, but O M G girl!"

"Um, this is not the time," was all I could muster through clenched teeth.

"Five pm today *is the time*," Scott responded seriously. "Kiddo, this is your opportunity to explore the expat life, to have an amazing adventure. To travel the world! It's all you've ever talked about since I met you. Charly, you have to take—"

"Gotta go. Kai is on the other line—"

"Tell him I say—"

"Will do."

Click.

"Hello? Kai?"

"Charly."

"Um, hi, you wanted to tell me something? That's neat, (*neat? moron!*) I have something to tell you too."

"Well, who wants to go first?" he laughed at the soft awkwardness of our conversation.

Kai was going to tell me he loved me. I could *feel* it in the little part of my stomach behind my belly button, and that part was *never* wrong. Had I stumbled upon the world's last perfect man? Um, yes.

Kai insisted I go first, "I've been offered a job in Bangkok. It starts at the end of August."

"Cool," Kai said, almost deadpan in tone. "Okay, my turn. Well, I don't know what's gotten into me, Charly. Maybe it was meeting you and hearing your stories of traveling after college—or how you want to live and work abroad and be an expat. But I just gave notice at work. I walked in, and just quit, basically. That's so not like me. But I need a change and I actually think you really inspired me."

"Oh, wow, thank you, Kai," I wasn't really sure what to say.

He continued, "So, yeah, I'm going to take the summer off, relax, and then, maybe in the fall, I'll go travelling for a year or so."

Oh.

No big deal.

Totally manageable.

"So, you like, didn't like your job?" I asked, moderately confused about Kai's plans to relax (*where?*) and take the summer off (again, *where?*) and then "maybe" in the fall, go travelling (um, like I said, mister…. *Where!?*).

It seriously annoyed me that someone I'd only just met was weighing so heavily in my thoughts and on my heart.

Love at first sight is not for the weak, I tell ya.

"I walked in to work this morning," Kai continued, "and I just *knew*. When there is doubt, there is no doubt. It's time for a change."

"Oh, of course," I had no idea what he meant.

Kai continued, "So, Charly, are you going to take the job in Bangkok?"

Uh…

Really?

Are we really having this conversation?

What am I supposed to say?

"I really don't know anything about Bangkok but, yes, I'm kind of thinking about it. The contract is only for six months, and it could be fun. I could do some travelling after."

I tried to sound casual as I did my best Jedi mind tricks to make Kai, like, oh I don't know, offer to come along?

"Well, Charly B," Kai sighed, "you and me just have bad timing, I guess."

Hmmm, not exactly the response I was hoping for.

Without hesitation I blurted out the first thought that popped up in my head — because I'm kind of an idiot like that, "Hey, Kai, if we're together in say, five months, when my contract starts, I *dunno*, you should come with me."

Pause.

Crap.
Damn.
Seriously?
Did I seriously just say that to a guy I met last night!?

I mean, I know there's the whole *love-at-first-sight thing*, but Kai could be a psychopath! What the hell have I just done? I've just invited a complete stranger to Bangkok with me.

Really.
Bangkok.
Honestly!
Stupid Dry Spell clouding my vision….
"You know what," Kai sighed. "What the hell, let's do it."
Whoa.

....and off we went.

10. The Last Ritual

"Well *that* happened fast," huffed Eden as she topped up my and Scott's champagne flutes. It was our last and final Thursday afternoon ritual before I left for Bangkok. The summer was coming to a close and I was on my way out of Boston. I had officially accepted the position of Public Relations Liaison for Edifice Luxe South Asian Hotels & Resorts.

I'd be touring thirty or so luxury properties over the next six months with groups of travel journalists, photographers, and magazine editors. My role was to take them on a complete tour of the hotels, wow them with its offerings and the surrounding area, and ensure positive coverage online and in print. I was beyond excited. After all, a job like this was why I applied to Edifice Luxe in the first place.

Exotic adventure in luxurious five-star settings.... and I get *paid! What more could a girl ask for?*

The spring and summer had been devoured by dating Kai, falling in love with Kai, naming our stunningly gorgeous hypothetical offspring, being embarrassed when I was caught doodling their names in my hot pink Moleskine, and slowly siphoning Liam & Olivia pieces from Alégra.

(If I was going to be an ambassador for the world's leading hotel chain, I'd better look good doing it. And besides, I knew Ali didn't mind.) The summer was *also* spent discovering what a perfect man Kai was, (and running myself ragged trying to keep up). In the near-six months that Kai and I had been together, I'd never waxed my legs so much, agonized so incessantly over the perfect outfit, or spent such an alarming percentage of my salary on lingerie and anti-ageing products. And that was *only* when he was in town: as promised, Kai had spent the summer 'relaxing'. That meant reconnecting with friends he'd not seen since college, visiting distant cousins in Scandinavia, and in July, Kai took a month-long scuba trip in Papua New Guinea. The rest of the time, however, he was at my side. It was a good balance of missing each other and time spent together. I felt it was the perfect way to ease into our relationship and I didn't mind Kai's travelling at all. After all, I valued my independence. I knew that things would change once we got to Bangkok—we'd be living together!

But before that happened, I had lots to do to prepare for my big move. There were friends and family to see, Pilates classes (okay, one class) to attend, and burritos to stack up on. I really was *not* confident that Bangkok would offer the same high-quality purveyors of Mexican food I'd become accustomed to. I tried to wean myself off of my favorite food but ended up just eating as much as I could in the fearful knowledge that it'd most likely be a long time before I had steady access to burritos again. I also didn't want Kai to find out just *how* enthusiastic I was about Mexican food... For some reason, Kai was under the impression that I was one of those organic vegetarian holistic health nuts.

I have no idea why. Well, okay, I have some idea why...

In addition to pretending that I was a total Pilates freak (*ugh, must* switch to pretending I practice yoga, I think that'll be way easier to fake) I may or may not have insinuated that I'm into holistic vegetarianism and other healthy, um, ways of like, eating, and stuff.

I worried a little that Kai might ask to sample one of the delicious vegan meals I'm always pretending I make. I worried even more about how I would conceal my infatuation with burritos.

Did I just say infatuation?

Oh crap.

I don't think I can go six months without burritos.

I thought I could, but I don't think it's gonna happen.

They must have <u>one</u> burrito place in Bangkok, right?

Am I going on and on about this a little too much?

Like, is this getting weird?

Okay.

Be calm.

I'll just ship over a box or two of frozen burritos…

…that should get me through the first couple weeks until I figure out the lay of the land.

But where will I keep them so Kai doesn't notice?

No, no, that won't work.

He'd think I'm a total freak.

Anything to declare?

Yes: a wack-load of burritos and seven jars of queso.

Okay, I'll admit… it's getting a bit weird.

"Daydreaming about opening a Mexican franchise in Bangkok, missy?" Scott smiled.

"What? Huh? No!" I stammered. "Sorry, Scott, what were you saying?"

"*I* was actually talking, darling," Eden said as she signaled sharply to the waitress to bring us another bottle of Moet and, in doing so, no doubt incurred the 18% gratuity charge normally reserved for groups of ten or larger. Eden continued, "I need to prepare you for working at Edifice Luxe Asia and for *expat life*."

Life abroad, I couldn't wait…

Exoticism.

Adventure.

Mangoes.

Wahoo!

Eden was originally a transfer from the EAME (Europe, Africa, Middle East) office but she'd also done a stint in Asia. She knew *all* about life overseas, especially how to adapt to a culture *within* a culture: that of expatriates.

"Oh, darling, you'll just love it," she began, "garden parties and champagne, heaps of social drama and weekend trips to the island, it's like living in a W. Somerset Maugham novel, but without the cholera."

"And the infidelity," I added obviously.

"Ha!" Eden scoffed.

I shot her a look...

She quickly remembered how sensitive I am to tales of cheating—thanks Ethan—and readjusted her response, "Oh, 'course not, darling, I'm sure you and your *luvey dovey* are exempt from such mortal sins. You two are so much better than that."

I felt a chill at the prospect... Eden's words were disturbingly prophetic and I changed the subject with enthusiasm, "What else, other than day-drinking, island hopping, and gossiping, will I be doing as a fabulous expat?"

Eden looked at me as though I'd just been offered a lifetime supply of Liam & Olivia, Dom Perignon, and size four hips, and scoffed, *is that all?*

"What *else* would you want?" Eden asked with much confusion and a raised eyebrow.

"Alright, alright," I gave in. I'd have to get the ins and outs of expat culture some other time. "Let's talk about the *actual* job. Fill me in! I want to know *everything* about the expat life. Don't leave anything out; I need to be prepared!"

My role would be very similar to Eden's old job, the one she'd had when I met her, so I knew she'd be able to tell me everything. Eden started with the nuts and bolts... living in a hotel... dealing with sales reps... satellite offices... sales targets... off-site training seminars... the importance of group bookings... the quirky "operational types" in the F&B department... it went on and on.

Eden told me how to give the perfect site inspection, how to appease unreasonable media requests, and always to remember the most important part of it all: the whole thing was ruled by, *The Director*. Eden leaned in and said sternly, "Everybody in Asia reports to *it*."

She was referring to Wilhelmina, the Director of Marketing at Edifice Luxe in Asia. Wilhelmina's reputation preceded her: she was known far and wide to be the worst person on the planet in the history of all time, *ever*. She was also Eden's old boss and they did *not* part on good terms. "That megalomaniac has zero class, I'm telling you, zero appreciation for the finesse required to coax an editor into writing a story on yet *another* tedious menu at some uppity spa no one gives a *shite* about."

Eden fanned herself elegantly by ruffling her loose indigo frock. She was stunning despite the foul words that fell from her perfectly put together pout, "And she's so hideous, I want to look at her and scream *Oh my god, was anyone else hurt?*"

"Alright there, saucebox," Scott said with a hint of seriousness. "You're at a *ten* and I need you at a *six*."

"I agree with Scott," I said. "Give the poor woman a break. There's gotta be a reason she's so huffy."

I could say that with confidence. I already knew that I was reporting to someone else: a Canadian guy whose reputation was about as soft and cuddly as they come.

"You're right, Charly," Eden sighed. "I should be nicer to her. After all, I would be quite agitated as well if I hadn't had a proper bowel movement without the use of industrial strength laxatives in a decade."

Eden laughed at her own joke, "I'm telling you, IBS couldn't have happened to a better person."

Scott and I shook our heads, sighed, and took a sip of our freshly poured Moet. There was no use. All we could do was sit back, relax, and hope that Eden's tirade would wrap up before my plane left for Bangkok the following week.

"I'm serious, guys! Do you know how embarrassing it was for me to pitch OM Luxe's new spa menu to CNN?"

OM Luxe.... Why was that familiar?

Eden pressed on despite the fact that Scott and I weren't really listening, "I was still working overseas. I think it was maybe three, no, almost four years ago. Anyway, it was the day the civil war broke out on that little tropical island, Jeeranam? Do you remember? It was awful!"

"Charly, are you listening? Anyway, she *forced* me to try and get a *serious* and *respected* journalist to cover a new spa menu. A spa menu!? I mean, *really!*" she huffed. I did my best *I'm listening* face while Eden pressed on, "CNN is in the middle of covering a critical war and I'm asking them do a story on *Macrobiotics!* It was very popular back then as you'll remember. I mean, these days, the whole world is *Paleo*, but that's totally beside the point. The whole thing—me hounding a respected journalist to drop what she's doing and cover a spa menu—it practically ruined my reputation and it was *entirely* Wilhelmina's fault! She *made* me do it!"

OM....

Luxe....

How do I know that name?

"Charly, you look like you're on another planet!" Eden exclaimed. "This stuff is important, darling. You're sure to cross paths with Wilhelmina, and she *hates* me by the way, so never, *ever*, mention the fact that we work together."

"Okay, okay," I waved a hand in surrender. I hadn't really been paying attention, truth be told.

Who did I know in the Maldives?

Eden pressed on, "Charly, darling, you *definitely* need to know about Jeeranam. It's only an hour's flight from Bangkok. You never know, you might end up there one day..."

I highly doubted I'd end up on a tiny little tropical island in the middle of nowhere—I wanted *fabulous urban expat* not *feral jungle dweller*—but I didn't protest.

Truth be told, I hadn't caught much of what Eden was saying. I was distracted for some reason...

OM Luxe...
The chicest brand by Edifice Luxe...
Why does this sound so familiar?
Did I know someone at OM Luxe?
Who did I know at OM Luxe?
Of course!
Tyler Kee!!

I instantly perked up, smoothed my hair, and blushed. My whizzing mind was corralled onto one single thought: Tyler Kee.

My super-hot Canadian fling (had it just been a fling or was it something more?). I couldn't help but wonder how he was doing. Was he still working at OM Luxe? Was he still based in the Maldives? Why hadn't I heard from him? Why was I wondering why I hadn't heard from him? Why should it matter?

Breathe, girl!

I censured myself for caring, for even *allowing* my mind to pause momentarily on him. It made no sense whatsoever. I mean, I was perfectly content with Kai, why was I thinking about Tyler? Tyler was in the *past*, Kai was the *future*. I wasn't going to get distracted by Tyler and his perfectly golden skin, pristinely sculpted shoulders, endless green eyes inviting me to...

Whoa. Seriously, get a grip.
Why am I pining for a burger when I've got NY sirloin?
Collect yourself, Charly!

"Ugh," whined Eden, "you're a useless nit with no attention span. Anyway, so this CNN reporter is in Jeeranam when the war breaks out, the whole world is watching, and there I am, trying to get him to do a story on the nutritional benefits of kale. *Fu.ck.ing Kale!*"

Scott and I burst out laughing unintentionally and Eden waved a hand at us to signify that she didn't care that *we* didn't care about her story. She just wanted to vent.

"I'm telling you Charly," Eden almost wailed. "I'm never again dealing with that *tuna melt*. She's a total disaster and utterly evil."

"I heard she can shrink heads," Scott added sarcastically without looking up from his lap. He was posed as though reading a serious work email on his BlackBerry but from my angle I could see he was playing Brick Breaker. "But what does that have to do with our little Charly over here?"

"Who? What?" Eden was perplexed. "I don't know, Scott, I don't know. *Come on now!* Where *is* our waitress? We're going to need another bottle before the day is through."

"And *that's* why I love you two," I smiled.

Eden and Scott were my *besties* at work and exactly like the older siblings I'd never been lucky enough to have. I couldn't help but make a very sad face as it dawned on me how lost I'd be without them.

"Don't give me that sad face. We can talk all the time. That's what Skype is for," Eden said softly but then added in a most British way, "and don't be a baby about it! It will be the most amazing journey of self-discovery, I promise you that. Besides, you've already been to Asia once. And look how well you did! Just try not to molest any minors this time."

"Oh *ha ha!*" I laughed. "He wasn't *that* young."

I pushed certain thoughts, *about certain people*, out of my head as we clinked our glasses together for the last time in a long time.

11. The Big Mango

Kai and I finally left for Bangkok at the end of August. In addition to a substantial portion of Alégra wardrobe, I brought everything I owned, which was basically one thing: Kermit the Dog, my precious (and slightly rotund) Boston Terrier. I couldn't bear to be apart from him and, thankfully, some of the properties I'd be working on were pet friendly so I'd be able to bring him along. For the times that Kermit was unable to come with me, Kai had agreed to look after him in our new place. There was nothing else to organize. I was all packed and ready to embark on my amazing journey of self-discovery with Kai, as per my plan. Perfect! And, at last, after a long night of crying (and drinking) with Nikki and Alégra, Kai and I left for the airport early in the morning. Our journey began.

"Here you go, babe," Kai handed me a small package as we boarded the plane. It was an oversized pale pink shawl and I completely adored it. "It can be your *airplane shawl*. I know you get cold on trips."

Kai had remembered some offhanded comment I'd made over a month ago.

Perfect man?

Yes.

Ohhhh yes.

"Thank you! I love my *airplane shawl*," I said as I kissed my favorite two-legged man (my four-legged man was just short enough to ride with us in the cabin. He slept soundly under the seat in front of me). I cuddled up to Kai and sighed happily. I *just knew* this was going to be the beginning of an incredible journey: an expat journey, a journey of love between Kai and me, and a journey of self-discovery...

¤ * § * ¤

Ugh, dry heave much?

Bangkok reeks. It is a vicious, evil, assault on the senses with open sewers and filthy waterways. Thanks, Bangkok, for teaching me the meaning of the word *stench*. I constantly worried that Kermit would develop asthma or maybe even herpes from the disgusting pollution; but Kai comforted me with the statistical improbability of that actually happening.

Still, it was really gross and I did not manage one deep honest outdoor breath in all the time we lived in Bangkok. The bars, the sex tourists (called *sexpats*), the non-stop action: Bangkok is wild. Not Eden, nor *anyone*, could have prepared me for life in Bangkok. Even if they'd told me, I wouldn't have believed them. But in hindsight, the most shocking thing about Bangkok was the way I left it... That comes later, though.

Three hours after landing, I was at work. I met my new boss at the Edifice Luxe Asia Pacific offices and, much to my relief, he was nothing like Wilhelmina, Eden's old (and scary sounding) boss. He was the head of communications for all of Asia Pacific and looked more like a man who had just climbed out of a nickel mine in Nova Scotia than a man who had climbed the corporate ladder in the hotel world. He was tall and strong with wispy blonde hair, and a kind, wrinkled face. He and his wife had left Australia to go backpacking for "just six months", that was three decades ago.

His name was Bob Sands, but everyone called him Sandy. My first assignment was to familiarize myself with the hotels, "Go get the lay of the land, Charly," said Sandy.

I was to visit all the hotels in the Bangkok area over the next couple of weeks and get to know the general managers, hotel managers, chefs, concierges, night managers, auditors, hostesses, on-site marketing teams, sales managers, the gift shop girl, porters, waitresses, sous chefs, front desk staff…the list went on and on.

"Think of yourself as our first point of contact when it comes to media," said Sandy with a voice that inspired confidence in me.

"At first I'll choose the writers and photographers for you. But once you get the hang of things, you can pitch your own assignments. Don't worry, these properties sell themselves. We just need you to play host, okay?"

"Okay!" I said cheerfully.

"Oh, and also I need you to study the region's top travel media because you'll need to know who's who."

I nodded; sounds easy enough.

"And," Sandy continued. "Of course, you're expected to attend all the events, whether it's a hotel opening or a door opening."

"Of course," I said.

"And," Sandy pressed on as I got a little dizzy. "Get to know the writers and editors and journalists and photographers and bloggers—and make them love you."

I laughed because obviously he was joking, *make them love me?*

But then it was Sandy's turn to laugh. "I don't care what you have to do. Every journalist who stays at our resorts *must* write a glowing review. We're in the age of online guest reviews and our hotels are judged by what some dipstick from Milwaukee says about us. We need good press and that's why we brought you in, Charly. We've got six months, and trust me, it's going to fly by."

"Great, of course, I'm your girl!"

Holy pressure!

Like seriously I haven't event adjusted to the time change yet!

But then Sandy smiled gently, "Charly, don't worry, you pretty much have free reign of the hotel when you're there, and a *very* generous budget, by the way. You'll get to know the journalists pretty quickly, too. Just wine and dine them; make sure they have an amazing time."

"Got it."

"Okay, so let's dig in. After you've spent this and next week familiarizing yourself with the Bangkok hotels, we'll get you working. You'll have a lot of smaller-scale assignments to start with—sometimes only one or two journalists for lunch and a site inspection—but we're building towards the big rebranding event at the Edifice Luxe Orient Royale here in Bangkok. It's a massive gala and you'll be the lead organizer. But don't worry, it's six months from now and by then you'll be an old pro."

Sandy winked at me reassuringly and I liked him immediately, "One more thing," he added. "Your weekly report *must* be submitted to me every Friday by noon."

"Friday, noon, got it!"

"Great! Welcome aboard," Sandy shook my hand and concluded by mentioning that I was welcome to bring a *plus-one* with me on my out-of-town assignments.

Kai was naturally very happy about this. A couple of days and a million meetings later, I felt mildly settled in to this strange new land. There was so much I wanted to see and do; but I was also eager to get going at work. I booked my first assignment: the pet unfriendly Edifice Luxe Grande on Sukhumvit Road in Bangkok. Kermit stayed with Kai in our loft and awaited my return. I hopped into a cab and half an hour later, I pulled into a graveled crescent driveway in front of the grandest property I'd ever seen.

Here's me falling in love with luxury... Unlike Bangkok, Edifice Luxe Hotels & Resorts were pristinely manicured, expertly manned, and smelled like freshly baked bread, peonies, and soft 600-thread-count linens. The grand foyer alone must have been five stories tall. Everything was gold and pink and bubbly.

Just how I like it.

Overall my first assignment went well. I only had one writer to host and I thanked Sandy for starting me off easy. The journalist assigned to me was a lovely middle-aged British woman who was married to a diplomat. She'd taken up writing as a way to pass the time and had been commissioned by an English-speaking spa magazine to review the hotel. She seemed genuinely impressed by its offerings.

On my end, I was truly happy to have met her: she had been an expat for longer than I'd been alive and I just knew she'd be a valuable resource on the topic of living in a foreign land.

"So, tell me everything!" I beamed as we had brunch on the first day. "How did you come to be here, what's the best part about being an expat, what's the worst, don't leave anything out!"

Sure, it was probably *me* who ought to be guiding the tour — here's the pool, here's the spa, there's the concierge and that's the garden — but I couldn't help it.

"Oh, my, Charly, you're really happy to be here, aren't you?"

She smiled as she dropped a tea bag in a small alabaster pot and delicately spread boysenberry preserve over a golden English muffin.

"That's great, but I don't know where to begin," she continued. "You really will have more fun discovering it all on your own. I bet that's why you embarked on this journey in the first place, right?"

I nodded sweetly and lifted a giant latte bowl to my lips in an effort to hide my annoyance at her refusal to share her expat wealth. I wanted answers... like, now! I was quickly approaching twenty-cough cough years old. I don't have time to waste travelling around trying to figure it all out.

The expat lady put down her teacup and smiled softly, "the one thing I can tell you for sure, is don't get sidetracked from *why* you initially went abroad. It's very easy to do that here, *especially* as a woman."

Okay, that made sense...

She continued slowly, "New arrivals risk becoming spiritually malleable when they're just trying to be accommodating. Don't become a victim of someone else's life plan."

Spiritually malleable?
A victim of someone else's life plan?
This isn't a yoga retreat, lady.

I only wished she was as helpful as she was sweet. None of that was useful so I smiled nicely and hoped the next two days would go by fast. I wanted the juicy stuff: where to go shopping, the best expat hangout, the latest gossip. I wanted it all and here's why: it didn't take long for me to become painfully aware of my place on the periphery of this weird and wild world.

I wanted in and I wanted it now. I didn't care that I hadn't even been in Bangkok for a week; I was on the outside and I didn't like it. It had never occurred to me to think about that sort of thing back home, surrounded by my safety net of friends, family, and familiarity. But here in this strange place, nobody knew me. I was no one to anybody.

Weirdsies.

At least I had the basics sorted out. My job was great so far and my salary had doubled thanks to an awesome package negotiated for me by Scott. I was in an amazing and mysterious (albeit stinky) new city with my perfect boyfriend who would someday be my perfect husband and probably the face of Prada's next print campaign.

Perfect.

Two days later I checked out of the hotel and headed to my new home: a modern split-level loft on the left bank of the Chao Praya River. Open concept, two stories, massive windows, spiral staircase: perfection. Having spent most of my expat life thus far in a hotel, I was eager to spend time with Kai, Kermit, and my new neighborhood. Upon hearing my keys jingle in the door, Kermit jumped up and down like an epileptic, while Kai remained in a vegetative state.

He looked exhausted and had clearly been very busy job hunting these past few days — or something that required a lot of hot-guy effort. I kissed both my guys and surveyed the loft: the moving boxes were neatly arranged in every room while only Kai's computer and Kermit's toys were unpacked. Exactly as I had left it.

"Been busy?" I teased.

"You have no idea," Kai said as he handed me a little gift bag.

"What's this?" I asked with a big smile.

"Just open it," Kai winked.

Inside was a hot pink LG Samsung smartphone. It was so completely my style and eerily appropriate I wondered if Kai was an alien or perhaps a cult leader. Either way, I made a mental note to touch his man parts later in gratitude, "I love it. You're the best. How'd you even know I needed one—"

"I just love my lady," he shrugged adorably. "The salesgirl told me that pink was the new black, or something like that..."

"Oh my gosh, thank you, baby!"

He shrugged, "Anyway, I thought you'd like a new phone to complement your new job. And look, I set it up for you. You can put all your documents in it too."

"And it's pink!"

Kai chuckled softly, "Yes, *and* it's pink."

The fact that Kai had managed to find time in his busy schedule of being the hottest guy on the planet to be *so* thoughtful was just too much. I had won the boyfriend lottery and quite frankly, I was jealous of myself.

"C'mon," he said. "Let's get out of the house. I'll show you the neighborhood."

"You bet!"

OMG I love my boyfriend!

As I recounted the past couple of days, Kai guided me to a nearby street market that was bustling with a kind of action I'd not yet experienced since arriving in Asia. We stopped abruptly at a food stall Kai obviously already knew about.

"*Som tam,*" Kai said as he pointed to vibrant green and red bits of papaya that glistened in fish oil. The food stall vendor tied a red band around a clear plastic take-away bag and handed it to us as Kai offered him the exact amount of change—without even looking at the strange currency that I was still having so much trouble with.

"*Kap kun krub,*" Kai said in perfect Thai.

When in the name of silk rompers did my boyfriend find the time to learn Thai? Kai maneuvered easily through the market as though he possessed a life-long familiarity with the area. It was amazing. Pungent odors and curious aromas revealed themselves at every turn through the narrow rows of chaotically organized stalls. Pinholes of afternoon light pierced through shabby overhead canopies illuminating the ground, the perspiration on the street vendors' necks, and sizzling meat on a stick that popped loudly as grease hit the fire. Everything tactile—every smell, every color, every sound—was amplified tenfold. It was a beautiful side of Bangkok I hadn't yet seen. Kai was so natural in this weird new world and I couldn't even buy a phone card.

And yes, I'd tried.

Talk about a total disaster.

While on my first assignment I'd wanted to call Alégra and Nikki to check in and say hi. I found a convenience store near the hotel and made the huge mistake of standing in line like a normal human being. In America, customers line up in a single file with at least one foot of space in between each other. In Thailand, not only is personal space measured in millimeters, but touching, gentle shoving, and taking over counter space with personal items *before* the customer has finished paying is totally acceptable.

Yucky!

I was in line and a man—who by American standards would have been considered two customers *behind me*—stood to my right shoulder with his breath circling my earlobe.

Ugh.

So rude!

Naturally, I gave the classic American passive aggressive look-over-the-shoulder as a signal that he was in my personal space.

Nothing.

So I turned slightly and gave the exaggerated-eye-roll and even cleared my throat a little to indicate that his socially deviant ways were *not* going to be tolerated.

Still nothing. This guy was clueless.

Finally, I took a step forward and tried to take up as much space as possible with my body: hands on hips, wide stance like I expected an earthquake at any moment, I even readjusted my Liam & Olivia bag with a wide angled swing over my shoulder in the hopes of scaring him off. No such luck.

No sooner had I stepped forward did he step forward too (*really!?*) and as he did he brought with him his convenience store groceries: a carton of milk and a plastic wrapped powdered pastry—*both* disgusting and both pressing *boldly* into the edge of my Liam & Olivia bag. I felt as though I just might jump out of my own skin. I mean, there's unforgivable and then there's *unforgivable.*

"Ah, ah, ahhhh, don't go there, darling," Eden reprimanded me when I told her of my lost-in-translation moment over the phone later that night. "You can't go meddling in other peoples' customs and social norms," Eden cautioned. "Culture is the living, breathing tapestry of a people's history and national identity, *even* the annoying parts. Just accept it. Believe it or not, you Americans drive me crazy sometimes with your constant opinion-giving and *howdy neighbor!* familiarity. What's that idiot saying you people have? Oh yes, "strangers are friends we haven't met yet". Okay, actually, they are *strangers."*

Whatever, Eden!

"Yeah, no, but, Americans are, like, normal and everyone else is—oh okay fine, fine, fine, fine, I get it."

"As much as you would like to," Eden said, "it isn't for *you* to say what is and what is *not* appropriate in your new host country."

"Fine, fine, fine! What's your advice?"

"Laugh it off. The sooner you do, the sooner you become an expat. Charly, trust me. You have to *let go* and stop being so entrenched in your own customs. That's why I moved to the States, to let it all go. I mean, seriously, as scary as it was at first, I've come to adore you freaks and your ability to put any kind of meat on a stick. It's brilliant. And just last week, I ate a pancake bigger than my face. I love this country!"

Eden was right, of course. I promised to be a better expat. Back at the market... Kai and I wove ourselves deeper into the mosaic of foreign gastronomy and bizarre market goods. Kai pointed to a stall that sold *Phad Thai* and another with fresh fruit.

"And over there," Kai said as he gently pushed a flyaway hair behind my ear and kissed the side of my forehead, "in that tucked-away little shop, you can find some funky artsy pieces I know you'll love."

"Aren't you the perfect tour guide," I smiled as I slid my arm through his and kissed him on the cheek.

"It's my backup plan in case the whole investment banking thing falls through," he laughed to himself softly.

I almost lost Kai at one point when I stopped to admire some orange tapestries and prints of a meditative Buddha.

Maybe getting into the whole Buddhist thing — maybe even revisiting yoga — would help me fit in to this strange new world?

Yes.

Perfect.

Every expat needs to go back home with a newly acquired skill. How had I forgotten that?!

You know, like all those douches who go to India come back vegetarian or whatever.

Perfect.

I'll come back as Buddhist yoga-master.

But a chic one.

Not, like, one with knotted hair that reeks of sandalwood.

Gross.

No, no, I'll come back enlightened and able to cook stuff in pineapples.

Ooooooh, or maybe I'll come back as Feng Shui expert – maybe I'll even open up a shop! Yeah, I'd love to work for myself.. That's the dream...

Or maybe Edifice Luxe would hire me to ensure all their villas are Feng Shui approved. That way I'd get to travel the world in luxury. Oh no, wait, how about Tai Chi? Or Wabi Sabi Zen? What about Taoism? Oooh I have so much to discover!!

"Hey, Miss Briar, over here," Kai beckoned softly and I skipped over to him apologetically, embarrassed about my inability to focus on one task at a time.

"Sorry babe, the sparkly Buddha pulled me in."

"No biggie," he shrugged.

An hour later Kai was still coasting effortlessly through the market while my tired footing was beginning to fumble along the uneven walkways and awkward passageways. As he pointed out a newsstand, water taxi station, and nearby corner store where I could buy imported wine, I began to feel more like I was on a guided tour and less like I was on a collaborative journey of discovery. Kai even seemed to receive a few familiar smiles along the way, particularly from a row of stalls where young Thai women sold "designer" bags.

The pretty Thai girls wore tiny denim skirts that, on the average American female, would look like sausage casing. I immediately disliked them. The shop girls were slim, demure, and as *interested* in Kai as they were *uninterested* in me. They smiled and giggled at my boyfriend and it made me proud to be on the arm of such a great catch—but also a little insecure... and rage-like with protective jealousy. *What was going on?* In three short days, Kai had seamlessly transitioned into the expat lifestyle, whereas I still felt like a tourist.

I tried not to let it bother me but an hour later I was *very* happy when Kai suggested we retreat back to our place with Phad Thai and spring rolls.

As the sun set over the Chao Praya River, we drained a bottle of Australian Pinot and talked about everything and nothing. It reminded me of the first night we met. Eventually, we fell into bed—with Kermit snoring at our feet—exhausted and happy. As I drifted off, I let those silly insecure thoughts about the girls from the market melt away, and instead surrendered to thoughts of love, contentment, and Kai.

12. The Buffer Snack

Hey Charly,

I know it's been awhile since we've been in touch... but yeah, so anyway I wanted to drop a line and see how you're doing. I am not the greatest at writing letters, so bear with me...

Anyway, I hope work is good, I heard you're a legit "expat" now... cool. I bet Bangkok is awesome, I'll have to visit one day...

I'm good... been travelling and whatnot. Not sure how much longer I'll stay here. But I guess the reason I'm writing is... I think about you more than I'd like to admit ;)

So yeah, come visit anytime...

xx

    ...I tucked what would become the first of many letters from *him* safely out of Kai's sight. Good thing I was working from home that day so Kai didn't pick up the mail!
    Gah!
    Breathe.
    That was a lifetime ago...
    That ship has sailed...

Let it go.

Just like harem pants... it's over.

Don't acknowledge it — don't respond — maybe he'll go away.

I couldn't believe September was already coming to a close. Work was going fabulously well and in fact ramping up with bigger media groups and more high profile hotels by the week.

Kai hadn't found a job yet (I wasn't entirely sure if he was still in the relaxing phase or in the actual looking for a job phase, but his investment banker bucks from his previous job were more than enough to keep him afloat for three lifetimes so it didn't really matter that much). Whenever he did decide to go back to work, I had faith that he'd have no trouble at all in finding something that he loved.

Being an expat, I'd noticed, was slowly shifting my outlook on things towards being more open to possibilities and unafraid of the unknown. For example, just because my contract was up in six months didn't mean we had to go home. Maybe I'd spend some time really getting into my yoga practice (by which I mean starting a yoga practice). Or, maybe I'd get a new offer to go somewhere else even *more* exotic and Kai would follow. Or, perhaps it'd be a good time to travel, you know, before we got engaged. The world was very much my oyster. And Kai's too, of course. Even Kermit loved Bangkok. Everything was perfect.

The telephone rang.

"Hello?"

"Hey, babe."

It was Kai.

He was on his way back from a networking luncheon for expat bankers — I have no idea, it was something a friend of a friend back home had set up for him. He'd said it might be good to mingle with "his kind" for a change. I'd teased him that he's not allowed to grow tired of all things luxury for as long as we're together. Barring that, he was welcome to go for lunch with his people.

"Hey, hun. How are you? How was the luncheon?"

"Whatever. Bunch of nerds. Anyway, I'm almost home... walking through the market, want anything?"

"Just you!"

"Done," he chuckled. "But I'm passing by that *Phad Thai* place you like. Sure you don't want some?"

"Okay, you *and* the *Phad Thai*. But you're having some too, right?"

"*Okay na ka*," he mused.

Kai had picked up so many Thai words in a matter of weeks, I was impressed. I still had yet to sign up for Thai language lessons — which I fully intended to do — but had been so busy with work. I'd get around to it eventually. Yes, must take Thai lessons. Maybe also silk screening classes — that seemed to be big here. Oh, and must find a yoga studio as well — but, like, a westernized one that caters to beginners. And, also, um, must find purveyor of authentic burritos. *Stop judging...*

Eleven minutes later Kai entered our loft and I couldn't help but stare. Caught somewhere between the Bangkok afternoon sun and our sleek track lighting, Kai was illuminated in such a way that made him look like either a Grecian god or a svelte water polo player. Either way... I'll take it!

On that day, like most, Kai wore all black, save for his crisp white shirt that shone like bleached teeth. His slim-fitted suit made his figure look like an upside down isosceles triangle that highlighted his obsessively landscaped shoulders and enviable Teutonic ancestry. Our kids will be immune to disease and sarcasm, of this I am sure.

Refusing to adopt the standard uniform of most bankers, Kai dressed more like a mod publishing magnate than a math nerd. Above his shoulders sat a pronounced jaw line that would make a prize Doberman envious, and a perfectly controlled mane. He had lightened his hair since moving to Bangkok (*when did he have time to do this?*) from Granny Smith apple to gleaming ocean pearl. (I'm pretty sure I have split ends longer than Kai's actual hair.)

I couldn't help but sigh adoringly as he casually slipped off his Ermenegildo Zegna loafers, casually using the other foot as leverage. He fingered his black blazer for keys, Marlborough Lights, and a BlackBerry, and tossed them easily on the wrought iron high table by the door.

"Oh, hey, you," Kai said softly as he looked up.

It was as though he hadn't expected me to be home and hadn't noticed that I'd been sitting directly in front of him for the last two and a half minutes. I could never tell if Kai was incredibly collected or a bit slow on the uptake. My hunger pangs instructed me that at that point, either one was okay. He glided toward me like an Apache helicopter undulating gracefully over virgin ground. *Ugh, he's almost too good looking.*

I readjusted myself on our overstuffed loveseat with hands outstretched as I took the plastic take-away bag from Kai. He headed towards the kitchen to open a new bottle of Pinot (and proceeded to tackily empty most of it into two large hand-blown indigo goblets I'd just bought). I cringed a little at his vino-pouring ignorance—just because the glasses are big doesn't mean you should see how much wine you can pour into them! But then I quickly shamed myself; everyone is allowed to have *one* flaw, I guess.

Let's not discuss my burrito addiction...

I began to dish the contents of the flimsy white container onto our big flat square plates (very blue, very chic, I got them at the market) and as I turned to toss the bag aside, I noticed there was another container in it.

"Oh, yes!" I exclaimed. "Did you get those super yummy vegetarian spring rolls, too? You are a prince among men, baby. Thank you! I *love* those spring rolls."

With the enthusiasm of a wino uncorking a free vintage, I unfastened the cardboard hook-and-eye of the take-away container as the left corner of Kai's Kiehl-moisturized lips birthed a little grimace.

"Um, excuse me! That moron street vendor forgot to put them *in* the box!" I mock-gasped at the sight of nothing more than spring roll remnants in an otherwise empty container. The idea that Kai had so thoughtfully attempted to procure spring rolls without success made me sad and I envisioned them alone and abandoned by the absentminded street vendor some sixteen stories below.

My poor orphan spring rolls wanting only to be eaten by me.

So sad.

So tragic.

(Yes, I know I'm nuts.)

But the romantic image of the lonely little spring rolls, longing to be dipped in sticky sweet and sour sauce, was interrupted by Kai's unabashed confession...

"Nope, I was really hungry so I got spring rolls."

Completely confused, I inquired as to their whereabouts. Completely unconfused, Kai responded that he had consumed them prior to entering our domicile.

"Between the market and home?"

"Yeah," he shrugged, "because I knew if I brought them home, I'd have to share with you. So I needed, like, a buffer snack."

"A buffer snack?"

"A buffer snack."

"A buffer snack?"

"For sure, babe. Guys get buffer snacks *all the time* to stave off their mighty man-hunger," Kai growled as he pounded his chest for effect and kissed my forehead.

Kai continued, "That way, guys are able to share *equitably* among the remains. Guy is full, girlfriend believes she's been shared with. Disaster averted, thanks to: The Buffer Snack."

Bemused by Kai's absurd rationale, I inquired further, "So this is, like, a preventative measure?"

Pleased that I was catching on, Kai nodded and continued, raising his eyebrows for emphasis, "Exactly. I dunno how hungry you're gonna be, so I gotta have a plan... "

"Oh, I see," I laughed. "So, it's a premeditated tactic to avoid sharing food with your insatiably ravenous girlfriend? Afraid I might bite your hand off like a hyena?"

"Or a honey badger..." Kai smiled.

"No more Animal Planet for you, *mister*."

"No, no, no," he laughed. "It's not you, it's me. I *need* the buffer snack, and if I don't get it, well kiddo, I'm not so sure I can share my *Phad Thai* with you. Plus this way, if you take too much *Phad Thai, mai ben rai*."

"Which means, *no big deal*."

"No big deal is *right*, my love," Kai moved in for a kiss and was playfully denied.

I teased, "You're a knuckle-dragger in a nice suit, you know?"

"Yep, and I'm going to drag you back to my cave later," growled Kai. I reminded him that he should enjoy his caveman privileges now because soon enough I'd be visiting out-of-town properties on media trips.

"The down side is that you'll be gone," said Kai. "But the up side is that I won't need to sneak around with my mistress... My sweet lady, *the Spring Roll*."

"Oh, so you're funny today!" I joked.

"I try," Kai said as he leaned over, kissed me, and threw a rejected beansprout in Kermit's direction.

"Me too, babe," I sighed with sympathy at the screen.

When it was time for bed I headed upstairs but was halted by Kai's soft voice, "Hey you, want some company up there?"

I turned around at the top of the spiral staircase and joked, "Maybe later, I need a minute first with my Buffer Boyfriend."

Kai laughed as I slipped into my Miss Piggy Pajamas and dove into bed (but not before double-checking to make sure that letter I'd received that day was safely hidden.) I wasn't sure how to how to feel about it; happy to hear from him or angry that he'd disrupted my perfect life with my perfect boyfriend?

Argh, so annoying.

It's not like he moved in next door, but he was in my thoughts now and I had no idea how to get him out. The whole thing was frustrating and made me wish he'd disappeared the way the *'gardner'* had.

Fully Booked / Genn Pardoe

13. The Constant 'Gardner'

After Ethan Charge I had a short but fun relationship with a guy named Greg Gardner. He was known as *The Constant Gardner* on account of his penchant for outdoor activities and preoccupation with women's, um, well, you know... Officially, we met in college at a Champagne & Cupcake garden party that Alégra was throwing in celebration of absolutely nothing, but we'd seen each other countless times and even had a few classes together. We had shared a few flirtatious smiles, lingering glances, and on a couple of occasions, he'd sat right beside me in lectures.

I was happy when that happened because he had the best aftershave I've ever smelled. It's always refreshing when one is attracted to someone outside of their regular "type" and The Constant Gardner was definitely not my type. But maybe that's because he came to me at a weird time in life...

I'd dumped Ethan two months before and my back was fully recovered from the unfortunate rendezvous with that meat-head who gave me the hernia.

As ready as I was to jump into a new relationship (like an idiot) I was still coasting—just a little bit—on that sweet post-breakup high. You know, that burst of unexpected energy you get a couple months after the split. It infuses you with a new lust for life, a refreshed outlook, a new haircut and a strong desire to try new things (by which I mean, touch new man parts).

See: rebound.

Whatever.... In my world it's called a "Post-breakup High".

Anyway, I figured I had another month or so of debauchery left before my adorable sexual anecdotes would become sad tales of a moderately easy girl. But since I'd just decided to embark on a life-changing journey of self-discovery, I felt confident in saying that, overall, things were looking up for Charly Briar.

Champagne & Cupcakes

Ali put me in charge of the cupcake table (a fatal error on her part) and as I unpacked a new box of red velvet and vanilla bean minis—awarding myself a sample of each—The Constant Gardner sidled up to me and whispered, "What's a nice girl like you doing in a dirty mind like mine?"

Really?

I laughed a bit and turned around to see a tall slender guy with an intentionally shaggy coif and sly hazel eyes. He wore cargo pants—which usually calls for a reading of my zero tolerance policy regarding fashion's biggest crimes—and a white v-neck tee. But what struck me most was that he was barefoot.

Weird yet oddly appealing....

"You don't even know me," I raised a curious eyebrow as he topped up my champagne flute.

"You don't even know *me*," he retorted half flirtatiously and half like a juvenile delinquent, which, I think we've established by now, I'm into.

The Constant Gardner smiled with his eyes and when he opened his mouth it was as though sex was falling out. He was so intriguing and unlike anyone I'd ever dated: a cargo-pant wearing political science major with mega-intelligence and a near-disdain for money and all things materialistic. I mean, Ethan was extremely smart, but only when it came to math and manipulation. Not exactly someone you want to be stuck on an island with...

But the Constant Gardner, *oh wow!*

He was opinionated and well-read and curious about every tiny aspect of life—his energy was infectious and he was so exciting to be around. Over the course of our short relationship we'd frequently stay up all night talking about everything from the viability of communism to how different the world would be if procreation depended on the female orgasm.

(*Think about it...*)

The Constant Gardner was so cool that I totally got over the cargo pant thing and even bought a pair for myself.

I know...

Ugh, I know...

¤ * § * ¤

"So," I smiled at the Constant Gardner as I sweetly licked vanilla bean icing off my finger—the Post-breakup High has always given me stupid levels of self-confidence, if only it could be bottled...

"How do you suggest we get to know each other?" I mused.

The Constant Gardner leaned in and whispered, "I'd like the chance to show your boyfriend how it's done."

"I don't have a boyfriend," I said in a faux *you're-boring-me* voice as I turned back to the cupcake table but was stopped by the Gardner as he slid his arm around my waist tightly.

"I find that *hard* to believe."

Okay, now you have my attention....

"Come with me, now," he said as he pressed his lips into the back of my neck and I swooned.

(The Constant Gardner gave me my first legitimate *swoon*. And, no, *that's* not a dirty metaphor. I really mean it, I swooned.) And, given the fact that I was super high on awesome-breakup-dust... well let's just say I followed him without hesitation to a private part of Ali's garden.

"What the heck happened?" Nikki and Alégra cornered me after the party was over.

"Quite frankly," I beamed, "He hijacked my hoo-ha!"

"You're demented!" Alégra tried to subdue her disapproving face but it was clear she was dying for gossip, "I can't believe you soiled my garden!"

I couldn't help but laugh.

"So," Nikki raised her eyebrows. "Did he soil *yours*?"

"Um, yes, it was fabulous and—" right at that moment I began to sense a very urgent and *very* severe burning sensation between my legs.

OMG!

What the hell is going on?

"What's the matter, Charly?" Nikki scrunched her nose. "Got ants in your pants?"

"That's so *not* funny," I winced painfully, "Alégra, do you use any weird fertilizer or, like, pesticides?"

"*Obviously*. I had an infestation of red ants last week and—"

Nikki burst out laughing and I ran to the shower.

Over the next—well, for a longer period of time than I'd care to admit—I endured ant bites, poison ivy, and one inexplicable case of soft bumps that still make an appearance every time I get too close to a compost bin. And yet, it was one of my more successful relationships. We never fought, never interfered in each other's lives, and we always got along really well. We went on some great outdoor hiking trips, too… Our relationship was probably so successful because we never worried about the future, we just had fun in the present. Even the end of our relationship arrived with minimal turbulence. The Constant Gardner won a scholarship to some prestigious law school in some Nordic country I had no interest in frequenting and that was that. We parted ways and eventually lost touch. And, although these days, I like to keep my outdoor activities to drinking on a patio, I'll always remember The Constant Gardner fondly and honestly, I've never looked at shrubbery in quite the same way.

14. I'm Not Paranoid, *Right?!*

It was official: my first full month in Bangkok!

It was Friday morning and I was looking forward to a full day working from home on my report. I was sure I'd be able to finish up early—as Sandy preferred to have reports in by noon—and I'd be able to get out and enjoy the city. Kai and Kermit were still sleeping so I quietly crept downstairs and left my two boys in bed. I loved my loft, I loved my job, I loved my dog, and of course, I loved my boyfriend. Everything was perfect. That is, except for one teeny tiny barely-worth-mentioning issue...

So annoying....

I hate talking about this...

The *only* issue in my perfect life was the *source* of the loft that Kai and I shared. Get ready for this: Kai had heard about the rental opportunity from...wait for it... his most recent ex-girlfriend.

Gets better...

The loft belonged to her.

No, really.

I know, I know...

Needless to say I was *not* thrilled about the opportunity when Kai first brought it up before we'd left Boston. However, I quickly came around when he mentioned the price, showed me the pictures, and promised that she would never ever — not even once — be in the country, let alone the city, let alone the loft, while were there.

But still....
Renting a loft from Kai's ex-girlfriend?
Gross....
But it is worry-worthy?
I mean, just how close were they?
Not very, Kai had assured me.

In fact, the only reason he knew about the loft was because his ex had sent out a mass email asking if anyone knew of anyone who'd like to sub-let her place while she was off saving the developing world through yoga (or something equally stupid).

Honestly, I didn't even care why she *happened* to be in Asia at the same time as us — I didn't want to know and I definitely didn't want to ask — what if it had something to do with supreme devastation on her part over the breakup with Kai?

Don't know, don't care.

Kai assured me she was in his past and since I trusted my boyfriend implicitly, I had no reason to doubt him. (Also, I'd grilled Scott about it endlessly and he let me know that yes, indeed, it *did* have something to do with aforementioned supreme devastation on her part over the breakup with Kai.)

Scott also told me that she was using her life's savings to travel and teach yoga and find herself and although he liked Bangkok, she wanted to get out and explore more.

Like, *really?* That's *so* cliché.

(Nikki, Alégra, and Eden assured me that *my* journey of self-discovery was way cooler than hers. It was also infinitely more original.)

It's true.

Being an expat on a mission is way more awesome than being unemployed and bendy. And, I'm sorry. I'm really not trying to be a bitch. But I did *not* like the sound of Kai's shady ex from the beginning. Having never met her, I was forced to base my opinion on the few facts I had: her name. Zoë van der Baque.

First of all, that is a 100% fake name if ever I've heard one. Sounds like the love child of a Swiss midget and a lesbian hippie — like, what kind of name is that!?

I didn't like it one bit.

Nor was I a big fan of the visual I got in my mind when I put the two names together: Kai & Zoë, Zoë & Kai. It either sounded like a mass-murdering sociopathic duo or a super-too-close-for-comfort brother / sister chef team at an annoyingly trendy vegan café.

But, being the terribly diplomatic person that I am, I decided to let the name marinate in my mind for a few days before making a final decision. I concluded that Zoë was probably not an *entirely* putrid person. In fact, in another dimension, we might have even been friends. (This, unfortunately, was proven to be an incorrect assumption when I proposed the hypothetical friendship to Kai. He practically shot scotch from his nostrils at the hilarity of such a scenario, "Um, no sweetie. You two would *not* have gotten along.")

Oh.

Okay.

Wait.

Why not?

Enter the crazy...

Was Zoë a departure from Kai's typical type of girl?

Was I?

Did Kai have a typical type of girl?

O

M

F

G

Make it stop!

Obviously, I stopped liking her after that.

And, well, actually, if you think about it, it's Kai's fault.

Whatever, I was willing to forgive him.

But not *her*.

And the thing that infuriated me most about this shady character was when I discovered that she had the *raving audacity* to leave a *welcome gift* for us at the loft. This proved to me that she was pure evil. What's worse, it was a set of adorable blue hand and bath towels. Naturally, I was enraged.

Thankfully, the chance to get Zoë back for such a brazen move presented itself to me when I ran out of toilet paper one day and was *forced* to use them as backup.

Still, I was left feeling unsatisfied. Zoë knew about me, but I didn't know the first thing about Zoë. I decided to take it up with Alégra. I signed into g-chat hopping she would be there.

kermitandcharly@gmail.com

Charly says:
    Alégra, are you there? I miss you!

Alégra says:
    Hi! I miss you too. Unpacked yet?

Charly says:
    Hardly... So how's work going? Are you president of Liam & Olivia yet?

Alégra says:
    Not yet. But I'm definitely the prettiest girl in my office. Are you the prettiest girl in yours?

Charly says:
    I really wouldn't know how to answer that, Ali....

Alégra says:
    Oh well. Guess what? Teddy and I just celebrated our six month anniversary and I've met the parents! It's for realsies! I think I might marry this guy!!

Charly says:
>Yay Ali, that's awesome, congratulations!! I'm so happy for you. Okay so I hate to turn it on me... but I'm having a mini-insecurity crisis about Kai's ex-girlfriend.

Alégra says:
>Np... is this Zoë van der Something?

Charly says:
>That's her. She hooked us up with the loft, as you know, and even gave us a housewarming gift.

Alégra says:
>How tacky!

Charly says:
>I know!

Alégra says:
>Are they in contact?

Charly says:
>I know that she texts him from time to time...

Alégra says:
>That's only a *textual* relationship – no biggie.

Charly says:
>But it's like, in the middle of the night sometimes.

Alégra says:
>That's because Evil never sleeps, honey, don't worry about it. Just think of her as a slutty shark... if she stops doing what she naturally does best, she'll sink and die. It's nothing personal, just remember that. Kai is like totally madly in love with you. That's obvious.

Alégra was so great at objectively analyzing men because she took a break between relationships (mostly because she needed time to come up with elaborate rationalizations as to why it didn't work out): "He's super busy with work. Being a part-time online poker player is like, grueling both mentally and emotionally."

OR

"We're just not on the same level and if he's more mentally connected to that hillbilly whore well, then, that's his journey… and who am *I* to stand in the way of true herpes-ridden love?"
OR
"He's gay."

All that midnight stalking, texting, and "randomly" bumping into exes had equipped Ali with a wealth of knowledge about the opposite sex and their curious behavior. She credits her work as being the inspiration for most romantic comedy movies and television shows that have come out over the past decade, "HBO owes me so much money it's not even funny."

¤ * § * ¤

I shook off my insecure thoughts about Kai's ex-girlfriend and tried to get back to a healthier mental place. I looked around the loft and sighed happily; despite the lack of unpacking efforts on both of our parts, the space was beautiful. It was completely open-concept with two stories of glass overlooking the river and most of the city. We had breathtaking views of just enough sunrise and sunset for the light to be a compliment to the space.

Despite the fact that the *source* of the loft was an annoying wacko named Zoë who I'm pretty sure had an ulterior motive in renting it to us (*how could she not!?*) I decided to just "let it go" and enjoy a peaceful morning.

I fixed myself a homemade latte with soy milk and rocket-fuel strength coffee from a French press and frother we'd bought the day before. It was a far cry from my beloved blend back home, but it did the trick. I perused the contents of the fridge and discovered that Kai had been living on Phad Thai and Heineken for the majority of my absence. I made a mental note to go grocery shopping as soon as I had finished my report.

I was getting the hang of this!

With a makeshift home office—a pub stool for a chair and a stack of boxes for a desk—I eased what would become my Friday morning ritual: innumerable homemade lattes, Edifice Luxe reports, and being extra quiet so that my two favorite boys could sleep-in upstairs. But before I could do any of that, my new cell phone rang.

Armed with the knowledge that only two people, Kai and Sandy, had the number, I was pretty sure Kai hadn't yet been reduced to calling me from the bedroom upstairs.

Mindful of a sleeping boyfriend not far away, I put on my professional but quiet voice, "This is Charly Briar."

"Halloooooooo?" said a cheerful young Thai woman's voice.

Wrong number.

"Hallloooooo? Who is this?" she inquired.

Um, who is this?

"Hallloooooo?" the voice didn't give up.

Despite the promise I'd ***literally*** just made to myself—the one where I was going to let things go and be calm, cool, and collected—my thoughts fell into a paranoid tailspin.

OMG!

It's one of those girls from the street market!

Why was she calling for Kai?

Was he having an affair and doing it daily on the fake Fendi bags?

Oh...

Wait.

Hold the phone... cray-cray.

That makes no sense.

I composed myself by sitting up straight and tucking my hair behind my ears as I do when faced with something really puzzling, (like Sudoku or Google Maps). Why would Kai's mistress be calling me? How did she get my number? And *why* was I so quick to assume that Kai had been knocking knock-off boots with a seductive street vendor? I couldn't help it. I was lost in a frisson of paranoia and doubt and my mind conjured up ridiculous cheating scenarios, shooting them at me like a rapid-fire death squad.

"Charly? Hallloooooooo?"

Who was this tortuous vixen?

I broke into cold sweats at the mental image of this brazen hoochy Gucci mamma. I had to say something but I didn't speak Thai—I'd been there for less than a month! I only knew one word, so I used it.

"Ka?"

"Ohhhhh," the girl giggled uncontrollably and spoke in Thai to someone on the other end as I mapped out how I was going to "deal" with her. I decided murder-suicide was my only option. As I was about to hang up and throw myself off the roof just to escape the agony of it all, the voice spoke again.

"Khun Charly, this is Child's Size, the secretary of Sandy."

Not Kai's mistress.

Obviously.

(I called her *Child's Size* because she was the tinniest girl I'd ever seen in my life. She was not a little person *per se*, but she may as well have been.)

The cartoon tee-shirts and hot pink flip flops she wore—not to mention her squeaky baby voice—didn't help either. As the embarrassed blood drained from my face, I was left with surprisingly little to say. So I offered up my only knowledge of Thai, again.

"Ka."

"Oh, you speak Thai now?"

Child's Size erupted once more and nestled the phone into her chest so that she could tell her colleague how hilarious I was.

I was mortified at mistaking my boss' secretary for my boyfriend's secret lover and so I politely inquired as to the reason for the phone call.

"Please check your email, Khun Charly. There is a big networking function next month. It is for hotel industry people and Khun Sandy would like to invite you and your *plus one*. Also, please send me the report, *ok na ka*?"

Cultural affectations aside, Child's Size—whose real name was unpronounceable and composed entirely of consonants—spoke English beautifully. Child's Size could converse in my native tongue with ease while I could barely manage five words in Thai. Concluding that I really needed to enroll in Thai language lessons, I sheepishly explained that the report would be finished shortly and I'd be happy to attend the networking function.

"*Okay na ka,*" Child's Size responded cheerily.

"Oh, O, Okay...."

I was painfully aware of my ignorance when it came to phone etiquette in Thailand.

"Ka..." Child's Size said.

"K-, Ka?"

Click.

It was a somewhat odd exchange but I shrugged and chalked it up to one of many lost-in-translation moments to come. I turned back to my laptop and rubbed the touch pad on my keyboard to bring the screen back up.

And, as I did, I guiltily brushed away my initial accusations during my conversation with Child's Size. I promised myself to stop being so jealous and paranoid... In my inbox was an e-vite to an event called "The Hoteliers' Ball" at a place called The British Club. There was also a note from Sandy in the subject that read "Great networking opportunity, see you there!" so ditching wasn't an option.

Damn.

Ugh, networking. Could there be anything more contrived and unnatural (and, um, a more thinly disguised excuse to hook up with colleagues) *See: Annual Retreat in Singapore, 17-year-old mega-hottie Tyler Kee.*

Cringe!
Well... Cringe happily...
But cringe nonetheless!
Moving on...

The invitees to the Hoteliers' Ball included local media, industry executives, travel agents, event organizers, tour operators, and basically anyone having anything to do with travel. The evening consisted of a cocktail reception at 7pm followed by a traditional English buffet (whatever that was), the past president's toast at 9pm, and dancing 'til late. While the itinerary itself didn't seem too painful I'd still rather take a handful of laxatives, drink a bottle of diarrhea-stopping medicine, and play *who would win in a fight?* in my stomach than network.

I *hate* networking.

It's never felt natural for me to speak to strangers and, in the past, I have always done everything I can to avoid people at networking functions. Unfortunately, I've learned that the best plan for avoiding people at networking functions is to linger by the cheese table or at the open bar. I later realized that makes me come across as a binge eater and / or functioning alcoholic, (two facts about myself I like to keep on the hush-hush). Thankfully, *plus ones* were invited and there was no mention of cheese. I entered the event into my fabulous new smartphone and drained the last of my homemade latte as I heard Kai rumble down the stairs.

"Hey, babe," he said.

Kai kissed me on the back of my head and made his way to the kitchen; I looked up to see him walk by in nothing but faded sweat pants resting just below his hips.

Wicked.

Hot.

With his back to me, I was able to admire my boyfriend's statuesque form without blatantly gawking. I wondered how Kai had already managed to find a gym and, clearly, visit it a couple of times.

How does the girl who has to push her teeny ponch back into her skinny jeans after too may burritos get the guy who looks as though he's been chiseled into life?

Seriously…. I rule.

We'd been together for months and months now, but Kai still fascinated me as though I'd never laid eyes on him. I strained my neck over the counter to admire my gorgeous man as he opened the fridge and bent down to search between the cartons of take-away food for his favorite morning beverage: organic lychee juice. It was Kai's morning staple and the *only* acceptable morning juice, according to him. I sighed and wondered if other girlfriends found their boyfriends to be just as gorgeous and just as flawless and just as awesome as I found Kai to be.

As Kai searched high and low I giggled quietly at the realization that the glasses he was looking for were still in one of the numerous boxes that were *supposed* to have been unpacked while I was away at work. But seeing him go through these ridiculously exaggerated movements was like watching a male model do calisthenics in the nude: *Too good to pass up…*

"Where are the glassy juice holders?" Kai asked more to himself. "Not the plastic ones but kind of like the plastic ones. Like the ones that are tall and glassy, you know? Where are they?"

So sexy.

"Um, I don't think they've been unpacked yet, babe," I laughed. "Would you like to use my mug? I can wash it out, it's no problem. I've finished my soy latte."

Kai made a face as though I'd just suggested he lick the floor of an outhouse. He put the juice back in the fridge and opted instead for a four-dollar bottle of water he had purchased the day before. He checked the expiry date (*why??*) and twisted the cap off disappointedly. Standing there, half naked, Kai drank deeply and deliberately. I waited patiently as he drained the water bottle of its contents.

Very patiently…

Somehow, Kai had the ability to make people feel as though he was always about to say something epic.

Finally, he cleared his throat and bestowed his message upon his attentive audience, "So, what's shakin'?"

I announced that I had finished my report on time, I had decided to take Thai language lessons *for real*, and would he like to be my *plus one* at a work party next month?

"Yep."

Ha! No lingering creepily at the cheese table for this girl!

"Oh, hey, by the way," Kai said as he made his way past me and back up the stairs towards the shower. "Nikki Temple called while you were out the other day."

"Great, thanks babe." I said as I contemplated the sea of boxes that desperately needed to be unpacked.

Kai stopped on the winding staircase and sighed almost quizzically, "She was really weird on the phone, acted like we'd never met. What's the deal with her anyway?"

"Oh, that's just Nikki," I answered truthfully. "*Her deal* would take ages to explain."

"Okay," Kai said with a smile of relief as he reached the top of the stairs but then turned and called down to me from. "So, I'm not like, being *paranoid* over nothing, right?"

"Trust me," I blushed. "You're good."

15. Here's the deal with Nikki Temple...

So, we've already established that Nikki Temple, in truth, is *not* Nikki Temple at all. She's Nicola Templeton, heiress to the Templeton Industries' fortune and in line to control the whole thing one day, if she ever wants to.
But wait,
there's more...
...much, much, more...

When Nikki was barely over a decade old she walked in on her father at his office getting a hand-job from a pretty young secretary. Without missing a beat she exclaimed, "So *that's* what shorthand means!"
(That's not the story but I love telling it!)
While this event would be traumatizing, to say the least, to most children, Nikki calmly proceeded to help herself to a cookie from her father's secret stash — the one he kept at the office just for her — and insisted that she was perfectly content to keep herself occupied with her New York Times Weekend edition and her cookie until they were, "Finished their meeting."
It was then that Nikki's father realized that his daughter needed to know the *truth*.
Here's where the story actually starts....

In the mixed-up chronicles of the dysfunctional Templeton family, what had just transpired was a bonding moment between father and daughter.

And you thought your family was weird...

Nikki's father excused his secretary (permanently) and took his daughter out for lunch to reveal the truth about her family, his infidelity, and the existence of a half-sister Nikki never knew she had.

Talk about drama!

Something about being caught red-handed, sort to speak, sent Dusty Templeton into a tailspin of truth-telling...

He confessed to a long life of cheating, stemming from a loveless childhood, drug-filled teen years, and alcohol-filled adult years. Even his wife didn't love him and had only entered into marriage for the financial benefits. (That much Nikki was already well-aware of.) Dusty even admitted that he no longer loved Nikki's mother.

Nikki assured her dad that she didn't really love her mom either. (This was because her mother just taken away TV privileges for a week and Nikki was *not* pleased.) In fact that's why she'd come down to her father's office in the first place; to appeal to a higher authority).

Then, out of the blue, Dusty's eyes filled with tears as he confessed to his biggest shame: fathering an illegitimate child almost exactly Nikki's age.

I know!

Crazy, right?

In a strange but true way, Dusty Templeton had never loved any woman until he met Nikki, his perfect daughter. He told her that and she believed him. It was the first honest thing he'd said in his life and Nikki could feel that. She didn't care about the drinking or the infidelity or even the half-sister. She loved her dad and that was that. Now, any adult woman would have rolled her eyes and written Dusty Templeton off as a disgusting excuse for a man...

And if Nikki had been more like her mother, she might have felt the same way. But Nikki was a true Templeton and adored her dad despite his mistakes. Dusty became her hero that day; a sad, wounded hero in need of his daughter's protection. (True, Nikki would spend her teen years acting out these deep-seeded daddy-issues—never making the connection until years later—but she chose sides that day, and never looked back.) Thus continues the confusing intricacies of father-daughter relationships...

(By the way, we don't tell Alégra about any of this. It would upset her and we know that she can't risk frown lines until they invent something stronger than what is currently on the market. It's not that Alégra wouldn't be able to handle the fact that Nikki's father was a philanderer or that Nikki regarded him as her hero despite his many flaws. It wasn't even the fact that Nikki had a half-sister no one knew about. It's the fact that Alégra *is* Nikki's half-sister! Oh yeah.)

Dun, dun, dunnnnn!

Here's the other half of the story: before Alégra was born, her mother had been the secretary to a very well-known industrialist, Dusty Templeton, President and CEO of Templeton Industries.

She was young and Nikki's father could be very persuasive... and let's be honest, what billionaire doesn't have a couple illegitimate kids hanging around? I'm not entirely sure about the details but apparently there was a big payoff—like a *big* payoff—to Alégra's mom and a trust established in Alégra's name that paid out monthly (which is what accounts for Alégra's stunning condo and immaculate wardrobe). All of this was on the condition that the truth be kept *hush hush* and of course, the easiest way to do that was to keep Ali in the dark. This left only her mother to carry the secret of Dusty Templeton's infidelity... *How crazy is that?!*

For such an enormous mess it sure was packaged up prettily: Alégra was told a wealthy aunt had set up the trust for her, her mother had long ago remarried a wonderful man, and both her education and a career of her choosing were guaranteed.

With such luck Alégra never really bothered to ask questions. *Would you?*

Okay, well, most people would. But Alégra wasn't most people... she believed in Easter egg hunts and the possibility of a perfect hair day (and prince charming). Years later we all met at Boston University. Although I'm sure it was a bit awkward at first for Nikki to lay eyes on her half sister — the product of her father's infidelity — we became the best of friends. Lucky for both Nikki and Alégra, they took after their mothers in terms of looks, so there was no resemblance whatsoever.

There was also the fact that Nikki had had her beautiful golden wavy locks chemically straightened and dyed midnight black (*which is insane*) and surgically rejected the gift of being well-endowed — a Templeton female trait — years before when she had decided to become Nikki Temple. To look at Nikki and Alégra was to look at complete opposites. It was hard to imagine them being friends, let alone sisters. But with no reason to be suspicious, Alégra never clued in. But Nikki confided in me almost immediately that she recognized her half-sister the second she'd laid eyes on her. It was in Nikki's blood to be suspicious. Unlike sweet Alégra who had enjoyed a life free of scandal, deceit, and secrets, Nikki was from one of the richest families in the world and well accustomed to duplicity and betrayal. The Templetons were always in the news for embezzlement, tax fraud, public drunkenness, or scandalous affairs, and from my count, Alégra was just one of seven illegitimate Templeton kids. Throughout her childhood, Nikki had frequently and unexpectedly come face to face with a dark Templeton secret: whether it was the cover up of an idiot cousin who'd been drunk driving and hit someone or a child born out of wedlock, there was always something... I once asked her if she missed the public life and being a member of *high society*... "Not at all," she assured me as she cleared her throat sagely. "There's an ancient Tibetan saying that goes something like: *mo money, mo problems*. And trust me, it's true."

16. Confessions of a Flatulent Girlfriend

I couldn't believe it was already the day of the Hoteliers' Ball. One whole month had passed: the loft was unpacked and starting to feel lived-in, I'd just finished another round of in-town assignments, and I was really getting the hang of being an expat.
Amazing!
I was so proud of how awesome Kai and I were settling in as an *expat couple* and also how easy it was to transition into working in PR. What was Eden always complaining about? This is awesome! I could do this forever!
I'd already garnered high-quality coverage for several hotels, Sandy was thrilled, and at this rate, I'd even be able to take some extra time for travelling with Kai over Christmas. There was so much of Thailand I wanted to explore.
I was also making great connections with local media and had yet to run into any of the slimy travel writers Eden had warned me about.
Maybe there'd be one at the Hoteliers' Ball?
I doubted it.

Kai was out all afternoon *manscaping*, and after finishing my report, I took the rest of the day off to relax and get ready for that evening. I was really excited to finally have a real expat night out; I'd been spending so much time at work hoping to impress my boss that I'd neglected a huge chunk of expat life... the parties!

Sure we'd gone out for dinner and explored Bangkok a bit, but I was starting to notice our lack of friends and social life. I hoped that the ball would change that. As I puttered around the loft that afternoon I felt pleased with myself. I was turning out to be quite the natural expat. I especially liked my Friday morning rituals: three homemade lattes, two walks for Kermit, two, or three, microwaveable burritos, (*I'd finally found them, yay!*) and one Edifice Luxe Media Report.

After I finished my work I set up my yoga mat and got into my favorite position, *Savasana,* in which I lay on my back and close my eyes sagely. Truth be told, it's pretty much the only pose I have mastered but without any formal training I'd say I'm well on my way to nirvana. When I meditated, I always envisioned moving towards an incredibly blissful and peaceful happy place...

Om.

Kai is there.

Om.

Kermit the Dog is there.

Om.

My ass is a size four.

Om.

Nobody knows that I'm lying when I say, "I never eat meat".

Om.

All of my ex-boyfriends have been shipped off to Azerbaijan.

Om.

All of Kai's ex-girlfriends have been mauled to death by polar bears.

Om.

(Now *that's* bliss.)

    I was really starting to get the hang of yoga and realized I was probably advanced enough to take my practice to an actual studio. Maybe, at some point. Perhaps next week. Anyway, I still had yet to sign up for Thai lessons and that should take priority. The important thing, though, was that I had already found a place that sold frozen burritos *and* given myself an at-home hair trim which, to the untrained eye, looked great. An hour or so later I was checking email and Alégra popped up.

kermitandcharly@gmail.com

Alégra says:
    Hi sweets. What's new?

Charly says:
    Well I was just yoga-ing and Kai is out get *manscaped*. Haircut, facial, and I'm not sure what else. Quite frankly, I don't know if I want to know! LOL

Alégra says:
    That's too cute. Well tell him I say hi when he gets back.

At that moment—*obviously* unbeknownst to me—Kai came through the door. He always went through the same routine of nonchalantly removing his loafers and tossing his keys on the table by the entrance. He meandered a bit in the kitchen, perused the contents of the fridge, flipped through junk mail, and finally plopped himself on the couch to watch yesterday's soccer highlights on mute while enjoying a Heineken.

Routine was the bedrock of Kai Kostigan's existence and regardless of me—or anyone else for that matter—certain things had to be done in a certain manner.

I, on the other hand, adapted my routine to accommodate Kai: when he was home, I would greet him and together we'd chat about our day and other couple-related topics like movies we should see and other couples who were breaking up. We'd always say *I saw that one coming* and be content in the knowledge that it would never happen to us.

But when Kai *wasn't* home I'd stay in my favorite Miss Piggy Pajamas well past noon, watch Kermit sun bathe on our balcony, gossip on g-chat with friends, and eat burritos. (Kai's opinion of burritos was like Alégra's opinion of men who wear capris: inexcusable.)

"They give you gas, and what is gas, if not a sign of weakness?" Kai had once proclaimed in a Buddha-esque manner as though it were the answer to a deep philosophical question. When I realized that my boyfriend was actually *above* farting I got a little bummed out. This meant endless nights of gurgling indigestion as I tried to stifle would-be toxic gas leaks from my under-area. Kai's wardrobe, his conversation, *even his pubic hair*, it was all perfectly controlled. I guess I was more of a free spirited type: I had no problem picking clothes out of the hamper so long as they were on the top layer and lacking stains on the front. Nor did I find it weird to only shave my legs when I had a good soak in a tub (twice a month, whether I needed it or not).

That's why monogamy was invented, people.

On that particular day I had consumed more than a few burritos and, well, combined with the soothing effects of my restful *Savasana*, I'm not ashamed to admit my lower intestines housed a veritable gale force just waiting to take flight. I figured I had another couple hours before Kai came home. I could relax, do my nails, shower, and pull myself together into one hot number (instead of one hot number two) well before he came home.

(Bless this open concept loft with its expansive windows that can air a place out in a matter of minutes—now *that's* Feng Shui.)

Charly says:
> Kai's great. He has started interviewing a little bit with jobs. Doesn't seem to excited about anything, job-wise I mean. We're great though.

Alégra says:
> Well, it will come with time I'm sure.

Charly says:
> I hope. I think he's starting to get discouraged. I don't know actually. I can't tell. It's not like he's in desperate need of a job and he did say he wants to take time off...

Alégra says:
> These things always happen for a reason....

Charly says:
> Thank you Ali.... I can't talk long. Kai will be home soon and I'm still in my pajamas.

Alégra says:
> Of course, it's "Savasana Friday". Did you also have burritos?

Charly says:
> Argh, don't remind me. I feel like I swallowed an angry lab mouse. Must get rid of evidence before Kai returns.

Alégra says:
> Gross. That is truly inelegant.

Charly says:
> I meant the wrapper!

(I did *not* mean the wrapper.)

Alégra says:
> Oh, right. I remember... Kai doesn't *approve* of burritos.

Charly says:
> He thinks they're ideologically unsound. They cause gas, which he frowns upon. He also frowns upon burping, vomiting, definitely Number Two's... basically the departure of any bodily gas or fluid is bad. He doesn't even really sweat. It's totally disturbing. LOL

Alégra says:
> OMG he's like a Stepford Husband, lol.

In retrospect, that's probably when Kai realized I was home. He must have seen me over the railing from the first floor and noticed that I was still in my pajamas. He probably finished the highlights before tossing out his empty Heineken and heading up the stairs slowly and silently. Of course, like some kind of revolting zoo animal, I *still* didn't realize he was home, so I kept talking about the riotous gas that was gaining momentum just behind my belly button.

Charly says:
> Ow, OMG cramps... I regret that third burrito.... 💣

Alégra says:
> Ewwww, three? You're such a filthy being. LOL

Charly says:
> Oh you're right. Who would date me?

Alégra says:
> Just be thankful Kai's not home!!

In hindsight, it was probably then that Kai rounded the top of our spiral staircase. I grabbed my stomach and keeled over at the hilarity of my conversation with Alégra. It was so awkward and funny I couldn't help but laugh. And then it happened.

I simultaneously felt my face tense and my bowels relax as I let out *the* most robust gaseous explosion ever known to man.

My bum roared like a motorcycle gearing up and I felt our brand new plush leather office chair—the one that Kai had *just* ordered from Bang & Olufsen—ripple wildly. It was like a Tibetan lunch bell and it was glorious.

Still oblivious to Kai's presence, I laughed hard at the gassy eruptions that continued to fly out from under me like a rocket with increasing intensity in the fight against gravity. As the feculent essence of digested burrito filled the room, I felt tears of laughter roll down my face while I thought of the intestinal symphony Kai would most definitely disapprove of.

I was *so* happy he wasn't home—

"Hey, babe," Kai said.

I jumped up like an obedient dolphin at an aquatics show. My eyes expanded beyond their sockets, my face became hot like a fire poker, and the sheer terror of being caught caused yet *another* series of rapid-fire eruptions that kept me hovering at least four inches above the chair as though I had a jet pack up my ass.

I swiveled softly above the chair from left to right, propelled by the force of my own gaseous expulsion.

Somebody kill me, now.

Ancient mystics claim that the secrets of levitation can be obtained only after years upon years of profound introspection and spiritual meditation. Well, I did it in three burritos and twenty minutes. Imagine that.

When will this end?

As I hovered there above the chair farting like a motorboat engine, it suddenly dawned on me. I just might have enough gas to fly back to Boston and pretend the whole Kai, Bangkok, expat thing never happened... because I'd *totally* be okay with that.

Ugh!

Somebody, anybody...

Just swoop through the window and assassinate me... now!

I will pay anything you want, just put me out of my misery.

Anyone?

You can even do it Baby Seal Styles, with a club...
Like the Canadians do...
Please. Just kill me.
Oh god... When will this end!?

Without turning to face Kai, I scanned the floor for a vortex to another dimension or at the very least, a black hole to nowhere. I was *more than* willing to abandon friends and family forever if it meant not having to turn around and face Kai.

No such luck.
Oh my god...
Please let me have an aneurism!
Spontaneous combustion?
Falling plane parts?
Anything!

After what seemed like an eternity, the exhaust clouds dissipated and I stopped levitating above the planet's surface propelled by my own personal *asstronautical* vessel. I swear I was up there so long I should have taken pictures for Google Earth. As I sank back into the chair with great relief one last tiny *shpleck!* squirted out from deep within the tiny air pocket between the leather chair and my Miss Piggy pajama bottoms.

Really?!

Faced with my own grisly fate — and with no vortex or samurai assassin in sight — I took the *only* viable option. I couldn't bear the thought of admitting defeat and facing Kai. I was sorry to have done it but I didn't see any other way. Desperation drives people to do crazy things and honestly, I'll regret it for the rest of my life. I took a deep breath and exclaimed, in utter shock, "Oh my god Kermit, that's so disgusting!"

Pure evil?
Maybe.
Brilliantly executed?
Of course.
Kai will never catch on.
There's just no way.

I shot a Hollywood-smile at Kai to confirm my awesomeness and clear away any doubt that I was capable of such a despicable deed. Kai was probably only in the room for the tail end of my *assquake* anyway. And let's be honest, that fart didn't even smell human in origin, so it's completely believable that it came from a dog's butt. I shot a glance at Kermit, who shifted uneasily as the wrongly accused tend to do. Poor little fur ball, he was *always* my scapegoat for missing leftovers and farting, and sometimes I even blamed him for missed trips to the gym. My favorite excuse killed two birds with one stone, "Oh, right, well, Kermit ate the leftovers so I scolded him and then obviously I *had* to stay here and watch him. This unfortunately meant that I missed my spinning class."

I smiled convincingly and prayed to every deity I could think of that Kermit wouldn't suddenly develop the ability to speak English, or any language really. Instead, he responded with a snort and rolled over, exactly what he normally did after farting.

Bless you furry one.

I turned to Kai and smiled again as I got up to kiss him hello.

"Nice try," Kai put his palm on my forehead and pushed me away gently. "Cripes, I can taste that!"

It wasn't that Kai made the joke. It was that he didn't even crack a smile while saying it. There he stood head-to-toe in some unpronounceable designer suit and gorgeously coifed hair, with a Kiehl's glow and a chiseled profile, just *oozing* excellence. There I sat, in Muppet pajamas with my hair in a messy bun atop one inch of un-dyed roots, having just allowed the vilest stench in the history of time to escape from my bum. I probably had burrito breath too.

(Okay, I'll admit that three burritos might have been a bit excessive, but it is beyond me how anyone can resist such a divine blend of cheese, bean, and beef. Like a warm little pillow of goodness inviting me to lay my head down on its soft tortilla exterior and take a little nap. The burrito is the finest of all snacks and quite frankly, it's their god-like deliciousness that keeps me from becoming an Atheist.)

"Oh, fine," I gave in. "Busted. I'm no lady, I suppose."

"You can say that again," Kai waved his hand in front of his nose, symbolically I hoped, and walked past me to the bathroom to partake in his late afternoon ritual: Shower # 3. Shower # 5 came before bed while Shower # 1 was naturally the nanosecond after he emerged from slumber in the morning. Any type of sexual activity or a trip to the gym accounted for Showers # 2 and # 4.

I know it's odd but I'm not about to start judging people's quirks...

I watched Kai glide across our bedroom silently as my embarrassment soon gave way to irritation and confusion. Was he *seriously* shunning me for farting? Surely there are more offensive things in the world than a gassy girlfriend, was it really worth fighting over? Still unconvinced that Kai was being entirely serious, I offered up my lips once again in salutation. Kai responded by floating by and pretending not to see. He went into the bathroom and turned the shower on. I looked to Kermit for support but he was clearly miffed at being blamed for the whole situation. I think my dog actually gave me screw-face but I couldn't be sure.

What the heck was going on?!

With the door closed and the shower turned on, I walked across the room and placed my ear to the door.

This can't be happening, our first fight, over a fart?

"Babe?" I said loud enough to be heard.

Nothing.

"Hunny?"

Silence.

"Kai!"

I *had* to rectify this situation before it got out of control. I turned the doorknob to the bathroom silently before pressing the door open and leaning into a steamy room that consisted of a standup shower, a tiny sink, and an unfortunately placed toilet. But before I was able to say anything I found myself standing directly over Kai who was, at that moment, sitting down on the toilet with his pants around his ankles.

"Get out!" he bellowed. Kai shooed me away with his day old copy of *The Wall Street Journal* and reached frantically for the door.

Flustered, I turned on my heels as I attempted to extricate myself from the awkward situation as quickly as possible.

Ack! Must get out of here!

I whipped around frantically just as Kai grabbed hold of the door and flung it shut which caused me to trip and smack my elbow on the door as I fell down.

"Owwwww!" I yelped as I crawled out the room. I could hear the door lock from the inside.

What the hell!?

Okay, now we're even, I thought as I rubbed my sore arm. Minutes passed. No sign of Kai. No noise. Nothing. I wondered if he had been lucky enough to find a vortex or an agreeable ninja assassin to put him out of his embarrassment. More minutes passed.

Breathe.

Focus.

First things first: open a window.

Okay, done.

Second: The Hoteliers' Ball.

Must get ready.

While Kai was in the bathroom for what seemed like an eternity, I changed into an air-tight black cocktail dress for the party that night. We (was Kai even coming?) had planned on grabbing drinks together before heading to the party. I threw on some simple makeup and picked out my favorite black stilettos.

Although I had wanted to look good that evening, I now mostly wanted to look good for the moment Kai came out of the bathroom just in case we were about to have our first fight.

Were we going to fight?

I had no idea. When we first got together, I mentioned to Kai that he was one of the most *unreadable people* I had ever met. He responded quizzically, "So you think I'm illiterate?"

Kai could be so confusing…

Finally, *eons* later, a showered Kai finally emerged from the bathroom wearing only jeans and flip flops and holding a wet newspaper. He didn't look very pleased. Well actually, I wasn't sure *what* he looked...

Did Kai have Relationship Botox?

He calmly closed the bathroom door behind him and floated across the room silently, like a pissed off male model on rollerblades.

Aha, so we are going to fight.

Is this serious? This can't be serious.

I decided that I would be the one to extinguish this thing before it really got ignited. Extending the olive branch of peace, I attempted to speak but was unceremoniously cut off, "Just forget about it, Charly."

Kai waved the newspaper he'd brought into the washroom with him like a royal prince dismissing a lowly servant.

Irritated, I retracted the olive branch of peace slightly by bringing up the fact that *he* had slammed the door on *me*, and in doing so, had caused actual physical harm (not to mention the emotional distress of being passed off as a disgusting low-class fart-machine). I sat down on the bed and crossed my arms tightly to signify that I had made a good point.

"*This* is why there should be *his* and *hers* bathrooms," sighed Kai as he ignored me once more and tucked his newspaper under his naked arm. I wondered why I had extended the olive branch to begin with.

"Let's just forget it," he continued. "I'm going to read my paper, have a beer, and be thankful that my girl saves us a ton of money by fumigating the loft herself."

"LOL you big asshole," I said under my breath.

Kai sniggered at his own joke and I seriously considered judo-chopping him in the larynx. I watched in disbelief as his carefully sculpted torso and faux-worn jeans passed by me without acknowledgment.

As he disappeared down the stairs he added casually over his shoulder, "I've just never had a girlfriend that, like, *did that*... it's just, like, kinda weird."

And that's when I let something *else* slip...

Without thinking I whined in my best, *most* childish tone, "Ohhhhhhhhh I'mmmmm Zoë. I save the planet *and* my ass smells like fucking couture perfume."

No really, I actually did say that.

Maybe Kai didn't hear me.

"Excuse me?" Kai snapped.

Okay maybe he did hear me.

Okay, 'cmon! It's not all my fault!

Ugh what is happening? I feel like I'm losing my mind.

At first I *loved* that Kai was gorgeous and always collected and completely put together. It made me proud to be on his arm. But lately he was turning into an annoyingly hygienic, boring, and judgmental robot with zero sense of humor.

What's worse, his perfections were only accentuating my flaws. There was Kai: gorgeous, smart, and funny with perfect friends and a perfect family and a perfect body and blah blah blah. And then there was me: a fashion-challenged dork with quirky friends and an even quirkier family.

I looked at the two-dimensional person in front of me and wondered, for the first time, what it was that initially attracted me to him.

Oh, yeah, I remember. I was initially attracted to all the things that are presently annoying the hell out of me.

I took a breath and composed myself on our bed, posing as naturally as my tortuously tight black cocktail dress would allow. I wasn't sure what to say. The truth was, in that moment, I felt embarrassed and insecure.

Oh crap.

If I was having concerns about our compatibility, it was entirely possible that Kai was having them as well.

As I cleared my throat to apologize for the unnecessary jab at his ex-girlfriend, Kai leaned his naked chest against the top three steps of the staircase and asked, "Why are you all dressed up?"

Completely deflated (literally and figuratively) I reminded Kai of The Hoteliers' Ball as a fat tear rolled down my cheek.

Great!

Crying!

Zoë probably never cried.

Kai certainly didn't.

Maybe Kai and Zoë should just run off together and never cry and never fart and have boring robot sex forever and ever.

Bleh!

The thought of them together having robot sex made another fat tear roll down my cheek although I have no idea why I'd be envious of robot sex. I mean that doesn't even sound appealing and in fact it is probably quite cold and painful—

Wait a tick.

What's going on?

I don't cry.

Like, I have never cried.

I just don't do it.

What was happening!?

What was this salty clear stuff running down my face?

What is going on!?

Weird and horrible all at the same time.

The more I tried not to cry, the harder the tears fell. They fell for the bruise on my elbow, they fell for the fact that I obviously wasn't good enough for Kai, and they fell for my fart. My stupid, little, fart.

How could a delicious little burrito (or three) cause so much sadness? They are <u>designed</u> for pleasure!

"Oh, no," Kai rushed over to me. "I'm so sorry, baby. I didn't mean to make you cry. You poor thing. It's not you. It's just that I'm very frustrated with a number of things...."

Oh okay. Wait...

Robot says what?

Kai's voice trailed off and I was left to wonder how I could live with someone yet apparently know so little about them. I had no idea that Kai was frustrated and certainly not *very* or with *a number* of things. What things? What was the *exact number* of things he was frustrated with? Did the things have anything to do with me or Zoë, or my fart? What does *very frustrated* mean? Was he very frustrated at the things, or by the number of the things?

What $!&^!%* things ???

Just before my head exploded into a splatter of brains and question marks all over our gorgeous new duvet, Kai kissed my forehead and signified the end of our would-be fight.

"Lemme just get ready," he tucked a flyaway behind my ear. "Don't cry. It's okay, everything's okay."

I smiled and, happy that our fight was over, I went for a real kiss but Kai was already heading off to the bathroom for another shower.

17. The Hoteliers' Ball

As Kai and I walked the short distance down the driveway of The British Club, (each wearing a sleek black outfit: mine a cocktail dress, his, a tailored suit), I tried to put our turbulent afternoon behind me. At least we could say we'd gotten our first fight under our belts and I was excited to move forward.

And what better way to do that then a party?

As we rounded the corner of the garden party, I heard informal laughter and clinking glasses. Soft music emanated from tiny outdoor speakers while perfectly strewn rows of white lights bounced softly in the early evening sky. Everything about The British Club had a soft feeling to it: the music, the flowing dresses of the female attendees, even the conversation seemed to linger tangibly before floating up gently into the air. It was the closest thing to an old-fashioned country club I had ever seen and I drew in a nervous breath as we came upon the loosely assembled circles of friends and colleagues. *Shit!* Nobody was nearly as dressed up as we were.

"Chill, sweetheart," Kai could sense that I was irked at being over-dressed and he softly pushed the small of my back to start me walking again.

Like a skilled animal trainer, Kai could always coax me out of any would-be-freak-out scenario. It worked. Sometimes I wondered if Kai was the Woman Whisperer.

I reignited my gait and strode confidently toward the crowd. Most everyone seemed older than us and they congregated in casual but distinct groups. At least Kai was by my side, I thought, as I tucked my arm in his for extra security and surveyed the crowd. Older men with soft white hair and gentle faces assembled by the hors d'oeuvres and spoke in deep voices.

They wore tailored shirts and tan linen trousers stretched to the limit over husky waistlines. Every belly laugh or hearty chuckle resulted in a good deal of alcohol falling out of thick scotch tumblers and down onto a perfectly manicured lawn. No one seemed to notice, or care. The older women grouped together as well. They were like sorority sisters who giggled and whispered with each other; sometimes even pointing at another party guest before erupting into stifled laughter. Their ever-so-slightly grey hair was assembled into beautiful loose chignons and ponytails that swayed softly when they laughed.

Their makeup was modest and they wore elegant a-lines and shift dresses. Both the older male and female expats seemed genuinely happy. Where the older women were dressed elegantly, the younger women either donned chic pantsuits or plain skirts and sweater sets.

The *pantsuits* congregated much like the older women while the *sweater sets* sat by themselves at tables covered in white linen and gold confetti. I guessed that they must be expat moms. Those women did not engage in lively conversation with each other like the professional expat women did, but instead seemed to absent mindedly down whatever wine was available while they hissed at their misbehaving children under their breath. I didn't see that many younger men at the party, but I guess that's because I didn't venture into the men's bathroom.

As I later discovered, that's where they all hung out, divvying up lines of cocaine, bragging about their latest extramarital conquests, and trying to snort as quietly as possible so their wives were none the wiser.

So *these* are expats, I thought. The people who leave their country, family, and the familiar all behind... And not just for two weeks' vacation, but to immerse themselves totally and completely in an unknown culture.

Finally.
I had officially arrived.
Actually.
Wait. No.
I had officially departed.

It suddenly hit me that I had undertaken a grand endeavor without really considering the consequences. True, we'd been in Thailand for almost two months but we really hadn't ventured out that much, and certainly not into expat territory.

I suddenly panicked.

What had I signed up for?

I didn't want to abandon my customs, I didn't want to fall out of touch with anything from back home, and I certainly didn't want to lose that closeness with my friends and family that I cherished so much.

Breathe.

I was at a place called The British Club surrounded by Europeans drinking California wine and everyone was speaking English. The only clue that I was in Thailand at all were the staff. *Mental meltdown averted.*

"I'll get us drinks," Kai said as he turned on his heels and walked towards a huge line-up. *Argh!*

Doesn't he know my rule about networking parties?
Stick together! Leave no girlfriend behind!

Kai walked away and I was left alone to ponder what it meant to be an expat and whether or not I was truly ready for it. I shifted uneasily like a six-year-old with bladder control issues in my too-tight dress, and stared at the ground.

I'm calm.
I'm freaked.

I'm calm.
I'm freaked.
This is why I hate networking parties.

With no social props such as a drink or cell phone with which to hide my obvious discomfort I was forced to resort to lighting one of Kai's cigarettes. I hardly ever smoked and when I did, it was always out of desperation.

Most people who casually smoke refer to themselves as Social Smokers. I, however, thought of myself as an Anti-Social Smoker: I only smoked when no one would talk to me or when I had no one to talk to. I gave one last hopeful glance around the party and lit up. I figured I had at least seven and a half minutes of looking like I had a purpose in life—to smoke—before I would once again be that overdressed loner girl with no wine and no one to talk to. An eternity passed. No Kai.

Why hadn't I just gone with him to get drinks?
What's wrong with me?
What's wrong with him?

More time passed. I looked down at the cigarette and guessed I had two minutes to go, three if I pushed it. This was torture. I began to worry that Kai might never come back. Eventually, I was smoking the filter and as I finally stubbed out my cigarette—convinced that Kai had been abducted by a gaggle of horny women or perhaps he'd decided to leave me because of my fart—a guy in faded jeans, a white v-neck tee, and well-kept brown loafers approached me.

"Tell me you've got another one of those," his smile revealed the nicest set of teeth available for purchase that I had ever seen.

Excellent!
A human!
My social savior!
Yippee!

His crisp American accent was a welcome sound and he extended a tanned arm with a vintage Breitling on it.

"I shouldn't smoke," the stranger said to me. "I promised my girlfriend I'd cut down, but hey, you know, she promised me she'd stop drinking before noon, so I guess we're both liars. Ha! Oh sorry, where are my manners? I'm Radden."

Hell of an opener.

Still trying to absorb all of the information bestowed upon me by the curious stranger, I found another one of Kai's cigarettes in my slouchy clutch, offered it to Radden, and gave him the lighter. Radden was intriguing, to be sure... There was something different about him but I couldn't place what it was. He seemed to both fit in *and* be an outlier at the same time. Even though he was one of *them*, he was different from them. Admittedly, he was kind of cute but honestly not my type. I mean, v-neck to a cocktail party? *Really?* Are you a diplomat's kid or something? I cocked my head at the stranger as we shared a moment of silence, sizing each other up with friendly half-smiles.

"Annnnd, what's your name, pretty girl?" he teased and I realized I hadn't reciprocated his salutation.

"I'm Charly Briar," I said with a blush. It'd been years since I'd met someone who knew literally nothing about me and I drank in the feeling deeply. In the past, there'd always been a connection or affiliation somehow; even Kai was introduced to me via Scott. This was so fresh and I relished the experience, "I just moved here," I continued with budding confidence. "I work for Edifice Luxe Hotels & Resorts... in media relations."

So yeah, like no big deal except for I'm completely amazing and I have the coolest job on the planet and if my wandering boyfriend ever shows up you'll see that he rocks, too.

So like, yeah, that's me in a nutshell.

"What about you?" I asked as I basked in the glow of well, me.

Radden ashed his cigarette to the side and looked at me as his lips parted into a smile, "I told you, I'm Radden. And don't make fun of my name, my parents were super artsy and shit."

I giggled, "No, I mean, what do you *do*?"

He looked at me again with a half-smile and a suspiciously raised eyebrow, "What do I do? Like, for fun? Or when the lights go out? Or when it's late at night and nobody's watching?"

"No," I couldn't help but giggle a little more. "Like for a living, you know, a job?"

"Why can't it all be connected?" he said as he took a step towards me and stared deep into my eyes, I felt a bit woozy.

Whoa.

Stop that right now, Mr. Friendly!

"Alright, alright, I'm a photographer *and* it is fun. Satisfied?"

"Yes," I affirmed with a smirk.

A smartass, huh?

I've met your type before.

Nothing new here.

Radden helped himself to two glasses of red wine from a passing server and offered one to me.

Um…

Hello?

Where in the name of strappy sandals was Kai??

Why was Kai getting drinks from the bar if waiters were circling?

"Okay, okay," Radden cleared his throat. "Here's the deal. I guess I'm what you'd call an *expat brat*. Born in New York but travelled constantly, you know, diplomat parents, the whole nine."

Diplomat parents! Did I call it or did I call it?

Radden continued, "I started shooting a couple years ago after I gave up on a career in amateur rugby and professional drinking. I shoot mostly for luxury travel magazines and yes, I know it's fluffy but, honestly, I love what I do."

"Mmm hmm," I smiled widely, suddenly unsure of what to say.

This guy was overwhelming in a new way and I wasn't sure if my footing was off because I was in heels standing on grass, or because of him. But since he was the sole purveyor of wine and the only person I had to talk to, I decided it was a good idea to do whatever I could to keep the conversation going…

I found out that Radden's mother was a New York wild child socialite who met his father, a British diplomat, in the seventies. As a child, he had been toted all over the world including Kenya, Mexico City, a brief stint in Jakarta, and most recently, Hong Kong. There had also been one or two years in London at some point. Radden's parents retired just outside of London and wintered in the Caymans. Radden was an only child.

"So tell me, Radden, what's the best thing about being an expat?" I asked the curious stranger.

"I'm looking at it," he smiled sexily.

The party? Me?

The booze? What!?

Where are you looking, curious man!?

Radden sighed and became a bit serious, "it's all I really know, so I couldn't compare to be honest. But I wouldn't trade it for the world. Better than being a tourist, that's for sure."

"Oh, why's that?" I asked.

"Well, a tourist seeks immediate gratification and takes a vacation to *get away* from home, whereas, an expat *is* home."

"Think of it as a relationship," Radden continued. "A tourist is very non-committal, emotionally unavailable at best. Just dabbling, really. But an expat, now *there's* a serial monogamist. He, *or she*, is committed to the experience, totally and completely. We don't just flirt with the culture, we dive, right, into it."

Now you're speaking my language.

A perverted version of it…

But my language nonetheless…

I *immediately* became sure that I truly wanted to be an expat, it all made sense now.

After all, I'd had lots of experience committing to one man after another, why couldn't I use the same approach to living abroad?

(I wasn't sure if the customs surrounding leaving a guy however, were reflected in the practice of leaving a country, but I gathered that's where the term "baggage" came from.)

Radden and I talked for some time and even had another cigarette and a second glass of wine. I told him about Kai and my decision to come to Bangkok with Edifice Luxe, what I was hoping for, and how it had gone so far. He told me about shooting in exotic locations all over the world and meeting amazing people. When the conversation naturally came to a pause I realized that Kai had been gone for too long and I couldn't keep monopolizing Radden's time without starting to look desperate.

"Are you sure you came here with a boyfriend?" he chuckled. "Maybe he's run off with a Thai lady-boy."

"Oh ha haa haaa," I retorted playfully.

Oh please don't let that be true!

Where in the name of bedazzled track pants worn ironically was Kai!?

Then it dawned on me.

Did he leave me because of the fart?

Oh no! Was I going to be alone forever?

"So, listen, pretty girl, I hate to leave you stranded here but I do have to get back to my friends," Radden gestured to a group of people I hadn't yet noticed. "You're welcome to join."

I surveyed the group: they were all gorgeous, stylishly dressed, and laughing in different accents. It was the United Nations of Awesome People and I wanted to be friends with them!

I hated being dependent on Kai for social survival.

"C'mon, girl. Let me steal you for a minute," Radden cooed with a smile. "A couple of my friends are writers, I'm sure you can turn on your PR charm and sucker them into writing some bullshit editorial for your little fancy pants hotel."

"*Hey!*" I faux-pouted.

He softly pinched my side and laughed, "I'm joking! But seriously, I gotta go. See over there? That cute girl with the horns and the pitchfork? That's my girlfriend, and she's a bit, how shall I say? *Stabby*. If I talk to another girl for too long she'll shellac my nuts so like, we gotta make a move here. Come over and meet everyone. Do it for my nuts, *please*."

"Ewww, *stop* saying nuts!" I blushed hard. "I'm sure my boyfriend is around here somewhere, I'll be fine, you go ahead. It was nice to meet you Radden and good luck with those, er, nuts."

As I was saying goodbye to my new acquaintance, Kai *finally* emerged with my long awaited Pinot. He slid his arm coolly around my unnaturally cinched waist and stared at Radden.

"Hey," said an unfazed Radden as he offered his hand to shake Kai's.

Kai—visibly chilled—shrugged and pointed out that he had a drink in one hand and *his* girlfriend in the other.

So cute. Wait.
Why do I find jealousy cute?
I should probably look into that.

"Cool," Radden returned the cold front to Kai as he stepped towards me and smiled softly. "Bye, pretty girl."

I watched Radden rejoin his group of friends and was about to suggest we follow in the spirit of networking when Kai spoke, "We're in Douche Bag City and *that* guy is the mayor."

I burst out giggling and faux-scolded Kai, "Nooooooooo."

I swayed gently and placed my palms on Kai's chest to steady myself, "This is *your* fault for taking so long!" I teased. "I was thirsty and the waiter guy kept coming around and around with the wine and then around and then the wine and then…"

"Okay, *Little Miss My-First-Cocktail*, you've done enough "networking" for tonight," Kai uncouthly scooped me up with both arms and started to carry me through the yard of The British Club in front of all the guests. "You're coming home with me, *pretty girl*."

I was totally embarrassed by Kai's lack of concern for what other people thought, but I surrendered into his arms anyway. On the way out, I caught sight of Radden smiling at me over Kai's shoulder. I couldn't help but smile back. That night Kai and I made love sloppily but passionately, and thankfully, without turbulence.

18. Speaking of Nuts

"The Nut" and I dated immediately after graduation. I was feeling melancholy about finally being an adult and having very little to show for it and, what's worse, the thought of being officially old was devastating. Magically, the universe handed me The Nut.

Disclaimer: I don't call him "The Nut" because of some sad physical dysfunction. I refer to him as "The Nut" because he was just that, *nuts*.

"Gimme yer number!" a drunken dirty blonde with big brown eyes yelled one night at a loud pub.
I was with Alégra, who had just cheated on her diet, and eaten more than once that day. So, naturally, she needed to have a faux *get-too-drunk-and-throw-up* outing.
Don't ask me... I just go where the party is.
"Excuse me?" I was slightly amused by the stranger's forwardness.
"You're a *stunner*. I want your number. Then I will call you. We will go out. Have dinner. From the looks of things, probably get hammered. And then, well, c'mon girl, you're not a baby, you know how this plays out..."
Wow.

I couldn't believe someone could be so rude, so arrogant, so, so hot... I found out later that The Nut was a sports agent, so it was in his nature to be rude and arrogant. The hot part was just a bonus. He graduated from Harvard two years before and came from a family of professional athletes and drinkers. Everyone in his family got along, had great jobs, a good education, and could hold their booze. I think if I would have brought The Nut home to my mother, she would have kidnapped him until he agreed to marry me.

"Fine, I'll give you my number." I conceded, having no intention of giving this nut-job my number.

"I knew you would," he smirked arrogantly as he immediately dialed the fake number I had given him. "Now, let's dance to your ring tone, *Woot! Woot!*"

Oh shit. Thankfully, at that moment, Alégra stepped in, "Excuse me, *please*, Charly is leaving, okay?"

"Oh, Charly?" he smiled as he disconnected the call to the fake number I'd given him. "Is that your name? Charly, Charly, Charly, I am *so* happy to be celebrating your birthday with you!"

Alégra and I exchanged confused glances.

"Bartender!" The Nut yelled. "My friend Charly is turning 37 today, it's a big one! She looks great for her age, huh? And with two divorces under her belt already! This kitty has got claws. Rrrrrrr! Can we please get some — what do you want Charly? Oh you want Jägerbombs? Okay papa will get you Jäggerbombs — excuse me, bartender? Six Jäggerbombs, please. Thanks so much."

"I'm 37? Two divorces? *Really!?*" I faux-scolded him as I placed my hand on his shoulder.

"Hey, cougar!!" The Nut yelled loud enough for people to stare. "Get your wrinkly paws off me!"

Alégra was disgusted and I totally in love.

19. Nikki & Alégra & Me and a Happy Place

Back in college, when graduation finally came around, we all helped each other pack. Nikki begrudgingly "welcomed" both Alégra and me into her apartment to box up the remainder of her belongings.

"Already done," she grumbled upon opening the door. Nikki looked completely exhausted but not from packing: her typically straight midnight black hair was unkempt and frazzled, and she looked even more emaciated than usual.

Must have been an awesome night out for Nikki!

"Hey, I recognize you," I joked. "Didn't you play the role of Child Prostitute #4 in the Broadway hit *Les Miserables*?"

"Ugh," Nikki faux-heaved. "I think I left my self-respect at the bar last night."

I laughed as I surveyed the effects of enthusiastic alcohol abuse on Nikki's tiny frame, "Seriously, Nikki, you look like you came to this country in the bottom of a boat."

"Hey, Charly, Comedy Central called, they want to give you your own show," Nikki gave me the finger but smirked cutely nonetheless.

I offered her a large take-away soy latte and she made the international symbol for *I've just smelled a rancid fart* but accepted the drink anyway.

"What do you have against dairy cows?" she scoffed.

"I've never gotten on board with milk," I shrugged.

"Dairy is full of mucus and hormones." Alégra, who was a die-hard vegan back then, shouted as she skipped upstairs with flattened boxes for packing, ready to get to work on Nikki's things.

"Don't you think you should pack your own crap?" I teased Nikki.

She shrugged, "I appreciate it, but I don't know why Alégra is bothering." Nikki then leaned in to make sure that Ali was out of earshot before she said in fake *hoity toity* accent, "Daddy Templeton is coming with his packers tomorrow anyway and I'm having everything shipped to my new abode."

"You're such a rich bitch," I mocked quietly, making sure that Alégra couldn't hear us.

Nikki grinned widely.

"Yeah, I am. What's *your* excuse?"

We both laughed at first but then realized it was somewhat bittersweet. We'd all stay friends of course, but we in so many ways; it was the end of an era. Nikki and I split a cigarette in Sunday afternoon silence as we looked around her place and smiled sadly. I just couldn't believe how fast it had gone by. But I guess that's life: there's no clear demarcation between one chapter ending and the next beginning. I know there's graduation and moving day and first day on the job and all sorts of stuff like that—but somehow it's never as you imagine it will be.

Somehow, the end of a chapter is only realized after it's over. It can never be savored the way it deserves to be savored.

Oh god...

I sound like one of those douchebags with a beaded necklace and a second-hand guitar...

Anyway, so out of nowhere Nikki and I heard a shriek from upstairs. It was coming from where Alégra was packing. It so high pitched and so horrific that the only possible explanation was that Alégra had just discovered she was a victim of identity theft by someone who shopped exclusively at big box stores.

"O M F G!!" Alégra shrieked. "Nikki, what has *happened*?" Alégra never used the F-word, not even in an acronym.

Something was *terribly* wrong and, considering she was addressing only Nikki, the only logical explanation became immediately clear: while packing Nikki's things, Alégra had somehow discovered the true identity of her father—who was *also* Nikki's father—Dusty Templeton. He was the man her mother had had an extramarital affair with, which resulted of course, in Alégra's birth *and* the end of her mother's marriage (not to mention, job). Alégra and Nikki were half-sisters but only one half of them had ever known about it.

OMFG!

Had everything changed in the blink of an eye?

"Aw, crap," Nikki eked the words out like a deflating air mattress. "Either she's discovered that my "pearl beads" she always borrows are not intended to be worn around the neck... or she found something to do with Daddy Templeton. Either way, I'm in a shitty situation."

"Beads? *Really?*" I said, totally grossed out.

Nikki waved her hand—directing the focus back to the more pressing issue—and we both sighed. We knew what the ramifications were if Alégra found out about Daddy Templeton: it was the end of her friendship with not just Nikki but me too. After all, I'd known all along but never said anything. And how could Ali stay friends with Nikki after finding out she'd been lied to by her own sister? Nikki loved Alégra and couldn't bear the thought of it all coming to an end over something so trivial.

This was bad.

We ran upstairs to face Alégra as Nikki's trademark even-keeled manner drain from her face like liberated bathwater down a drain. I started to become truly worried until I realized what Alégra was holding in her hand. I grabbed Nikki's shoulder just in time to stop her from revealing herself by accidently tumbling into a barrage of apologies on behalf of her father.

Up in Nikki's bedroom in absolute shock stood Alégra with wild disbelieving eyes firmly affixed on Nikki... and a college text book in her hand.

Nikki burst out laughing with relief, "Calm down, Alégra! You *knew* I was taking that course on Nihilism! It's not a big deal!"

It was no secret that Nikki was trying anything and everything to get over her one and only boyfriend—the one who dumped her for a cheerleader. (Those were the only details we were given as she refused to discuss it further.)

Nikki was so relieved to discover that this whole debacle had nothing to do with her secret identity and everything to do with some stupid course she was taking. She flopped on the bed and lit another cigarette, exhaled deeply, and flicked the ashes in the half-drunk soy latte I had brought her, much to my annoyance.

"But, but," Alégra huffed. "I didn't know you were having an affair with the professor!"

I shot a glance to Nikki for verification and she rolled her eyes. Alégra continued to scold Nikki, "His number—and a *very* inappropriate note—it's all in here in the course textbook."

"So?" Nikki shrugged. "Who cares? I'm about to graduate. I'm old enough to sleep with my professor. And he's not just a professor, by the way, he's the author of that book you're holding. He's actually very famous."

Alégra ignored Nikki's efforts to sell us on her affair and asked flatly, "Are you taking drugs?"

"Is that like, a serious question?" Nikki asked with a half-smile.

"Well," Alégra put her hands on her hips. "What else would propel you to such a, such a, such a *gauche* and gloomy state as to date this weirdo? You must be on drugs!"

I couldn't help but laugh.

"First of all," Nikki dropped her cigarette in the latte and got up to take the book from Alégra's grasp. "I only do drugs ironically, like the way Charly wears 80s clothing ironically, *we hope*. Anyway, it's not meant to be taken seriously."

Alégra waved her hand and persisted, "We're not talking about Charly! Are you, or are you not, having an affair with your professor who teaches—of all things—a course in Nihilism?"

I was still trying to catch my breath.

From what I gathered, Nikki was doing more than just her homework in her Nihilism 101 course and it seemed Alégra had a big problem with this...

"Nikki, you're making love to a *nihilist!* They literally do not care about anything! Don't you get how messed up that is?! What's the point? What kind of future are you expecting with this guy?"

Nikki rolled her eyes and lit another cigarette, "Ali DeVrees, *enough!* First of all, let's get one thing straight: we're not *making love*, we're banging. Believe me, there's no future in that, and I'm *perfectly* happy that way. And besides, who cares? What does that prove? I can sleep with whoever I want. You've never cared before."

"It proves, *Nikki*, that after much time and excruciating pain, I have finally found the source of your depression!"

Alégra cheered, as if finding the source of a friend's depression was a great and happy achievement. I stole a drag from Nikki's cigarette while she shook her head and censured Alégra.

"Pollyanna, I certainly hope you hide your crazy when you go on dates with all these trust fund boys. Or, are they closet freaks like you?"

Alégra waved another dismissive hand at Nikki and grabbed the book back, "You're the one who is addicted to the dark side. *You're* the freak!"

Ali read the blurb of Nikki's book out loud...

> Who Cares Who Cares?
> by Hank Zero
>
> ~ Free yourself from the chains of emotion, the burden of feeling, and the shackles of sentiment. ~
>
> Imagine paralyzing your emotions the way Botox paralyzes your face... now you can! True freedom is only possible once you've let go of all that debilitating happiness!
>
> Once you master my 12-step program and understand that nothing is connected or meaningful, you'll be free to navigate any situation... without feelings!
>
> Who cares? Not me.

As I clutched my sides and let out deep belly laughs, Nikki tore the book again from Alégra's disappointing grasp as Ali exclaimed, "*This* is why you're so, so," Alégra struggled to find the right word.

"So free from sadness and despair?" Nikki shot back, clearly insulted at Ali's judgment.

Apparently she had yet to read the chapter on dealing with skepticism.

"How is he, like, in bed, by the way?" I asked, desperately hoping to change the subject.

"Neither here nor there," even Nikki missed the brilliant irony of having a love affair with a nihilist.

This only made me laugh harder. What followed was an intervention-style lecture from Alégra on the importance of daily affirmations to maintain optimism, even in times of crisis.

"But I'm not in a crisis!" Nikki protested. "Where did you get this idea that I'm in crisis? Jeez, Pollyanna. Just because I don't bounce around giggling all the time—like *some* people—doesn't mean I'm depressed!"

Nikki's words fell on deaf ears... As Alégra talked passionately about the power of positivity, Nikki made a *help me!* face in my direction.

I sat silently with a big latte and an even bigger smile. Alégra stressed the importance of having a "Happy Place" to go to; hers was a lovely little town with friendly neighbors and free pedicures.

"When faced with a challenge," Alégra explained with perfect posture, "I will go to my Happy Place, it's a little picturesque town up the in the mountains—maybe Vermont—with rosy-cheeked townspeople and Sherpas. The weather is always clement and it's *always* pleasant. I love to drift off to my Happy Place when I find myself facing times of stress…"

Nikki interrupted in a deadpan tone. "Tell me, Ali, how many Ambien does it take to become a resident of Happy Town?"

"Not Happy Town, Happy **Place**!" Alégra surrendered as she couldn't help but giggle, too. "Oh, I so badly wish you were coming backpacking with me and Charly this summer!"

Nikki explained again that she was starting her own business and wouldn't be able to join us on our summer tour of Europe. As it turned out, Nikki was quite the entrepreneur and, with the help of Daddy Templeton, had set up her own importing/exporting company. In just one year—and still in school—she had become one of the biggest suppliers of sleepwear and undergarments to Victoria's Secret. She called her company *Face-to-Face Lingerie*.

"That is positively tacky," Alégra said, completely disgusted. "What other way *is* there to make love?"

"Oh, Ali, what are we going to do with you?" we all laughed and Nikki promised to join us on our next adventure.

Fully Booked / Genn Pardoe

20. Turn-down Service

I spent the weeks that followed the Hoteliers' Ball working on in-town projects and getting to know my new city (and being content that our first fight, nicknamed *"Burritogate"*, had blown over). Kai and I were a happy little expat couple and everything was perfect. Work-wise, I focused on city-hotels and booked three press tours in a row.

They were easy assignments that required only a walk-through of the hotel or a short photo shoot with a photographer. They'd stay overnight to get the full Edifice Luxe experience and I'd go home to Kai. I'd always go back the next day in time for lunch before they checked out to make sure everything went well.

Overall the media seemed really pleased with their experience. This made me feel confident as the time neared to the big media trips I'd eventually have to host at the Edifice Luxe Orient Royale. I was really beginning to fall in love with the amazing paradox of Bangkok: the elegance and grandeur of the city's hotels contrasted sharply with the grit of the street action, it was sublime. I sometimes felt as though the volume on everything in Bangkok had been turned up—the smell, the noise, the color—it's all vivid and vibrant. It felt more *real* somehow, than back home.

Back home everything is clean and anodyne: fish look like fish sticks, garbage goes in bins, and there is a quiet but respected *order* to things.

But in Bangkok, chickens hang in storefront windows with their faces intact and garbage is everywhere, even floating by in the Chao Praya River; there is no order. Life ebbs and flows in between friction and harmony as easily as the days change.

"Babe, can I talk to you for a second?" Kai stared into his coffee one morning like it had the cure to his melancholy (or a million dollar gift certificate to Kiehl's) in the bottom.

I could tell he was becoming increasingly frustrated at the job hunt—I guessed that the shininess and excitement of being able to do whatever he wanted was wearing off—Kai wanted to join the working world again but was having trouble finding a way in.

"I'm starting to feel shitty about not working," he said. "I wanted to take time off, and that's great, I'm happy I did."

"Me too, babe."

He continued, "You know I've never had a chunk of time off since I graduated, never really travelled, and I've really appreciated this time. But I need to go back to work... it's slowly driving me crazy being unemployed."

"Oh, babe, is there anything I can do?" I asked with genuine concern.

"Can we get out of Bangkok for like, a couple weeks, or whatever?" Kai said with a sad look on his face.

"Of course we can!" I was so happy to be able to offer a solution.

Before the big media trips started, I knew that I had some preliminary site inspections to do—sort of like test runs—at out-of-town resorts. I had to visit the hotels I'd be taking big groups of journalists to so that I'd be familiar and comfortable with the resort grounds, the staff, and the amenities. Sandy, my boss, didn't want me showing up at an Edifice Luxe five-star resort with 20 travel writers and not knowing where the front desk was. So, in an effort to get the preliminary site inspections off my To Do List *and* help Kai shake off his melancholy, I immediately booked all of my out-of-town hotel visits and put Kermit in boarding at the super swanky Expat Terrier Hotel.

When I dropped Kermit off he licked my cheek, jumped out of my arms, and trotted away happily to greet a kiddie pool filled with fellow terriers. They snorted in salutation and Kermit plopped his pudgy figure in the pool beside them. They looked like a bunch of collegial retirees in a plunge pool in Boca Raton and I felt confident leaving him among friends.

And off we went.

During late October and early November, Kai and I visited resorts in Malaysia, Laos, Cambodia, and even made our way over to Sri Lanka. Some of the resorts were set upon expansive plots of land—one of them was on a tea plantation—while others were century-old residences transformed into chic boutique hotels.

Each resort was more impressive than the last and I was surprised at how much I was falling for the local culture: there's nothing like the dusty crunch your sandals make as you wade through street markets.

The exoticism of it all is overwhelming and to know that as an outsider, I was only getting a pinhole view of the whole picture, was positively addictive. After a day of wandering through the local attractions, we'd head back to lap up the luxury of Edifice Luxe. The food, the views, the duvets (*the duvets!*).

After traipsing around the streets of Vientienne with Kai one day, I settled into a rosewater tub back in the room and thought about how lucky I was to have this job. When I started a couple months back, I was in a constant state of awe. Slowly but surely I was transitioning into a constant state of gratitude.

Even Kai seemed to cheer up and be happy for a moment. We found ourselves in a blissful little bubble of contentedness. This blissful little bubble, however, was popped the moment Kai *insisted* we go to the Maldives.

The Maldives?
The Maldives!
Ah, the Maldives.

Possibly the tiniest *&%#!! island on the planet and also the island where Tyler Kee lived and worked.

Of all places!

Hmmm, how to get out of this one...

There was no way I could risk Kai meeting Tyler Kee. If Kai was half as jealous as I, er, could be, then meeting an ex-lover would not go over well.

I mean, it's not like I was *with* Kai when Tyler and I hooked up — heck, I didn't even know Kai back then. But let's be honest, how mega-awkward would that encounter be?

Oh, hey, Kai, I'd love you to meet the child I molested right before I met you. How much time before I met you?

Oh, let's just say his hand prints on my boobs had barely faded when you and I got together.

As you can see, he's inexcusably good looking and yes, there actually is a shockingly large difference between your stamina, six pack, sex drive... and his. What a difference a decade makes...

Um, yeah... Anyway. Not thinking about that...

Miraculously, I managed to talk Kai out of going to the Maldives and he reluctantly settled for a stopover in Singapore on our way back to Bangkok. It proved to be an amazing trip. Well, at least for me it was. Kai was still pouting about the Maldives and all the work I'd put in to making sure he had a great time seemed useless. He was increasingly miserable and all he talked about was his inability to find a job...

"I thought you'd been to Singapore before, at that conference? Less than a year ago?" Kai sulked as we backtracked down Orchard Road for the third time in search of our hotel. "Why don't you know where anything is?"

I had to act fast; the truth was that Tyler and I never left the hotel room, "Singapore is like, a *huge* country, Kai," I huffed. His sulkiness was starting to irritate me.

"It's very easy to get disoriented," I continued. "And besides, I was in conferences all day."

Kai never did pick up on my creative truth, but he spent the rest of the trip aloof and distant.

All this over the Maldives?

Talk about a first world problem!

While I toured the hotel with the housekeeping staff to learn about the signature Edifice Luxe Turn-Down service, Kai was at the hotel bar. While I sampled 14 different types of curry from the hotel's renowned Indian chef, Kai was off exploring a nearby market. While I had projectile diarrhea the next day thanks to curry overload, Kai went golfing.

So maybe it wasn't all bad.

¤ * § * ¤

"Are you happy here?" I asked Kai when we finally got home.

"Um, sure babe," he answered absent-mindedly. "I just want to focus on the job hunt, okay?"

"Fine," I shot back, feeling rejected. "How about I schedule a couple out-of-town media trips so I'll be out of your hair?"

He'll never go for that. That's ridiculous.

He wants me around.

Obviously.

"That'd be great."

I'm sorry, what?

Oblivious to the fact that he'd just hurt my feelings, Kai continued without missing a beat, "Plus, it's FIFA season, there's probably no reception wherever you're going. Please, I just need space. It's not you. Honestly. I just want to chill out and watch FIFA."

As in, soccer?

First Burritogate.

Next the Maldives.

Now it's FIFA?

Really?

We went to bed in silence and I couldn't decide if I was more disappointed in Kai's inability to articulate *why* exactly he needed space, the fact that he needed space at all, or the fact that he hadn't grasped that my offer to leave him alone was rhetorical. The next week Kermit and I left for Railay.

21. The Nut, Part II

...three hours later we had lost Alégra and I was on the back of a motorbike headed to an Asian-themed bar called The Happy Snapper. I will spare you the details, mostly because I don't remember them, but suffice it to say, do you have any idea how hard it is to get ejected from an establishment that *already* has pillows on the floor? *I do.*

"Hey Charly, Charly Beans, Beaners! Give me yer gum," The Nut said as we came up for air in between make-out sessions and smiled at me.

"I already did, silly," I returned the smile and ran my hands through his hair.

He was big and strong and I wondered if he played rugby or maybe just threw truck tires around for fun.

"Oh, yeah," he tongued his own mouth and fished out a stick of gum, and stuck it my mouth. "Thanks, Beans!"

"You're disgusting!"

"You love it!"

Next thing I remember, I was being manhandled by a very understanding but curt bouncer, "You horny idiots can't be doing this shit in here. I know one of you has a bed, somewhere, I hope..."

The next morning I awoke in a state of dehydration so intense that I was pretty sure my liver was writing me a *Dear John* letter in the other room. I glanced around and foggily tried to put together the last few scenes of the night. The Nut was beside me but at least we were in *my* bed. Okay, I thought, we're off to a good start. I much prefer, no, I *insist* on being in my bed. I have no time for the Walk of Shame (or the Prance of Pride, as Nikki likes to call it). I'd much rather bid a polite adieu to my guest and crawl to the nearest toilet / shower / takeout menu than stroll through the streets draped in last night's disgrace. I surveyed the naked boy beside me.

Hmmm, pretty cute, actually.

I gave myself a self high-five but clapped louder than I meant to, and slowly, The Nut started to wake. He rolled over and, even in the haziness of the morning, he looked incredibly handsome. I only hoped my mascara wasn't smeared across my face.

Never a good look.

He opened his eyes and smiled at me. Perhaps something meaningful would evolve from this, I wondered. I hoped.

"Well," he said as he pulled on a grey tee-shirt and faux-yawned. "I got what I wanted… see you later or whatever."

Gasp!

I was about to sick Kermit on The Nut's nuts when he reached around and grabbed one of my over-stuffed pillows and whacked me in the head, "Beaners! Are you crazy? *As if* I'd let you go. C'mon, let's get breakfast, cutie." And we did.

22. Dear Sanity, I miss you so much

Scott says:
    Hey, girl, how's it going?

Charly says:
    Hey fruitcake, all is good. I'm on Railay Beach right now, not far from Krabi. I'm on a media trip at an upscale spa slash animal sanctuary slash eco-lodge properties. They're releasing a family of turtles tomorrow as a sign of their commitment to preserving local wildlife.

Scott says:
    Oh that's great.

Charly says:
    Yup, a bunch of local fisherman rounded them up last week from the other side of Railay, nobody is meant to know this, obviously.

Scott says:
    Classic Edifice Luxe bs. LOL... Is Kai there too?

Charly says:
    Nope, he stayed back in Bangers to watch FIFA. Apparently the satellite won't pick it up here.

Scott says:
    Right on. Got his priorities in order I see, ☺

Charly says:
    Whatever... anyway, how are you? How's Boston? What's new? I miss my daily dose of gossip!

Scott says:
> Well... Eden, as I'm sure you'll be hearing soon, is considering two offers right now. One of them is in Jeeranam, that's super close to you. The other is in Croatia, I think... not sure which one she'll go for.

Charly says:
> Oh, wow, I had no idea. That's amazing! Well I hope she chooses Jeeranam! What about you?

Scott says:
> Well... I'm thinking, just thinking, about an offer from Singapore.

Charly says:
> OMG do it. We would all be in the same time zone!

As we chatted, I felt a growing sense of longing for Scott, for home, for anything familiar. I wasn't really homesick but Kai had been my only outlet, aside from work, over the last couple of months. And, as Kai's frustration grew with not being able to find a job, he became increasingly distant.

To make matters worse, I'd already used up all of my in-town projects. The only thing I had to look forward to over the coming months was more time away from Kai. At least I had Kermit with me on this trip.

I sank into a cushy overstuffed love seat and uncorked a bottle of Pinot from the mini-bar. It was only noon but my six journalists weren't arriving until late the following day, so I figured I had time to relax. An hour later and halfway through my Pinot, I put on my Miss Piggy pajamas and called upon my fuzzy travel companion, who dutifully hopped, with a little help, onto my lap. I gently stroked Kermit's head and wondered why it hurt so much when I was away from Kai.

I then wondered if he actually *wanted* to be away from me. With growing insecurity (and growing gulps of wine), I wondered if it was me who *made him* want to be away from um, me.

Ugh.

Head hurts.

The worst part about worrying alone is that unwarranted worries can blister into unfounded fears in a matter of moments. Once ignited and doused with Pinot, those fears spread like wildfire, asphyxiating all self-assurance and blackening out all confidence. And, in no time (particularly when well-lubricated, as I was increasingly becoming), unfounded fears can blossom into devastatingly undeniable truths. As I drank an entire bottle of wine, I began to question myself deeply and interrogatively, even turning my cell phone ringer to silent so that I could think. I just needed to think.

Think.

Think.

Think.

I just needed to get to the bottom of this unnamable issue between Kai and me. What had been the catalyst? Was it really just about his inability to find a job? Or, was there something more?

There's got to be something more.

Oh, crap, it's me. It has to be me. I've done something (or haven't done something) and Kai is mad at me. But what was it? What did I do? Ugh, this is all my fault. I just know it. Damn, I've never felt like this before. *This sucks.*

If it weren't for me unintentionally passing out, I felt as though I was quite close to discovering what it was about me that drove Kai away. Sometime after dinner I awoke up from my impromptu nap to discover that my helpless, self-loathing and frustrated demeanor had been replaced by an insane level of anger.

We're talking the kind of anger that scares kids...

Apparently, all it took was an empty stomach and a bottle of wine for my fears to morph into pure, unfiltered crazy. Imagine that. The only thought I could hold on to was: damn Kai for making me feel this way! The other thought, of course, was: more wine please. Kermit judged me—I'm sure of it—as I rummaged around the mini-bar, like a raccoon in a dump, for more wine. I needed something to suspend my sadness and prolong my anger...

Equipped with the knowledge that only *one* bottle of red wine and *one* bottle of white wine were placed in each Edifice Luxe standard room (and I'd already gone through my preferred grape), I begrudgingly took hold of the *other* Pinot and uncorked it. Now, there are certain things that I promised myself I would *never* do unless I was in a state of extreme torture. They are as follows:

1. Admit that I find Taco Bell to be the greatest culinary invention of all time
2. Talk to my dad about favorite positions
3. Use a hobo's dental floss
4. Drink the *Other* Pinot
5. Drink my own urine (or any urine, I mean, at that point, does it really matter?)

I dug into the snack-bar in an effort to subdue the gut rot that clenched my insides the way a child clings to his favorite teddy: relentlessly and with conviction. I found wasabi-coated peas and a blue mango.

A blue mango!?C'mon!

Haven't you people heard of honey-roasted peanuts and / or salt & vinegar chips?

Dear Edifice Luxe, I'm really starting to grow tired of all this quirky, hipster-chic crap…

Who's in charge of the mini-bar menu?

Zooey Deschanel?

I resentfully cracked open the can of peas, took one bite of the blue mango, and emptied the bottle of wine into my mouth.

Classy.

Kermit watched this pathetic process take place from his comfy little spot on the bed; he leaned on one paw more than the other with his head cocked ever so slightly to the right. It reminded me of the stance Kai took when he was confused.

Oh, sad sigh…

I missed Kai.

Kermit blinked silently while I paced the room and darted out onto the balcony for an occasional cigarette. (Recently I had expanded my smoking repertoire from Anti-Social Smoker to Social, P.M.S.ing, and Drunk Smoker.) I continued to munch on the stupid *hipster peanuts* and soft mango while I drank the rest of the mini-bar for several hours in sad silence.

I had done so much thinking all day that I got to a point where I was just staring out the window, watching the sun set as darkness enveloped the beach. I just couldn't figure out how we'd gone from amazing to awful so quickly, and so suddenly. When 11pm came and went it was marked by my realization that I was out of wine rather than the hour's usual demarcation: a punctual call from Kai to say goodnight. He *always* called at 11pm on the dot when he was away from me but since I didn't notice—due to said state of pain and inebriation—I decided to venture outside. Kermit needed a break from peeing on the balcony, anyway.

Thailand was in its monsoon season and with Kermit in one hand and a ridiculously large and ridiculously blue paisley-colored hotel umbrella in the other, I headed toward the beach. I tried my best to keep Kermit dry and away from the wet sand and I think he was thankful for that. I had noticed that wet sand was among his greatest fears. (I can only assume that a worldwide kibble shortage would be number one on the list.)

I stopped when I reached the beachfront and looked out over the darkness that blanketed the small inlet on which I was staying (which now felt more like *marooned*).

Only the fading lights of the long-tail boats taking the last of the day's tourists back to the mainland could be seen. There were no waves that night and I guessed that the few restaurants on the beach would already be closed. I started wandering in no particular direction. Eventually I found myself on the backside of Railay. It was still raining heavily and the overgrown trees provided minimal shelter.

At one point I tripped on an exposed tree root and had to put Kermit down quickly so as to avoid falling on him. He stood in the pouring rain, his feet sinking in the sand, blinking at me as rain drops ran down his cheeks. He looked at me like I was the worst dog-mother in the whole world, "That'll half-ta-wait," I slurred as I bent down to pick him up."

I kissed Kermit's damp forehead and promised to get him a yellow fisherman's hat once back on the mainland.

"I'm currently dealing with being the worst girlfriend in the world and I can only carry around so much guilt at any given time. I'm Irish, Kermit, not *Catholic*... there's a limit to the things I can legitimately feel guilty about at any one time."

Realizing that I was embarking on a one-sided drunken dialogue with my dog, I refocused my blurry sights on the soggy path that stretched out before me. Barely lit huts served as makeshift bars, each with only two or three patrons. I had no idea where to go so I carried on to the end of the beach and settled for a bar that looked the driest with the least amount of annoying backpackers and/or sex tourists.

An old Thai man, presumably the bartender, waved me in and confirmed that his bar was still serving.

"Dog, dog," the bartender pointed animatedly at Kermit, who had chosen a spot under a gently swaying hammock. He was visibly irate with each swing of the hammock that did not favor his endeavors to stay dry.

I responded without thinking, "Argh, c'mon, it's a *beach bar*. No part of your bar is not, like, on a beach. How can you not let the dogs on your premisesss? Kermit and I are together, we're a team, *sir*, like gay men and theme parties, like hangovers and bacon, like—"

Eeks. Did I sound as thought as I drunk I did?

"No, no... dog *can* come here," the old man said as he pointed to the chair next to me.

Oops.

Talk less.
Smile more.

I hoisted Kermit on top of a bar stool and offered a genuine *thank you* in Thai to the man. (I had yet to take up Thai lessons, but my vocabulary seemed to expanding on its own.) I rubbed Kermit's belly for warmth and wondered if the same rules of hypothermia apply for dog-to-human-body-warmth. I was sure it couldn't hurt. The old man smiled at Kermit and took a FIFA tee-shirt from the previous year off the wall. He handed it to me to wrap around my wet pup.

"No good if sick," he said. "No good. Must keep dog happy. Good boy."

"Thank you," I said. "Thank you so much, I really—"

Um, what in the name of faded denim?

I had been under the impression that there was "No FIFA in Railay".

Kai had told me there was no reception for FIFA in Railay. *Kai* had stayed in Bangkok to watch the FIFA game. *Kai* had personally *promised* me that that's why he stayed. To watch the %*$#@) game! Seeing the animated expression on my face, the man asked excitedly, "Oh! You like FIFA?"

"Ka," I lied, as my throat started to burn painfully.

Oh no. Here come the venomous fireballs of rage.

The bartender walked over to a carefully protected large screen T.V. and, after a moment, the satellite link connected and a soccer game began to play.

Adding insult to injury, it was in real time.

Kai's testicles are going to make great bookends.
Why would he do this?
Why would he lie?
What possible reason would he have to lie to me?
Okay, Charly.
Breathe.
Focus....

You are definitely in a rational and objective mental place right now, so just let the answer come naturally.

Open your mind.

Ommmm.

Just let it happen.

Here it comes… It's coming…

Allow the answer to —

Kai stayed behind in Bangkok and lied about the FIFA game because he is cheating on me.

Ta Da!

"Really?!" I half questioned, half stated.

"Yes! Yes! Leally. Leally good!!" said the bartender.

It was then that I remembered I hadn't heard from Kai that night. He hadn't even called at 11pm like he always did.

Of course he hadn't.

Why would he call?

He was out with someone else.

But who?

Had he met someone at the Hoteliers' Ball? Is *that* why he took so long getting the drinks? The girls from the market near our loft? What about a well-known adversary from the past, like that good-for-nothing philanthropic yoga bitch, Zoë van der Baque?

No, no, it *couldn't* be her. She was in some unpronounceable country curing malaria or some other disease that had *blatantly* already been cured… *Then who?* I ordered a bucket of whiskey, stroked Kermit's head, and watched the FIFA game in disbelief.

Pause for a Painful & Embarrassing Memory from Charly Briar's Dating Past: The Professor

One summer in college I took a course abroad for a month. It was in England and the course was on the influence that 19th century travel literature had had on the construction of the modern European concept of self.

Oh, yeah, that's right.

I used to be a major geek.

Come to think of it, enrolling in that summer course was probably what planted the seed in my mind about the romantic and exotic life abroad. About expat-life. About amazing journeys of self-discovery. I guess it was my first time really diving into a culture other than my own. It was only England, so it was safe, but it was far enough away from home that I could be who I wanted to be. And that summer, I was the gal pal of a much older British man.

Well not that much.

Just a little bit much.

Like, nine years much.

That's not much.

¤ * § * ¤

"Darling, what *is* running through that little mind of yours?" my professor brought me out my own thoughts and back into our slowly moving airplane as it docked in Heathrow.

"Oh, nothing," I said casually.

My professor and I were coming back from a weekend on the *continent* exploring wine and food (food, by the way, that I could *never* afford on my student budget). I had welcomed the friendly invitation from my professor at that time because I genuinely believed his intentions were strictly platonic. (He was good, but that summer I desired only the *greats*: Kipling, Theroux, Maugham... Like I said, I used to be a geek.)

The one thing my professor definitely had going for him, though, was that he looked *exactly* like one of the characters in the books we discussed, as though he'd just walked off the set of *The English Patient*. He was a strong, well-travelled, and sturdy man who almost always wore khakis, a crisp white shirt, and beautiful oxblood loafers. He was in his (very) late twenties but already a respected—and highly sought after—professor. It was mid-day when we landed and I was happy to be getting back to London.

I had lots of work to do and I couldn't wait to ditch it all in favor of spending the afternoon at the Tate Modern...

Oh, I love London!

"Is it always so rainy in London?" I frowned as I leaned over to look out the window; we were still in the plane taxiing along the runway.

"It is what it is, my dear," he said poetically and gathered his coat around his shoulders dramatically.

I frowned even more—I hate rain.

"Well, never mind," my professor continued. "At least you are here with your ravishing smile and New World pluck to brighten it up!" (I never really understood much of what he said but I didn't care.) "Come along now," he urged. "The Tate will still be there tomorrow. Let's dispose of our luggage and *immediately* head out for dinner. I'm famished."

We stopped by my professor's house on the way to dinner. Now, "stopping by" a professor's house (let alone going out for dinner with one) is something I'd never dream of doing back home. But in Europe, the rules about that sort of thing were more casual.

In Europe, it wasn't at all bizarre for a professor to socialize with his or her students. And since our relationship had been entirely platonic thus far—we'd had separate rooms on our trip of course and never even so much as flirted with each other—I had no reason to believe anything was going on in that dusty British mind of his... My professor's house was *stunning*.

It was an old Victorian-style skinny townhouse that reached three stories tall. It was completely open concept except for the kitchen which was about as big as the shoebox my new Liam & Olivia boots came in. Classic English, I thought. But then I rounded the corner to see all of the ethnographic trinkets and souvenirs my professor had picked up during his years of anthropological study in over thirty countries.

Oh, god... my parents would love it if I ended up with this dork.

"So, *this* is where you live?" I asked as I surveyed his six-volume book collection on indigenous mating habits of grain farmers in the sub-Saharan between 1775 and 1783.

"Tis," he said as he heaved his heavy suitcase out of the way. "Well then, shall we?"

I tucked my chin down into the high collar of my camel trench as we walked briskly through the grayness of early evening. It was summer but chilly with intermittent bursts of rain.

I totally get why there are so many depressed writers from England. And also why the British are so, um, uptight...

(I'd be tense too if I was always damp.)

I surveyed the streets of my professor's neighborhood and took in the scent of beer and cigarettes. It smelled of camaraderie and good, uncomplicated times. On the sidewalk, stylishly dressed twenty-somethings hustled past each other in click-clacking stilettos and designer dress shoes, almost everyone had their hands in their pockets for warmth.

My professor opened the doors to a chic bistro and ushered me in. Inside, the modest décor was overpowered by animated chatter and tables hosting three times their normal capacity.

Voices erupted in endless variations of British accents while hearty gulps of wine and beer were devoured. We followed our waiter to the back of the restaurant and were seated at a table for dwarves.

"It's, um, quite lively," he practically yelled at me across the table with a frown.

"Oh, what? No, it's fine!" I yelled back.

I had about three heart attacks and one stroke as I perused the menu. The cost of the course and travel to England had practically asphyxiated my financial freedom that summer and I foresaw a lot of Cup-O-Noodles in my future.

As if reading my mind, my professor winked at me and said, "By the way, this dinner is on me. Count is as part of the trip, which, I promised, was on me. So, not to worry."

"Oh, thank you, that's very sweet of you," I said genuinely.

"No, no, thank *you*, Charly," he smiled. "I appreciate you coming with me to the continent for a little weekend away. Life as an academic is so solitary and lonely; the last thing I want to do is travel by myself. I'm glad you came. You're a lovely friend."

We ordered a Meatlovers' Pizza and a half-carafe of heavy Cab Sav to share. Not my personal choice but whatever...

"Oh, bugger, I forget," my professor said as he sucked spicy pizza sauce off his thumb, "You're not a vegetarian are you?"

"Me? No way," I said as I drank a gulp of wine.

"Me neither," he said. "I've tried to give meat up but I invariably fail. It seems that I always want things more when I've given them up." He winked conspiratorially at me and continued, "There's an Oscar Wilde quote: *I can resist anything, except temptation.* I love it, it's *so* me!"

Coming from an American man, *it's so me* would have been, straight up, the gayest thing a guy could ever say. Coming from my gorgeous, travelled, British professor? Hot. He looked at me for a long time and I couldn't help but blush. Three half-carafes later we had practically closed the restaurant.

"Oh, dear," my professor said as he wiped a tear from his eye as he laughed wholeheartedly at something hilarious I had just said but that neither of us could remember. "I've not closed down a place in ages. Alright, alright, shall we get going?"

"Yes, please! I'm jet bagged and half in the lag, wait, no, that came out backwards," I giggled as we gathered our coats and headed out into the night. We were both chilled to the bone by the time we reached his door.

"Allow me," my professor fingered the keys sloppily, his hands nearly paralyzed by the frigidity of the night air. Finally we pushed through the door and into an equally sub-zero climate.

"Oh, g-g-god," I stuttered as I took off my coat and rubbed my bare arms feverishly in an effort to warm up. "I guess I'm going to have to get used to the lack of heat in this country."

No wonder these people are so grey looking.

I feel like I have scurvy just from the walk home.

"Now, Charly," he said sternly, "Go upstairs right now and put on some sensible clothes. There's no way I'm sending you out on a night like this, you'll get washed away! I'll make a fire and pour us a nightcap. Run along now."

(Because we'd come straight from the airport, I had a change of clothes with me.)

Minutes later I was warm, dry, and overlooking a crackling fire, an opened bottle of Pinot, and a behemoth piece of brie that glistened as the fire warmed the room.

OMG is that cheese for me?

Whoa, talk about a man after my heart.

My professor was sitting with one leg crossed over the other and an open arm resting across the top of his couch. He's remained in the clothes he'd worn to dinner but unfastened the top two buttons of his shirt to revel a tuff of chest hair that he appeared to be very proud of. He'd also managed to grow a five o'clock shadow in the short time I'd been upstairs changing.

Manly.

Impressive.

I scuttled over and tucked myself into the nook right under his arm, but not before collecting my wine and a massive gob of cheese.

"Don't worry, darling," he cooed deeply as he brushed my hair with his hand and I took a generous sip of wine. "All warm now."

Suddenly, the wine hit me.

Really hard.

Like, *really* hard.

The room started spinning and out of the corner of my eye I caught sight of three fireplaces.

"Oh," I said wearily as I replaced my half-drunk wine glass. "I think I've had too much. Maybe I should lie down. I should go home. I need to sleep this off."

"No," he shushed gently. "Don't go to sleep, if you go to bed too tipsy, you're sure to be rapaciously hung over in the morning. Would you like to stay up and watch a movie in my room?"

That made sense to me.

Of course it made sense to me...

...because I'm an idiot!

I leaned on my professor's shoulder as we trudged down a winding staircase to his room. It was even colder down on the ground floor and completely dark. I palmed my way along the wall until I came to a stubborn little light switch, the kind that in America are only found in Heritage Homes.

The bedroom was crisp and minimalist in design, totally unlike the rest of the house. It felt very British, colonial even. In the middle of the room was a King Size bed that was almost entirely hidden under an enormous white duvet.

I climbed on top of the huge mound of softness as my professor turned off the big light and plugged in a string of miniscule white ones.

"Oh, soooo nice and commmfy," I said.

Stop talking.

Don't be a dumbass...

Too late...
You're slurring.

"Feel better?" he smiled and put a DVD in the player—yes, that's how old he was. "I knew you'd stop spinning once you got yourself all cozy and warm."

"Where are your pajamas?" I slurred.

Um, I thought I had just decided to stop talking??

My professor raised a curious eyebrow, "Oh, well, *obviously* I hadn't thought that far ahead. Would you like me to put them on?"

I nodded.

No! Why?!
He might get the wrong idea!
Besides, nothing's going to happen.
He's so much older.
I mean, it's not illegal or anything like that.
It's just weird!

I couldn't help but notice my professor stumbling a bit. He chuckled at his own inebriation; he pulled at his belt unsuccessfully but then gave up and opted instead for taking off his white dress shirt. I shoved the duvet aside and sat up on my knees, "Come here you drunken old man."

"Old!" He burst out laughing, "I'm not even thirty yet! Next month..."

Yes, there was actually a time when I considered that to be old...

Anyway we both keeled over laughing at each other's ridiculousness and *literally* out of nowhere we started kissing. I mean, I did not see this coming.

No one could have.

We fell back onto the soft bed, me in my pajamas and him in his half undone dress shirt and pants. He wrapped his arms around me the way Fabio does in those cheesy romance novels and his tongue went deep into my mouth (and all over my neck and even part of my face) but in some way, it was really adorable.

Actually, it was probably ugly as hell.

After an unknown amount of time, my pajama bottoms and his shirt had found their way onto the floor and I needed to come up for air. We were like high school kids (really skanky high school kids with a lot of chest hair and mostly developed breasts, respectively). We were having the kind of makeout session that goes on forever and makes you forget that there's a world that exists beyond that moment.

"Whoa! I think I need some water," I gasped when I was finally able catch my breath.

My professor just smiled drunkenly at me in reply and went into the bathroom, returning a moment later with a full glass. I drank deeply and wiped my forehead.

"Sweating out the vino, are we?" he teased.

"Oh, shut up," I laughed as I pulled him towards me.

"Oh, darling, you are *exquisite*," he whispered. No one had *ever* said that to me before and it was empowering beyond articulation. I let all my reservations fly out the window.

After all, where better to have a mildly inappropriate fling than European summer school? I undid my professor's belt and slid off his pants awkwardly. He kicked them to the floor to reveal a set of snug, white briefs.

Um, excuse me?

Okay.

What?

It took all my strength to keep from bursting out into laughter.

I mean, there's old school and then there's *old school*.

I had to keep things moving before he noticed my shock. I'd deal with the man-panties, or *manties*, later. I pulled him towards me, and again, we kissed for an eternity.

Now for the goods.

I ran my fingers along the waistband of his manties and started to slide them… ahem… slide them… um, I ran my fingers along the waistband of his manties and started to slide them…

What the hell?

They wouldn't budge. His underwear was super-glued to his torso like a Ken doll and they refused to move and inch. My professor rolled off of me and made his way to his feet. He stood at the side of the bed, "Oh, I guess I'm a little sweaty too," he laughed awkwardly, almost embarrassed. "Is *this* what you're looking for?" He pointed to his tightly packed man bits.

"Yes!" I applauded drunkenly.

Stupid!

Stupid!

"Alright, darling," he removed his underwear in one swift movement but bent down as he did, so I *still* had yet to see anything.

And then I did.

Um, what in the name of reverse French manicures!?

"Oh," he chuckled casually. "It's nice *hmm*? I don't shave, or trim, never have."

Between my professor's legs was the biggest and most ferocious black clown's wig I'd ever seen in my life. I could not catch one glimpse, not *one tiny glimpse*, of a penis.

It was as though he had super-glued a black Santa's beard to his crotch. It was like one of those prize-winning ebony poodles was taking a nap on his dick. It was like an ebony chia pet, a worn out *brillo* pad, the collective beard of ten thousand gypsies...

I was truly speechless.

I mean,

I,

Um,

Uh,

I got nothing...

Then a profound realization hit me like a ton of bricks: I was face-to-face with pubic hair that was *literally* older than me. I quickly did the math and realized that my professor's pubic hair was in high school when I was just past being a toddler.

!&*@()#@!!

I suddenly gagged.

Blegh!

"It's not a problem, *is it*?" my professor asked in a tone that suggested if it *was* a problem, it was *my* problem.

"What? Pube? Huh? No! I *love* it!" I stuttered, unable to face the gorilla-sized bush that stared at me with its wiry, twisty, hairs...

Why did you say you love it?!

Good one!

Now Black Beard will never go away!

"Well then, let's get to it, shall we?" he sounded so enthusiastic it was almost sweet.

Sweet until I looked down again and realized that his pubes could probably be braided, maybe even dreaded, and most definitely worn in a *chignon*.

I wondered if any previous girls had lost their lives due to suffocation down there, it seemed entirely possible. Hell, maybe there even was a girl *living* in there, there was no way to tell. Suffice it to say I faked extreme-drunkenness and took a cab home *immediately*.

I spent the rest of the summer exploring England on my own and, upon my return, had a very difficult time explaining to my university professor *parents* why I'd flunked out of a class I so desperately wanted to get into. Overall it certainly proved to be an interesting trip, and one thing is for sure, I never acted so stupidly around men and booze again.

24. Hello, you must be my Dignity. I've been looking for you.

Unsure of how I stumbled back to my eco-hut, I woke up sometime around mid-morning to the stench of regurgitated blue mango, Kermit whining with crossed legs, and a persistent knock at the door.

Ignoring the mango issue, I opened the door, allowed Kermit to escape, and smiled sheepishly at the front desk representative who drew in a breath at the sight of me.

"Package for you, Khun Charly," he said in his best *I'm judging you as a person and as a dog owner* tone.

"Kapkunka," I mustered.

Inside was a dried blue rose.

Oh my god.

It took me a moment to register but I quickly realized it was from the bouquet that Kai sent me right after we met. I had no idea that he'd kept a rose, let alone brought it to Thailand. I was speechless. I couldn't believe it.

And, had I not lost all bodily fluids hours ago, I would have cried. There was also a letter.

Dear Charly,

I'm so sorry I've been distant lately. It's not your fault, not at all. I've been so deflated from not being able to find a job, I've been trying to hide it but I think I've been taking it out on you. I stayed back this weekend to chill out and get things in perspective.

It has been difficult with you being so busy with your job while I stay at home like an unemployed hausfrau with no prospects, no social life, and no friends of my own. In no way do I want to pin this on you, I'm happy for you, I truly am, I am just not used to being the helpless one, the dependent one.

But that's all ended now; I just received a phone call and I've been offered a full time job! It's such a great offer, I accepted immediately. I'm so happy but this whole thing has made me realize how difficult I've been making things for you.

I love you and am thankful for your support, you've been great and I hope we can put this difficult time behind us. I can't wait 'til you get home...

You're my girl,
Kai

I immediately reached for my phone to call Kai, and in doing so, set in motion a flicker of images from the previous night. Foggy memories began to flash in my consciousness like choppy snippets of an old 8mm reel.

Uh oh.

First, I remembered turning my phone to silent, probably the reason I thought Kai didn't call. Dammit. Second, I remembered the *other* Pinot. Yikes. Third, I remembered the FIFA game...

Double uh-oh.

This is bad...

Really bad...

I flipped open my phone and gasped: Seven.

Seven missed calls.

No voicemail.

OMG.

I frantically flipped up my laptop and gasped.

The sent page from my email account appeared in front of me, as did the drunken email I sent to Kai last night.

> To: "Kai Kostigan"
> From: me
> Subject: (none)
>
> Kai Kostigan - The Telephone. Have you two met? Well I had a very interessting night... I watched the FIFA game. Hmmm, pretty amaizing considering there's no statelite reception in Railay! Isn't taht the reason you stayed in Bangkok? To watch the gme? Are you even <u>looking</u> for a job?
>
> You nevr would've done this to Zoë! I know it... Why are you doing this to me? Is it because you're still in love with Zoë?
>
> The LEAST you could've done is to tell me you wanted didn't want to be with me. Why are you mad at me? And how am I suposed to know if you don't communicate??? This silent treatment is so immature.
>
> Next time don't scapegoat a FIFA game, that's so shitty of you. At least let me know *why* you're angry doing this to me, you droopy bag of douche.
>
> CB.

My stomach clenched worse than the time I tried to take on a Mexican buffet, and lost. Then my phone rang.

Shit. Shit. Shit.

I was nowhere *near* prepared to speak to Kai. My face was still on fire from the horrible email I had sent the night before. I felt awful, what could I say to him?

Damn. Damn. Damn.

Also, I do not like to cover too many topics at once and this conversation was going to be quite expansive in subject matter with various headings including:

1. Sorry I'm a drunken asshole.
2. Congratulations on the job!
3. Thank you so much for the package. It's really, really, sweet.
4. Yes, I *did* turn my cell to silent and then accuse you of not calling in a vicious email I don't recall sending.
5. Despite all evidence to the contrary, I'm not jealous of your ex, I *swear*.
6. Droopy douche bag? Hmm, no don't remember calling you that, must've been a typo or auto-correct, maybe I meant I, er, um, need to douche?
7. You're the best boyfriend!
8. When does your job start?

Crap. Crap. Crap.

Maybe the email gods had taken pity on me and lost my nasty message in cyber space. Maybe Kai hadn't checked his email yet. Maybe his account was hacked by identity thieves who had changed his password. Maybe Kai was calling to say he had been blinded in a freak accident and as such, had no access to email.

That would be great!

Maybe the phone would stop ringing – right – about – *now*.

No such luck.

The phone continued to ring and I finally stopped pacing. I would either have to move to Iceland, or answer it.

"Hello?" I said pathetically.

"Hi, Charly," a male voice drawled deeply in reply.

The voice did not belong to Kai.

Hallelujah.

But who was it?

Telemarketer?

"Who is this?" I croaked as I found my way back to bed and dove in under the covers—hoping to find a black hole.

He laughed softly, "Rad."

Who?

Wrong number for sure.

"Rad?" I repeated, clearly trying to place the name.

Unfazed at receiving a completely vacant reception, he pressed on, "It's me, Radden, the photographer with the *stabby* girlfriend. I met you at The Hoteliers' Ball."

"Oh, hi, Radden," I was so relieved it wasn't Kai that I didn't even bother to wonder why or how he had my number. "How are you?"

He got to the point fast, "I'm here, just got in."

Here where?

Just got what?

What in the name of summer scarves was he talking about?

I rubbed my head and sat up in bed, as I did, I caught a glimpse of myself in the mirror across the room — I was truly shocked that it didn't crack.

The impending blowout with Kai and Radden's curious phone call were all too much for me to process. I kept the phone to my ear but gazed vacantly at nothing in particular.

"Pretty girl, are you there?" Radden said softly. "You invited me, remember? Well, you pitched one of the publications I work for, and the editor sent me."

Argh, of course!

The media tour!

Radden teased, "either I've got the wrong Charly Briar or *somebody* dabbled in one of Railay's famous whiskey buckets last night."

"The latter," I moaned as I leaned back and pulled the covers over my head; I could hear Radden laughing at my expense.

How could I be so stupid as to get so unbelievably drunk when I had to host a media group today?

Just then a fresh round of bile swirled about in my stomach and promised to surface within minutes, maybe seconds. I hastily told Radden I'd meet him in an hour and rushed off the phone. He responded by laughing and promised to tease me later.

As evidence of the previous night evacuated my stomach and cascaded onto the pristine Moroccan tiled bathroom floor, I scolded myself harshly for writing that horrible email to Kai.

It was so clear what I had to do: I would have to cut my trip short and fix things with Kai. My top priority *must* be to head back to Bangkok and pay him a surprise congratulations slash apology visit. But first, I needed a plan.

A plan:

1. Meet the journalists, about six or so, and host a fabulous lunch in the hotel's main restaurant.
2. Try not to barf.
3. Lead a site inspection of the hotel grounds and invite the journalists to dinner.
4. Go back to my room for a mid-afternoon barf and nap.
5. Duck out after dinner and catch the last flight back to Bangkok.

Perfect.

Satisfied with my plan, I hopped in the shower and tried to wash both my guilt and the smell of whiskey off of me… Twenty minutes later, I emerged feeling better about the smell but still guilty as hell.

Okay. Breathe.

Kai and I would be just fine; all couples go through a rough patch. And besides, he'd already admitted it was his fault. I'm sure my email will be totally understandable and forgotten by the time I get home tonight.

Perfect.

Still drenched from the shower and severely lacking motor skills, I searched the room and found a towel just in time to hear a soft knock at the door.

Shit!

Who is it now?

Oops.

Kermit!

I had let Kermit out when I'd opened the door to the bellboy. I was sure it was someone returning my little guy. I tied my wet hair up in a messy bun above my head, wrapped the towel around myself tight and—possibly still a bit drunkenly—flung the door open, ready to apologize for whatever Kermit had eaten or wherever he had pooped.

"Hey, Chuckles," Radden was smiling with his eyes behind aviator sunglasses as his camera slung easily across his body. Faded jeans, grey v-neck, and flip flops: it's not a good look, it's a *great* one.

Damn.

Double damn.

And then there was me. I looked so, so, *so* utterly crappy (not to mention half naked). I could never pull off that awesomely emaciated and sexy hungover look that Nikki was so good at. I just looked soggy and half-drunk.

"What the hell are you doing here?" I half moaned and half smiled. "I'm meeting you guys in an hour!"

Radden returned the smile and made as though he was coming in to the room. To my surprise this caused me to flutter awkwardly—could have been his presence, could have been the monumental hangover—hard to say.

Radden stopped just close enough to lean on the door frame, "I found your little friend."

Kermit scuffled in from behind Radden. He snorted at me rudely and trotted towards the bed.

"Oh, thank you," I said relieved as I tried to tighten my towel as casually as possible.

"No worries," he said softly and then moved even closer towards me. "Hey, pretty girl, is that a piece of blue mango on your forehead?"

"What!?" I gasped, mortified.

Radden's smile softened. "I never knew there *was* such a thing as blue mango. It smells, um, funky."

Double gasp!

"Don't worry about the mango," I said trying to sound as casual as possible as I palmed my forehead.

How could I not know that blue mango wasn't a real thing!?

That's so gross!

OMG!

"Um, yeah, so," Radden smiled and looked at the ground. I thought I caught a blush but I couldn't be sure. "Sorry, I shouldn't have come by I just thought you'd want your little guy back. The bellboy told me he was yours, I, um, it doesn't matter. Let's catch up after you get dressed. You look like you had a rough night, *Jackie Daniels.*"

"Ha ha," I managed. "Don't mind my hideous appearance; I must look like a catastrophe."

Charly, stop blatantly fishing for a compliment!

Much to my mortification, Radden just smiled and turned away from me. He moved towards the veranda stairs.

Ugh…

awkward.

I thanked him again for bringing Kermit back to me and said I'd be at the lobby with the other journalists shortly…

I started to close the door—my feelings slightly bruised that Radden hadn't picked up on my request for a compliment—but at the last second he whipped around and snapped a picture of me. He then snickered loudly.

"I'm going to kill you!" I burst out laughing.

Radden smirked and took off his sunglasses to look at his camera's digital screen and the picture he'd just taken.

"Yikes! You're right. You *are* hideous. I think you broke my camera, Chuckles!"

"Ha, ha, *Shutterbug!*" I shot back as I felt my face start to burn with embarrassment. "Take your *Funsaver* elsewhere."

"Oh, shut up, you look like a million bucks and you know it," Radden smiled, turned on his heels, and strolled coolly down the path into the lush palms. I smiled at my new friend; it was sweet of him to lift my spirits especially considering the hellish time I'd had last night.

Amazingly, everything went according to plan. The writers and photographers were easy to get along with and they loved the resort. Some spent time reviewing the spa and the food, others took hundreds of pictures of the surrounding area, and, I was even able to arrange an interview with the General Manager for the editor-in-chief of the Bangkok Post.

Wow. Imagine how efficient I'd be if I wasn't hungover!

I excused myself early—citing another media trip back in Bangkok as the reason of my early departure—without arising any suspicion. Kermit and I boarded the last plane from Krabi airport later that evening and I was home before midnight. Of course I was nervous to see Kai after my immature email but I felt as though his new job and demonstrated desire to move forward would override all of that. Every couple fights. It's normal. It's fine. We'll get through this. As Kermit and I finally got out of the cab I was truly happy to be back in Bangkok and couldn't wait to wrap my arms around Kai.

Fully Booked / Genn Pardoe

25. Ethan Charge, Conclusion

Ethan was two years older than me and when he graduated he was recruited by a top-tier consulting firm. He moved into a gorgeous condo on the other side Boston but hardly spent any time there. Ethan traveled constantly for work—New York, London, Hong Kong—from Monday to Friday he was essentially out of touch. Sometimes it was weeks at a time. I didn't mind because I was so busy with school. And, I understood that he had a small window of opportunity to make a name for himself within the firm. He worked so hard and I was so proud of him. Often I would call his hotel room at 3am and he wouldn't be there because he was still at the office working on a case.

Such dedication.

Over the two years that we dated, I never really had any suspicions about Ethan's fidelity. He was beyond charming, my parents adored him, and aside from his complete and relative non-existence from Monday to Friday, he was always there for me. We planned to move in together as soon as I was finished school and sometimes he would even drop hints about an engagement ring as a graduation present.

Way to lock it down, me!

Everything was perfect. I mean, *okay, fine,* I will admit it... Ethan could sometimes be *somewhat* passionate about things, from time to time. We had our crazy fights but every couple does. It's totally normal and besides, Ethan was really, truly, intellectually gifted and it's difficult for people *that* smart to communicate their feelings in a non-violent way.

Right?

I always forgave him for his outbursts, binge drinking, and periods of unexplained absence and even helped him rearrange his art collection every time I visited because he had punched a new hole in the wall. I mean, some girls can't talk without gesticulating animatedly, Ethan couldn't express himself without using his hands against the wall.

(No really, I was actually that stupid back then.)

Rather than consider that Ethan *might* not be coloring with a full crayon box, I dutifully hung up his pictures, praising myself for being such a good art curator and girlfriend. But if anyone is to blame, it's Harry Winston, not Ethan Charge. Ethan dangled that rock in front of me like a genetically modified carrot in front of an emaciated work horse. There were even pictures of it that he'd toss in the garbage every time we fought as a symbol of my disqualification from the marriage race.

What an asshole, right?

But when we made up he would print out a new image of the ring and "accidentally" leave it around his condo for me to see.

And it wasn't just the ring. It was the dinners and the trips and the professions of endless, eternal love. It was the desire to have children and travel the world together and eventually, grow old and spend our golden years reflecting on a life of partnership, commitment, and love.

Everything was planned but nothing was real. In hindsight, I suspect it was my upcoming graduation—and plans to move in together—that put a real monkey wrench in his busy schedule of infidelity, because that's when things really started to go south...

⌑ * § * ⌑

One day Ethan was working on an in-town project and I decided to take Friday off classes and surprise him for lunch. Nikki and I drove to his office and hung out at a café nearby.

"Do you think he'll be psyched to see you?" asked Nikki.

Nikki literally couldn't care less but she was my only friend with a car and I needed a ride. I had no problem getting her to drive me when I mentioned skipping class.

"Oh, look, there he is!" I squealed and Nikki rolled her eyes.

Ethan was walking briskly on the opposite side of the street heading towards his office. His massive figure looked totally out of place in a tailored suit.

I dialed Ethan's cell and waited for his phone to ring. After a couple of seconds Nikki and I watched Ethan finger his jacket pockets for his cell.

"Oh, it's ringing!" I announced happily.

Even I surprised myself at how giddy I was after two years of dating. Ethan retrieved his cell phone, flipped it up to see who was calling, frowned, and promptly flipped it closed again. On my end, the connection died.

I was mortified.

I looked to Nikki, the girl who wasn't even shocked by the renaissance of summertime moccasins (yet again) and watched her eyes pop out of her head. I *had* to say something to dilute the undeniably rising tension.

"He's probably on his way to an important meeting."

Nikki stared at me as though she'd just walked in on a school teacher pleasuring herself during recess. There's really nothing that can be said, but it sure is curious. Ethan, who still hadn't spotted Nikki or me, finished crossing the street and strode up to a gorgeous brunette girl.

"Who the hell is that?" Nikki asked sharply.

"His assistant, I've met her a billion times, she's a total sweetie," I said absent-mindedly as I stared down at my own phone.

Had I dialed Ethan's number incorrectly?

"Um, Charly," Nikki jabbed me in the arm.

Was Ethan suffering from temporary illiteracy and couldn't read the caller ID saying that it was me?

"Ms. Briar," Nikki said louder.

Was Ethan having a nervous breakdown from working so hard?

"Charly-Briar-my-gawd-will-you-look-at-this!" when Nikki's Boston accent came out, *something* was wrong.

I looked up to see Ethan open-mouth kissing his assistant. Eyes closed. Tongues everywhere. He even had one of his big gorilla hands on her near-exposed breast.

Boobus escapus!
Breathe.
Compose.
Attack.

Now, I had always believed that, should I find myself in such a situation, I would know exactly what to do: death-by-blunt-object. It's so obvious. But I was paralyzed. I just sat there frozen as Ethan and his assistant went at it. They groped each other passionately for what seemed like an eternity and I literally didn't know where to look, so I watched. Finally they stopped and carried on their way back to the office together.

(It's not like the movies by the way, an anvil did not fall on his head and his assistant did not take one step off the curb and immediately get *pancaked* by truck.)

Um, what the @%#&*!!??*

Two minutes later Ethan texted to say he was sorry that he had missed my call, he had been in a meeting.

"I went through something like this once, with a guy cheating on me," Nikki said as she tried to console me.

"Did he ever stop?" I moaned, still remotely hopeful.

Please please please...

Tell me he stopped...

"No!" Nikki scoffed as though I'd just asked her if gravity can be outsmarted. "Once a cheater *always* a cheater. Charly, I broke up with him. You *have* to break up with Ethan. Do you understand that? Tell me you understand that."

"I know, you're right," she *was* right.

There's no way she's right!

"So," I wondered, "Do you ever see him, that guy who cheated on you?"

"Once in a while," said Nikki as she polished off her latte and placed her palms on the table to get up, "Now he cheats on his girlfriend with me."

Oh.

"People don't change, Charly," Nikki sighed sympathetically. "Not unless there's something worth changing for. And if Ethan doesn't think you're worth changing for, well, fuck him."

Fully Booked / Genn Pardoe

26. Hunny, I'm home!

"Who the *fuck* are you?" I couldn't help but scream.

Kai is comfortably on the couch next to an impossibly gorgeous brunette. She is wearing chic khaki cargos and a fitted wraparound white cotton top. She sports a pixie cut and funky earrings (the kind you get from some indigenous tribe while you're on an intrepid backpacking adventure in Burma, or the accessories department at a cheapo tween store). She is tanned, tiny, and her perfectly round breasts invade my airspace.

She is Zoë van der Baque.

She must die.

"Whoa, Charly, um, what are you doing home so early?" Kai jumped up and headed towards me with a *very* surprised look on his face.

"You must be Charly, I'm pleased to meet you," the must-be-Zoë-girl extended her right hand in salutation.

Did I just seriously walk in on Kai having an affair?
Is that girl Zoë?
Wait a tick...I have absolutely no clue what Zoë looks like!
Argh! Who the hell is that girl?
Were my worst fears honestly just confirmed?
What the hell is going on?!

With my mouth still gaping open in shock, I reluctantly shook the girl's hand (all the time wondering if I was shaking a hand that had just been stroking my boyfriend's man parts). I scanned Kai's crotch but, unfortunately, there's no such thing as hand job tread marks. Plus, he had his pants on.

Where was the CSI Vagina crew when I needed them?
This could not be Zoë.
Zoë was in Sri Lanka or Pakistan or somewhere…
Anywhere…
But not here.
But she really fit the image I had in mind of her…
It must be her!
What in the name of relaxed denim was she doing in our loft when I wasn't home?
No.
No I'm wrong.
Not Zoë.
It wasn't Zoë, it couldn't be.
Could it be?

Time was moving at a glacial pace.

The mystery girl spoke again.

"Mind if I freshen up in the bathroom? I'd really like to splash some water on my face after such a long trip."

"Sure, Zoë," said Kai as he moved toward me and planted a kiss on my disbelieving forehead.

Planted a kiss?
That's so not him!
But that is Zoë!
What was going on!?

"Thanks Kyle," said Zoë.

Whoa.
Wait.
What?
Who's Kyle?
Okay, what the hell is going on?

Clearly, I had wandered into someone else's nightmare. I was so confused. The last time things made sense I was leaving a media trip early to come home and patch things up with my boyfriend. Four hours later there I was, standing in our loft (well, the loft that we were subletting from his ex) who, apparently, was at that moment, spending time *alone* with my boyfriend.

Huh!?

Kai called up the stairs towards the bathroom, "Zoë, you can use the hand towels you gave us."

(I thought of the time I needed toilet paper and those stupid hand towels were the only option available.) As Zoë fell out of sight, I turned towards Kai, who smiled casually back at me.

"Sweetheart, don't be so dramatic," he half pleaded and half rolled his eyes. "Zoë happened to be in town and only wanted to stop in for a Chai Latte."

Chai Latte?

Is that a joke?

Are you coming off a cleanse or something?

What's next, Kai?

Are you going to tell me that you're not really a banker, but in fact, a chocolatier from Bruges!?

"Kai," I began, "one *happens to be in town* in Boston, or even in New York, but *not* in Bangkok! What the hell is going on, Kai? Or should I say, *Kyle*?"

My guilty boyfriend tried to put his arms around me but I brushed him away angrily. I was so beyond furious and I seriously considered storming out, but then, how would I stab Zoë in the face and clobber Kai to death with the nearest blunt object?

I really didn't know what to do.

What a dilemma...

I wasn't sure what the protocol was for this type of thing and at that moment I felt as though I really needed my girlfriends. They were always the voice of rationality and in this situation they would have known exactly what to do.

I felt lost and directionless without them, as though I couldn't breathe, I had no idea what to do. So I did the most natural thing. I threw down my bags, thrust Kermit into Kai's arms, and stormed into the kitchen to open a bottle of wine. I'd need the excuse of "duress" if there were going to be bodies... and blood...

Kai put Kermit gently down on the sofa and moved toward me like an animal control worker. He cooed as though I were some kind of rabid wolverine.

Which quite frankly, I might as well have been.

"Sweetheart, you *know* my full name is Kyle..." he began.

Um, no I did not!

"...I changed it because 'Kai' sounds cooler..."

That's so lame!

"...and Zoë *was* honestly just passing by..."

Yeah... sure, and I'm a vegetarian pilates hottie with no rage issues...

"...Charly, there's no need to be dramatic."

Dramatic!

What?

Me?

Who's being dramatic?

I hate being called dramatic.

Especially when I am about to be *very* dramatic.

Just who, exactly, did Kai fucking Kostigan think he was dealing with? This wasn't my first time around the track. I had learned long ago that throwing crazy-maniac-temper-tantrums should be reserved for special occasions — and Kai and I were going to have a *really* special occasion — but not while Zoë was around. That would be uncouth.

So, moving as calmly as possible, I fixed myself a glass of wine and, through bared my teeth (like a serial killer or a baby gorilla).

I asked slowly, "What is going on Kai? And *don't* lie to me."

Inside my heart was breaking and I just couldn't believe his was happening. I just couldn't believe it...

Was Kai really about to break my heart?

"It's not what you think, Charly," Kai promised. "Zoë *was* passing through. She called to see if she could stop in because she had *big news*."

Kai gently took the wine bottle from my *rigor mortis* grasp—I stared at him hard. I just couldn't believe what was going on. I sneered at him, "Big news? Like, she's still in love with you and wants you back!"

I slammed my wine glass on the counter and it shattered on impact, slicing open my hand and drawing gushing blood immediately.

"Owweee!" I yelped.

Blood ran everywhere and Kai passed out. He fell to the floor like a ton of designer label bricks and his eyes rolled back into his head. Kai had always hated the sight of blood.

"Just great," I smirked meanly at his lifeless body.

There I stood, in the middle of the kitchen, with a cheating boyfriend unconscious at my feet while his ex-girlfriend was upstairs wiping her face with towels she had given us as a gift that I'd once used to wipe my own ass with.

Now, how often can you say that?

"F - M - L," I said to Kermit.

Kermit nodded. After an eternity, Zoë came back downstairs.

Kai was still unconscious on the floor and I was coolly on my second glass of wine.

"Oh *nooooo*! What happened?" Zoë's squeal sounded like a lab rat with shampoo in its eyes.

"Never mind that," I pointed to the body. "So, my dear, Kai tells me you have big news?"

My teeth were grinding so hard it was audible.

"I do! But, er," Zoë grimaced. "Is Kyle okay? Are you okay?"

"*Kai* is just fine," I snapped. "Thank you for your concern, Zoë."

With a pointed stiletto on either side of my comatose boyfriend's body, I felt like a fashionable champion hunter standing over my defeated game.

Moments of painful silence passed before Zoë finally seemed to catch on to the immense awkwardness of the situation. There was no way to be sure, though, she obviously had no soul.

"Charly, look, I…"

"Please Zoë, just explain yourself."

My smile was so big and fake it must have seemed as though I was either going to rip out Zoë's jugular with my komodo dragon talons, or stab her with a spoon.

What the hell happened to the code among women?
Girls shouldn't prey on other girls' boyfriends.
Period.

I mean, truthfully, Kai could have been on fire and I still would have insisted on hearing Zoë's *big news* before tending to him. I didn't think he deserved my attention anyway. As calmly as possible, as though I was welcoming the editorial team of Architectural Digest magazine into our loft for a photo shoot. I posed against the counter and smiled faux-warmly at Zoë.

"I want to explain," Zoë began nervously.

I gently placed my bloody hand — still gushing blood from the smash of the wine glass — on her clean ivory top.

"Then do that," I smiled meanly — I couldn't help it.

Sensing that her body would never be found if she didn't explain herself quickly, Zoë backed away from me and stared at the floor guiltily. When she finally conjured up the courage to talk she was interrupted by Kai's slow moaning as he regained consciousness. Instinctively — and on behalf of *all* girls everywhere who have ever been cheated on — I knee-jerked the toe of my pointy stiletto into what I prayed were Kai's testicles, and he passed out again. Zoë's eyes looked as though they might fall out of her head and roll across the floor.

Did I go too far?
Did I say too much?
Maybe…
Probably…

Whatever.
Who cares…
You'd do exactly the same thing…
Anyone would have…

"You were saying, Zoë?"

The perky pixie looked utterly frozen. All I could do was smile as Zoë tried to sputter out her pathetic excuse for slithering into our perfect relationship and splitting it open like a gutted fish. An eternity passed. Finally, she spoke, "Charly," Zoë coughed and looked down at the floor, "I'm a lesbian."

Sandbag!

kermitandcharly@gmail.com

Nikki says:
> Buahahaha, that's awesome. You're a total psycho *and* a homophobe.

Charly says:
> Oh my god, I am not! And you would have thought the same thing!

Nikki says:
> Um, no crazy pants, I would not have done the same thing. Why? Because I don't do serial *monotony*. I don't get jealous or crazy or fantasize about my boyfriend's lesbian ex-girlfriend eyeballs rolling across the floor.

Charly says:
> I'm such a jerk. Why does this *always* happen to me?

Nikki says:
> Oh don't worry so much. So, did you really kick Kai in the balls?

Charly says:
> With my pointy stilettos.

Nikki says:
> Priceless, just priceless.

Charly says:
> My life is a mess.

Nikki says:
> LOL it really is. Kidding… it'll all be fine. Hey, by the way, random question: you don't think Alégra has caught on to the whole Templeton thing, do you?

Charly says:
> No, I don't think so. I hope not, at least. What makes you think that?

Nikki says:
> I dunno, just a feeling. Okay, I gotta jet.

Charly says:
> Okay, lady, talk soon.

Nikki says:
> You too. And hey, Killah, you might want to switch to moccasins if you ever hope to procreate with this guy.

27. Ethan Charge, Conclusion *Again*

In addition to temporarily turning me on to guys who look like violent male Swedish models, Ethan provided the inspiration I needed to embark on a whirlwind jet-setting journey of self-discovery.

It was back in college and I had broken up with him exactly seven days earlier. The week leading up to that point had been, well, interesting. Ethan was calling 20 times a day, at all hours, always drunk. He pleaded with me to take him back and even argued that I had been mistaken when I saw him and his assistant making out... *right in front of me.*

At first I really *wanted* to believe him. After all, we had spent two years together and made plans for the future. The temptation to just forget it and move on with him (yes, I said it, *with* him) was almost overwhelming.

Sometimes it's easier to deal with the devil you know; so much less effort. But thankfully, Alégra and Nikki were there to be my backbone when I wasn't strong enough. They took me out for an amazing night at the Fairmount where I met the coolest girl—who I'd later come to know as Eden—at a fabulous party. It was then, on that night, that everything finally dawned on me...

"It's over, Ethan, just leave me alone," I said sternly during our fourth conversation that night. He was pleading hysterically and I was swaying drunkenly from my night at the Fairmont.

"No, Charly! I love you, don't you understand? We're supposed to be together! What's wrong with you? Is there someone else? There's someone else, *I know it!*"

"No, Ethan, if you recall, *you* cheated. Not me. Now seriously, just leave me alone."

"Never!"

His reaction scared the hell out of me and for the first time I saw with picture perfect clarity exactly *what sort* of relationship I had been in for the last two years. I needed to tell Ethan something that would make him leave me alone, for good.

"Well, do whatever you want!" I screamed with all the force in my lungs. "You'll never find me. I'm, um, I'm leaving the country! Yes, that's it! I'm going to be a jet-setting hotel PR girl! It'll be fabulous and you'll never hear from me again!"

Now, I'll admit I wasn't really thinking through the implications of that statement but it seemed to do the trick. Ethan was finally grasping that things were over between us.

"I just can't believe you're doing this," he sobbed. "Don't you see what you're doing to me?"

"You did this to yourself, asshole," I said without emotion.

"Don't you see that I *need* you?" he gasped in between fits of hyperventilating. "Don't you see that I can't breathe without you?"

Although Ethan's reaction was hyper-dramatic and totally unjustified (it was *him* cheating on *me*) I could see that he was tormented, twisted, and broken. I felt immense sympathy for him. After all, I never wanted to feel as though I couldn't function without someone, (and I certainly did not *ever* want to make myself sound like a raving lunatic just to convey that message). I hoped, more than anything else, that I would never make anyone pity me the way I pitied Ethan.

28. Such a pity...

When Kai eventually came to, Zoë was gone and I was upstairs erasing the nasty email I had sent the night before; I couldn't believe that he hadn't checked his email yet! *Thank you, Karma, I won't forget this.*

"Hey," Kai said as he hobbled up the stairs. "What's up?"

What's up?

What's up?

What's *up*?

I didn't even know where to begin. The weeks of percolating tension, near-fights (the Maldives, FIFA, the fart, *eeks!*), and the fact I had just apparently fully transitioned into a ball-kicking, paranoid freak. It was *way* too much for me to process and I wanted to wipe the slate clean and start fresh. I prayed that Kai wanted the same.

"Look, Kai, I am —" he cut me off.

"Why don't you just congratulate me on my new job, Charly? I assume *that* is why you randomly appeared here, *unexpected*, and not to render me infertile and give Zoë a level seven heart attack."

I stared at the ground as Kai moaned his way into bed, "You're *such* a child," he said under his breath as he rolled over pretended to sleep. "And, yes, if you're thinking it, because you *always* do, Zoë *never* would have acted like this."

Excuse me?

Since I had, at that moment, what is medically referred to as a "rage blackout", I cannot be sure *exactly* what happened next. But I *can* deduce what set it off: hearing that perfect little princess' name for the hundredth time. I was so tired of her!

Even though I had complete faith that it was over between them because, well, the whole lesbian thing, I couldn't stand the fact that Zoë had become deified in Kai's mind. It was driving me crazy trying to live up to her, so, naturally, I took it out on Kai.

"You think you're so perfect with your Kiehl's facial products, your obsessively landscaped pubes, and your Ermanagilda Zenya — or whatever the hell they're called — loafers. Is there even a person below that superficial veneer or are you mainly comprised of hair gel and protein shakes?"

Without missing a beat, as though he'd been waiting to say it for months, Kai scoffed, "That's hilarious coming from you, Charly Briar! You work for a luxury hotel brand that builds palatial atrocities in third world countries. You're obsessed with labels."

"Are you kidding me right now?" I yelled. "That's not even close to being true. You're just angry and I get that, I understand, I was an idiot… but I think you're being silly — *and* mean."

"Oh really?" Kai shot back at me, "Be honest, Charly, you won't even leave the house without a piece of Liam & Olivia on. You're only happy when I'm giving you presents like that stupid phone or the airplane shawl. All of it. It's all bullshit. Without all your little toys, do you even know who you are?"

Wow. Ouch.

Breathe.

Thankfully none of that was true…

Right?

"Look," I sighed, "Kai, I'm sorry, congratulations on the job, that's what I meant to say, and yes, *that* is why I'm here."

Sensing I was in retreat, Kai half-smiled, sat up, and beckoned me towards him.

"Thank you. Look, I'm sorry. I lost my mind there for a moment. I love you. Truly, I am sorry. I didn't mean it."

"I love you too, Kai," I said as I fought back tears.

I was happy at least that we were on the same team again. It's not easy being a fabulous *expat couple* and most don't make it. Most people get caught up in trivial mini-fights and silly non-issues. But we weren't most people. We were Kai Kostigan and Charly-Briar-soon-to-be-Charly-Kostigan. We were super-couple extraordinaire, we were practically the greatest couple ever, actually, we were going to be together forever, we were—"The job is back in New York, I start next week."

We were through.

❑ * § * ❑

"I'm so tired of hearing you cry, Charly." Kai said from a hotel in New York a week later.

"That's a *horrible* thing to say," I bellowed at him.

Recently I had begun to wonder if I'd hallucinated our entire relationship.

"I want to be with you my whole life, please Kai, I love you." I pleaded pathetically through snot-filled gasps of air.

I was choking on my own disbelief; the full extent of Kai leaving had just begun to sink in and I was drowning in my own apoplectic rage.

What happened to our love?

When we were together I felt immense joy all of the time, and suddenly that joy was gone. Kai had taken that from me—so easily it seemed—and I hated him for that. And if that wasn't enough, Kai also took my dog.

My dog!

My *dog!*

My *#&%(@ dog!*

Kai agreed to take Kermit because I still had out-of-town, pet unfriendly resorts to visit and no one else could take care of him.

Oh, and also, if only I hadn't been frantically trying to please Kai when I'd booked all those in-town assignments, I'd have been able to book them now and still have Kermit.

Thanks for nothing, Universe.
We are so on the outs.
Stupid Universe.

Kai promised to take good care of Kermit and said I could pick him up as soon as I came home. The thought of losing both my two-legged *and* four-legged loves at the same time was too much. And… the fact that I was *still* living in Zoë's loft was really the crap icing on my bullshit cake.

Just great!

The temptation to take up drunken tight-rope walking over a cesspool of mutant alligators was very strong…

¤ * § * ¤

"*Why* are you doing this? Why have you *done* this?" I wailed at Kai the next time we spoke. I hated him for what he did. He took our picture perfect future and discarded it like it was trash, like it was less than nothing. What's worse, he was increasingly avoiding talking to me on the phone. I was so confused. How had we gone from a fart to a fight to a full-on break-up in a matter of weeks? Why did I have no say in the matter? Where did this all come from?

I knew Kai despised dramatics more than anything so when I actually was able to get him on the phone, I tried to be as calm as I could. I drew in a few controlled breaths, collected my thoughts, and tried to whisper, "Look, I know you followed me to Asia."

My voice was so shaky that I didn't notice Kai cringing in disagreement. He was silent; forcing me to wonder what he was thinking.

I continued, even more shakily, "Now, we have to make a choice. Why are you not asking me to make that choice with you? To follow you? To move to New York with you?"

"That's not my call," he said it dryly and without emotion.

"So, it doesn't matter to you if I come to New York you or not?" I said through gritted teeth.

Silence.

I caught a glimpse of my reflection in the mirror: my face was purple with fury and my whole body was shaking uncontrollably. My long hair was scrunched atop my head in a messy bird's nest and bobbling around. My eyes were raw and puffy and my lips were chapped from making that awful *crying smiley face* that people make only when they are truly heartbroken.

I looked like a laboratory panda bear that had received a forced-overdose of pharmaceutical cocaine and was brought back to life, only to die again from rabies.

F.

M.

L.

For reals.

I couldn't help it, I fell to the floor sobbing and gasping hysterically, "Don't you see I can't breathe without you?! I'm dying, I think, I think, I think I'm dying, I can't breathe."

It was all I had left.

It was so pathetic.

"Get it together. You're acting crazy," Kai said angrily. "I would *never* ask you to move anywhere for me."

It was completely incomprehensible to me how he could remain so calm.

"But you did it for me," I protested pitifully.

He sighed again, "No, I didn't, it was a move, *a calculated move,* on my part. I needed time to re-group and realign my priorities."

Huh?

"Go to hell," I said slowly; it was my turn to be calm, even though I was faking it.

"I meant job-wise, Charly. *Jesus*, I just needed some time to clear my head, and anyway, I'm not interested in speaking with you when you're acting like this."

"*Acting*" *like this??*

I literally did 'Jazz Hands' I was so furious...

"So go," I said meanly.

"Well, clearly, I already *have* gone. C'mon, Charly, you knew Bangkok wasn't working for me. But I love you, and I would be very happy, *obviously*, if you came along when your contract is up. But I'm not going to ask you to do it. I just, like, hope that you do. But I'm not asking."

Men talk in this twisted language and they call us crazy?

"Came along?" I couldn't help but scoff rudely.

"What the hell, Charly? Are you upset because I love you more than anything or is it that I finally—*finally!*—have found a great job?"

Silence.

Not giving him the satisfaction...

He'll have to work for it.

Kai continued, "Do you know how depressed I was in Bangkok? My god, Charly, put things in perspective, you're coming back in no time. Did you honestly think you were going to stay out there forever?"

Um, kinda!

Kai continued, "You'll be back in, like, two months. Get over yourself. Come to NY and find a job here. Besides, New York is infinitely better than Boston."

Whoa, there!

Watch your mouth, boy.

Kai responded to my silence with increasing agitation, "Charly, you're driving me nuts. Why can't you be happy for me?"

I let a minute go by in silence as I thought about this. I was pretty sure I *had* been supportive of Kai.

Obviously I wasn't happy about him moving back to New York with no input on my part, but I distinctly remember saying congratulations.

That counts, right?

"Hello?" Kai's voice brought me in to the moment. "Still there, Charly? Hello? Can you hear me?"

"Yes!" I snapped back to reality and back to our conversation.

I could hear him exhaling cigarette smoke and pacing on a hardwood floor. I wondered where Kermit was at that point; he always hated when Kai and I fought.

"I need to know what our future is," I said gently.

"Our future is," Kai hesitated. "Take it as it comes."

Take it as it comes?

C'mon!

What in the name of retro aviators was this moron talking about?

I thought Kai wasn't the type of guy to mind-fuck the hell out of me. Apparently I was wrong. *Argh, what to do now?* I needed to put a shape or label to us. I needed to define us somehow. "Take it as it comes" was *not* an option. Without pausing for a moment to consider a rational (or sane) response, I blurted out the first thing that came into my hyper-emotionally charged head, "Marry me or we're done."

Oops.

I have no idea what possessed me to use *the ultimate ultimatum*, the bottom line of *all* bottom lines, the epitome of boy-kryptonite, but I couldn't take it back. I had no choice but to run with it.

"I'm serious Kai, you can't ask me to move to New York without some semblance of a future for us, can you?"

Brilliant.

Silence.

For a long time.

Oh boy...

For too long of a time...

Eeks...

Finally, he spoke, "Look, Charly, I *love* you. I *want* to be with you. At this point, I am pretty sure that I want to be with you for the rest of my life. But, if it doesn't work out, I don't want to be held accountable."

I was more confused than ever, "But, so, *what*!? I don't get it. You *want* to be with me and you *think that* I'm the *one* that you will want to marry?"

"Totally," Kai answered calmly. "But, if we ended up breaking up, I wouldn't want to be called a liar because I had seemingly deceived you or whatever."

Who says "totally" and "whatever" at a time like this?
Is he, like, a thirteen year old girl?
And what the hell was he talking about?
I was confused, beyond hurt, and *really* offended.

Why was this all on him? Why wasn't this a joint decision? Why didn't I have a say? I gathered myself calmly and attempted to clarify the situation.

"So, you *do* think that we will get married?" I was terrified of what the answer would be.

To my simultaneous shock and relief, Kai said, "Of course I do."
Oh my god!

Suddenly, all of my worries, sadness, and bad hair—they were all gone. Okay… so it wasn't exactly *the dream* proposal but I could deal. The point was that we were going to make it work. I was never more sure that Kai was *the one* at that very moment. I burst into tears of joy and began to tell Kai how much I loved him, but he interrupted me.

"…however, Charly, I don't want to verbally confirm it for fear that it might come back to bite me in the ass, you know, in case we break up."

Wait.
What?
Enough!
Charly Briar has a limit!

I am officially getting off this rollercoaster.
This insane rollercoaster of games and bullshit!
Charly Briar is a lot of things, but she is no sucker.

I'm not going to live someone else's life. And, fine, maybe I *don't* have it all figured out and, fine, maybe I *am* flighty and flaky. And *fine*, maybe I have *slight* interest in luxury and labels and things like that; but that doesn't make me an asshole.

Am I right?!

And it certainly doesn't mean I have to take second best. I want a guy who wants to be with *me* above all else, not just when it's convenient for him. *I* come first, not some stupid *wanker banker* (yep, Eden called it) who doesn't even care when he's breaking my heart. I decided right then and there that I would take the proverbial ball and put it squarely back in *my* court.

"You know what, that's fine, Kai, it's totally fine."

I wasn't going to fight for someone who half-heartedly wanted to be with me. Enough is enough.

I took a deep breath and channeled my old self, the confident girl I apparently had lost sight of. I turned my attention to Kai and calmly asked, "Can I please keep your track pants, the Abercrombie & Fitch ones? You left them here, in the loft. You know, the ones you used to wear all the time. Please, can I keep those?"

"Oh, sure," Kai said as his voice softened. "Charly, my love, my life, my girl. Of *course* you can keep my track pants—wear them as much as you like—until you come back and live with me in New York. That's adorable. Aw, babe, you must miss me, huh? Is that why you want to keep them? To wear them?"

"No," I said sweetly. "I want to keep your track pants in case I have the desire to dress up like a *fucking douchebag!*"

I hung up and melted into a puddle.

But at least it was *my* puddle.

kermitandcharly@gmail.com

Nikki says:
>So are you two broken up, or not?

Charly says:
>Don't ask me, I have no idea... I'm going to assume yes. I have never been in this situation before. So much ambiguity. I hate it.

Nikki says:
>Kai was obviously absent from school the day they teach you how to be, oh, I dunno, a normal fucking human being. Screw him, who cares?

Charly says:
>I care! I love him. I thought he was the one.

Nikki says:
>I could tell you guys wouldn't last. Too obsessed with perfection if you ask me.

Charly says:
>What's wrong with a gorgeous, smart, ambitious and perfect-in-every-way man?

Nikki says:
>Kai *wasn't* perfect.

Charly says:
>Um, yes, he was. And you're going to feel like a horse's arse when we get back together.

Nikki says:
>You're not getting back together and I hope you'll seriously take a break before jumping into yet another relationship, Ms. Serial Monogamist.

Charly says:
>Excuse me? Kai and I *are* getting back together! Well at least I hope we do. Oh crap, I don't know. I don't know about anything!

Nikki says:
>Why would you want to get back together? I'd rather watch *Gigli* every day for the rest of my life than spend my time terrified I'm not good enough for my "perfect" boyfriend... and you *did* do that by the way.

Charly says:
> Um, *hello*? Sympathy please! I've been crying for days, I look like a homeless crack-addicted muppet.

Nikki says:
> Charly! Pick yourself up, go buy a vibrator, and move on! You're loved by your friends back home, you're fabulous, you're amazing, and you're *better off* without that penis-masseuse!

Charly says:
> I just don't understand why this happened to me.

Nikki says:
> Save it for group therapy... no more feeling sorry for yourself!

Charly says:
> But he was the perfect man! He *is* the perfect man!

Nikki says:
> Do you ever listen to yourself? What about *you*? What about what you want? Don't look for the person you want to marry—*be* the person you want to marry. You're better than this. And besides, if Kai is so perfect, why did he jump ship for no good reason?

Oh.
Right.
Shit.

Nikki had a majorly solid point there. Still, I spent the next week with my face buried deep in my pillow bawling my eyes out. I wasn't *there* yet and I couldn't even begin to put this on Kai. I was still at the stage where this was all my fault or, at the very least, a catastrophic blunder on the part of the universe. I kept replaying the night in Railay over and over again in my head. If *only* I hadn't turned my phone to silent, if *only* I hadn't drowned my unfounded paranoia with two bottles of wine and a bucket of whiskey (and a blue mango—*why??*), if *only* I hadn't felt the need to rush back to Bangkok... if only.

No dog.
No boyfriend.
No hair.
Oh, yeah, *that*.

The *one* outing I'd managed to make in the past week entailed a trip to Starbucks and an impromptu drop-in at a salon, *just to look*. The hairstylist said I'd look great with a "shattered bob". I said that sounded about right and went for it.

As the young Thai woman finished up and spun my chair around to face the mirror, I had what is commonly referred to as a stroke-due-to-shock.

"What do you think?" the peppy Asian hipster cheered.

What do I think??
What do I think!!
What do I #%&@ think?!*
Where do I even begin?

I think it screams: "I just got dumped and rather than cry about it, I'm going to chop off all my hair to symbolize just how *fucking fabulous* I am because I don't need a boyfriend, I don't need anybody, hell, *I don't even need hair!*"

I said thanks and left the salon in tears.

Tears. *Yuck.*

I never cry over ex-boyfriends (or hair!).
Ever! What was wrong with me?

In a flash I had gone from a never-crier to a one-woman-waterworks-festival. This had *literally* never happened to me before and I was utterly confused. I mean, honestly, I have a jar of peanut butter back home that is older than my relationship with Kai.

I need to put things in perspective!

Something was going on, this wasn't right; I wasn't reacting the way I normally did after a breakup.

What had changed?
What had happened?
What was going on?
Why am I asking these questions over and over again?

The next month followed much the same way: a total haze. I threw myself into work and when I wasn't working, well, I was shopping, crying, or drinking.

What else could I do?

I decided that I'd need to revamp my entire wardrobe: anything that reminded me of Kai *had* to go. Anything that he'd touched, complimented, criticized, or basically ever laid eyes on, was chucked.

I set about accumulating my new must-have accessories for starting one's life over: super sexy knee-high boots from Liam & Olivia, a chic cashmere knee-length wraparound sweater, three armfuls of blouses and adorable tees, and a bountiful array of cosmetics and hair care products.

Oh, *and* I also picked up five or six (or seven or eight) skinny jeans, all colors, obviously. I also bought lots of new lingerie. I couldn't bear the thought of having *anything* on or near my hoo-ha that Kai had touched. I needed new underwear that wasn't soiled.

With heartbreak, that is.

It went on and on like this for weeks. Work, shop, drink, sleep, repeat. I'd already lost 10 pounds (a total upside to crippling depression) and I was sort of starting to get used to my new coif. I was coping. At best. And then, all of a sudden, Christmas was fast approaching. I'd decided to stay in Bangkok to get as much work done as possible. The faster I got through my media trips, the faster I could go home and forget this mango-flavored nightmare ever happened. At least that's what I told everyone back in Boston—that I just wanted to work through Christmas so I could get home to friends and family faster. The truth, however, was that I couldn't stand to face anyone that I knew. And I wanted to be left alone.

Christmas in Bangkok...

Just great...

You know what?

Fuck you, Santa.

Yeah, I said it.

What have you done for me lately?

Nothing.

That's what.

This sad little thought made me drink a lot and take what I hoped were a couple of Zanax. (Turned out not to be Zanax.)

Hours later, as I vomited ramen noodles, wine, and imposter relaxation pills, I suddenly saw an upside.

"Hey," I said to my gaunt reflection in the mirror as I wiped away a smidge of barf. "Maybe this is *that* life-changing moment you've been looking for, Charly. You know, the one that will lead to an amazing journey of self-discovery. Sure it didn't come in the neat little package you'd hoped, but maybe, just maybe, *this* is the moment that changes everything."

"Hey, self," I said to myself. "Maybe you're right."

As I crawled into bed, and pulled the covers tight around my head, I was comforted with the notion that the one good thing about hitting rock bottom is that it provides a pretty solid foundation to rebuild upon. I closed my eyes somewhat happily for the first time in a long time.

"No, no, no, silly," said my future self to my sleeping self. "Things are going to get so much worse."

29. Let's Do Lunch

Charly B,

Sooo I'm writing to you, again, lol, in the hopes that you didn't get my first letter because I don't want to look like a weirdo, or a stalker, because I'm not! Okay awkward... I hope you're not mad at me (or married! LOL) I just honestly wanted to see how you're doing.

So, yeah, I'm doing really well. Work is awesome. Still traveling a bunch. I was dating this girl for awhile, I mean, it didn't work out, but I've realized that's cool... and I've learned something about love... You have to be crazy brave... like you have to jump in headfirst no snorkel... with no regard for what comes out the other end.

Anyway, ride 'er til she hits the beach, I guess, eh? Well it's stupid but that's my new motto, LOL. So in the spirit of that, Ms. Briar, have we hit the beach yet? I didn't think our story is done... but if I'm wrong, hey, cool, tell me to go take a hike... at least I tried...

Either way, I would love to know how you're doing. I miss you... kinda :)

xx
me

...*as if* I have the mental capacity to deal with that right now... Besides, my phone was ringing.

"Hello," I croaked like an Amazonian swamp toad.
Wow.

Here's a tip: Don't smoke a million cigarettes and then drink a barrel of wine and then throw up and then pick up the phone.

"You sound like a dirty pirate," Radden burst out laughing.
Really, Universe?
Really!?
"Good morning, Radden," I smiled and my lips cracked.
Oh, god it's bad.
Really bad.
"What are you doing today? Wanna meet for lunch?" he got right to the point.
Um, gee lemme think...
Hells no.
I moaned in reluctance and rolled over. It was Saturday morning and the only thing I wanted to do was sleep all weekend and hide from the world.

"C'mon!" Radden pressed on cheerily. "It's actually work related. Please, Charly, you'd be doing me a favor. I need to ask you something. Please..."

"Argh," I pulled the duvet over my head further and crumpled up the letter I had just read five times. "Ugh, just ask me the favor over the phone."

Radden paused and then chuckled, "No deal. Let me bribe you with lunch. My treat, c'mon. It's at the Mariott, best club sandwich in the city. Am I selling it?"

"Hmmm," I paused.

I really did not feel like getting out of bed.

"I will stalk you until you say yes, Chuckles!"

Sigh, why wouldn't Kai stalk me?

"I give up!" I caved happily. "Alright well, if you throw in a spicy Caesar and I'm there."

"Change up that dorky Caesar for a proper Thai beer and I'll pick you up myself," Radden offered.

"Really?"

"Really. *Dork.*"

Thirty minutes later I was on the back of a motorbike whizzing in and out of Bangkok traffic (not to mention regretting wearing a short pale pink shift dress).

I had purposely chosen a loose and thigh-bearing frock, not to be alluring, but to minimize the overwhelming evidence of my profound perspiration. It was stiflingly hot that day and I was really trying to pull it together for my first social encounter with a human in what felt like eons.

I topped off my outfit with over-sized Jackie O sunglasses in the hopes that they would cover my puffy red eyes and what I feared were permanent pillow creases in my cheeks. I put my new haircut into a bobby-pinned *do* in an effort to look moderately chic. And I didn't bother with any makeup beyond tinted lip-gloss—it would probably just slide off my face anyway. Radden parked on the sidewalk outside the Mariott and suggested we find a spot on the patio.

Really?

Are you being serious right now, Radden?

An entire air conditioned hotel I have to sit on the stiflingly hot patio? Ugh.

Radden sat beneath an umbrella and took his keys and cigarettes out of faded jean pockets and tossed them on the table. He fanned himself with his white polo shirt and sat down, stretched out his legs, and relaxed with a big happy sigh. His blue shoes were casual, like the kind surfers wear on land, and he had no watch or jewelry of any kind.

"So, pretty girl," Radden smiled approvingly at me. "What's the good word? What you have been up to?"

Radden seemed to fluctuate between two go-to nicknames for me: pretty girl and Chuckles.

I felt as though it might be somewhat rehearsed but accepted it anyhow. *Whatever*. I'll take any attention I can get right now.

"Oh, you know, nothing much," I couldn't help but launch into a much rehearsed soliloquy about how extremely busy and ridiculously fabulous I'd been since last we met.

(And by extremely busy and ridiculously fabulous I mean I've been drowning in devastation over the loss of my one-true-love and the thought of being out in public makes me want to take a bath with a toaster.)

Radden made the international symbol for *no big deal* and then suddenly realized, "Oh, my gosh, I'm so rude. I forgot to give you the classic clichéd *expat hello*."

Time slowed as Radden stood up.

Huh?

I instinctively rose as well and stood in front of him, unsure of what the heck he was up to. Radden took control and reached forward to grab me by the shoulders softly and double-kissed me on my cheeks.

"I, um," I was frozen despite the incredible heat. "Um, yes, I."

Needless to say, Radden's kisses caught me totally off guard and I instinctively put my hand on his shoulders, partly to steady myself and partly to push him away, it was too much. I opened my eyes—which I did not remember closing—and sat back down, flustered.

"Um, yes, well," my eyes blinked and my stomach fluttered.

Radden's scent lingered around me. I'd never smelled *anything* like him. It wasn't a particular cologne, per se, or even body wash or after shave, it was all three, and *then* some. He smelled of things I had no idea about: being an *expat brat*, going to boarding school, living a traveled life. I had never done, seen, or experienced any of those things. It was intoxicating. But I wasn't stupid. I knew what my brain was up to. I was clearly in the *dear-god-why-can't-one-male-just-one-member-of-the-male-species-find-me-attractive?* stage.

It wasn't Radden.

It was my infinite sadness, my profound emptiness, and my inconsolable heart that were telling me to seek out affection.

My heart, most of all, wanted to be useful again. My heart wanted me to place Kai's hand on top of her, like I always did when we snuggled in front of the T.V. My heart wanted me to draw little pictures of her when I signed notes next to his name.

♥Kai♥

I tried to reason with my heart and explain that this wasn't my fault, and someday, she would have the capacity to love and be loved again, but my heart wouldn't listen. She kept insisting that she was out of love, she had no more to give, and that she would forever belong to Kai.

That last jab really hurt me because I worried that it was true.

"So, pretty girl, how's work going?" Radden's voice brought me back to the moment.

"Oh, you know, same old, same old," I said casually, wondering if I might spontaneously combust from the heat and his kiss and my bottomless depression.

"So," Radden pressed on. "How's that male model Viking-type guy with the scarily perfect jaw structure you were with when I met you at the Hoteliers' Ball? Seemed German-*ish*? Karl?"

Now I was *sure* I would spontaneously combust. I let out a sigh which erupted into a near-unstoppable verbal avalanche. I would have given anything to *not* talk about Kai but, as luck would have it, I was forced to.

Ugh.

Seriously?

Okay... deep breath...

"Kai, his name was Kai. Well, I suppose technically his name still *is* Kai, or Kyle, um, as I have recently discovered. Ugh, I dunno. Well, anyway, whatever, we're not together anymore. He's American by the way, not German, and he went back—"

"Oh my god, can you hear that?" Radden smiled widely as he lifted his beer to his lips. "All the expat men in Bangkok have simultaneously broken into a *Happy Dance*."

"Oh, yeah, ha!" I shrugged with a little smile.

Radden did a geeky *raise the roof* gesture and I couldn't help myself, I had to laugh.

Okay, okay, fine… he was *kind* of cute.

Then he collected himself and asked, "Jeez, it's hot, *huh*?"

I nodded as Radden readjusted his polo and wiped his moist upper lip with the back of his hand. I squinted up towards where the sun *ought* to be; there is no sun in Bangkok thanks to the dense layer of smog that blocks it out. That day was no different. It was flat and grey but I had no intention of taking my sunglasses off. Thankfully, neither did Radden. It's always awkward when one person has their sunglasses on and the other doesn't. It's even *more* awkward when one of those people has bloodshot eyeballs and crusty mascara smear leftover from two weeks ago.

Radden looked at me intently from behind his Ray Bans (this was *before* the trendy renaissance the brand has enjoyed in recent years — it was retro, cool even).

We chatted about the hotel industry, photography, and expat life. It was refreshing to get out of my own head, if even for a short time. After almost an hour we decided to order lunch. Radden had a burger and another beer and I ordered the same. After the waiter left Radden leaned in and whispered in a mock-gossipy girl voice, "OMG, girlfriend, you're not going to order a pathetic little salad that you'll barely pick at?"

"Fuck vegetables," I giggled a bit for the first time in weeks.

"Whoa! I like it! High-five, Chuckles," Radden laughed and held his palm up in anticipation of mine.

I echoed his smile and brought my palm to meet his. We spent the rest of lunch drinking beer and enjoying small talk. It was such a relief to momentarily suspend my self-imposed seclusion from society.

It was also nice to talk to someone who didn't know my past, who wasn't going to lecture me about jumping into relationships again, or putting Kai on a pedestal, or everything else I've apparently done wrong. Radden really couldn't care less. And it was nice for me too, sitting with someone I knew absolutely nothing about. We had no history, no expectations, and we only went as deep in conversation as we wanted.

Ahhhh.

The blessed clean slate.

I totally "get" expats (and fugitives) now.

"So, listen, Chuckles," Radden's smile was so friendly and easy it was like silk and cashmere all rolled into one. "I need to ask you for a favor."

"Sure thing, Shutterbug," I said.

(Radden told me that he hated that term, so I made sure to tease him with it often.)

"LOL Miss Media Handler. Listen, have you done your media tour at the Grand Luxe Beach Spa & Resort in Koh Samui yet?"

"No, actually," I said of the massive Edifice Luxe resort my boss had *just* booked me at. "That's weird that you'd bring it up. If you can believe it, I'll be there over Christmas in less than three weeks.

The resort wants to promote their holiday events so that Americans and Europeans fly over here for their two weeks off. They have this big promotion, *New Traditions* or something like that, not sure. Anyway, yes, Christmas, you can definitely come if you want to. I assume that is what you were asking?"

"Oh, crap," Radden sighed. "Well, yeah, that's what I was asking, but Christmas, hmm, hard to pull off. The girlfriend's parents are coming into town. I was hoping to get on a media trip to that resort before the holidays."

"Oh, too bad," I sighed as well. "I'm only able to bring media when I'm there, and my boss Sandy already booked me during Christmas, so—"

Wait?

What?
Girlfriend?
Oh...
Right.
Of course...
I remember now...
A girlfriend...

I had conveniently forgotten. Radden had a girlfriend. He was attached. There was a girl attached to him. Blah blah blah. Everyone has a significant other except for ugly dumb Charly.

Ugh!

And then I remembered. Radden had pointed to a group of girls at the Hoteliers' Ball but I wasn't sure which one was his girlfriend. Three of them were model types who probably also had PhD's and saved dolphins on the weekend before going to underground indie bars to drink organic beer and enjoy being ridiculously cool. The one other girl had been a *titch* more human-looking: she was cute but just a little on the chunky side with a somewhat vacant look—as though she was from an agrarian community or maybe she'd had a scuba diving accident whilst on high school grad trip...

In my head, *that* girl was Radden's girlfriend.

I smiled at this thought. Radden smiled back—completely unaware of why I was smiling. This made me smile more.

He said, "Well listen, if I can get out of it somehow, can I come along? I really need some shots from that hotel for one of the magazines I work for. I'm on deadline—it's stupid, it's my fault, long story, anyway I messed up and the bottom line is that I'd love not to fork out the cash to get down there."

He shot me his famous half-smile and I couldn't help but smile back, "You got it, Pontiac," I joked as I reached in my bag for a cigarette—I'd progressed to only smoking during waking hours.

"Oh my god, *Pontiac*?" Radden burst out laughing as he lit my cigarette for me and one for himself. "I can't believe you just said that. My dad says that. You're such a dork."

"Happy to be one!" I said as we clinked our bottles and eased into just another Bangkok afternoon amongst a couple of expats.

◻ * § * ◻

The next day I got a text from Radden saying he'd love to come to the resort if that was still an option. He said there had been a change of plans: his girlfriend would be going home to visit her family so his schedule had freed up.

Interesting.

I immediately texted Radden back to say sure, I'd be able to add him to the media list—twenty-five in total, my biggest group yet—and sorry to hear about his girlfriend.

He texted back to say thanks. I wondered how long Radden and his girlfriend had been together. I wondered if she was going back home for Christmas because they'd had a fight. I wondered if they fought often. And what they fought about...

Hmmm...

I wonder...

I was brought back into the room by my phone ringing.

"Hello?"

"Hi, babe,"

It was Kai.

As in, Kai Kostigan my ex-boyfriend.

Seriously!

Seriously?

Seriously!?

"Oh, hi," I tried to sound as unimpressed as possible.

It was my first conversation with Kai in what felt like forever, "So, what's new?"

I was torn between finding Kai's phone call very presumptuous—as though I only existed when he had time for me—and wanting to jump through the phone into his arms. In so many ways I still couldn't believe that we were broken up.

We'd spent so much time away from each other before coming to Bangkok that the feeling of having distance between us wasn't all that unfamiliar. But of course, this was different...

And despite his soft tone, I was beginning to feel that the possibility of us getting back together was dwindling with every passing day. I couldn't decide which type of break up was worse: the one that fizzles out over months like a dull continuous pain, or the devastating blow that you just don't see coming. My break up with Kai felt as though it was both.

Crazily, I still had not received confirmation one way or the other. I mean, the last thing I said to him was that I want to wear his track pants and dress up like a douche bag. That's really not definitive...

Kai and I chatted as though no time had passed at all. The conversation was free and easy and it freaked me out. I thought we were broken up? What was he doing? Why was he chatting with me like we were okay? I couldn't help but listen intently as Kai told me all about life back in New York and how Kermit was adjusting wonderfully—I needed a clue as to how he truly felt.

So frustrating!

Kai continued... he said his new job was going really well, he'd found a new condo that he *just knew* I'd love, he was back hanging out with his old friends, he can't believe how much he'd missed New York... *oh blah blah blah!* What about me!? This hot and cold was driving me nuts. Did he want to be together or not?

It was infuriating to think that he was so happy while I remained in a stinky city, alone and devastated. I didn't even have a dog (or hair!) to comfort me. And every time I put my key in the door to enter the loft, I felt sick to my stomach. This wasn't a home anymore. It was a rented space from my ex-boyfriend's ex-girlfriend turned altruistic lesbian who is now probably traumatized for life. Just seven weeks ago he was happy, we were happy. Well, at least *I* was happy. It suddenly dawned on me that Kai might never have felt as deeply about me as I did about him. This was *not* acceptable.

I *had* to do something to get his attention. I *had* to make him miss me. I *had* to make him care. I decided to reprise an oldie but a goodie that I *just knew* would sting.

It *had* to.

"Well, I should get going. I'm off shortly," I said with a huff. "More jet-setting and whatnot."

Whatnot?

Who says whatnot?

"Oh, that's great, that's really great." Kai sounded totally deflated.

Fantastic!

"So everything's going really well for you, huh?" he asked.

I chuckled, pleased with myself, "Oh yes, yes, yes, yes, everything's going *extremely* well if you know what I mean. Pretty, pretty, fabulous. So, *yeah.*"

Okay, seriously you sound like a complete doofus.

It's so obvious that you're morbidly depressed and trying to hide it!

"So when are you off again?" Kai asked nervously.

"Next week," I said with all the confidence of a big, fat faker.

I couldn't let Kai know how sad I was so I just prattled on like I was the coolest thing since Nutella.

"I'm off to Edifice Luxe's biggest resort in Thailand. I'm going to be spending the holidays there with a media group. It's my biggest media trip yet and like, honestly, it's going to be huge."

Shut up, shut up!

You're over-selling it!

"Kai, like, I'm telling you. *Huge.* I'm beyond excited. Like, *beyond.* Because, it's like, *huge.* You know, so, *yeah.* After this trip, who knows? I'll probably stay here forever because it's just like, wow, you know, it's going so insanely well."

OMG I sound like a complete idiot.

And yet I couldn't stop... "It's crazy, actually, how great everything is what with all the friends I have. Girls, guys, you know, a lot of friends, good, very good friends...."

Why *oh why* must I always work so hard to portray this ridiculously grandiose and fabulous life?

It's exhausting!

Can't I just say something like… "When I finish my contract, I'll be returning to Boston and I'll continue working for Edifice Luxe and yes, probably one day I'll start dating again and although I'm really hurt right now, ultimately, I'll be okay."

But no.

I have to embark on these insanely convoluted journeys of self-discovery and whirlwind jet-setting tours with garden parties at fabulous expat country clubs. Everything has to be magnificent and splendid and perfect. There has to be fashion and gossip and luxury and exoticism—my god, I sound like nutbar.

"Oh," Kai said softly and sadly. "You must be bummed about having to work over Christmas."

"I am not," I said quickly.

I was!

"Like I said, I'll be among friends…" I said coolly.

I wouldn't be!

"…it'll actually be awesome…"

It'll actually be crappy!

"…and I'm super excited to spend Christmas you know, chilling on a beach. I mean, how cool is that?"

Not very! You'll be all alone!

"Oh, that's too bad," Kai said with increasing awkwardness. "I was actually, um, thinking about coming to see you. I know it's crazy, but I really miss you, Charly, I was thinking maybe this whole thing was a mistake— uh, um, anyway, I guess it would be weird if I was your *plus one* at the resort. Because I would happily come…"

"Kai, it would be weird," I heard myself say.

It wouldn't be!

"Oh, well," sighed Kai sadly. "I just thought that maybe we could—"

"Keep in touch?" I cut him off. "You bet!"
What are you doing, you complete fruitcake?
He's reaching out to you!
Why are you rejecting him?
Did you fall down stairs?
Electrocute yourself?
Lobotomize yourself?
Eat some car tires?
Lick shoeshine?
Blackout?

I wished Kai a Merry Christmas and rushed off the phone. I sat down on my bed and started to cry silently. The love of my life just upped and ran away to New York with my dog, I wasn't going to see my friends or family for the holidays, my Pinot-marinated liver had just posted itself on Craigslist as "free to a good home", I lived in my ex-boyfriend's ex-girlfriend's loft...

Could it get any worse?

Oh... yes, it could...

I'd be spending Christmas working at Edifice Luxe's *most* romantic hotel with total strangers. If ever there was a time I wanted to tie a Louisiana grilled flank steak around my neck and swan dive naked into piranha infested waters... that was it.

Pause for a Super Painful Memory Courtesy of Kai f@*#ing Kostigan

Argh.
Must I tell this story?
It's so embarrassing.
Okay.

Back in Boston when Kai and I were together and everything was fabulous—before we left for Bangkok and before everything went horribly wrong—we decided to go for dinner at a Thai restaurant.

"I should really expand my Thai food repertoire," Kai said as he ordered a Heineken from the waitress. "I've only ever delved into that noodle dish. What's it called?"

"Phad Thai?" I offered.

"That's the one, babe." Kai said as he gently took hold of my finger tips and kissed them. I stared at my new gorgeous boyfriend and smiled.

"Well, this menu looks great," I said happily. "How about spring rolls? And, let's see, ooh, let's try the coconut curry, that looks good too."

"Sure, baby, whatever you want," Kai said as he scooped up my hand from the side of the table and nibbled at the inside of my wrist.

So romantic.
So sweet.
So full of it.

"I'm really excited for our adventure," I said of Thailand. We weren't leaving for another month but it was pretty much all I could think about. This was going to be such an amazing journey I could hardly wait. No more boring Boston with its dank pubs and grey landscape. It was a brave new world and I couldn't wait to dive in and wrap myself up in it.

"Me too babe," Kai smiled softly. "You know what? In the spirit of adventure, I think I'll try something spicy."

"Oh, how very intrepid of you!" I teased. Kai ordered Phad Thai with hot chilies and I had the curry. After dinner we took the long way home and along the way Kai suggested we pop into his favorite wine bar. Two hours later we arrived home (barely) and stumbled quietly into the condo I shared with Alégra.

"Oh my god, let's do it right here," a tipsy Kai whispered in my ear.

"Shhh," I giggled. "Don't wake Ali!"

Kai put his index finger to my lips softly and led me into the kitchen, away from the bedroom.

"Shhh," he mimicked. "Don't wake Kermit!"

Once in the kitchen, Kai hoisted me onto the granite island and tugged at my wraparound dress.

I'll spare you the x-rated details of a newly in love couple, but let's just say it got hot, hot, hot… wait a second, it got *really* hot, like, too hot…

"Holy shit, something's burning!" I squealed. I no doubt ripped half the hair off Kai's head as I removed his face from my situation.

"Jesus, Charly!" he half-yelled. "What the hell?"

"It's bbbbburning," I stammered. "What the ffffff did you eat?"

There was an insanely hot pulsating feeling *down there* and it felt as though someone had quite literally scorched my earth.

In an instant we knew.

Hot chilies. *Gah!*

I sprinted to the shower, turned it to cold, and jumped in as I was still pulling off my dress.

"Ohhhh, my god, that feels better," I yelped. Kermit had waddled his way into the bathroom to see what the commotion was and stared at me with sleepy eyes. "Kermit go back to bed, it's fine. Kai, I hate you!"

"Oh, no, Charly," Kai tried not to laugh. "I'm so sorry."

"I'm-going-to-kill-you!" I screeched as I tried awkwardly to angle my *situation* closer to the shower head.

"Shut up, you two!" Alégra moaned from the other room.

"Sorry, Ali!" we both whined.

Oh, god, it burns.

Scrubbing only seemed to further ignite the pain.

Cripes! It's as though the chilies are <u>embedded</u> in there.

This is torture!

"I totally forgot, Phad Thai with chilies, *my bad*," Kai leaned against the bathroom frame, offering condolences while trying not to chuckle.

"Yes, Kai," I scolded while I scrubbed. "*Your* bad!"

"What the hell is wrong with you two?" Alégra appeared in the doorway, sleepily hiding inside her massive white terrycloth robe. She picked Kermit up and he turned to nuzzle his head in her neck.

"Ali, he put chilies on my hoo ha!" I wailed.

"You guys are sick freaks."

Ali shook her head, turned on her heels, and took Kermit to bed.

"Oh god oh god oh god please make it stop," I pleaded.

I seriously think that's the most religious I've ever been.

"Hey," said Kai when we were alone again. He tugged away the shower curtains gently and whispered, "Want some company? Your chilies are my chilies, and if you've got 'em on your junk well, I want 'em there too."

"Get in here!" I smiled and pulled Kai into the shower, clothes and all.

31. It's Beginning to Look a lot like Christmas

Um, it really wasn't.

The Edifice Luxe property in Koh Samui I'd be spending Christmas at was decorated to an unbearable level of kitsch. There were flashy green and red light bulbs dangling off everything that stood still long enough to be lit up, neon Santa animatronic figurines that belted out "Ho! Ho! Ho!" without warning, and festive, Christmas-y versions of traditional Thai dishes: Egg Nog *Tom Yum* Spicy Shrimp Soup, Gingerbread Fried Rice, and Yule Tide Christmas Cake with papaya.

Ick!

It was Christmas Eve and since I had arrived on the flight before the media group like always, I took the opportunity to stroll around the property and check out the beach. If I was going to be working over Christmas, I thought, I might as well enjoy myself. I put on a blue one-piece swim suit (*bikinis are for people with boobs*), and pale pink cover-up and set off walking barefoot towards the water. My hair was finally starting to grow in and, for the first time in my life, I had a real beach body thanks to my inability to eat due to crippling sadness.

Ahhh, profound lack of appetite: the upside to heartbreak!

Aside from the hideous decorations that peppered the grounds, the resort *was* gorgeous. As I made my way to the beach I took in the soft breeze that fluttered through large palms. I smiled into the warm sun.

It was a bit surreal to be in a tropical climate for Christmas, but it was undeniably beautiful and incredibly luxurious.

As I walked the beach, I half-eavesdropped on the many conversations I heard along the way. Young couples stretched their barely covered bodies along colorful towels and discussed what they should do for lunch, if they would go scuba diving tomorrow, and how much they loved each other. Small families consisting of mom, dad, and diaper-clad toddler were preoccupied with their own happiness by the water as little waves lapped up the beach like a thirsty puppy. Even the *sexpats*—with little Thai girlfriends sitting dutifully on their lap—laughed and teased each other playfully. It was truly picturesque and I became cognizant of the fact that I was looking in on love, from the outside. Then something strange happened...

For the first time in ages, the sight of love didn't make me want to volunteer as that person who gets attacked by police dogs in training. Up until a week, ago I was numb and raw and wouldn't have even noticed the happy couples along the beach. (And if I did, I would have thrown sand in their faces. Just joking. Not really.)

But today, for the first time, I felt hopeful and energized at the sight of love. It was finally dawning on me that if I wanted to be happy again, that's a choice only *I* could make; it was up to me and all I had to do was say *yes*.

Yes to happiness. Yes to healing. And one day, yes to love. The rest will fall into place. I am responsible for my happiness. No one else. Not even Kai. It took me being thousands of miles away from home to remember a saying I'd heard a thousand times: it always works out in the end. If it hasn't worked out yet, well, it's not the end yet. I exhaled deeply and scanned the beach with a smile. A real smile.

"Hey, pretty girl." I knew who it was without turning around, but of course I did anyway.

"Hey Radden," I smiled. "Glad you arrived safely."

"I come bearing beer!" he announced happily.

"Ah, my hero," I smiled.

Radden was wearing board shorts and a purple polo tee with his camera strung 'round his body, as always.

He would have looked like a dorky tourist save for the fact that the camera had a telephoto lens and he carried an extra camera bag on each shoulder. Radden tossed his bags and shoes to one side as he smirked, "So, do you mind if I go topless? I'm roasting."

"Um, I think it would be okay, we're on a beach, and you're a guy," I smiled as I put my sun glasses back on and accepted a bottle of Tiger beer from my new friend.

We sat side by side in the sand as Radden unraveled his polo tee-shirt to reveal a set of abs and arms that quite frankly, I was not prepared for. I tried very hard to pretend I didn't notice but couldn't help blurting out, "All *that* from holding a camera? Wow, Shutterbug, I might take up photography."

"Ha! You're a funny one," Radden laughed in subtle disbelief. Then he teased, "What are you hiding under that granny cover up? A freakish goiter?"

"Ew!" I laughed as he nudged my arm with his and I fell back a bit. "No!"

"Oh, wait, I get it, you're just soooo hot that you're afraid you're going to be kidnapped and sold into sex slavery if you show a little skin."

"No!" I pouted but continued to smile; it felt good to be joking around with someone.

Radden grabbed my cover-up and tugged at it playfully, "Too bad. I would for sure put a bid in on *that*."

I actually took that as a compliment, like being sold as a sex slave was a good thing, and not a global human rights crisis. Holy crap I was desperate for validation. We spent the next half hour catching up.

"Sorry to hear about your girlfriend," I offered genuine condolence at the fact that she had decided not to spend Christmas with him.

Well, fine.. okay... it was as genuine as I could muster...

"Aw, naw, it's fine," said Radden. "We've been together for five years, it's just a lull, we'll be fine. She'll be back in two weeks. Everybody needs time to vent and chill out, or whatever, you know? I do miss her a lot, though."

To my shock I felt jealous of Radden's girlfriend. Not jealous in the way I was of Zoë (which was crazy, I'll admit) but jealous of how sweet he was being to her. Even though they were going through a rough patch, he had nothing but kind words to say about her. He could have criticized her or expressed frustration and she'd never have known. But he didn't. What's more, he had no doubt that they'd work out their issues. His loyalty was admirable. It was so sweet and hopeful and it gave me a great deal of faith. It also made me wonder what Kai was saying about me. We had left things so ambiguous.

At first it seemed like we were broken up, but our last conversation—where he'd offered to fly all the way here just to see me—left me confused and unsure. I really didn't know what Kai was thinking or saying about me, or about us. Hearing Radden speak so sweetly about his girlfriend gave me hope...

"Alright, Chuckles, let's go grab some lunch," Radden suggested as we finished our beer.

"Sure, just let me go change."

I was feeling so light and happy, and definitely very expat-ish, I just *had* to call Eden for a quick gossip session.

"Eden, hi!!" I said excitedly. "Did I wake you?"

"No, no it's fine, darling, it's not as though it's the *bloody* middle of the night." Eden said sleepily but clearly happy to hear from me.

"I'm shocked you're home!" I exclaimed. Eden was normally out on the town searching for her next conquest.

"You know what I've discovered, darling?" she gasped. "I'm not as young as I used to be. And, like, quite frankly, it's *exhausting* being me."

I couldn't help but laugh.

"I'm serious!" she continued. "I have to limit my whoring to the weekends now, well, and Thursdays. I've even started taking a B-12 supplement. Anyway, how are you?"

"I'm great! A little birdie told me you're thinking of taking a job in Jeeranam?"

"Oh, well, yes I am." Eden seemed to be waking up a bit. "Except that awful Wilhelmina—that marketing director I can't stand—she'll be there. Anyway, I'm still thinking about it. Hey, you should come too! Let me talk to Scott about putting you up for a role once there's something available."

"Amazing! Thank you! Now listen," I got to the point of my call. "I have quick *expat question* for you, what do I wear to lunch with Radden and the other journalists?"

"Radden?"

I blushed at hearing his name.

Why did I blush?

Do I like him?

No!

Of course not.

That's crazy talk.

"Who the hell, or *what* the hell, is a *Radden*?"

Double yikes!

Eden pressed on, "Oh. My. God. Charly Briar tell me you're not shagging one of those awful playboy travel writer types. Ugh they're such *slimeballs*."

"No, Eden! Not at all. Nothing like that. He's a photographer," I corrected her.

It's not!

"Bah! Charly Briar! That is literally one hundred times worse," Eden laughed.

"We're not sleeping together, not even close," I assured Eden. "He's got a girlfriend and we're just friends."

"Mmm hmm," said Eden with great skepticism.

"Oh, stop it!" I laughed.

"Don't say I didn't warn you my little darling," Eden laughed. "Photographers: worst of the worst."

"Anyway, thank you Eden, you're the greatest big sister I never had; now can we please move on? I've got a huge media group arriving soon and I want to look fabulous and expat-ish. This is my biggest and most important media group yet. Do I wear sandals? Flats? Linen? Silk? A dress? Pants? *Help!*"

Eden was the expert on all things *expat*, "Oh, lucky me," scoffed Eden. "She finally calls me up and, not only is it the middle of the night, but it's to ask about flip flops. That's *infinitely* more exciting than sex."

"Eden, please!" I begged.

"Alright, alright," she conceded. "First of all, it's linen all the way. And you might want to lose the sandals—but for heaven's sakes, make sure you've had a proper pedicure first. You want to be one *with* the natives, not one *of* the natives."

"Ha, ha, okay but seriously, thank you, Eden!"

"Oh, and lastly, throw on a *swish* scarf, perhaps Hermès. Think Betty Draper, not Ugly Betty."

Why would I think Ugly Betty?

"Got it," I confirmed.

"Now listen," Eden continued. "Have fun but *do not*, I repeat, *do not* get involved with this vacuous photographer playboy. They are trouble. I've told you this. All he'll give you is a broken heart and syphilis."

"Very funny," I said absent-mindedly as I rummaged in my suitcase for an Hermes scarf.

Maybe someone broke into my luggage and left it there?

"We're not going to get together. Nothing is going to happen. I'm not interested. Well, at least not in that way, I mean he's great but seriously, no, I promise, it's not like that, Eden, seriously. I'm a changed woman! And besides, *as if* I'm remotely close to being over that asshole who shall remain nameless by which I mean Kai…"

"And the babbling awards go to... Don't say I didn't warn you, Charly. Now go play expat. Ugh, I'm actually raving jealous. Boston is frigid and boring and I miss you terribly! It's not fair that you get to romp around tropical Asia without me. The more I think of it, the more I'm sure I'm going to look into a role for you in Jeeranam when your current contract is up. I want you there with me. It's settled."

"Thank you Eden!"

"Repay me by *not* hooking up with Radiator."

"*Radden*," I smiled as I corrected her. "And I'd *never* do that. He's not single. *And* he's my *one* friend here. *And* I'm not over Kai. *And* Radden's not attracted to me!"

"Mmm hmm," Eden said sleepily. "Good thing we're not in court."

I dismissed my friend's skepticism, "I miss you, Eden. Hurry up and get here! I *really* hope you take that job."

"Well I *really* hope I can find a job for you at the same resort that I end up at!" she said. "Now go away and have fun! Ciao ciao."

I threw on a pair of white linen pants, a pale grey tank, and a hot pink belt. I messed around with a scarf for about ten minutes before abandoning the idea entirely. Instead I opted for a colorful chunky necklace I'd picked up at a market near my loft and a gold cuff that Alégra had given me as a birthday present last year. I threw on my sun glasses and set off. Within a minute I rounded the corner of the hotel courtyard. It was decorated to delirium with fake Christmas trees and an ice sculpture of what I can only assume was once Rudolph. I spotted Radden sitting by himself under a thatched roof at a little outdoor bar reading *The New York Times*. He had also changed and clearly showered (*I knew I forgot something!*), and was wearing his signature faded jeans and a white polo shirt.

"You look very *expat-y*, Chuckles."

"Oh, thank you," I said nonchalantly.

I rule.

Well technically Eden rules.

"No shoes, huh?" Radden asked and I was about to become extremely embarrassed when —

"Me neither."

Yes!

I gave myself a mental self-high-five for awesomeness and sat down beside Radden for what ended up being a fantastically long lunch. By mid-afternoon the other writers and photographers of my media group were starting to trickle in. I was surprised to recognize so many editors and well known photographers. Normally the magazines sent junior writers and freelancers on press trips like the one I was hosting.

Especially over Christmas.

And since I'd always dealt with the booking manager or assignment editors when I made my pitches, I never really knew exactly who was going to show up. Writers and photographers would often be assigned at the last minute based on availability and other, more time-sensitive stories.

Corporate office would naturally prefer to have senior editors and photographers visit the hotel and I knew both the general manager and my boss back in Bangkok would be happy about the turnout of such high caliber media. Radden knew everyone and everyone knew him. This instantly made me feel at ease. It's quite daunting to host twenty-five people you haven't really met yet, and somehow, Radden's approval of me legitimized my presence as one of the "cool" PR girls.

I liked the group right away and I could tell they liked me. One by one, the girls kissed Radden on the cheek and the guys did that high-five-hand-shake-hug thing that guys do. Everyone seemed super friendly and there was a palpable lack of ego — this made me feel even more at ease. Radden naturally fit into the role of host which made sense considering he knew everyone and no one knew me. I truly didn't mind that Radden was taking on the role of welcoming committee; in fact I was thankful for the chance to relax and meet new people.

With Radden's social stamp of approval I could sit back and enjoy myself. He introduced me to the group: there was an editor for an Asian luxury lifestyle magazine, a girl who produced a travel television show, a guy who published a group of travel websites, there were a couple of photographers, and the girl who sat down beside me was a freelance writer—all expatriates.

"Hi doll, I'm Laney Booth," said a bubbly girl with a southern accent. "I'm a freelance writer for about six of the magazines you contacted. They sent me as a kind of, buy-one-get-six-free type of deal, *ha!* I'm going to do a piece about the spa, the gardens, the amazing guest service… oh gosh I can't even remember what else! Well, I'm just so glad to be here… Anyway, you must be Charly, thanks ever so much for putting this together!"

I liked Laney immediately. She had jet black wavy hair and massively pink sunglasses. She wore a bright blue dress that hung breezily over a round frame and when she laughed, her whole body wiggled.

"I hear you're a virgin," Laney mused as she lit a cigarette and passed the lighter back to a fellow writer.

"I'm sorry?" I asked with much confusion.

"You practically just got here, to Asia, *right*? You're brand new to the expat life?"

"Oh, yes!" I laughed as my cheeks reddened a little. "I am new here and I love it!"

It was only a half lie: On the one hand I didn't *love* the fact that I was dog-less, hairless, and Kai-less. On the other hand, I *did* love the parties, the Pinot, and the fresh chance to redesign myself entirely from the inside out. Being an expat, I had realized, was a second chance for me to become who I was meant to be in the first place.

Oh, yes… I like that!
A second chance to be the real me.
Sign.
Me.
Up.

"I'll bet, *darln'*," Laney's southern twang brought me back to the conversation. She sank back into a rattan chair and accepted a highly ornamented cocktail from a waitress, "Hunny, let me tell you something. Back home I was a failing journalism student at a community college that only my hillbilly friends had heard of. Here, I'm a well-known writer with a condo in Singapore and a boyfriend in, well, just about every port. Imagine that!"

"Amen sister!" another girl joined the conversation as her and Laney clinked glasses.

I *liked* these girls!

"So, um," I cleared my throat, feeling the need to take charge even just a little bit. "Should I take you ladies on a tour of the resort? I know it's in your itinerary and I thought maybe we could do a site inspection before you go for your spa treatments and —"

Laney raised her index finger and smiled a big southern smile...

"Charly, baby, I do this for a living. If I have to endure another frangipani facial or rosewater salts bath, my ass will sprout flowers."

I couldn't help but laugh.

"Don't worry, *darln'*," Laney continued. "We are here to relax and *not* be at home with our families for Christmas. Am I right ladies?"

This time, two girls chimed in, "Amen sister!"

I liked these girls a lot; they were so welcoming and free spirited. If this was expat life, sign me up. We chatted for another hour or so and in that time I learned the following things:

1. These girls were gorgeous, cool, and *bona fide* expats for at least three years each,
2. not one of them looked a day over twenty-five (even though they all were),
3. they all seemed to have something, or someone, at home they'd rather not talk about,

4. their approach to relationships was pretty much, *if I need to stand on a hill to get reception to call you, do not consider us monogamous*, and
5. where's the vino?

I was impressed. I was in awe. I was envious. Wait a tick, just wait one hot second... *I was one of them!* Well, at least I was well on my way... I'd obviously been approaching this expat thing all wrong... having a boyfriend was like having a boat anchor... yeah, totally! I turned my attention back to the group but promised to circle back on this crucial realization at a later date...

Since nobody wanted a tour of the hotel and Radden and his photographer friends had long since left us to take some shots before they lost the afternoon sun, the girls and I gabbed our way through the next couple of hours. I was insistent they tell me everything about what it was like to be an expat *woman*.

"You have to pick and choose your cultural battles," said an intelligent-looking skinny blonde girl in a khaki dress and gladiator flats. "You have to let go of familiar customs, you know, in order to navigate this place, culturally I mean."

"Yes, but," a tiny dark haired French girl in green capris and a tight white polo tee-shirt disagreed gently. "Other times, your own customs and traditions are just *too integral* to the essence of what makes you, *you*. So you must hold on to those."

A couple of the girls nodded and *mmm hmm'd* in agreement. I could tell they had a strong bond.

"Life, as an expat," Laney began in her intoxicating southern drawl. "Is a see-saw between fitting in and staying true to yourself. It's the very process—of resistance and surrender—that reveals *who you truly are*... I mean, at home, so much of who you are is already decided for you. Am I right? Whether it's high school or college, or your family or friends, or what town you come from, or who you've dated—I mean, it's just dizzying how many ways a woman can be socially pigeon-holed before she gets going in life. It's some real bullshit if you ask me."

Everyone laughed in agreement.

"As an expat, however," Laney pressed on. "You have the freedom to *discover* who you are without all that extra baggage. You can really truly *create* yourself."

Oooh, I loved that.

Laney accepted another blue drink with half a pineapple hanging off the side of it.

She took a sip and continued to drawl in her heavy accent, "Oh, and Charly *darln'*, the transient lifestyle of amazing parties, exotic travel, hot men with no last names, and zero accountability for anything you ever do? Well that ain't bad either!"

We all clinked our glasses in agreement and this time, I joined in, "Amen sister!"

32. The Nut, Conclusion

For the next six months, we stayed together, we partied together, we did everything together. It was amazing. We always had fun and never worried too much about the future, even though it was implicit that we would be together. I worried sometimes that I was falling in love with him but maybe he didn't feel the same way. As far as I knew, it was all fun for him, until one night...

"Psssst," said a very drunken boy outside my door.

I rolled over and pretended I was asleep. Sometimes one is just too tired to entertain visitors. But he was relentless.

"Charly!" The Nut faux-whispered loud enough to be heard by everyone in the hallway, I'm sure. "Charly Bean, Bean-Bean, Beaners!"

"Go away, *crazy*! I'm sleeping!"

I moaned and pulled myself up out of bed and headed towards the door.

"Argh! You two are a couple of horny baboons!" moaned Alégra from her bedroom.

"Sorry, Ali!" I whispered.

"Beans," The Nut pleaded. "Lemme in, you know you want to."

Even though he was behind my front door, I could tell he was smiling. The Nut always spoke with a smile, it was irresistible.

"No, I don't," I teased as I padded down the hallway.

"Beaners!" he exclaimed loudly as I opened the door to a very drunk man in a half open dress shirt and jeans. "I can see seven of you and you are allllll hawt!"

"Thank you, Captain Ron Bacardi," I laughed as I adjusted a midnight wedgie from my Miss Piggy pajamas. It would never have occurred to me to hide wedgies, farts, or anything really from him. The Nut never cared about that stuff.

"Come on in and *shhhh!!* Ali is sleeping."

"Well, I'm trying to!" moaned Ali.

The Nut followed me to my room and asked for something to drink on the way. By the time I had returned from the kitchen with a glass of water and two Advil, he was passed out in my bed with nothing on but half of his pants and one dirty white sock. His cell phone was in his hand and he was mid-text.

Too tempting...

I knew it was wrong but I gently took the phone from his hand and stole a quick glance at the text he was composing: "I love you so much, Beaners."

Oh boy.

I never told The Nut about the text, possibly because I wasn't ready to acknowledge it. It freaked me out and on some level, I honestly would have rather seen a text that said something about my ass or how fun I was to hang out with.

Very strange for Charly Briar, I know, I know...

But the truth was that The Nut was not the kind of guy I'd ever fall in love with, and his admission of love for me was like a sandbag to the head. There was nothing wrong with him — in fact, he was a great guy — but he wasn't *my* guy and he was never going to be, no matter what he did.

Now, I am a firm believer in love at first sight and although it was definitely *wow you're hot we should makeout* at first sight, it never grew from there. There was something about him I just couldn't take seriously. The text left me nervous and flustered and I somehow felt that I owed The Nut an *I love you* back.

So, rather than have fun, like we had been before, I started looking for things to love about him. And even though there were lots of things that I liked, I didn't find any that I *loved*. But of course, like an idiot, I told him I did, all the time. Only one week after his text message, I dropped the L-bomb back on the Nut.

In hilariously ironic fashion, he looked shocked and awkwardly said it back. We still keep in touch but let's just say it kind of dissolved from there…

Note to Boys: there's a *right* time and a *wrong* time to tell a girl you love her!

The Nut and I never actually broke up. An amazing job opportunity came up for him and I do *not* do trans-Atlantic long distance relationships. Be that as it may, I genuinely wanted him to be happy, even if that meant being without me. And to be honest, it came as a bit of a relief.

Fully Booked / Genn Pardoe

33. Merry Kissmas!

"Did you guys bang!?"

These were the first words I heard on Christmas Day.

I had scheduled a wake-up call for 9am and found it hard to believe that this was a standard Edifice Luxe greeting. I knew they differed from property to property, but somehow *did you guys bang* just didn't seem as though it would be in accordance with E.L. brand standards. I was pretty sure it wasn't my mom, either, because she generally opted for something more traditional along the lines of, "Charly... *this* is your mother," as if she was channeling Darth Vader or an airplane pilot. Also, my mom had the unique ability to *only* call when I was either completely inebriated or with a guy. How she knew what I was up to, I'll never know. I just prayed I didn't develop the same creepy intuition when I had children. Considering I wasn't drunk and there was no one in my bed, I was pretty sure it wasn't mom.

"Who is this?" I moaned just starting to take in my surroundings.

"It's your doctor," said the sardonic female voice. "Bad news, you've got herpes."

I hadn't heard Nikki's voice since coming to Bangkok and it was refreshing to see she hadn't lost her delicate embrace of the English language.

"Yay! Nikki!" I exclaimed. "I've missed you! How are you?"

"Did – you – guys – bang?"

Nikki *never* wasted any time getting to the good stuff. She would have been a great interrogator. It took me a second to register *who* exactly she was talking about. Eden must have tattled about my friendship with Radden.

"Oh, Radden? No! *Mygodno!*"

"And why not?" she shot back.

"And a Merry Christmas to you, Nikki. I hope you're not surrounded by little children at a family gathering or, oh god, you're not like, at church, are you?"

"*Me* at church? Christ no. And it's Christmas Eve, I'm fourteen hours *behind* you, remember? And in *no* time zone would I find myself in a place of worship, you know that. I'm pretty sure I would burst into flames as soon as I passed the threshold."

"Oh, right, I remember…"

Nikki had last stepped foot inside a church when she was eleven years old. It was Christmas and she was playing Mother Mary in the Nativity play. She had the loin cloths, a swaddled baby Jesus in her arms, the whole nine yards… As she was walking on stage she stubbed her toe on the wooden manger, and in front of the whole congregation accidentally blurted out, *"Son of a Whore!"*

Not a good look considering her surroundings…

"Anyway," quipped Nikki impatiently, "I'm leaving for a date in, like, five minutes. Give me the goods on this photographer guy."

"You've got a date… on Christmas Eve?"

"Yes, I do. It's with that professor who wrote the book on nihilism, Hank Zero. We hooked up at BU, remember? Anyway, nihilists don't believe in Christmas so it doesn't count, and besides, I prefer to be drunk before I face my family. We're just going to a pub, no big deal."

"*Huge* deal!" I exclaimed.

"Hey, listen, *do not* tell Alégra that I'm seeing Hank. I'm serious. You know she gets mental about that kind of stuff. And I'll *know* if you told her because you're the *only* person I'm telling. Okay?"

"Okay!" I promised.

"Anyway," Nikki continued, "tell me all about this Radden guy. I'm putting you on speaker phone while I get ready. Do you think a nihilist cares what you wear, or is that like, an obvious *no*?"

I had *never* heard Nikki talk like this. She was babbling all over the place. She was bubbly, even! There were two things I knew for sure about Nikki Temple and she was defying them both at that moment:

1. She cared more about what bark was made of than any date anyone had *ever* been on, and
2. she cared less about what she wore, *especially* for a boy.

There was only *one* possible explanation...

"You're in love!" I squealed as I shot up in my big comfy bed and pulled the soft duvet around me.

"What? No! That's retarded, well, no, I'm mean, no, I'm not, like, well, whatever," Nikki stammered.

Being in love was clearly flustering Nikki beyond words. I had never heard her talk like this before. It was contagious and I burst out laughing.

"Nikki's in love, Nikki's in love!" I chanted happily.

"I'm not in love!" Nikki protested. "Eww, don't make me go bulimic again."

"Nikki's in love, Nikki's in love!" I continued.

This was epic, this was legendary; love had never happened to Nikki before and I was thrilled to hear about it.

"I'm never going to talk to you again," she said dryly. "I swear."

Wow, she had it bad. The fact that Nikki, the *most* cynical girl on the planet, could find love, gave me hope.

"Yeah, yeah, laugh it up. Anyway, listen," Nikki turned serious as she took the phone off speaker. "I'm out the door in a sec, are you going to tell me about this guy or not?"

I didn't really have a choice at that point.

"Fine," I began. "But let me *assure* you that *nothing* happened."

The truth was that I *did* have dinner with Radden...

Just him, me, and twenty-four writers, photographers, and editors. And it was amazing. I'd had so much fun letting loose and forgetting about all the drama over the last couple of months. It was the first time in a long time that I'd lived *in the moment* and it was fun. I was alive again. I could feel again. I even went to bed without the aid of (too much) alcohol or over-the-counter sleep aids.

I slept soundly—alone—and woke up feeling like a princess in an Edifice Luxe signature King sized bed surrounded by silky pillows and plush duvets. The sun shone through my window and the essence of exotic flora from the lagoon below filled my room. Life is beautiful...

"You're full of shit," Nikki faux-believed me. "Maybe you didn't bump uglies with this camera dude, *per se*, but *something* happened. I can hear it in your voice. Now, you've only got two minutes left before Hank gets here to pick me up, and this is costing a fortune, although quite frankly, I don't pay for it... Daddy Templeton does. Anyway, not the point... *go!*"

I decided to appease Nikki even though, truthfully, there wasn't much to say, "Okay, okay. We're hung out last night... along with, like, twenty or so other people! This is my job, Nikki, I'm not on vacation."

"Okay there, Officer Briar."

"Ha, ha, okay, I'll admit it, I'm having *lots* of fun and Radden is *very* cool, but he's not my type."

"Mmmm hmmm," Nikki said in disbelief.

"Nikki, his job is to take pictures. That's literally *all* he does. And you know how I feel about anyone making a living out of what the rest of us do for fun. Not acceptable."

"Charly!? You get drunk with people who write articles in airplane magazines about hotels and spas—that's *your* job."

"And I'm very good at it," I grinned from ear-to-ear at the irony. "Anyway, in more exciting news, I'm really starting to get over Kai... I think."

"Cool," said Nikki nonchalantly. "But I still don't believe you."

"Well, believe it, I *am* getting over Kai."

"Not that," Nikki scoffed, but quickly added, "congrats, though, he's a douche. Kai has the maturity of a leaky garbage bag, and you need to *drop, him, off*. But I'm talking about Radden. You like this guy, or he likes you. I'm not sure which. But something... *something*... is going to happen. I can feel it."

"No, no, I honestly don't think—"

"Charly," Nikki's voice turned serious. "Just don't make this guy your boyfriend by default, okay?"

"Of course not," I promised. "But Nikki it's not—"

"Okay, Hank is here. I gotta go. Merry Christmas, Charly!"

"You too, Nikki. Miss you!"

An hour later I rounded the corner of the hotel's outdoor eating area to find Radden at a table by himself. He was reading *The New York Times* and he seemed comfortably settled in enough that I assumed he was on his second coffee. I instinctively smoothed my white linen knee-length dress with my palms and corrected my posture.

"Hi, Chuckles," Radden said when he spotted me.

Radden had one of the biggest, most genuine smiles I'd ever seen. It was in stark contrast to Kai's standard greeting of pursed lips and squinty eyes—as though he had a lemon in his mouth and smoke in his eyes. (Add that to my list of things I didn't miss about that sourpuss.)

"Merry Christmas, Radden," I said as I helped myself to some water from a perspiring glass on the table.

"You too," Radden said. "So, have fun last night?"

"I did, very much," I said as I squeezed two lemon wedges into my water.

"Yeah, they're awesome," he smiled. "Hey, so listen, we were thinking of renting a boat, just like a little tin can type thing. We can all pile in and find a place to go snorkeling. You in?"

I immediately knew I was *in*.

"I definitely want to come! And thanks for the invite!"

"Oh, please," he waved a hand. "It's nothing. You're doing *me* a favor by having me here. It's so great to just *get away*, you know?"

I couldn't help but smile. It seemed very odd to me to want to get away from what seemed like a perfect life. Radden was a professional five-star island hopper (with bajillionaire parents and condos in Bangkok, London and New York) who took pictures of cool stuff all day long—what is there to get away from, exactly? It sounded like a pretty sweet deal to me. As Radden and I discussed the different islands we should visit, a waitress in a somewhat revealing Mrs. Claus outfit appeared and took my order of a soy latte and large orange juice.

"You can go to buffet now, okay *na ka*? Merry Kissmas!" the Thai girl turned on her tiny little heels (but not before smiling sexily at Radden) and skipped away flirtatiously.

"Oh, look at you, *Romeo*!" I teased.

Radden blushed and swatted away the compliment, "And *now* you know why my girlfriend wants to leave Asia. Trust me, it's not me, it's the fact that I'm white and male. It's ridiculous."

I immediately empathized with this girl. I told Radden all about Kai and the girls from the market near our condo. I told him how it made me feel insecure and just a little bit jealous. (Naturally, I left out the psycho violent fantasies I'd had about the market girls; it was Christmas after all). He nodded and agreed that there is an awful double standard in Asia.

"Expat men are like kings here while expat women are, well, kind of out of place," Radden sympathized. "For that reason I'm really glad that you met Laney and the girls. You'll want a solid group of chicks to hang out with if you're going to stay here long term. You'll need your little female wolf pack!"

"You're right," I smiled. "I'm okay being a woman here. But try being a *single* woman! I get asked all the time *where's your husband?* and *why do you work?* and, oh, my favorite, *did your family send you away to Asia because you did something wrong?*"

Radden smiled kindly and told me he'd heard it all before—at least I wasn't the only girl subjected to this annoying treatment.

"I'm so glad I met those girls," I continued. "I can see why they all stick together."

Radden chuckled, "Aw, well, I'm glad you're in our little group, Chuckles. You are a welcome addition."

"Thank you," I smiled.

"Owange joosh and soy latte, *na ka*," announced the waitress as she returned and placed the beverages on the table.

"*Kap kun ka*", I said in thanks.

The waitress started to leave but stopped herself, turned around, and bent over me and my loose linen dress. She put her face just inches above my belly button and again, she said, "Merry Kissmas!"

And as she did, she giggled animatedly and waved to my stomach in a gesture that was totally perplexing until all of a sudden, it wasn't. She was saying *Merry Kissmas* to my unborn child. She thought I was pregnant.

Oh, for the love of popped collars!

One step forward, two steps back in this place, huh?

Breathe.

Okay, now, anyone who has *ever* been unceremoniously dumped by the love of their life and fallen into *such* a depressive state that alcohol, hysterical fits of dry heaving, and a complete loss of appetite has become as natural as *breathing* understands what I went through.

Experiencing *such* extreme and involuntary body mutation does not produce a killer bikini body but rather, a skeletal frame of unevenly distributed fat and lack thereof. Any body parts that aren't already permanently affixed by bone or cartilage become sunken in. This renders hipbones, knee-caps, and resistant cellulite all the more prominent. So, fine, I'll admit, maybe I had the teeniest tiniest *ponch*.

But a baby bump?

A baby bump!!

I looked down as beyond-embarrassed blood flooded my face. I smoothed my dress once again, this time over the one teeny tiny miniscule bit of tummy that emerged beyond the surface of an otherwise completely flat abs. I had lost almost 15 pounds, my face was sunken in, my bum was a pancake, my boobs were *what boobs?*, and the only protrusion on my entire body, aside from my nose and elbows, was my itsy bitsy ponch.

The irony of course was that the only reason it was visible *at all* was because everything else was gone. At that moment I felt that life was unfair in about a hundred different ways.

"sofaphg woagesup caofehba bsfareupg na ka!" Radden barked something in Thai at the waitress who immediately looked down to the ground.

Apparently now it was her turn to feel embarrassed. Her wild giggling stopped abruptly and her flawless olive skin went a blotchy shade of pomegranate. She turned around slowly and sauntered away, clearly deflated.

"What did you—" I began to ask but Radden put his hand on mine to stop me.

"Don't *ever* listen to anyone. You're gorgeous and she's an idiot and besides, you're way tougher than that. Don't let it get to you. Okay, Charly?"

"Sure, sure," I waved a hand nonchalantly.

I was beyond mortified at having to rely on Radden to rescue me from a waitress who totally baby-shamed me.

Who does that!?

"Look at me, Charly, I am serious," Radden pressed on. "You cannot let that stuff get to you. You're one tough cookie."

I laughed softly in response but kept my gaze down, still embarrassed.

"But a *beautiful* cookie," Radden added. "Like a homemade cookie that's all gooey and warm, none of that store-bought bull shit."

I started to laugh a bit more.

"Okay, okay, thank you Radden. I feel better. Thank you for your ridiculous cookie analogy. I don't know why, but that made me feel better."

"Because you're a good cookie," he smiled softly.

"I think that's *good egg*," I corrected.

"Oh, shush it, smarty pants," Radden put his arm around me and I let out a happy sigh of relief. "Aw, Chuckles needs a hug!"

I laughed more and put my arms around my new friend — it felt good to get a hug.

"Listen, Charly, I know you're going through a breakup," Radden said as we hugged. "And you're relatively new to the expat life. And you're working on Christmas. And you're away from friends and family. That's a lot to take in all at once."

I nodded in agreement.

Radden continued, "Don't be so hard on yourself. Just chill, you know? You gotta be *easy like Sunday morning*! Do you some yoga or whatever it is you chicks do to not be mental."

"Psychology major?" I teased.

"Ha!" Radden guffawed. "More like complete *drop-out*."

We cruised the buffet together and I opted for copious amounts of bacon, two bagels, cheese, a Western omelet, and a hardboiled egg. Not exactly the traditional Christmas breakfast of my childhood but thanks to Radden's kind words I was enjoying having an actual appetite for the first time in over six weeks.

We returned to the table as a *new* waitress was topping up my orange juice. I didn't bother saying thank you.

"So, what's the plan after you're done your contract with Edifice Luxe?" Radden caught me off guard.

The truth was that I'd initially thought I would return to Boston. But of course that was when Kai was in the picture... Maybe we'd get back together and maybe we wouldn't; I was getting tired of waiting around for him to make up his mind. And then I realized I was waiting for him to make up his mind about my future...

Which is stupid...
I see that now...

In fact, the further away I got from our last phone call, the more I realized what complete jerk he was. Leaving, then offering to come back, then saying he missed me, then not coming back.

Eeks, what a headache.

The whole experience had been a blow to the ego (not to mention shattering for my heart) but the truth was that, if Kai wasn't the one for me, I should stop wasting time worrying about it. My soul mate was out there, *somewhere*, and every second I wasted on Kai was a second I could be spending on finding that person or, even more importantly, finding myself.

You know what?
Maybe I'll stay in Asia just a bit longer...

"Well," I began, "actually, I was thinking —"

"Charly, is *that* you?" a sweet sounding female voice beckoned.

It was coming from behind a fruit display of mini pineapple Christmas trees and a Menorah made of blueberries. I scanned the breakfast tables and saw no one. Must be another *Charlie*....

"Anyway, Radden, sorry, I thought I heard my name. So, yeah as I was saying, I'm seriously thinking of staying in Asia for a while. It was an adjustment at first, but I really do love it here now."

"That's great," smiled Radden.

"Yeah, I mean. Maybe even looking for a transfer within Edifice Luxe. I'd really like to head over to Jeeranam. My colleague and friend, Eden, is accepting a job there, and I might like to check it out. Jeeranam is totally secluded, and I've always worked in corporate, so it'd be really cool to be based at a resort and —"

"Charly?" that voice was at it again.

"Weird, I just heard it too," Radden said as he looked around.

"*So* weird," I shrugged. "I don't see anyone. So, anyway, yes, I mean I *love* the freedom that comes with this job but maybe I'd like to be settled at a resort for a while. Maybe in marketing, although I really am enjoying PR. I feel as though I've come a long —"

"Charly! Charly *Briar*? Is that you?"

I turned around and instantly became winded from the shock of seeing her. Dear Universe, you've *got* to be kidding me.

"Charly! I *knew* it was you!" the girl's eyes narrowed as she turned her eagle-eye focus to Radden. "Uh, um, *wow*, jeez, this must be *so* awkward for you running into me after everything that's happened with Kai, in *my* loft, and here you are with, well whatever, anyway I didn't mean to interrupt."

"Then why did you?" Radden asked coldly as he stared the girl down with hard eyes.

Although I appreciated Radden sticking up for me, it couldn't have been to a worse person...

"Radden," I said as calmly as I could considering I was having four panic attacks at once, "Meet Zoë. Zoë, meet Radden."

Honestly, I'd rather be bobbing for apples in a lobster tank.

¤ * § * ¤

Despite an astronomically awkward introduction between Radden and Zoë during which I somehow forgot the words for: "Radden is a photographer and seeing as *this* is one of the many hotels I run PR for, he was invited along with *twenty or so* other members of the media for a press junket. They should be here shortly and despite how this looks — the two of us sitting together at a table on Christmas morning at a romantic resort — there's actually *nothing* shady happening, and Zoë, could you just *please* go back to the muddy little hole you squiggled out of? Thank you," the trip actually was a huge success. I landed in back in Bangkok on the 29th of December and when I turned on my phone I saw that I had a message from Kai. It'd been weeks since I'd heard from him so I eagerly returned the call from the cab on my way home.

"Hey, it's me," I said quickly. "Merry belated Christmas."

OMG.

Really?

I was somewhat nervous considering I'd just run into Kai's perfect ex-girlfriend with a *really* good looking guy on my arm (not that it's *any* of Kai's business, quite frankly) but I'll admit that it *looked* suspicious. Nothing happened between Radden and me and that evil pixie midget *must* have been able to see that. Still, as Kai's little pet, Zoë had the power to mess with my future in terms of Kai and me getting back together. (Which I'm not even sure I wanted — but it's good to keep one's options open.) I just *had* to trust that even though Zoë wasn't on the same team as me anymore, she was still on the same side. After all, she dated Kai too.

"Merry belated Christmas, Charly." Kai said in a tone that instilled great nervousness in me.

"Um, you called?" I said, hating myself for succumbing to his games. "I saw that you, um, called?"

"Did I call?" Kai seemed disoriented, sedated even.

"Kai, what's up?"

"I have something to tell you Charly," he said.

Oh shit.

He knows about Radden and me.

But there is no Radden and me!

"Yes?" I said with great fear.

This tension was too much for me to handle and I was just about to come clean about the mistaken case of me and Radden when —

"I lost Kermit."

Of *all* the things I expected Kai to say, "I lost the most important, most precious furry man in your life" was *not* one of them. Not even close. My heart sank. No, my heart plummeted. The thought of my little Kermit, my tiny baby with his wet nose and wiggly bum, roaming the streets of New York, lost and completely terrified, it was too much for me to handle. I burst into tears.

"I'm so, so, so sorry, Charly."

"How could you let this happen?" I sobbed.

What followed was a lengthy exchange of accusatory questions and frantic apologies.

Kai promised that he would do his best to search for Kermit — who apparently had shimmied out of his leash mid-walk and bolted — but I was too furious to listen. I felt so helpless being stuck half way around the world. I wanted to reach through the phone and throttle Kai. And then go find Kermit. I was at a complete loss of what to do or how to react. None of this would have happened if Kai didn't leave for New York. I told him so and he was forced to agree.

"Yeah, I know, I know, I know... you're right, babe. Honestly, I should *not* have left; I have no idea what I was thinking. Everything's turned to shit without you. This never would've happened if I didn't leave."

It was the first time that Kai's voice had a hint of humanity to it. I couldn't believe he was fully and completely admitting that it had been a mistake to leave me. Major breakthrough!

Maybe this was the beginning of us getting back together. I wasn't even sure if I wanted to get back together, but I was definitely sure I wanted Kai to *want to* get back together. He cleared his throat in a way that signified he was about to acknowledge that he was *totally* wrong and that we were meant to be together.

"You're right," Kai began slowly and sweetly. "This would *not* have happened if I didn't leave. And I'm so sorry for that. And, also, you probably wouldn't have spent Christmas fucking that douchebag photographer, *either.*"

Just, great.

34. The Ball Drops

Ok Miss Briar, now you're, like, in serious trouble, lol.

Jeez, for a girl who works in communications you pretty much suck at this whole pen pal thing... I've written a couple times and I'm not getting so much as a text to say "leave me alone!"

You're starting to give a guy a complex, and honestly, if you refuse to be on Facebook, how am I supposed to stalk you? Joking... but seriously, drop a bro a line, would ya?

I hope you're doing well, that's all. And I'm sure you've figured it out by now... you've gotten under my skin, Charly, and quite frankly, you're harder to forget than I thought you'd be... I find myself not wanting to forget you... Actually, I'm missing you more and more as days go by. It isn't supposed to work like that...

It's, like, every time something funny happens, I want to laugh with you. When I'm bummed out about something, I want to call you. I wonder what you're doing, and if you're happy. I hope you are.

Anyway, I'm starting to sound like a serious weirdo... so despite all this gushy talk, which is so not my style btw, this is my last letter...

xx
Me.

I couldn't even possibly begin to deal with *that* right now. So much had happened, so much time had passed. I was so emotionally exhausted from recent events—it was official, Kai and I were over—I just needed to be alone for a while. For, like, a century or two. I put the letter aside, but, unlike the other letters he had sent me, I didn't hide this one. There was no need to. I didn't have to tuck it away somewhere secretive so that Kai wouldn't find it. That's because there was no Kai.

Kai was my ex-boyfriend.
I was Kai's ex-girlfriend.
Ugh.

"Oh, Kai Kostigan? Yes, I know him," I said to the mirror. "He's my ex-boyfriend."

Words I never thought I'd say…

When we first met, Kai referenced his relationship with Zoë as *that ship has sailed*. Now, I too, was on that ship. Kai would eventually meet some new girl and move on. She'd ask about his life *before* and I'd have no more importance in the story than Zoë did. The thought of this made my stomach churn.

"Oh, I dated some girl named Charly, it didn't work out," Kai would say casually over breakfast in bed one morning. "Before Charly, there was Zoë the lesbian."

Then they'd laugh about it and have a passionate makeout session and probably get married that afternoon and have a hundred babies. That's it. That's how I go down in Kai's history: Post-lesbian Beantown girl with slouchy boots and hyper-neurosis.

Great.

I cringed at all that wasted effort, the lost time, and the stupid little fart that started it all… Anyway, doesn't matter. The Kai & Charly chapter had come to a close and it was time to look forward. My contract would be completed in three months. I had to spend one month debriefing in the Bangkok office but what happens after that, I wasn't entirely sure.

I was still toying around with the idea of staying on as an expat in this strange land. After all, I'd only just begun to delve in to this new world and, rather than being scared off by a bumpy start, I felt as though I should force myself to focus on all of the amazing aspects of my current situation. I made a list of all the amazing aspects of my current situation:

1. I don't really know anyone in Bangkok so there are no expectations of who I *ought* to be.
2. So that means...
3. I can start fresh.
4. I can re-invent myself.
5. I can be *any* Charly I want to be.
6. And what better time to wipe the slate clean than New Year's Eve?

This thought was scary and thrilling all at once. I could wipe the slate clean and start over with a blank canvas, new brushes, and a fresh set of paint. And, what better way to kick off the new me than by going to Radden's New Year's party with a whole new set of friends? *Brilliant!* Radden had insisted that I come to his loft for New Year's Eve, and since I had nowhere else to be that night (and there are fewer things *more* pathetic than a newly single girl staying home alone on December 31st) so I immediately agreed.

¤ * § * ¤

"To the new me," I cheered to the girl in the mirror on New Year's Eve as I began to get ready.

I put on my Backtrack Soundtrack—the one that went from the nineties to Motown—and slipped on a simple black three-quarter-length dress with a high neckline and plunging V down the back. I couldn't wear a bra with the dress but it's not as though my deflated boobs needed one.

Thank you very <u>little</u>, Kai.
Anyway... Moving on...

I tied up the soft ribbons on my brand new indigo strappy-stilettos and put on shimmery New Year's Eve-appropriate makeup, but not too much. I pinned my hair into a faux-fringe and actually managed to pull off a pretty cute coif. The final touches included a gold cuff (both Alégra and Eden had told me that bangles were for high-school kids) and a spritz of some no-name perfume I'd recently found at the market. It was a blend of classically safe vanilla with a hint of wild lotus; it smelled like *expat* and it perfectly encapsulated *the new* Charly Briar. I looked in the mirror again and, for the first time in a long time, I smiled genuinely at the girl looking back at me. I admired my dewy reflection (a blessed change from pasty and pale) as my playlist shifted into Motown tunes. I poured myself a pre-party Pinot in celebration. (It's not drinking alone if you're planning on meeting up with people later, by the way.)

"Well, hey there good looking," I said to myself as I started to rock out a bit, just a little bit, to the tunes of Marvin Gaye's Party People. I did little twirls and hip shakes. I have no idea what my moves looked like—probably like the last moments of a gopher dying from rat poison—but it didn't matter. I was alone and, finally, it wasn't asphyxiating, it was *freeing*.

Radden's loft was on the other side of the Chao Praya River from where I lived so I took a cab there. I didn't want to risk messing up my carefully constructed coif on the back of a motorbike. I could smell expat party smells as soon as I got off the elevator: lemongrass candles that take ages to burn, imported French perfume, and expensive champagne. All of these foreign fragrances eked out of Radden's doorway at the end of the hall and wafted towards me slowly. I floated towards the intoxicating smells like Sleeping Beauty towards the spinning needle that totes knocked her out: completely hypnotized and cautious but mostly euphoric.

"Chuckles!" a very inebriated Radden stood in the doorway as I approached it. "Oh, hello pretty girl! I'm so glad you made it!"

He reached for me drunkenly and wrapped me up in his arms in salutation. But just as quickly, he let go and whisked me in to the party. It was 10pm and Radden's loft — which was at least twice the size of mine — was wall-to-wall expatriates. I rounded the corner to be greeted by a huge open space illuminated by golden Chinese mini-patio lanterns and indoor-safe Tiki torches.

Festive voices were loud and happy, and just a little diluted by the sound of funky African drums and house beats. First impression: overwhelmed. Walking into Radden's loft was like walking into the home of Indiana Jones and Kofi Anan's lovechild; him and his girlfriend had obviously travelled the world together, and along the way, picked up every trinket and artifact of *every* culture they'd come across. It was like walking into a private art collection curated by two lovers. I found it interesting, though, that there were no pics of Radden *or* his girlfriend.

I continued to survey the space. Radden and his girlfriend lived in a *hard loft* which means that the walls were concrete and the ceiling was unfinished. Where my loft was crisp and white, Radden's was stark and grey. Not that there was much opportunity to look at the walls: every available space was ornamented with ebony tribal masks and vibrant tapestries: there was a throw rug I *swear* was made of Woolly Mammoth, and in the corner was the biggest didgeridoo I've ever seen. In another corner was a mess of travel guides; one of them opened to a page on scuba diving in Papua New Guinea and another depicting hang gliding in the Azores. There was also a gigantic mound of Nepalese yarn in the corner by the fire place, and a natural sponge from the ocean as big as my bathtub.

Jeez, did you two <u>bother</u> to leave anything behind in the third world?

Radden sensed my shyness at my new surroundings and slurred, "Get in here, Chuckles, and join the party, you look fantastic!"

Radden looked pretty good himself: khakis, loafers, and a pale blue dress shirt rolled up to the elbows and undone one button too many. Unlike the over-dressed disaster I had been at the British Club, I was relieved to see that everyone at Radden's party was in appropriate attire: stylish frocks, tailored shirts, and even a couple of die-hard New Year's Eve types with taffeta skirts and seventies-style tuxedos (worn ironically, I *hoped*).

"Thank you, Shutterbug," I smiled as Radden took my hand, led me into the party, and handed me a glass of Pinot. I greatly appreciated that he remembered my beverage of choice.

"The other pretty girls are in the kitchen, go join your people."

I was grateful to be able to leave the main party area just as quickly as I had entered it. I needed to ease into expat socializing and was anxious to see the new gal pals I'd met on the trip over Christmas. With modern slabs of smooth granite contradicting rocky backsplashes and sleek faucets, Radden's kitchen looked as though it had been carved out of a cave.

The mixture of rich dark colors with cold metallic fixtures; it was straight out of an old James Bond movie where the evil villain has an ultra-modern lab deep underground, "This is the coolest kitchen I've ever seen," I cooed.

"I know!" said Laney as she kissed my cheeks hello and gave me a warm hug in salutation.

We all sat on different edge of the massive counter top island; I said hi to the rest of the girls and briefly caught up on the last couple of days of gossip.

"Hey," whispered one them and we all leaned in conspiratorially. "Has anyone noticed who's *not* at this party?"

"I know," said another with a raised eyebrow.

"Mmm hmm," said the intelligent looking blonde as she sipped on pink champagne in a mini bottle with a hot pink straw.

"Well, I mean, on the one hand it's somewhat unexpected," said Laney. "On the other, are we really *that* shocked? It was bound to happen eventually."

"Who are we talking about?" I asked curiously as the intelligent looking blonde offered me a sip of her champagne. "Oh, that's good!"

Two ginger-haired girls with cute bobs in almost identical blue frocks looked over their shoulders and craned their necks towards me to whisper, "Radden's girlfriend."

"Oh," I said. "I thought maybe she'd be back by now. Is she not coming back until after the holidays?"

The two ginger girls looked at each other and giggled almost mutedly before hiding their smiles behind sips of champagne.

"Oh, sweetie, no," said Laney quietly. "That's just what he tells people. I mean, it *is* true, she's visiting family, but not because it's Christmas."

"Oh, really?" I said curiously.

"Oh, really!" exclaimed Laney, trying to keep her voice down. "Here's the skinny on Radden's girlfriend: she *never* liked the expat life and has been *dying* to get back home since they moved to Bangkok."

"Are you serious?" I asked.

Okay, what kind of dipstick doesn't prefer the expat life?
It's so much better!

Laney continued, "Oh yeah, to be honest, she's been trying to domesticate him since they met. Talk about *Mission: Impossible*! Anyway, her trips back home have become longer and longer. Nowadays, it's more like she lives back home in New York and visits Radden only once in a while."

I made a sad face to signify that I was empathetic towards significant others who want to be back home in *stupid old* New York with friends and family and familiarity and blah blah blah.

Nothing against New York. I love New York. Just not the total dipshit who can't make up his mind who lives there...

"What she never realized is that you just can't unscramble a scrambled egg. And that," Laney nodded her head in Radden's direction. "Is one *scrambled* egg."

I found it *very* curious that Radden had not divulged the severity of his relationship status to me. Maybe it was because of what I was going through with Kai, maybe he was afraid it would come true if he talked about it, or maybe he was just private. I couldn't decide if the reason Radden hadn't told me about his relationship troubles had to do with me, or him.

"Oh, well, I am sorry to hear about their troubles," I said as genuine-sounding as I could muster.

"Well, whatever," said one of the gingers. "Radden needs to let go of her. A fish and a bird can love each other, but it doesn't mean they can live together happily ever after."

She had a really good point.

(I immediately envisioned myself as a beautiful raven soaring free above the earth and Kai, as one of those gross sucker fish, who just swim around all day being aloof and non-committal.)

"And, besides," the other ginger leaned in. "She can't hog him to herself when she barely uses him! Let him go or, at least, share the wealth, girl!"

They all giggled except for Laney, "Aw, poor girl, that's not fair. Be nice to her. It's not her fault she doesn't enjoy life abroad."

Um yes it is!

"*She's* not being fair *to us!* Radden is hot—have you seen his arms? *My god!* And, did you know that he rock climbs too? That's, like, so sexy. I think he does a bit of writing too. And anyway, the point is, he actually *is* one of the few good guys out there. It's unfair to keep him off the market like that. She's greedy, plain and simple. That's all there is to it."

Laney's face softened into a little mischievous smile as she caved in, "Well, I'm not going to argue with that."

"I never liked her," admitted the intelligent looking blonde as she took the conversation in a decidedly blunt direction. "I've had more engaging dialogue with bubble wrap."

"I know!" squealed yet another, encouraged by the admission of her friend. "I never got what he saw in her. She's kind of chunky!

"I know!" hissed Laney, completely surrendering to the fun of being mean. "Like, after a certain point, they're not *skinny jeans* anymore, *darln'*. I don't care what The Gap tells you!"

"And, I'm not trying to be a bitch, but she honestly smelled like kibble, *I swear!*" said another girl as she burst into laughter, taking a few of the girls down with her in a full-on giggle-fit. All of a sudden, the kitchen became a gossip-bomb shelter and I did *not* want to step outside of it. The girls and I eventually moved past Radden's girlfriend and found other topics of conversation including, of course, my situation.

"What about you, Charly?" one of the gingers asked. "Where's your beau this eve?"

"Oh, yeah, not so much," I stared at the floor. "We broke up almost six weeks ago actually. Anyway, he's back in New York."

All of the girls made sad faces and offered me more wine. One of them even gave me a hug and offered a kindly, "*Fuck that.*"

"Don't worry," the intelligent looking blonde girl said. "Ruin is the road to recovery. It's all for the best, you'll see."

"And, sometimes, rejection is the universe's form of protection," added one of the gingers. "There really is a reason for this, I promise."

"And, also, he's a complete *shitstain*," said Laney bluntly.

We all laughed and agreed, and blessedly, changed topics. Eventually we tuned in to the rest of the party just in time to hear the countdown to midnight begin. We all hustled to get out onto Radden's balcony and I rang in the New Year with new friends and a new outlook on life: everything was going to be just fine. I realized that if I surrendered to the universe and stopped planning so much, who I *was* and who I *wanted* to be would eventually be the same person. I was thrilled, I was excited, I was… hammered. The next morning I woke up in Radden's bed with a hangover the size of Tokyo and a text message beeping in my purse.

Fully Booked / Genn Pardoe

35. What a Dirty Clean Slate You Have...

```
Hapy Neew Yr.
Sory I'm am ashol.
I love us. Kai.
```

I was about to respond to Kai—although what exactly I wanted to say I'm not sure—when my phone rang, "Hello?"

"Spill it."

"*You* spill it," I shot back at Nikki.

I was in Radden's bed, it was January 1st, and I was dying slowly of every type of alcohol poisoning ever been invented.

W.

T.

F?

"What are *you* talking about?" Nikki retorted.

I may have been rapaciously hungover, but I *still* remembered the latest gossip: Nikki was in love with the famous nihilist, Hank Zero. She'd had a date with him on Christmas Eve and I'd yet to hear how it went.

"Your date," I reminded her. "You reignited your little flame, the famous nihilist, Hank Zero, *remember?*"

"You bag of hammers!" scolded Nikki. "Alégra is on the phone. We called you on three-way."

"Hi, Charly, Happy New Year!" Alégra chimed in. "Nikki, I'm going to *kill* you."

"Oh, shit, sorry Nik."

I opened my eyes with great pain and took stock of my surroundings: The sun was beaming in through the windows—*Radden's* windows—and I had more questions than answers.

I had just woken up to Kai's drunken text message.

I had just spilled the beans on Nikki dating that nihilist guy.

Oh yeah, and I was in Radden's %^*&#^ bed!

I pulled the duvet over my head in the hopes that everyone would go away.

"Charly!?" bellowed Nikki. "Are you there?"

I faux-cried, "I love you two but *why* are you calling me at this time? It's like, zero o'clock in the morning. I just went to bed."

My dry lips and mouth stuck together audibly, making more noise than my actual voice.

Sexy.

"It's three in the afternoon your time, I checked," Nikki was clearly unimpressed with my state.

"And, we called to wish you a Happy New Year," added Alégra somewhat awkwardly, as though half her brain was occupied with scheming up a plan to punish Nikki for not telling her about the nihilist.

"Whrrr rrrrrr you guys?" I moaned, still utterly confused and sounding more like a drunken pirate than a fabulous expat.

"Hey, Captain Morgan, wake up. We're at my place and we want to know what you got up to last night, how you're doing, when you're coming home, the usual," said Nikki. "And this is costing like a hundred bucks a minute... so spill it!"

Without thinking I quipped back at her, "What do you care? I thought Daddy Templeton took care of it."

"*What* did you say?!"

"What did you *say*!?"

"Uh, what *did* I say?"

As soon as the words fell from my mouth I wished I could suck them back in again. Did I just blow Nikki's super-secret identity and reveal to Alégra that it was Nikki's father, Dusty Templeton, who seduced Alégra's mother out of a job and got her pregnant resulting in, um, Alégra? Did I seriously just reveal that Nikki and Alégra are half-sisters?

!^&#@%!!?*

I could hear Alégra breathing deeply, trying to compose herself.

"Look, I already knew—" Alégra began but was interrupted by Nikki.

She already knew?!

What the what?!

"Alégra," Nikki moaned guiltily. "It doesn't matter, I'm sorry, I just—"

"Close your mouth Nicola," Alégra said sharply.

I had *never* heard Alégra talk like that. A whole minute passed without a word from anyone. Finally, Alégra spoke again, "Look, I *knew* already. I knew all about it. I just didn't know that *you* knew, Charly. How could you do this to me? You're a secret-keeper!"

"Oh, my, god, Alégra," I started to say. "I'm so unbelievably sorry."

"Whatever, Charly!" Alégra shot back at me. "I can't believe you. Oh, and the other reason I called, by the way... I'm getting married, yes, MARRIED. Teddy proposed—you'd know that if you checked in once in a while. I can't even believe how mad I am at you right now!"

And with that, Alégra slammed the phone down.

She knew all along?
She's getting married?
Huh?
What is going on?
How did I get myself so out of the loop with my friends and everything familiar?

"Nikki, oh my god you have to do something!" I cried.

"I'm sure it'll be fine, but listen, I gotta go."

And then Nikki hung up.

Happy New Year, New Me.

Radden, Kai or Alégra... I literally could *not* decide which crisis to address first. This was *not* the fabulous new start I had been hoping for. My thoughts were interrupted by a cheery male voice.

"Happy New Year, pretty girl," Radden rounded the corner with a mug of tea in his hand and offered it to me.

Of *all* the remedies I turn to when hung over: water, pain killers, cold pizza, hot pizza, Diet Coke, instant noodles, television, Chinese food, pajamas, texting, hiding under the blanket, movies, sex, potato chips, French fries, tater tots (anything potato based will do), 'hair of the dog', cheese, water again, spicy food, moaning about my agony to anyone who will listen, Mexican food, swearing off drinking and threatening to take my own life in an unnecessarily creative way... tea is/was/will never be one of them.

"Yuck."

"It's herbal, from Nepal, it'll kick your hangover. Trust me."
Double yuck.
That was the first thing I said to Radden after we spent the night together.
OMG!
We spent the night together!
Did we spend the night together?
Why don't I remember if we spent the night together?!
It eventually came back to me as it usually does, in increasingly fast snippets, like an old film reel.
Everybody left.
We were in the kitchen. I was sitting on the island in the center of the room. Radden stood in front of my knees, then between them.
OMG.
OMG.
OMG.
It's all coming back to me.
The snippets became faster and faster and more intense, as though accompanied by a quickening heartbeat. It was tension-filled. Just the two of us. His fingertips brushed the tops of my thighs. We talked only a little but stared at each other a lot. He said I looked great. I blushed and looked down.

Our finger tips touched and I *know* we both felt a jolt of electricity run through our bodies. He told me he was thrilled that I came to his party. I said thank you for inviting me as I tugged on his belt pulling come closer.

He put his lips close to my ear and whispered that despite us both being somewhat tied up with other people, he was happy I was in his life and he wanted more of me. Hearing him say that sent me flying.

Again, he stepped closer towards me and brought his lips closer to my neck. He pulled my hair back and whispered to me, *Charly, you can go crash in my room, I'll take the couch.*
Oh.
Right.
Of course!
Whoa.
Radden really is a good guy!
Nothing happened.
Hmmm.

Not the path I would have taken...
....but I guess I can respect his decision.
Kind of.
Well, let's be honest.
It's not like he's an angel.
I am in his bed after all.
This made me feel better.

I made little snow angels in his duvet to stake my claim and yes, if I'd have been a terrier, I would have peed a little. Obviously, I *had* to make my presence known in the House of Radden. But of course I'm not a terrier (although it remains to be seen if I'm a huge bitch), so I did the next best thing: I left two bobby pins on the bathroom sink. Was it immature? Yes. Did it feel badass? Hells yeah.

Oh, give me a break!
I've just been dumped.
It's not like he's married.
Oh god I hope he's not married.
And whatever, nothing happened!
Well.
Nothing-ish...
After taking a shower I felt like a human again.
A shameful human, but a human nonetheless.

I returned to Radden's bedroom to see him standing in the corner by his desk, playing with a camera. He was only wearing track pants.

Argh!
So many ways to interpret this situation!
At the very least it's moderately inappropriate.
Well..
At least on his end that is.
What's my role here?
So confused!

"How come you never take my picture?" I asked as I got back into his bed. I had *no* choice: there was nowhere else to sit comfortably in the entire bedroom and besides, I was only wearing only a towel.

"Ohhhh no, no, no...." Radden laughed to himself. "That would not be very wise."

"Why not?" I asked as I propped myself up against a couple of pillows and pulled the duvet up tight under my arms.

Radden continued to smile to himself as he put the camera down gently, turned around, and walked towards me slowly. He came around the side of the bed and lay on top of the duvet facing me. He was far enough way that legitimately, we could "just" be talking. I mean, I'd spent tons of nights in Alégra's bed gossiping and hanging out. It didn't make us lovers or anything like that. And besides, Radden wasn't even touching me (nor did it seem like he was going to make any effort to do so). I couldn't help but inch towards him.

"Because, pretty girl," Radden said with a mischievous smile as he moved closer too. "If I took your picture, I would have a hard time, *just* taking your picture."

"You think so?" I asked as my temperature rose and I found myself leaning towards him.

"I know so," Radden blushed and looked away but continued to move his body closer to mine. "You know what I think of you, Ms. Briar?"

"What?" I smiled as Radden inched close enough to whisper in my ear softly. I felt his lips against my ear.

"This girl is going to be the death of me."

"Hope so," I smiled.

36. The Come Down's a Bitch

I spent the next four days at Radden's place doing nothing beyond taking up space in his California King sized bed. It was heaven. It was the break from my life I so desperately needed and I was thankful for him. We laughed and ate and napped and wrapped ourselves up in each other. We got completely lost in our stories and spent most nights awake and most days sleeping. We drank and lounged and smoked cigarettes on the balcony.

We put on music and then searched the loft for the best spot, acoustically, to lie down and listen to it. And finally, he took my picture. It was the most indulgent four days of my life and completely unlike anything I'd ever experienced. For four days we shut the world out. For four days, we were perfect.

That's the time I'll remember.

Eventually, though, we hauled ourselves back into civilization. Back to our lives. Back to our *condition*, as Radden called it. He had to go away on assignment for a week. I went to meet Laney for lunch at the Mariott.

I pushed through the heavy doors towards the patio—I knew now that that's where expats ate lunch—and made my way over to say hello to my new friend.

"Hi, lady!"

We double-cheek kissed hello and I sat down. Laney folded her menu, put it to the side and without warning, she exclaimed, "Well somebody's glowing! Who's been in your pants, missy?"

Um...
Radden!
Radden's been in my pants!
Yippee!

I immediately blushed and waved a dismissive hand, "Oh, god, nobody! Ha! That's so funny as if that'd ever happen, like, no way!"

May have over-sold it a bit.

I was thankful that Laney had left the New Year's party relatively early (from what I could remember) and she'd had no idea that I stayed at Radden's that night—or the next four days. I was glad I didn't have to explain myself to her, or to anyone, because I had absolutely no clue how to articulate it.

With Radden and me, it felt best to let everything happen organically. Like a slow moving song that kept playing over and over; I didn't want to put words to it for fear I'd lose that unbelievable feeling. Forget the emotional outcome—I wasn't even there yet—I was still fumbling around in elation from it all. The only thing that *wasn't* amazing was saying goodbye to Radden; I'm pretty sure we would have stayed in that bed for eternity if it weren't for the fact that he had to go away on assignment and I had to get back to work. We'd lingered in the kitchen as he made coffee, we'd lingered on the couch as we drank it, and finally, we'd lingered in the doorway, kissing goodbye.

It took three hours to get out of his loft and every second of it was bursting with bittersweet bliss. I floated back to my condo and I couldn't wait to see him again. As I happily strolled through the market close to home I took in the smells of mango, sweet-and-sour sauce, and fresh BBQ. I felt renewed and happy and I laughed to myself that Radden's not even my usual type of guy, he's just so—

"Hellooooooo, space cadet," Laney laughed. "Care to come back to earth? I asked you how work was going."

"Oh, my gosh I'm so sorry, I must still be hung over from the New Year's party! Ha! Um, yes, work. Well, it's fine. I am coming to the end of my list of media trips. Good and steady media coverage though, the boss is happy."

Why am I rambling? Distracted much? Pull it together!

I tried to collect myself, "Actually I *do* have that massive hotel rebranding coming up in a month which, of course, I'd love you to attend! It's at the Edifice Luxe Orient Royale in Bangkok and it's my biggest event so far. It's a huge party with hundreds of people. I have to start organizing it soon."

"That's exciting," said Laney with a big smile at the mention of a party. "Yes, of course I'll be there, you know me!"

"Great!"

"So, you're not leaving after your contract is finished, are you?" Laney asked as we both ordered another round of mango smoothies, sans alcohol.

Yes, <u>without</u> alcohol!

I know!

Shocking!

Unheard of, even!

Ladies and gentlemen, Charly Briar is officially getting her life together!

Today, a mango smoothie...

Tomorrow, the world...

"I really hope not," I said. "I only have six weeks left in my current contract. The party at the Edifice Luxe Orient Royale is my last big function. It has to go well! Anyway, yeah, that's it. I can't believe how fast it's gone by... I don't want to leave!"

I was half-pleading with the universe. It was true. I'd recently come to realize that life was much more fun when I got out of my head and explored a bit. Plus, I didn't want to leave my new friends. And I really should see what happens with Radden. It'd be the right thing to do... I made a note to talk to my boss Sandy before my contract was up.

◘ * § * ◘

My phone rang as I fidgeted with the keys to my loft.

"Charly?"

"Oh, hi Sandy, I was actually just about to call you."

"Perfect! Listen, our Director of Marketing is in town visiting from Jeeranam. She's got some extra time and I want you to meet her. Can you make it to the office by 4:30pm? She's always looking to add people to her team in Jeeranam and your contract will be up soon."

Jeeranam! That's where Eden was headed!

My ticket to extending my stay as an expat!

"Absolutely, thanks very much Sandy."

I hopped in the shower, blew out my hair, and selected a fresh blue wrap-dress. I really wasn't ready to give up on expat-life yet. Despite a bumpy start—on which I wholeheartedly blamed Kai—I was really getting into the swing of things. I had new friends, a good job, a fabulous city, and a potentially new guy.

Everything's coming up Charly!

I threw on some basic makeup and hit the streets, hailed a motorbike taxi, and zipped up my *soi* to the water-taxi stand that would take me across the river. Once there I skipped up the steps to the sky train and rode the four short stops to Edifice Luxe Head Office. It's funny, just a couple of months ago, the process of negotiating the fare with a motorbike driver or finding my way to the correct water-taxi stand would have been a nightmare. Everything was foreign and challenging and required frustrating effort. I think I even used to sweat more back then.

But since losing Kai something unexpected had happened: I could no longer rely on someone else to remember which stop I had to get off at, or remind me to tell the taxi driver which *soi* to turn down. True, I no longer had the security of Kai on my arm, but the reality was that I had been missing out on so much by empowering him to make all the decisions for me.

Maybe I could blame him for the way he left, or the way we ended it, but it suddenly dawned on me that the real fault was mine: I looked to Kai to solve all my problems and take charge of my destiny.

Some journey of self-discovery!

Hours later I pushed through the heavy gold doors of the Edifice Luxe headquarters. I felt fresh and reborn. I also felt a sense of repentance and resolve... I wasn't going to rely on other people, *especially* boyfriends, to guide me through life anymore. It was up to me.

"Charly!"

I was greeted by a happy looking Sandy.

"Quick quick quick she's waiting for you!"

Uh, okay can I catch my breath first?

Sandy half-pushed, half-dragged me down the hallway of the EL offices and I'm not entirely sure my feet touched the ground on the way.

"She hates to be kept waiting," he hushed.

I'd never seen him like this.

"Who?" I whispered back.

Sandy's response was a gentle pat on my back and the words *good luck kiddo* as I practically tripped my way into an airy, spacious office and came upon *the* most elegant woman on the planet. The Director of Marketing, I presumed. I could see that she was engrossed in whatever she was writing with her thick Mont Blanc pen (worth more than my credit limit), but I couldn't decipher whether or not she wanted me to introduce myself or wait silently.

"I, um, hello, I am Charly Briar," I said.

No response.

Okay...

Wait silently.

Finally, she half-acknowledged me.

"Sit," she said to whatever she was writing. "I'll be with you in a moment Ms. Brown."

"Um, Briar, my *last* name is Briar, um, my first name is, er, never mind," I sat down as a wave of unexpected nervousness washed over me.

The woman in front of me was wearing elegant black trousers, a white blouse with a high collar, and fabulous red Prada loafers. Her chunky David Yurman bangle had big blue sapphires that caught the light and caused irreversible damage to my retinas. Her short and stylish coif was somewhere between blonde and grey and her skin was flawless. An eternity passed. Finally she put her pen down and looked up.

"I am the Director of Marketing and my name is Wilhelmina."

Wilhelmina from Edifice Luxe?

Wilhelmina from Edifice Luxe who tortured Eden?

Wilhelmina from Edifice Luxe who tortured Eden and would never, under any circumstances give me a job?

Oh no!

Oh no!!

Oh no!!!

"Oh yes," she grinned cruelly and I think I saw two horns make an appearance on her head but I couldn't be sure. "I see here from your CV that you worked in Boston?"

"Um," I stuttered.

"And I assume that you worked *closely* with Eden Quinn?"

"Er, well, not exactly…" I felt dizzy and nauseous and worried that I might pee all over her Armani Casa carpeted floor.

"Hmmm?"

"Oh, I barely know Eden, I wouldn't really say that we are friends, well, more like acquaintances, I don't, um, really know…"

"That's funny," she said in a tone that suggested it was not funny at all.

A wave of anxiety and whizzing confusion swarmed me like a slow-moving cyclone of killer bees. I was unable to speak and, for a brief moment, I couldn't hear anything except a loud buzzing in my ears.

I quickly glanced over her shoulder at a big bay window. I seriously considered propelling myself through the glass and swan diving into the Chao Praya River, but then I realized that was crazy, the windows were surely reinforced. I tried to collect myself, I *had* to get my grounding.

"So," said Wilhelmina. "Tell me about yourself."

"Well," I began with confidence, "I've always had a love of travel, ever since I can remember."

"Well, I'd hope so," she frowned at me like I was an idiot. "As a means to escape the transient, post-modern world in which we live, or as an extension of the inherent and inexorable impermanence of the human experience?"

I had roughly a 5% understanding of what Wilhelmina had just sad and I suddenly became aware of how small and alone I was.

"I guess I just like travel," I said as I searched her office for a black hole to another dimension.

"Fascinating," Wilhelmina stared at me as though it was the most un-fascinating thing on the planet.

This was not going well.

The next forty-five minutes went pretty much the same: unnecessarily wordy questions on her part followed by awkward, monosyllabic answers on mine.

I thought she just wanted to meet!

What is this interrogation?

We shook hands and she said that meeting me had been an "interesting use of her time".

Eden was right!

This woman probably had no reflection.

I collected my things, which now seemed cheap and pitiful in comparison to Wilhelmina's refined style and grace, and walked out of the office, completely deflated.

I spent the rest of the day wandering the streets and coming down from my Radden-high. I recapped the last couple of days…

I'd accidentally revealed that Nikki and Alégra were half-sisters, Alégra was apparently getting married, I'd yet to return the text from Kai (or even acknowledge it), Kermit was missing, I'd just blown an interview, and I had to plan a huge party at the Edifice Luxe Orient Royale, and honestly, I had no idea where to start.

Well this day went from kickass to ass kicking.

Pause for a Painful Memory Courtesy of Slipped Disc Guy

I suppose I knew that, at some point, I was going to have to bring up Slipped Disc Guy. While he was not exactly *the* catalyst for my embarking on a journey of self-discovery and idiotically using serial dating as a crutch (which proved to be more of a hindrance to finding myself, truth be told) he *is* part of the story. Actually, in hindsight, he was a pretty important part of my journey, maybe even the first step, so I guess he deserves some credit.

Ah, hindsight.

Love it or hate it, hindsight helps to pin point *the exact* moment where you've stopped thinking rationally and started acting like a laboratory panda on Vicodin. Hindsight, if used correctly, can help to avoid the same mistakes in the future. It's a very helpful tool and I hope to learn how to use it one day.

Anyway, it was three days *before* the big party at the Fairmont and just shortly *after* I had ended things with Ethan... I hadn't yet come up with the brilliant idea to go to jet-setting, nor had I decided to become a serial dater. Nor, *obviously*, had my back started to spasm in hernia-esque fashion.

Sigh, those were simple days...

¤ * § * ¤

As I sat on Slipped Disc Guy's apartment balcony watching the sun come up I looked at the person sitting next to me and realized he was a complete stranger. Now, rather than take this as a nano-moment of sobriety and jump ship, run home, and harass my friends incessantly for the next three weeks about whether or not they thought I was a total hussy, I took the opportunity to ask his opinion on my life.

"So, why do you think I couldn't see that my ex was a bad guy? I mean, it was *so* obvious."

Slipped Disc Guy sighed like a drunken little Buddha, placed his beer down beside him, and said, "Because you made him up."

"Excuse me?"

(Of course I didn't *realize* that he was speaking metaphorically. That would have saved me *a lot* of time.)

Slipped Disc Guy continued, "What I mean is, you *made* him into the person you wanted him to be. Nothing means anything until we *give it* meaning."

"What are you talking about? Forgive me," I sighed. "I've been drinking heavily for the past decade or, so, what the hell are you talking about?"

Slipped Disc Guy smiled and said, "Okay, look, you had no concept of me before tonight, right? We didn't know each other — so how could you have any feelings, good or bad — about me? I didn't exist to you, so you couldn't possibly care one way or another about me. I wasn't in your reality."

"Go on," I said, happy that Slipped Disc Guy was speaking more slowly and with hand gestures.

"Now, I *am* in your reality, I *do* exist to you. And um, let's be honest, we're most likely going to part ways, in, oh, about an hour or so."

"True," I agreed as I tried to stop seeing double.

(It *was* true: he was far too short for me and besides, one never pairs up with their rebound in any long term situation. It just *isn't* done.)

"And, to you, I'll forever be that one-night-stand guy, right?" continued Slipped Disc Guy. "But to someone else, maybe I'll be a boyfriend, or even a husband one day."

"So," I began. "You didn't exist before tonight... according to me? Therefore, I couldn't possibly have any feelings about you."

"Exactly."

"Okay, how does this relate to Ethan?"

"Well," Slipped Disc Guy said. "Before you met Ethan, you had no concept of him, either. No feelings, good or bad, same thing as me. He didn't exist in your consciousness, so you couldn't have cared, one or another, about him. But then you *did* meet him. And, let me guess, he fed you some bullshit line about the future and the two of you together and kids and marriage and all that crap, right?"

"Er, *right*," I nodded reluctantly.

"And I'm guessing then, out of nowhere, he'd rip it away from you—this image, this false promise of the future—if you did something he didn't like. Right?"

Ugh, this guy was good.

"Right!"

"And, yet," Slipped Disc Guy warned, "based on no tangible evidence whatsoever, you became a curator of sorts and created a whole future with him."

I nodded as he continued.

"Then you fed that false future back to him—*projected* it on to him even—and probably got angry when he didn't live up to it."

"Wow, you're very insightful," I said.

"Aw, thanks," said Slipped Disc Guy.

"I guess I'm just too creative—and not in a good way."

"No, Charly," Slipped Disc Guy smiled. "You're imaginative, just like every other woman. And please, don't take that the wrong way. It's why we adore you, but, also *kinda* why you drive us nuts. But it's not *all* your fault. Men can't help themselves when it comes to dropping lines about the future—it works every time. It's almost too easy."

"Oh, my gosh, you're totally right. I get it now." I squinted at the rising sun and continued, "I was *always* projecting this false future onto him. Then of course he didn't live up to it..."

"And *that's* why you got so frustrated," Slipped Disc Guy continued. "You kept looking for validation and reciprocation... from a fantasy. You saw what you wanted to see."

"Okay, you're really good!" I said honestly.

Slipped Disc Guy smiled and continued, "I'm not *that* good. It's just obvious that you built Ethan up to be bigger, and *clearly* better, than he was, based on what *you* wanted."

"Oh, god, you're right. Am I'm one of those nutso girls?" I said asked semi-frantically.

"No!" he burst out laughing. "No, Charly, if anything, you're normal. Honestly, you're totally normal."

"How fantastic for me," I groaned.

"Do you want the good news?" he continued.

"Sure," I said dryly.

"Nobody has power over us unless we *give* it to them. And we do *that* by projecting an unrealistic image onto them, usually derived from our own insecurities."

"Okay, Oprah, I get it, *you teach people how to treat you*, right?"

"Yes, exactly! Charly, listen to me, you do *not* miss Ethan. You only miss the meaning you've injected *into* him and the life you projected *onto* him. You don't miss him, you miss the mirage you created of him."

"Wow, you're really smart," I had to admit.

"Psychology major."

"Wow, that's like, super original," I teased as I stretched my arms out and tried to massage my lower back.

It was really starting to ache for some reason — maybe I'd pulled a muscle dancing the night before?

Did I slip and fall and not remember it?

Oh well, no big deal...

It's not like I've given myself a hernia!

"Listen, I gotta get going," I smiled awkwardly as I started to sober up and decide where the nearest purveyor of painkillers was en route home.

Slipped Disc Guy smiled and kissed me on the cheek, "See ya 'round, Chestnut Haired Girl."

/ Fully Booked / Genn Pardoe

38. Step And Repeat

All of a sudden I was knee-deep in the middle of organizing my biggest media event *ever* at the Edifice Luxe Orient Royale in Bangkok. It was my final big *hurrah* and the perfect way to end my contract. It was also a huge distraction that required all my attention. This was a good thing because I really needed to keep my mind busy so as not to obsess over Kai, Kermit, Alégra, Nikki, *have I forgotten anyone?*

Oh yeah, Wilhelmina.

Ugh.

Anyway, the shindig was so big and so involved that I had to stay at the hotel for two days prior to the event *and* two days afterwards. I had pre-party meetings, follow-up meetings, and a special debrief luncheon that I would be hosting in a couple of weeks at an EL branding event in Bangkok.

Sandy had even flown in some fancy pants "brand team" comprised of marketing and PR reps from different Edifice Luxe offices all over the world just to see my party! Well, okay *technically*, they were there to attend the re-branding of the hotel but *I* was the one organizing the party to mark it.

Go me!

I knew the event was of critical importance because, instead of putting me up in a standard room (the kind I normally got when hosting one or two members of the media), I was sent to a deluxe royal suite.

Pressure much?

Add to that, the re-branding party coincided with Bangkok Fashion Week and naturally, the Edifice Luxe Orient Royale—the grandest hotel in all of Bangkok—was hosting. This meant that essentially I was organizing two parties in one.

Yikes!

From the guest list to the flowers to the appetizers to the VIP's to the lighting to the speeches, everything had to be perfect. Then came the media... not only did I have to reach out to all my regular contacts, I also had to enlist fashion bloggers (*rolling of the eyes*) and mainstream media. Calling on the latter was probably the most terrifying thing I've ever done. Eden was right: a great way to feel like an idiot is by calling CNN and asking them to come to "your little fashion party". (Their words, not mine.)

But that's okay, I managed to secure Thailand's national newspapers *and* a BBC reporter—although she warned me that she wouldn't be covering the event for BBC—she *did* however, have a personal lifestyle blog and "might" be able to squeeze in a mention. I told her that even a tweet from the event would be "hugely appreciated".

And that's how I sold my soul for a tweet...

All together I had forty-five media coming. I felt as though I'd achieved some sort of magic number of media attendees and my boss and his boss (and her boss and her boss' boss) were all very happy with me. This in turn, made me happy. I really wanted to pull off a great event and a large number of media to complement the over three hundred *regular people* I had coming was the first step to achieving that, not to mention ending my contract on a high note. Sandy had joked, "Are you sure you can handle that much ego in one room?"

Of course, some writers and photographers wouldn't show up, some wouldn't write anything, and some would be hammered in the hotel bar the whole time, but that's PR…

To combat my would-be absentees, Laney rallied a bunch of her journalist friends from the Foreign Correspondents' Club which, to be honest, I had mixed feelings about. In spite of the fact that the FCC was nothing short of an iconic institution in Asia, the Bangkok chapter was nothing more than a clubhouse for gritty, hardcore war correspondents that drank and swore too much. Now, as the PR rep for the world's most luxurious hotel brand, my *ilk* was mainly comprised of Ayurvedic spa reviewers and writers whose most recent article discussed the renaissance of Ylang Ylang in facial serums. Members of the media who frequented the FCC, on the other hand, could more easily identify a Vietnamese drug lord than a lotus blossom pumice stone.

You can see where I was going with this…

I was thankful to Laney for padding my media list with her friends, but the thought of a gaggle of dusty war correspondents romping through my refined soirée (in their cargo pants — oh god, WHY are they *always* in cargo pants?!), made me envision a foul-mouthed, gin-soaked bull running through a dainty china shop.

"Oh *darlin'* calm yerself," Laney had laughed at me. "They just came back from the *field*. I'm sure they're rearing for some refinement after a tough assignment."

"Rearing for refinement? This is a disaster waiting to happen," I moaned. "What 'field' are we talking about here, by the way?"

"Oh, I don't know, Charly," Laney said absent mindedly as she checked out her new Clementine manicure. "Palestine?"

"Great," I couldn't help but laugh out loud. "I'm sure they'll have some upbeat stories to share with the fashion bloggers."

Laney assured me that her friends would behave and if anything, their presence would give my party more "street cred".

Ugh, Laney…

Among who exactly?

The branding team at Edifice Luxe didn't want to hear about ordinance and malaria.

Whatever.

Breathe.

Moving on....

I'd enlisted Radden to gather up some photographers—preferably hot ones—for the media pit at my red carpet entrance. They'd be taking pictures of the VIP guests, socialites, and fashionistas as they walked the carpet.

Things with Radden were going *amazingly* well, by the way. We'd both been insanely busy with work but had managed to spend a bunch of nights together since New Year's Eve and kept in touch by texting and calling each other like high school kids pretty much every other second. *Eeeee so smitten!* I'd finally realized that a healthy relationship requires both people to create the space required to grow.

And, as for Radden's girlfriend (who still had yet to return to the continent) she was on the outs he assured me, just like Kai, who was fast becoming a distant memory, diluted by both the passage of time and the awesomeness of *my* new boyfriend.

Well, not boyfriend, *yet.*

Too soon. *Obviously.*

Radden can't be my boyfriend *and* his soon-to-be ex-girlfriend's boyfriend. Oh god that makes no sense... Anyway, it doesn't matter because I wasn't "going there" at this point in time. Besides, I was much too busy rolling out the red carpet with the help of the hotel's event manager and her crew... I lay yellow marking tape for the photographers' pit and called over some extra hands to help me erect the step-and-repeat. *Ah the step-and-repeat...*

The step-and-repeat was the VIP port of entry—the gateway even—to the entire evening. Bangkok's society members and fashionable elite would enter on a red carpet and pause in front of a huge backdrop, the "step-and-repeat", to be photographed by the photographers.

The backdrop was sponsored by Johnny Walker (like everything else in Bangkok) and sported the beautiful emblem of Edifice Luxe Orient Royale: a teal blue and violet lotus with the name of the hotel in shimmery gold underneath. Making a stunning first impression among the impression-makers was easily the most crucial aspect of my entire event. It had to be assembled, managed, and executed with flawless precision. There are two simple rules for the step-and-repeat: no one can stand for too long and no one can fall over and/or accidentally reveal a boob. I enlisted one girl from the hotel's event team to usher attention-grabbing socialites off the carpet following their half minute or so of posing and I put another girl on "wardrobe malfunction alert".

(Two years ago a cousin of a Thai royal had had an unfortunate case of *boobus escapus* on the step-and-repeat and, let's just say, she's no longer seen at large social functions...)

Thousands upon thousands of flashes of light would capture the VIP's as they entered: there was no room for error. Everything had to be perfect. The step-and-repeat not only set the tone for the entire evening, it was the first impression of my event, and it would live in the Bangkok society pages for weeks, months even, and possibly eternity. The events manager and I hummed and hawwed about every aspect of the VIP entrance for an hour or so.

We finally got to stand back and admired our work: this was going to be an amazing entrance experience to an even more amazing party. I couldn't wait to add the night sky and a million flashing bulbs to the atmosphere. I stepped back and looked at the red carpet.

I imagined myself walking down it, maybe with Radden....
Seriously...
Charly...
Focus.

At 3pm I walked across the hotel lobby — still illuminated by the afternoon sun shining through an expansive glass ceiling — to check on the preparations taking place in the dedicated media room.

It was well-equipped with press kits, electrical outlets, and extra charging devices for every type of smart phone out there (seriously without fail on *every* trip I've ever hosted there's at least one reporter who forgets their phone charger—like, is this your first time away from mommy?).

I also made sure there was ample water (flat and sparkling) and carbohydrate-heavy hors d'oeuvres for my starving little drunken writers. (Do I know my journos or do I know my journos!?)

"The room looks great," I said to the set-up team. "I really appreciate all the work you've done."

(Sandy was right—I *did* feel like an "old pro". Those were the word's he'd said to me on my very first day at EL and I couldn't believe how fast the time had flown by.) I thanked the team again and walked away with the events manager to go over the guest list and discuss VIP's, mega-VIP's, and *regular people*. By 4pm the flowers arrived. I've never really been a horticultural enthusiast but it was hard not to be impressed as one hundred over-sized teal vases of huge blossoming flowers were paraded by me, "Wow," I couldn't help but gawk.

"Charly, *girl*, what did you expect?" The events manager teased, "This is the Edifice Luxe Orient Royale, not a roadside motel!"

I blushed a little, "I am just so happy. This is really beautiful, everything is so great. Thank you."

"Not to worry my dear," she said. "Why don't you head up to your suite and get ready. Guests will start arriving in an hour and you have to be *on*. You've got a long night ahead of you!"

I thanked her and headed upstairs to take a quick bath after which I threw on my *backtrack soundtrack* as I got dressed. For the evening I had chosen a different route than my standard black-on-black dress and pumps.

I'd splurged on a shimmery grey shift dress with a deep scoop all the way down my back. The sleeves were three-quarter length and the neck was high but loose. (I prayed for an evening free of spills and promised to only drink clear beverages.)

I opted for cream stilettos and chunky bracelets to match. Simple makeup with dark eyes and pale lips, and a poufy coif tamed with a sparkly headband.

As my soundtrack switched from eighties pop to easy listening seventies tunes there was a knock at the door.

"Who is it?"

"Room service," teased Radden in a high-pitched voice. "I'm here to fluff your pillow, wink wink."

"Hey, you!" I ran to the door excitedly and whipped it open. "What are you doing here?"

"Just wanted to say hi, pretty girl," Radden said as he pulled me in his arms and we kissed.

I smiled at Radden, "come on in, just getting ready."

"You look ready to me," Radden said as he wrapped his arms around me again. His gaze held mine for a couple more moments as I melted into a puddle of smitten goo. *Sigh*.

"Make yourself useful," I winked. "I've got wine, whiskey, whatever you want. Pour us a drink?"

"Sure thing," Radden flashed his little crooked half-smile and walked across the room. He was in his classic attire: jeans and a v-neck with two cameras and a bag slung across his body.

"Do you have Chang?" Radden asked as he rummaged through the mini bar looking for Thailand's most popular beverage aside from whiskey, *elephant beer*.

Radden pulled out a brown bottle with a green label and two elephants on it, popped the top and took a swig.

(I liked that he drank the local beer and had always found it a bit snobby that Kai insisted on Heineken *only*.)

Radden walked over with a glass of champagne for me, "Nothing red on that dress tonight, cutie."

"Oh, yes, thank you. Well, you already know me so well," I smiled as I took the flute. We clinked glasses and kissed until it was time to go to the party...

Happy sigh...

By nightfall my party was out of control in the best possible way. It was jammed with wall-to-wall celebrities, socialites, and fashion royalty. I had yet to see any mega-VIP's arrive, but I knew they'd be late so I wasn't worried.

Super typical...

In the grand foyer, the tens of thousands of twinkling lights that lined the party perimeter both inside and out rivaled the stars. The music was soft but building in tempo and the scent of hundreds of exotic flowers in bloom mingled seductively among the guests. The attendees were dressed in next year's fashions and every single person looked at least five pounds underweight.

Perfect.

By 8pm the chatter was just loud enough to be considered bubbly but not percolating over the rim; everything glowed *just right*. It was slick and sophisticated and it was all my creation.

Self-high-five!

"Charly, you've done it," Sandy exclaimed from at least twenty feet away as he strode towards me as at least eight minions turned on their heels dutifully and followed. The brand team, I guessed: two from New York, one from London, three from Singapore, one from Dubai and the other from — oh my good god you've *got* to be kidding me — the other was Wilhelmina.

Ugh, talk about a skunk at a garden party!

My stomach turned as my eyes met Wilhelmina's: I had barely gotten over the disastrous meet-and-greet interview slash firing squad session I'd just had with her.

She'd shamed me to an unbearable level and made me feel like a useless PR twit, but what could I do?

Wilhelmina was the queen of Edifice Luxe and I had to kiss ass if I ever wanted any chance of extending my stay in expat-land. I took a deep breath and prepared for a head on collision with the world's meanest human (if in fact, she *was* human, which I wholeheartedly doubted).

She was just so %&#^%* mean!

"Charly, my dear," Wilhelmina exclaimed joyfully as she extended two David Yurman-clad arms and grabbed my shoulders, kissing my cheeks with emphasis. "You've done it! Amazing job, just absolute perfection."

Okay, did she screw on a different head today? Where was the condescending dragon lady I'd met just a couple weeks ago? The one with the icy cold reception and dead-behind-the-eyes stare? Who was this Wilhelmina-imposter in from of me? Was this her lovely twin? Had she had an aneurism? A lobotomy? A brain transplant? Struck by lightning? I was completely caught off guard but managed to eke out a breathless *thank you* and attempted to introduce myself to the rest of the brand team. I barely got to the girl from Dubai when Wilhelmina grabbed the part of my arm just above the elbow and pinched hard (*oh wait, there she is! There's the crazy witch!*) and summoned the group, "Everyone? Everyone! Let's go to the step-and-repeat; it's Charly's pièce de resistance, *isn't it?*"

First of all, who pinches that part above the elbow on someone else? And secondly, you're damn right it's my pièce de resistance, you walking canker sore.

Prepare to be blown away by my extreme awesomeness.

I wriggled my arm out of her cold lobster clasp and regained control of the group with confidence.

"It would be my pleasure. Please follow me."

Sandy, Wilhelmina (who looked as though she desperately wanted to prove I was incompetent), and the minions click-clacked behind me as I strode confidently across the massive room. As I came upon the step-and-repeat, I allowed a barely visible smile of victory to emerge as I took in the scene that unfolded before me: a line-up extending down carpeted stairs and out onto the street, stunningly gorgeous men and women anxiously awaiting to have their picture taken, onlookers gasping and gossiping and generally clamoring over each other to get a piece of the action, and beautiful people posing in front of a photographers' pit that was stuffed to the max thanks to Radden (who was busy snapping away).

Everything looked amazing.

Ta-da!

I know no one noticed—especially the higher ups—but I was truly grateful to the two girls I'd assigned to wardrobe and line duty. They were completely on their game and running the step-and-repeat like a well-oiled machine. The first girl gave a totally inconspicuous "once over" to the celebs-in-waiting while the second girl ushered them on and off the carpet for their fifteen seconds of fame. (Getting them *off* the carpet was most assuredly the toughest part of her job.)

"I, um," Wilhelmina was speechless.

"Thank you," I said with pride.

Sandy reached over and extended his hand to shake mine. "Good job, kiddo," he winked and then turned to the group. "Come on guys, let's allow our future Head of PR to get back to work."

Aw... I love Sandy...

Wilhelmina outright laughed at Sandy's prediction but I didn't care. My boss gave me one more smile and then shepherded the group away (which I appreciated greatly). I smiled to myself and allowed a moment of pause to take it all in. I smiled at Radden too, who was busy with his group of friends and colleagues, shouting directions at the celebs and socialites: turn left, give us more hip, look over here, smile for us.

"Hey Rad," one of his photographer friends shouted over the rest. "Why don't you jump in there and take a pic with your girlfriend."

A couple other photographers chimed in and I blushed. It really wasn't appropriate for me to be in front of the step-and-repeat time but I appreciated the thought. Maybe later that night we could snap a couple pictures by the backdrop; but I had to let the guests go through first. In fact, I was a little surprised at the amateur suggestion from Radden's colleague.

I looked to Radden and noticed that he was blushing, as well, obviously embarrassed by the thought.

"Dude, how are you going to leave your lady hanging?" one of his friends said. "Just hop up there."

Jeez, has this guy ever been to a fancy function before?

There was *no way* I was going to hop in front of the line of VIP's to snap a smooch with my boyfriend—even though, let's be honest, I was *dying* to!

I made eye contact with the event team girl (the one in charge of monitoring the line) and shook my head at her as subtly as possible.

She acknowledged me and waved to a blue-eyed socialite standing on the step-and-repeat, beckoning her to hurry up and keep the line moving. To everyone's shock, the blue-eyed girl just stood there smiling.

"C'mon! Just one shot *loverboy*," Radden's friend teased and others joined in, even making kissy noises.

Well, I guess we were outed!

"Alright, *jeez man*," Radden sighed, clearly annoyed. "It's not like I'm *working* or anything. Make it quick."

Yikes, somebody was a bit pissy.

Radden rolled his eyes as he sauntered up to the step-and-repeat from the left. I was on the right side of the group and resigned myself to the fact that this *was* going to happen. *Eeks, I hope nobody from work sees!*

I hustled up quickly, tugging at my dress along the way and handing my champagne flute to the wardrobe girl. The line monitor girl was now making bigger gestures to the blue-eyed girl who refused to leave the view of the photographers. The girl was pretty, a bit chunky maybe compared to the anorexic models and waif-like royalty, but more worrisome than that, I wondered why I didn't recognize her. *Sure*, the list of VIP's was practically endless but I was confident I'd memorized most of them—if not invited them to the party myself. I found it odd that a mystery girl had snuck in somehow but I really didn't have time to worry about it.

"Charly!" I turned around to see Laney running towards me.

Oh cripes, I can't deal with this right now.

I was sure one of Laney's drunken war correspondent friends was being ejected from the party.

"Hold on!" I mouthed in Laney's direction.

"Charly, *no!!*" Laney's voice almost boomed as her gait graduated from a jog to a near-sprint.

"Radden," his friends egged on. "C'mon, man, give us a kiss for the camera."

Everyone just calm down!

Between Radden not wanting to monopolize the step-and-repeat, some random blue-eyed demi-socialite hogging the spotlight, and Laney running towards me full steam ahead, I was starting to feel the pressure mount.

Breathe.

Focus.

One crisis at a time.

I signaled to the line monitor girl that it was okay to call out to the blue-eyed girl and tell her that her time was *up*, we *had* to keep things rolling. Next, I turned to shush Laney—I'd deal with her and whatever her emergency was in a second. Finally, I took my first steps onto the step-and-repeat in front of fifty or so flashing cameras and about three hundred and fifty or so VIP guests.

"That's my man, *soooo* romantic," the blue-eyed girl teased as Radden hustled up, wrapped his arms around her, and planted a kiss on her lips. His friends cheered as I pretty much had a category seven heart attack, and honestly, I may or may not have peed myself.

What the fuck what the fuck what the fuck?

Seriously…

What…

the…

fuck!

That's when Laney finally caught up to me and explained that Radden's girlfriend had landed back in Bangkok earlier that day.

Just perfect.

Three hours later, Radden was banging on my hotel room door. I was in my pajamas, calm, collected, and *not* drunk.

No, *really*. I wasn't.

See?

Progress!

I opened the door slightly as I held my oolong tea and sighed at the man-child in front of me. It had all happened so fast—Radden and me—that I'd barely had time to fall for him before I found myself being profoundly disappointed by him.

"Charly, I don't know what to say!!" Radden exclaimed, completely drunk and totally exasperated. "I didn't know she was back! I'm so, *so* sorry. But I couldn't exactly end a five year relationship on a god damn step-and-repeat! Please don't do this—I was completely *stranded* out there. It's not my fault! It's the step-and-repeat—"

"Radden," I smiled coolly as I exhaled. "*Step-and-repeat, step-and-repeat, step-and-repeat...* I mean, those words have honestly lost all meaning. And, as of this moment, so have you. Goodnight. Good luck. Goodbye."

I shut the door and sighed again. It was a sad sigh, but it wasn't a hopeless one. It was just the kind of sigh one gives when one has come to the end of a chapter.

39. Singapore... Take Two

And... cut to me running away, again. This time to Singapore and, lucky for me, just in time for the annual Edifice Luxe conference.

Again.

The event at the Edifice Luxe Orient Royale had gone perfectly well and I'd succeeded at ending my contract on a high note. But there was no sign of an offer to stay on. Nothing from Wilhelmina. And no other prospects to speak of.

On any level...

I still had a couple of weeks left in my contract but it was pretty light at work: handover notes, debriefing, and generally wrapping up. It was all over, I couldn't believe it. I was just getting the hang of expat life and pretty soon it would be taken from me — all too soon. At least I could have one final blow-out weekend in Singapore before it all ended...

The time had come again for the annual conference and I'd asked Sandy to put me on the list which he happily did — thankfully. Eden and Scott would be there so I figured, why not?

Singapore-with-friends beats alone-in-Bangkok any day. It would be fun and besides, there was quite a lot on my plate that I was trying to forget. In fact it was an ever-expanding list:

1. No job
2. No Kai
3. No Kermit
4. No Hair (okay, just let me be dramatic)
5. No Radden
6. (Number 5 is just irritating. He didn't break my heart—not by a long shot—but he sure busted my ego. C'mon, Universe! Why can't I have an awesome rebound *just once!?*)
7. No friends (Nikki and Alégra hated me, I was sure of it. I hadn't spoken to them in weeks. I couldn't believe Ali was getting married and I had, like, no idea what was going on! Fine, fine, it might have been partly my fault...) And, the most terrifying of all...
8. No boyfriend and (yikes!) zero prospects.

Just me.
All alone.
Solo.
Reservations for... one.
Fawwwwwk.

Suffice it to say that I was *very* thankful for the few friends I still *did* have. Eden, who was now based in Jeeranam, would be at the conference. And Scott had accepted a job offer in Singapore so he'd be there too.

Thank heavens.

I was *very* much looking forward to taking a vacation from myself and I hoped that it would be a chance to wipe the slate clean and start with a fresh canvas.

Um. Again.

Yes, I know, <u>I know</u>, I've said this before!

The flight was long and I landed mid-afternoon. Singapore was as I had left it just over eleven months ago. My god, had it only been a year? Not even! So much had happened and yet, here I was, back where I started.

Sigh.

As I walked out of the underground metro that took me from the airport to Orchard Grove, a familiar scent washed over me. It was fresh and fragrant, clean and bright. Minutes later I came upon the Raffles Courtyard and immediately perked up as I spotted Eden and Scott.

It had been over six months since we'd seen each other and Eden was as regal as ever, always managing to somehow sit in the center of any room she occupied. The first thing I noticed was that her hair was chopped off. She sported a chin-length coif, just like me. Eden's coral blouse and white linen pants contrasted with her espresso bean skin and she looked radiant.

I watched her, laughing elegantly — despite the fact that she was probably telling an exceptionally rude joke — as she brushed a flyaway hair from her face, causing at least ten orange and red skinny bracelets to jingle.

Beside her sat Scott, whom I had also missed dearly over the past six months. Scott wore a tan dress shirt unbuttoned by two notches and brown linen pants. His bare ankles poked out from below his cuffs and above his loafers. He looked a little bit older but still as handsome as the last time I had seen him. Scott was officially in his mid-thirties and steadily moving towards the top of his career, and *apparently* he had a new friend. A pudgy little white French bulldog sat obediently beside him.

Must ask him about his new little friend!

As I approached my two work friends I felt a great sense of warmth wash over me. It had been so long since I'd seen people who actually *wanted* to see me, who actually *wanted* to be around me, who weren't full of shit... Eden's back was to me and it was Scott who noticed me first.

"As I live and breathe," he exclaimed.

I lifted the hem of my flowy violet dress and curtsied.

"Ladies," I said as I kissed and hugged them both, stuffed my hands back into the pockets of my dress, and plopped down between my two former colleagues and friends.

We caught up on the latest gossip and recounted our afternoons back at the Fairmont when we should have been working. It was so good to see them both.

"And, who is *this*?" I inquired excitedly about the little French bulldog beside Scott.

"Oh, well, this little guy is my new boyfriend's dog, Harvey Milkbone."

"Cute! And, congratulations on the new man!" I sighed. "Oh, this little doggie makes me miss my Kermit…"

Since I wasn't speaking to Kai, I had no idea whether or not he'd found Kermit (or even if he was looking.) It was so awful that, to be honest, I was still in total Kermit-denial. I just didn't want to face the fact that my little furry baby was gone. I knew it was immature not to deal with it head on, but as long as I didn't bring it up, it didn't exist. I just couldn't face it. It was too horrible. I'd deal with it with when I got home…

"Well, actually, sweetie," Scott became serious, "I *do* have something to tell you, it's about Kermit."

Okay…

I guess I wouldn't be able to wait until I got home.

"Yes? Tell me!"

"He's fine, totally fine," said Scott happily.

"What!?" I couldn't help but squeal. "That is amazing. That makes me so happy!"

"He was found in Central Park," Scott continued, "he's absolutely fine. Kai told me a couple of weeks ago. He said he's been trying to reach you but you haven't answered—anyway it doesn't matter. Kermit is just fine."

"Oh, wow," a rush of gratitude and joy washed over me. "That's so great!"

"There's more…" Eden and Scott looked at each other.

"What?" I asked impatiently.

"Some girl found him, and, um, he had tags, so, naturally, she called Kai because of the info on Kermit's tags…"

"Great! Whatever, who cares? I'm so happy Kermit is okay," I raised my glass, cheered the table, and took a big swig of my Singapore Sling...

"And now that girl and Kai are, um, dating."

... and then I spat out my Singapore Sling.

"Are you kidding me? My DOG?! MY dog!? MY DOG?! So, what, Kermit is like some kind of K-9 cupid? That's just fan-fucking-tastic. How long have they known each other? Five minutes? Do they even know each other's middle names? Somebody, please, tell me where I can volunteer for the Blind People's Axe Throwing Competition."

Kai had a new girlfriend already!
Of course he did!
That's just great... really, really, great.
Good for him.
^&@$?%*$#!!!*

Scott and Eden looked at each other awkwardly and decided the time was right to bring up the little surprise they had for me.

"Eden," Scott urged. "Isn't there, ahem, something you can do to help out poor Charly here?"

"I don't need help," I protested. "I just need a cattle prod and some rope."

"*Huh?*" Scott and Eden asked in unison.

"Nothing," I waved my hand, totally deflated. "I am a victim of my own stupidity."

"Yes, my sweets, it's true." Scott leaned over and kissed me on the forehead. "This year, it's very true, you *have* been karma's little punch line!"

"I really am!" I laughed.

"Listen, Charly," Eden said. "I have something for you."

"Not a date, I hope!"

I couldn't help but laugh. The thought of Kai getting a girlfriend because *he* lost *my* dog made me chuckle. At least I had Kermit back and I'd been with *that* furry little fella a lot longer than any man!

I thought about the image of Kermit and me maybe getting married one day—after all, he was my longest relationship—oh my god, I should totally marry Kermit! I burst out laughing and then suddenly stopped myself.

Enter lightning bolt.

In college, years earlier, Nikki had told me that one day, I would laugh at the things that once made me cry. And she was right.

Oh.

My.

God.

Everything was going to be okay.

I couldn't help but laugh.

Like, really hard.

"Okay, Ms. Giggles!" Scott brought me back as he handed me a manila envelope, "I'm glad you're happy. Listen, I've got something for you. Take this."

"I promise, I will open it later," I assured him. "Can we just relax and have fun for the afternoon? It's been a crazy six months."

Scott frowned somewhat, but Eden responded in classic big-sister fashion, "Of course we can, darling. You just enjoy yourself. You've had a tough go. Just make sure that you open that letter... *Trust me, you won't be disappointed.*"

"Thank you, guys," I smiled at my friends. "I just need to put the pause button on life for a bit."

I slid the manila envelope in my bag and forgot about it until weeks later.

❑ * § * ❑

A week later the conference was over and I kissed Scott and Eden goodbye. I promised I would open Scott's letter on the plane ride home. I couldn't believe it was over. My life as an expat.

Over.

Done.

Finito.

Well, almost.

Not for another seven hours…

My flight wasn't leaving until later that evening so I spent the morning wandering the pristine streets of Singapore and enjoying my last day as an expat.

Around mid-morning I ventured into a little deli in search of a sandwich but was halted by a familiar voice.

"Hey, Goldilocks."

Universe, you must be joking.

I smiled. I would recognize that voice anywhere: it was Tyler Kee. I turned around slowly and surveyed the affair I'd had exactly one year ago.

Of course Tyler was in Singapore; he was at the Edifice Luxe Retreat!

Considering that neither of us ever went to the seminars, I wasn't surprised we hadn't crossed paths over the past week. There he stood with his hands in the pockets of faded jeans that frayed as they reached grey flip flops, a plain white tee that showed off airbrushed quality muscles, naturally high-lighted blonde hair, a yummily toasted marshmallow tan, and sparkly emerald green eyes. Enter the fuzzy clouds and glittery rainbows…

C'mon, universe!

"Oh, hi, wow, Tyler," I stopped dead in my tracks as my stomach froze and my heart raced at super-sonic speed.

He looked a little older and, if possible, had become *even* more attractive. Tyler had the type of magnetism that was impossible to ignore. In a flash, I was brought back to a year ago. I instantly recalled every detail of our short time together with crystal clear clarity and I wanted to throw my arms around Tyler. It was all I could do to hold myself back from him; I felt my cheeks reddening. I looked at the ground and smiled.

"Got time for a real brunch, Goldilocks?"

"Of course," I looked up at him and we locked eyes.

We found a little café near the corner of Orchard and Scotts Rd. and sat outside watching shoppers clash with expats at the busy intersection. Tyler and I spent some time catching up on each other's lives over the past year, and in doing so, invariably reduced once meaningful events (and people) down to nothing more than lessons learned.

On Tyler's part, he had received an offer from another resort (it was a promotion, so he took it immediately), he'd dated some girl briefly but it didn't work out, and he'd broken his finger during an unfortunate water skiing accident

On my part, I had taken a job in Bangkok, dated some guy briefly but it didn't work out, and was now moving back home to Boston to most likely get back into copywriting for hotels. But this time, it was with deep gratitude and a dash of humility. No more grandiose plans and fabulous journeys of self-discovery for Charly Briar; just plain old good-enough-for-me life.

Wow.

I shocked myself at how the most eventful year of my life could be reduced to something so casual. Sitting there, with Tyler, I found myself barely able to remember the majority of once-dramatic events that had so recently dominated my life.

"So, that guy," Tyler leaned in and smiled deeply. "Is he still in the picture?"

"No," I confirmed. "We just weren't right for each other."

As soon as I heard the words fall out of my mouth I knew, for the first time, that they were true. Just a week ago, Scott and Eden had confirmed that I'd lost Kai *for good*; but rather than cry about it, I actually felt *blessed* to finally get some closure.

I know,
I know…
I know!!
The C-word…
Closure.
Barf.

"So can I ask you something? What was it that you saw in him?" asked Tyler with genuine interest.

"I saw what I wanted to see," I shrugged. "I think I projected a lot of what I wanted onto him. In the end, it wasn't anything that I couldn't recover from. No big deal."

"Yeah, same here," Tyler sighed. "That girl, the one I was with, same thing. No big deal."

I wondered if Tyler's no-big-deal-girl was like my no-big-deal-Kai. But then I realized it didn't matter. In a couple of hours I'd be on my way home to Kermit and hopefully, patching things up with Alégra and Nikki. I smiled.

"What?" Tyler asked as he smiled and casually took hold of my hand softly.

"Nothing, really," I looked at him. "It's just nice to see you."

"You too, Goldilocks, I had a feeling I might bump into you," Tyler smiled conspiratorially at me. "You know, once in a while, I missed you."

"Yeah, right," I laughed defensively. "You probably had, like, a billion girlfriends between last February and like, five minutes ago. They were probably more age-appropriate too."

"Maybe…" Tyler's eyes sparkled cheekily. "But it doesn't change the fact that I missed you. And, hey, I'm not pleased that you never wrote me back. You did get my letters, *right?*"

"Yes, I did. I'm sorry, Tyler," I said honestly. "I really didn't know what to say."

"I figured you were married or something."

"Ha!" I forced a laugh. "I don't think so. Hey, maybe I'll come visit you in… wait, where are you now?"

"Jeeranam," Tyler responded as he took one last sip of coffee.

"Oh, wow," I had no idea. "My friend Eden just transferred there."

"Yup. I've met Eden, she's cool. *Quite* the party girl!"

OMG.

Eden and Tyler knew each other!

I wondered why she hadn't mentioned it. She *must* have known that I would be *very* interested in that type of information. Maybe she didn't realize he was *the* Tyler Kee? Perhaps it had something to do with the manila envelope Scott had handed me. I wondered if it was all connected.

But I had no time to think about that because out of nowhere I noticed that Tyler was sitting so close to me that our legs were almost touching and all of a sudden without warning I was seconds away from passing out.

Oh sweet, sweet, fleeting love.
How had we missed this chance?
We were so close...

Tyler leaned in and extended his fingertips just enough so that they brushed against the inside of my bare knees and near-whispered into my ear, "Charly, why aren't you transferring, too?"

I had no idea what to say, in part because I didn't know how to answer his question, in part because I had lost all feeling in my body and at the same time, was bursting with joy and elation.

"I, um," I looked down at the sidewalk, and out at the people on the street, everything seemed to be slowing down... starting to spin and get totally out of control...

"I, um, I didn't think it was an option," I stuttered. I wasn't sure if we were talking about Jeeranam anymore.

"Oh, it's an *option*," Tyler said without hesitation as he palmed the back of my thigh and moved in closer toward me. Now I was *sure* we weren't talking about Jeeranam. I was about to remind Tyler, *and myself,* that I was headed home in a matter of hours, that this was impossible, that it was too overwhelming. But Tyler spoke for me, "Oh well, never mind... Hmmm. Right girl, wrong time, eh?"

All I could do was smile in sad agreement.

"Listen, Charly, you should at least visit Jeeranam. It's an amazing place. *Truly.*"

"Maybe I will," I smiled as I gathered up my things.

"You won't," Tyler's smile faded as he tossed some bills on the table and got up.

"You never know..." I sighed and was about to speak again when he put my face in between his hands and rested his lips gently on mine.

I closed my eyes and the whole world melted away. It was as though no time at all had passed since last February. I couldn't comprehend how I held so much passion for someone I'd barely spent any time with. But it was undeniable.

Eventually, we parted lips and Tyler looked at me intently, my head still in his hands "Hey Goldilocks, if this feels *just right*, then why can't it work?"

I couldn't say anything, I was in falling and being crushed, all at the same time, "I *will* see you again," I promised.

Ugh, why couldn't Tyler and I just work out?

"Don't make promises you can't keep," he said sadly as he wrapped me up in his arms and pulled me to his chest. I put my head on his shoulder and sighed. Tyler was much taller than me and I felt protected and safe in his arms. I didn't want it to end.

"Well," I looked up at him. "I *want* to see you again."

"That's good enough for me," Tyler smiled as he slowly let me sink away from his embrace, "*for now*... but I can't miss you forever. It's no fun."

There was nothing to say so I just looked at him and smiled sadly. Slowly, Tyler turned and started to walk away, "Hey, Tyler!" I called as he crossed the street. He looked over his shoulder and raised an eyebrow. "Happy Birthday."

Tyler Kee turned casually, raised a hand over his head in acknowledgement, and disappeared into the busy Singapore traffic.

Fully Booked / Genn Pardoe

Epilogue

kermitandcharly@gmail.com

Charly says:
    Alégra? I need to talk to you …

Alégra says:
    I'm busy planning my wedding, not sure if you heard, but I'm getting married. What can I do for you, Charly?

Charly says:
    You can accept my apology…

Alégra says:
    What?

Charly says:
    I'm so sorry, Alégra, I have had my head up my own ass. I hope you can forgive me I'm sorry about the whole Templeton thing—I mean, that was just awful of me, I really do apologize.

Alégra says:
    Oh heavens, Charly, there's nothing to forgive, you big nit wit. Nikki and I just miss you, that's all. Now listen, no pressure, but what is going on with you? When are you coming home? Soon, I hope!! I mean, it's totally fine, but Nikki—of all people—has been stuck planning my wedding. Is there anything more unnatural?

Charly says:
    Message received, loud and clear! I'm on the next flight.

~ Your presence is requested at the wedding of ~
Alégra DeVrees & Teddy Colbourne

I spent all of March redeeming myself for being a crappy bridesmaid and an even worse friend. The wedding was beautiful, *stunning*, actually. It was understated and elegant, just like Alégra. Teddy and Alégra decided to have the ceremony at night with just close friends and family.

They exchanged vows below a canopy of lilies and tiny white lights and, in typical *Alégra Fashion*, everyone was dressed in super-formal attire. Nikki and I both wore shoulder-baring black Maxi dresses with subtle pearl cuffs and sparkly headbands.

(Nikki was *not* pleased about having to wear a headband but did so anyway.)

The ceremony was short and afterwards, a band played as guests mingled and munched on hors d'oeuvres before a three-course dinner.

"I'm so happy we're all back together again," I said to Nikki when we were seated at the dinner table.

"Me too, Charly, we missed you," Nikki said as she wrapped her arms around me in very un-Nikki-like-fashion. "Oh, hey, it's speech time."

A few minutes later, I was up.

"...both Nikki and I have always regarded Alégra as our little sister. But I think that, when all is said and done, we actually look up to her. Alégra is the type of person who not only puts others first, she lifts them up, and she makes them shine. Alégra, you are stylish, graceful, and wise beyond your years, *and*, you have eternal patience—especially with me—and I love you for that. I am so thankful to have a friend like you. You are humble and giving, and I admire you. So, tonight I want to say congratulations, but mostly, I want to say, *thank you*."

Everyone raised a glass in unison and I was shocked to see tears in Nikki's eyes.

It was official: Alégra DeVrees was happily married, Nikki was happily single, and I was just happy that the three of us were best friends again.

At the end of the night (and pretty much the beginning of the morning) the three of us found ourselves sitting on the porch. Alégra's new hubby was inside packing for their honeymoon and had insisted that she come out to say goodnight to us.

"So Charlyyyy," sing-songed Nikki as she drained the contents of her second Moet bottle (not the mini kind). "Did you find whatever it was that you were looking for out there in the big world?"

"Nope," I said honestly as I stole a drag from her cigarette. "But I was looking for the wrong things anyway."

"What!" Alégra squealed drunkenly. "Noooooo Charly, whyyyy? What a waste!"

"It wasn't a waste, Alégra. I was looking for escapism—to escape from myself—and I was wrapping it up in pretty little boxes called 'expat' and 'girlfriend'. It was always *and off we went*. I had this ridiculous fixation on *we*; it was never *me*. No matter how far I traveled, I was looking for someone else to tell me who I was. I was never going it alone."

"Um, excuse me ladies?" said a man's voice out of nowhere.

The three of us looked up and I almost fell over.

"Kai," I said in shock. "Is that *really* you?"

A gaunt blond man with unkempt hair and a crooked nose was standing in front of me; the only indication that this man was *indeed* Kai was that, attached to him was a long leash, and at the end of that leash was a spastic Boston Terrier eagerly trying to make his way over to me.

"Kermit!!"

I ran over to my little companion as he licked my face frantically.

"Look," said Kai. "I won't stay long, I just knew you'd be at Alégra's wedding—congrats by the way, Ali—and I wanted to give you your little man back. Sorry it took me so long. Charly I just wanted to—"

"No, no, it's fine, Kai. It's okay," I smiled and gave my ex-boyfriend a genuine hug. "Thank you very much for making the trip from New York, I really appreciate it."

I looked up, and for the first time, I realized that Kai wasn't who I thought he was; he was who I'd *made* him out to be. In reality, Kai Kostigan was just an average-looking nice guy with whom things did not work out, and that's okay. We shared another quick hug and talked for a couple of minutes while Nikki and Alégra pretended not to stare but blatantly stared.

"All the best, Charly," said Kai as he started to walk away. "I really mean that. You're a great girl."

After we said our goodbyes to Kai, Kermit and I joined the girls again on the steps.

"That literally did *not* just happen," said Alégra in disbelief. "First of all, I remember Kai being *way* better looking than that, and secondly, are you okay, Charly? What about your happy ending?"

"Happy ending?" Nikki interrupted with a big chuckle. "She's not a Rub & Tug, Ali."

"You know what I mean," said Alégra, faux-annoyed. "Are you okay, Charly?"

"Of course I am," I smiled.

"But, but, but," Alégra couldn't wrap her head around the fact that sometimes, we don't get storybook endings, and we *never* will.

Ever.
Like… ever.
Seriously.
Like, <u>ever</u>.
And that's okay.
Honestly.
I promise.

"Not everything gets wrapped up in a pretty Tiffany bow, Ali. I'm okay with things being over between Kai and me. I promise, I will be okay."

"But what if you never left?" pleaded Alégra. "What if you followed him to New York? Maybe you two would still be together!"

"What if I had your boobs and Nikki's butt?" I scoffed. "Well, then, I'd have an entirely new range of employment choices, wouldn't I? Alégra, these are questions that I'll never know the answers to, so honestly, they just don't matter."

"But I thought you guys were going to end up together! It's so sad that you two weren't strong enough to hold on." Alégra whined as Nikki rolled her eyes but smiled lovingly.

I pulled Kermit up on to my lap and let him lick my face again. I hugged him tight and sighed.

"Ali, holding on doesn't require strength... letting go, on the other hand, that's where you find out what you're made of. And besides, I've got all that I need right here. Isn't that right, Kermit?"

Kermit snorted in approval and Alégra was stumped, "Well, at least you found yourself," said Alégra, wanting to be sure of at least one thing. "You did, right? You did find yourself?"

"Um, not really," I smiled as I stole a drag of Nikki's cigarette. "But that's okay, I've learned my lessons. I won't make the same mistakes again."

"Yeah, right!" Nikki burst out laughing and fell over.

I playfully waved her away as she struggled to get up and kiss me on my forehead. Then she rubbed my head and slurred, "Oh, *that's* my happy place, it's so kooky in there."

I chuckled and rubbed Kermit's head; he seemed quite happy to be back with his ladies. On my end, I was beyond thrilled to have my little furry man back. That's all I really wanted. Amazing how my journey home took me to the other side of the world...

All I really needed was right in front of me, I just didn't see it.

"Sooooo listen, Charly," Alégra swayed back and forth as her tiara teetered on her head. (Of course she wore a tiara!) "Lemme get this straight: you are *not* going to go run off again and you *are* going to stop jumping into ridiculous relationships?"

"Yes, I will, I promise."

"Liar!" scoffed Nikki.

"Shut up, Nikki!!" Alégra interrupted before I had the chance to respond, "Charly promissssed! She's not going anywherrrr! Charrrrly, rrrrr you?"

"Eeks, Ali! I've never seen a pirate in a wedding dress," Nikki chuckled and fell over again.

"I mean it! Shush up Nikki!" Ali said drunkenly. "Charly, just answer me!"

I had no answer for Nikki or Alégra. I didn't even have one for myself. And for the first time, I was okay with that. All I could do was raise my champagne flute and cheers to the most important people in my life.

The next day Kermit and I woke up in our old condo. Alégra was packing her things; she and Teddy would be moving in together when they got back from their honeymoon. I figured I should start *unpacking* my things (not to mention find a new roommate). I wasn't sure what the next step would be, but I knew *I'd* be the one to decide what it was. While unpacking, I came across the manila envelope that Scott had given me back in Singapore. I'd completely forgotten to look at it.

"Might as well have a look, huh?" I said to Kermit who seemed to say *don't do it, don't do it, please, I can't take any more!*

"Oh, relax," I said to Kermit. "It's not like this'll change anything…"

> From: Scott Lansdowne (s.lansdowne@edificeluxe.com)
> To: Charly Briar (c.briar@edificeluxe.com)
> Subject: Interested?
>
> Attachment 📎 Media Outreach Manager – Job Description
>
> Hey Charly,
>
> Okay, I'm starting to feel as though I work in HR...
>
> Check this out: one year contract based out of our newly rebuilt property in Jeeranam – the one damaged by the war there, it's not even open yet – you'd be in charge of corporate social responsibility and sustainable tourism resurgence initiatives...
>
> This is the *real* deal when it comes to expat lifestyle, you'd literally be living on an island! Obviously, Miss Bat-shit Crazy Pants (a.k.a. Eden) will be there too.
>
> Oh, and, btw, Eden isn't the only person you know who will be there... Here's me *wink winking* at you about a certain younger gentleman... *you cougar!!*
>
> Lemme know – job starts ASAP. Btw, dogs are totally welcome, so bring Kermit!
>
> xx
>
> *Scott Lansdowne,*
> *Manager, Sales & Marketing, Bumi~Spa~Aquas*
> *Edifice Luxe Global ~ Singapore Headquarters*

….and off I went.

Thank you...

There are so many people who helped bring this book to life. But first and foremost: thank you Laura Watson. Thank you for my beautiful illustrations (all bajillion of them) and your eagle-eye editing. But mostly, thank you for your zen-like patience with me. Where did they make you? You are so completely and truly wonderful! *Thank you thank you thank you!*

To Kim Bernot, Lul Hassan, Jessica Millar, Marah Smith, Mae-Lynn Slater, Lindsey Higgs, Kathy Fischer, and Toni Rufo: thank you for everything, especially the wine.

Thank you to my mom and dad, I love you both. Thank you to my little sister, the person with bar none the most inexcusable laugh on the planet (whose smile and love and joy are contagious and I just couldn't live without you). I'm glad you weren't a boy, or twins.

And for SDM, thank you for turning my "I *want* to be a writer" into "I *am* a writer". The crooked road I travel on has always been homeward bound, and that home is you. MHIYH.

Fully Booked / Genn Pardoe

The author lives with her best friend and their two Boston Terriers, President Bartlett and Kermit the Dog. Take a look for her next book, *Not Bitter*, coming out in 2014. You can get in touch with the author at kermit and charly at gmail dot com.

Made in the USA
Lexington, KY
30 June 2013